BURN

BURN

FOOLISH KINGDOMS
DARK SEASONS WORLD

3

NATALIA JASTER

Books by Natalia Jaster

FOOLISH KINGDOMS SERIES
Trick (Book 1)
Ruin (Book 2)
Burn (Book 3)
Dare (Book 4)
Lie (Book 5)
Dream (Book 6)

VICIOUS FAERIES SERIES
Kiss the Fae (Book 1)
Hunt the Fae (Book 2)
Curse the Fae (Book 3)
Defy the Fae (Book 4)

SELFISH MYTHS SERIES
Touch (Book 1)
Torn (Book 2)
Tempt (Book 3)
Transcend (Book 4)

To all the jesters who came before.
Poet thanks you for the inspiration.
Except for the clothes.

Never tempt a jester.

I

Poet

esters were dangerous. But princesses were fatal. 'Twas a lesson she taught me long ago.

Such a cruel story. So easy to remember.

Does this tale ring familiar? Allow me to remind you.

Once, I had watched her from the shadows. After, I'd targeted
her for mockery, ridicule, and scorn. Ah, how I'd relished her furious glares.

And later, her chaste moans.

I'd wanted to make her scowl, craving the delectable heat of her
anger. I'd fetishized every blush, tremble, and gasp.

We had been enemies back then. I was the seductive, silver-tongued
jester prowling after a willful, tenacious princess to the point of obsession. There was a time when I preyed on her vulnerabilities, for
they had amused me greatly. From behind a mask, I coveted each
forbidden part of her. I sought to trick that heiress, yet how quickly
she had ruined me, and how hotly we burned because of it.

What happened next, you wonder? Can you not guess?

My mask slipped, as did her crown.

Oh, and then. We became something unexpected, a force of nature that consumed two kingdoms like a brushfire. Whenever her mouth yielded beneath mine, her taste lingered for days. Whenever she opened her naked thighs for my hips, her broken cries ignited my pulse. Whenever her lovely cunt quivered around my cock, her pleasure ignited my very being.

Every moment torched the flesh, simmered the blood, and melted the body. Indeed, the blaze grew hotter until we breathed the same sweltering air. We became a tale for campfires, yet not the sort that warmed hearts. Rather, ours was a story that kindled the soul.

She reigned whilst I seduced. She sat on a throne whilst I dominated the shadows.

That was all. That was everything.

Then she was gone, taken from me as if we might be so pitifully snuffed out. Yet it hadn't extinguished that flame. Nay, our enemies had only stoked it higher. Separate the jester from his princess, and he would turn this cursed world to cinders.

This tale wasn't over. The only difference between then and now was I had no pity left. Death and decadence awaited.

I would find her, fuck her, and fight for her. This had started with a ribbon. Wicked hell, it would end with fire.

I had many rules, and the most vital one was this. When a jester worshiped his princess, he was ready to die for her. But when a jester lost his princess, he was eager to kill for her.

2

Poet

Standing at the princess's bedside, I inhaled the addictive scent of green apples wafting from the pillows. The aroma poured into my nostrils like an opiate, its effect potent and immediate. I sank to my knees, my joints shaking either from exhaustion, deprivation, or indignation. Really, I couldn't say.

Or mayhap it was something else. Something more. Something worse. An intrinsic force, deep-seated in my being.

Fuck. I could practically taste the scent on my tongue, taste *her* on my tongue.

Taking a deep whiff, I pulled the essence into my lungs, the muscles of my chest inflating. Drugged, I held my breath, held her in.

You have to let me go.

Nay. Not possible, sweeting.

Then again, I hardly relished asphyxiating and turning purple. Neither would do well for my complexion. Releasing the fragrance, I blew out a gale of air, my body caving with the effort.

Three days. Three days since her broken voice gusted into my ear, telling me to give her up. Dozens of hours since the princess turned from my arms and fled. Thousands of minutes since I sliced my way toward her in a raging panic, desperate to reach my thorn before she disappeared. Only to have her stop me. Only to watch her ride away. She had vanished from my sight like mist. A force of nature, impossible to hold on to.

Gone, as if she'd never existed. As though I hadn't just been clasping her, clutching her in a death grip, furious to protect my princess, to keep her close, keep her safe.

Who would do that now? Who would warm her, feed her, touch her? Who would draw a blade for her? Who would make her scowl and smile? Who would give her pleasure, bring an orgasm to her lips, wring a laugh from her obstinate mouth?

Aye. Three fucking days since my bones shattered, since my fingers felt her skin, since everything.

Sometimes when I turned a corner, my pulse pounded like a drum, and I expected to see her waiting with a stubborn glower, her gray eyes slitting and lips pursing, about to lash me with a reprimand for something naughty I'd done or said. Then I would stop in my tracks, stare at the empty room—the library wing, the throne room, the bedroom, every-fucking-where—and the vacant space where she should have been reminded me. Then my blood would boil, and my knuckles would curl.

Sometimes when I twisted in my sheets, my greedy fingers would reach out to grab my thorn, yank her from dreams, and haul her against me, so that I might tear the nightgown from her body and take what was mine, give what she wanted, and destroy our sleep. My hands would seek out her freckled shoulders, those luscious tits, and the wet crease of her pussy. My touch would extend for her prim and proper mouth, her swollen little clit, her sharp cheekbones.

Then I would grasp at nothing other than tangled quilts, and my sense would return, as well as my fury. In that moment, silence would suffocate the room. And the absence of her breathing would cause my eyes to sting.

She had a distinct voice whenever I pumped inside her, a symphony of private sounds that only my snapping hips could pull from her. She would utter such unique noises, each one particular to the things I did to her. My tongue sweeping over her cunt. My cock pitching through her soaked walls. My lips clamping onto hers and hauling her into a bone-deep kiss, from which her shaky moans and cries of rapture would echo in my head long after I awakened.

Now I felt the void of them like a chasm, a bottomless thing. Naturally.

Yet it was the memory of her words that did the most damage. Her righteous lectures, every time she disagreed with me, and each moment her vocal cords tightened in annoyance or exasperation because I was misbehaving, taunting her wickedly, or being a general pain in the ass. Every time she had spoken out against an injustice, brandished her words like thorns against an enemy, or raised that commanding voice to a crowded hall. Those memories pierced me through.

Blades cut deeply. Yet the pain was temporary.

But words. Oh, those lasted longer. They were underrated, for they made victims bleed eternally.

She was gone. Three days, and she was gone. I could no longer tell morning from night. Every hour dissolved into the next, thick and stifling.

Only one thing kept me upright. Only one person gave me air.

That person was sleeping across the hall. However tempted I felt, I couldn't wake him in the dead of the night. Dreaming was a challenge for Nicu, a feat I could relate to considering how I'd thrashed in my own bed, unconsciously tearing the blankets to shreds. My son—our son—deserved whatever precious slumber he managed to get.

In the meantime, I would do the midnight suffering for us both. I would carry that burden.

Outside Briar's suite, footfalls echoed through the cavernous halls. Armor and chainmail clanked from the distant wings and corridors of the castle. The night watch patrolled this fortress like hawks. More so, after the shitshow of the past few days. Everyone remained on edge, anticipating yet another bloodbath. Such a shame. For what each courtier should truly worry about was running into me. In my presence, no one was safe.

Moonlight dripped through the glass doors leading to the balcony. Eventide glazed the chamber walls in indigo, the color like ink from one of her quill pens. And these fucking sheets still smelled of her, crisp and tart.

My jaw hardened. I had almost forgotten why I'd come here. Reaching into my coat pocket, I withdrew a precious object. Once long ago, I'd done this same thing, except it had been a ribbon on her pillow, the band of fabric meant to target her for harsh reasons. Tonight, I would offer something different.

Nightfall shaded the rose, turning it from decadent red to a vicious scarlet. The petals puckered, not yet ripe enough to open. Like needles, a neat row of thorns sprouted from the stem.

When Spring arrived for Reaper's Fest, the king and queen had brought gifts, gestures of goodwill despite its recent history with Autumn. My origin Season was nothing if not boastful about its natural resources.

This flower, in particular.

My black fingernails flashed in the dark as I twisted the rose between my digits. Such softness. Such sharpness. That both coexisted was the cleverest of deceptions, the sort of combination I appreciated. This blossom could be a weapon if it needed to.

Or it could be a seduction. Like someone I knew well.

Sweet Thorn.

My lips twitched. My free fingers flexed into a fist, the red ribbon bracelet entwining my wrist pulling taut, withstanding the pressure. Indeed, it would take more than mere tension to sever the cord.

Back to the rose. In Spring, the most potent flowers existed, more than in any other Season. They possessed their own duplicitous magic, from the sinful to malicious.

Some varieties of roses intoxicated people to the point of sexual

14

gluttony, which could be a kink or a danger, depending on the person's restraint.

Whilst others had protective effects, such as mending broken hearts.

Or the blossoms yielded even more potent benefits.

Most Spring blooms infused with sinful magic, the princess would disapprove of. But this lovely gem, she would feel differently about—were she here.

I draped the rose on her pillow, taking care to keep the thorns from puncturing the textile. Like ribbons, masks, and crowns, the flower was a weapon. For each relic hid its true nature. Each was a force to be reckoned with.

Beyond the balcony doors, clouds rumbled, and thunder grumbled over the maple pasture. Lightning split the sky like a thin, white knife. It cleaved through the firmament whilst fog hung over the wheat fields, yet the earth remained as dry as a husk. It wouldn't rain. Not tonight.

Just as well. That would cut short the fun.

With slow purpose, I stood. Extending my arm, I slid the back of my finger over the rose's stem, then hissed as one of the thorns bit into my flesh.

The blood came easily, beading to the surface like a ruby. Oftentimes, the people of this virtuous kingdom overlooked how exquisite pain could be. All but one Royal who'd been taught the raptures of it.

Still. If I wasn't careful, the fluid would dribble onto my silk shirt. Bringing the droplet to my lips, I swiped my tongue over the wound. Savory salt dissolved on my palate, and I closed my eyes, envisioning myself smearing this tiny bead on her lower lip and then licking it clean. How I would enjoy that privilege.

More thunder rasped from outside. Like a well-timed cue, it erased the fantasy, taking that rare moment of bliss with it.

In its wake, black hatred flowed through my veins, enough to numb the ache. A muscle ticked in my jaw. Inclining my head at the empty bed, I whispered, "Forgive me, Your Highness."

Though I doubted she would do such a thing. No matter my reasons, and no matter how ferocious she'd felt the night of that battle in the courtyard, my princess had more sense than I did. She wouldn't forgive what I was about to do. Not even for the price of a perfect rose.

The coat buffeted my calves as I whipped around and stalked to the door. The heels of my boots fell silent against the area rug. I moved without sound, without breath, and without mercy.

Outside her suite, eventide cloaked the wood-paneled corridor in the Royal wing. My eyes clicked across the passages, scanning for guards or nobles. None, as expected, for I'd memorized the patrol's schedule.

Like a jester, I bled into the darkness. Like a specter, I maneuvered quietly and slipped into corners unseen. Like a man experienced in treason, I prowled toward a forbidden, felonious place.

No need to worry about making a sound. The restless, thundering sky was doing enough of that. And soon enough, when it was over and I was finished with my latest prey, the shouts would blot out my departure. I was hardly a fool without a plan. To that violent end, the racket would be so loud, no one would hear me leave. For I intended to make this newest target scream until their lungs shredded.

My booted feet moved quicker, carrying me from one end of the Royal wing to another, where guests from visiting Seasons resided, sleeping deeply and unaware of my approach. As I charged across the passage, my chin dipped, and I slit my eyes like the daggers strapped under my coat. Precautions, really. On this night, I had another type of weapon in mind.

You're mine, bitch.

Those words from several days ago returned to me like an infection—noxious and deadly. Before Briar was banished, I'd stood at a Royal's desk in one of the guest chambers and made that brutal promise.

Time to make good on my vow. Time to make a king burn.

Poet

I flattened my back against an adjacent wall and glimpsed the mezzanine located off the guest foyer. Summer's security detail migrated from one end of the wing to the other, unable to keep their asses still. This temperamental brood was notorious for their antsy nature, which tended to make them careless. As they were hardly known in The Dark Seasons for being prone to idleness, they paced the hallways like deep-sea creatures, constantly in motion despite the glazed looks in their eyes. Even at midnight, these fools were wound more tightly than barbed wire. It was difficult to tell whether they feared an attack or were spoiling for one.

Then again, every soul in this castle was on edge. The courtyard battle between Autumn's knights and the Masters, not to mention the spectacle of Briar's departure, had achieved the bare minimum in terms of settling the kingdom's nerves. The court had been walking on glass shards, the residents casting one another dubious glances.

No thanks to the miserable fuckwit at the top of my kill list. He'd done a superior job of injecting doubt into the public's mind about where to place their loyalties. Benevolent Autumn proved no less susceptible than any other nation. Trust had become a forgotten virtue. Now everyone was a potential adversary, not the least of all the Court Jester of Spring.

Even more reason to be careful during the next thirty minutes. Before stealing into Briar's suite, I'd checked on Nicu to make certain he was sleeping, only to find him and Tumble snuggled in bed between Posy and Vale. The ladies had taken quickly to coddling and pampering my son with the attention he deserved, seeking to divert him.

As for a certain First Knight, it wasn't Aire's turn in the watch rotation. That made it easy to come and go from Nicu's chambers without being questioned.

The agitated Summer soldiers continued to wear out the polish in the wood floor, their burnished capes trimmed in reptilian skin and snapping like sails, and their curved swords flashing in the dark. Regularly, they vacated the immediate vicinity, and all the better for this jester. I wasn't in the mood to wait, much less—worst case scenario—be forced to either flirt with these bastards or slit their necks quietly.

The knights stomped around the corner. One glance from the king's suite, one mere second of neglect. That was enough.

I drifted like smoke past their gazes and ghosted to the entrance. After a quick twist of the unbolted lever—what a fucking ignoramus, this king—I stepped inside the antechamber. The quarters greeted me like the inside of a tomb, the vast apartment obscured in sooty black and reeking of bigotry.

Papers littered Rhys's desk, yet the red ribbon I'd left him was gone. Because Summer acted viscerally more than logically, I imagined he'd swept it into the rubbish basket, having assumed a servant dropped it there by accident. Rhys viewed the world with a broader lens and rarely gave credit to the small details, such as the resemblance between that ribbon and my bracelet.

He hadn't made the connection. I'd wager his pecker on it.

And splendid. The king's absence meant he was consistent, both in stench as well as routine. Upon confirming the guest suite was vacant, my wolfish lips tilted. I swerved from the room and slipped out of the foyer a second before one of the knights returned to his station beside the entrance.

One corner, then another. Leaning my shoulder against a random wainscoted wall caused a hidden panel to swivel open, through which I passed. The confidential outlet required nocturnal vision, the channel so murky it was impossible to see my hand in front of my fucking face. I counted my steps, then turned west, then east. At which point, the conduit descended farther into the earth and tunneled beneath the castle. Eventually, skylights bled luminescence into the cavity and illuminated exposed tree roots laced in cobwebs.

My boots whispered over the bricks. Thunder clapped through the clouds, the rumble strong enough to penetrate the insulated passage.

At length, the slope inclined and ended at a wall of bark. I pushed against the facade, which groaned open like a door, the motion throwing dust into the air. I stepped through the exit—the partition camouflaged within a tree trunk—and into the maple pasture at the south end of grounds.

The towering trees packed themselves closely together, shrouding certain pockets from being seen by the parapets' night watch. Nonetheless, my eyes scrolled across the vista. A swatch of wind battered the leaves, sending a hissing noise through the expanse. Normally, fauna grazed in this area, but the resident foxes and their wild kin must have taken shelter from the restless sky.

My gaze sliced across every shrub and creeper, then clicked to a halt on a figure traveling deeper into the enclosure. Well, well. That hadn't taken long. Indeed, a creature of unlucky habit. The Royal cocksucker had a nasty penchant for behaving as restlessly as his soldiers.

Big mistake, sweeting. One among many.

I choked the edge of the open door in my grip, a pair of leather gloves straining over my fingers. Savagery caused my molars to clamp together, the pressure hard enough to crack enamel.

Since leaving my little token of affection on Rhys's desk, I had been watching him. From above the rim of my chalice, from across crowded halls, from the back of the throne room—and from the center of it—I'd pinned my gaze on his sneering profile.

I had planned. And I had waited.

I'd kept track of his schedule and studied his patterns. Wisely and understandably, his wife preferred to have her own chambers, separate from her husband. Even so, Rhys hadn't ventured once to Giselle's suite for a single night of mandatory procreation.

Nay, but the prick did emerge from his lair to roam the maple pasture like a wraith in the dead of night. Summer's culture of fitfulness was no secret among the continent, and the turbulent king was rumored to work off his unrest with evening walks so often he threatened to burn holes into the grass.

Perhaps thoughts of Briar and all the brilliant trouble she'd caused had kept him awake. Oh, but I hoped so. It would be just like my tenacious princess to torment this man even in his slumber. She'd accomplished that many times with me, though for very different, graphic reasons involving her moans.

In any case, it had been easy to track Rhys here once before. It would be easier to make him regret it.

My fingers released the door. Without looking away from the retreating figure, I closed the partition behind me and trailed after my prey.

Rhys strode around the trunks, his linen mantle billowing like a goody trail for predators. For Seasons' bloody sake. I couldn't help sneering at the fabric's color palette. Who the fuck paired aubergine with lemon yellow?

From the lower branches, the maple's maroon leaves trembled above his head. Stringy layers of hair hung like dead slugs down his back, the hue somewhere between tar black and shit brown.

Another blade of lightning pierced the firmament. On a night like this, I should be naked and entangled with Briar. But if she couldn't be here, safe and sated, the next few minutes would have to compensate. If I couldn't make my princess sigh, I'd make a king wail.

Thus, I quickened my pace whilst drawing flint and a steel striker from inside my coat.

Rhys paused at one tree and ran his palm over the trunk, then proceeded around a bend. I narrowed my eyes. His actions hardly seemed casual. Nay, they appeared intentional.

This wasn't merely a restless jaunt. He was looking for something. Pity for him. The fucker would be reduced to a carcass before he found it.

Crouching low, I glimpsed the clouds and noted the seconds that ticked by. One flash of lightning, then fifteen seconds later, another. In The Dark Seasons, such Autumn flashes were as predictable as ocean tides in Summer. I'd gotten to know their rhythm, as I'd gotten to know Rhys's weaknesses.

Because jesters had timing and kinetics on their side, I clenched the flint and steel in one hand and maneuvered with the other. Snatching a maple seed off the ground, its size as substantial as a pome fruit, I juggled the orb and tossed it to a neighboring tree. The seed bounced off the trunk, catching Rhys's attention.

His head whipped sideways. Like a proper victim, he pursued the noise and stalled beneath the looming maple.

It happened swiftly and beautifully. I counted once more, hardened my features into stone, and scraped the flint and steel together.

A lone spark flared to life. I flung the sizzling object toward the branches above Rhys's head. The blaze ignited at the same moment another ray of lightning cut through the heavens.

One instant Rhys festered there like a tumor. The next, the trunk detonated into flames, which snaked down the column and snatched the thin fibers of His Majesty's very flammable ensemble.

The shriek that ripped from his lungs played a melody in my ears. Summer bleated like a juvenile, his wail shearing through the pasture. Alas for him, thunder swallowed the noise like candy, so that no one heard him but me.

Fire licked his clothing and scorched his hair. He scrambled back and forth whilst slapping his skull. "Fuck!" he growled. "What the fuck!"

Narcotic pleasure fused through my veins. I stood and witnessed the king scurry across the pasture, the charred stench of his mustache filling my lungs.

He would melt and then flake to ash. And when it was over, I'd scatter the cinders across the nearest trough of pig shit.

"Never steal from a jester," I hissed under my breath.

My eyes blurred from the sting of smoke. Regardless, I relished the sight of Rhys's form broiling like tomorrow's dinner, the pyre roasting a path from his scalp to his arms. One blessed fact about that atrocious choice of fabric he wore. It burned easily.

My nostrils flared. Satisfaction thickened my blood.

It would appear an accident. Lightning had struck the tree, they would say. That had created a string of flames that turned His Majesty into a pan-fried steak.

If every court had one thing in common, it was their belief in the almighty Seasons. No one questioned the will of nature. If it had decided Rhys's time had come, despite being in his prime, so be it.

They would not doubt his death or place blame on those with obvious motives. They wouldn't suspect sympathizers of Autumn's princess, nor her lover or mother. They'd have no cause to.

Still, the night watch would make the rounds, patrolling this corner at any moment. Seeing the fire, they would sound the horn alarm and rush to the king's aid. Alas, to no avail. He'd be unrecognizable by then, but I shouldn't be around to answer questions.

As much as I fancied the show, I forced myself to stalk backward, to leave him there. Yet as I did, Briar's features swam before my eyes, and memories invaded my head like a gruesome vignette.

Her face in the courtyard, when she had witnessed the carnage of her people. Her face moments later, when Rhys had appeared and she'd tried to attack him. Her face in the Royal suite, features twisting in fear as she worried about what would happen to her. Her face in the bathtub, flushing and slackening with pleasure whilst I pistoned my cock into her tight wetness. Her face the next morning, creasing in anguish as her title was stripped from her, along with everything she held dear.

This king had done that to my thorn.

My boots halted. Nay, burning wasn't enough. My dagger would peel the raw, singed, blistered flesh from his bones. I would make him feel a wild agony the likes of which he'd never thought possible. For my princess, I would make him weep.

Instead of retreating, I felt my limbs stalking toward the smoke, approaching the burning tree, drawing nearer to Rhys's howls. My mind bellowed some type of objection, some form of warning. Yet I couldn't hear the precise words, couldn't hear anything lucidly above the sound of my own growls.

For a moment, the king's voice dissolved, and the pasture faded, and everything in my vision turned red. The scarlet of a ribbon and a rose. And then like a trap, Rhys leaped from the inferno, and his scorched hands launched around my throat.

4

Poet

everal unfortunate sensations followed. Oxygen drained from my lungs, the deprivation singeing my flesh. Smoke stung my eyes, and the neighboring blaze flung embers into the atmosphere, its temperature scorching my profile.

All the whilst, fingers clamped onto my neck like a noose. At once, the heinous sight of Rhys's face popped from the combustion, a stubborn motherfucker who just refused to die.

The king's features contorted. Black pupils swallowed his irises and flashed with recognition. "You," he snarled. "How dare you!"

"I dare rather easily, sweeting," I gritted into his face, squeezing out the words in between slices of air. "The problem is you keep failing to cooperate and fuck off."

"The audacity! To think a flame against Summer would work." His drool flew into my face as our foreheads mashed together. "Hasn't anyone educated you, peasant? Of all Seasons, Summer cannot burn. We are the blood of our ancestors, born of heat and flames." Rhys curled his digits into my throat, cutting off all remaining threads of oxygen. "We can't burn because we *created* fire!"

Nice to know this usurper hadn't lost his sense of supremacy, even while being fileted. If I didn't want his heart and cock roasting on a spit like appetizers, I would applaud the fucker's vanity.

Nonetheless, this paltry excuse for a ruler was right. How else to explain how little the fire had touched him? Not a single inch of the blaze had scalded his features.

Rhys burrowed his fingernails into my trachea. My lungs failed to pump, and looming trees grew hazy around the edges, maple leaves reducing to blots of color as my vision swam. As it did, the king wheezed into my ear, his respirations choppy.

"Decided to avenge your sympathizing autumn heiress like a faithful lapdog, did you?" he gloated. "Haven't learned your place yet? Whores like you eventually lose their luster, but kings are forged of gold, and their legacies reign for eternity. You will never know that glory." His visage crinkled like cheap papier-mâché. "And now, neither will Briar. Your worthless cunt of a princess is *gone*."

Her name on his lips blasted through me, and the mention of gold tipped the scales. Memories of that courtyard battle crashed over me. I saw my princess collapse as Vex jammed a dagger into her gut, the Master goldsmith attacking under Rhys's influence, acting on the king's command.

He had made her suffer. He'd made her cry. He made her bleed.

Because of him, she almost died. Because of him, she lost her throne.

Briar.

"One impertinent slut down." Summer's digits trenched into my throat. "One more to go—"

My skull slammed against his, the impact shattering his cranium. As the king staggered backward with a shriek, he released my throat, and my reflexes exploded into motion.

I was on him before he could squeak out another sound. In a dizzying sequence, I twisted and lashed out. My limbs moved so quickly, it disorientated Rhys, my arms and legs whipping into the air. Within seconds, I jabbed his temple with my elbow, then pivoted to catch his own neck in a vise grip, at which point my heel snagged around his calf, and I windmilled him off the ground. A guttural screech vaulted from Rhys's throat as he smacked into the earth, his head crashing against the grass, inches from the dancing flames.

Blood spattered his face, though hardly up to my standards. I wanted him disfigured, maimed beyond recognition to his own kingdom. Yet it wasn't my attack or the bone-crunching landing that made him shriek.

Nay, it was the blisters frothing across his arms. A chunk of his mantle had disintegrated and split open at the chest, revealing the mess of skin beneath. Tendrils of smoke curled from his flesh, the surface bubbling. The fire had gotten him after all, incinerating Rhys from navel to nipple.

Not enough. Not nearly enough to satisfy me.

The pissant roared and lurched upright, his fingers whisking out a knife. With a lazy kick, I knocked the weapon from his grasp, the motion so rudimentary I felt insulted. Truly, he should have known better than to test a jester's reflexes, if I could remotely call that paltry attempt a test.

Squatting above him, I slipped a dagger from the harness at my ankle. Like liquid satin, I trailed the blade's tip slowly and gently along the pink, foaming surface of his torso, the motions akin to a tease. I scarcely made impact on the raw and sensitive flesh, yet Rhys bleated as if being eaten alive.

My eyelids hooded. *That's right, sweeting. Shout for me.*
Do it for her.

Whilst he cried out, I murmured a soft rhyme. "Summer can't burn, you say? It doesn't look that way." Sweat poured down the king's neck, which shuddered under my ministrations. "Someone should have taught you. Jesters have many talents, including how to juggle the most fatal of weapons." Then my voice narrowed to a hiss, "You created fire, but jesters swallow it."

My fingers choked the dagger's hilt, the way he'd tried to choke me. Lightly, I inched the tip into one of the blisters. A high-pitched wail bolted from Rhys's mouth, then another as I sliced the dagger another inch.

I would be as patient as a lover while paring the burned skin from his skeleton. For I had plenty of experience with foreplay. By the end, he would beg for it to be over. Then he would never say her name again.

Leaning over, I let my silken voice purr into his ear. "You ruined her. So now I get to ruin you."

I locked my muscles, primed to retaliate, ready to shear him clean. Yet as the bonfire snapped and popped, the flying embers reminded me of freckles. And those freckles brought the princess's face to the surface again.

As a figure stepped into the pasture, my head snapped up, and my ribs constricted. I felt her like my breath, like my blood, like my pulse. Briar stood there, backlit against the burning maple. A black gown hugged her body, yet no crown sat upon her head. Still, her chin leveled high, poised and regal. Fuck, but she looked marvelous whilst standing among the flames, with her feet bare, her braid unraveled, and firelight brushing her lips.

The world evaporated, engulfed by her presence. Across the distance, her gray eyes clung to mine, imploring something.

To end Rhys? To spare him?

Hardly the latter. But mayhap not the former either.

She opened her mouth to explain, to tell me what she needed, and my heart stalled in anticipation. Just then, chaos broke through the pasture. A set of hands grappled my shoulders and hauled me off Rhys's flailing body.

"Stop!" a woman's voice commanded. "Poet, stop!"

I blinked, and the princess evanesced, vanishing like a hallucination. It hadn't been real. But the fingers shackling me were certainly no figment.

In a flash, I tore free. Executing a few choice motions, I ripped from the female's grasp, veered to face her whilst flipping the dagger in my fingers, and halted.

Shit.

Queen Avalea wavered from the impact of my movements. Beneath a jacquard robe, her chest rose and fell in rapid pants. I must have looked murderous because she lifted her palms in a placating gesture. "It's me. Poet, it's me." Her throat bobbed, and though she spoke calmly, panic strained beneath her words.

I clenched the dagger, frenzied breaths piping from my lungs. Had I not been distracted by a fantasy, I would have heard Briar's mother coming. To that end, I would have been swift to evade her grip.

Behind us, Rhys's shouts thinned to tortured grunts. Even in torment, he sounded offended, livid as if his title should have rendered him immune to pain. In this fucker's mind, only lower beings knew anguish.

The queen's frantic gaze darted to the lump of coal behind me, then leveled on my glare. "What have you done?" she whispered.

The demand radiated from her, though it did nothing to stifle my wrath. I'd had the king on his fucking back. My knife had been so close to shearing him like a lamb.

But then her lips moved, soundless and urgent.

Not like this, she mouthed. *Not without Briar.*

The plea relaxed my grip on the weapon. An instant later, another figure swooped into the pasture, this one larger and taller. Like a bird of prey, Aire sped through the trees, his shirt hanging open and a pair of broadswords braced in his fists. Despite the scene, he stalled with the lethal grace of a raptor.

Shock widened the man's dark blue eyes as he beheld the evidence of treason, the damage I'd done to Summer. "Seasons almighty," he muttered. Not one to mince words—much less use many words at all— Aire hesitated with a grimace. It might be Rhys of Summer, a man who deserved no less, but he was still a king whose demise would mean violent repercussions. So before Avalea could issue the order, the First Knight flew into action and hastened to the Royal's aid.

Shouts cannoned from the rafters. Only now did the night watch along the parapet walks register the mushroom of smoke. However, the alarm didn't sound, the massive horn that normally signaled intruders and natural disasters failing to echo through the castle. In its place, a smaller instrument blew across the grounds, its rhythm indicating flames but no attackers.

I considered that oversight and glanced Avalea's way. She'd stopped them from raising hell and alerting the court of a greater threat. Astute as ever, especially since her suite overlooked this area. She must have noticed the blaze first and signaled to the patrol that a fire had broken out, a circumstance that didn't warrant awakening the knights.

On that note, the queen processed Aire's presence with brief astonishment before remembering the man's uncanny ability to perceive things others couldn't. Grumpy exterior aside, the First Knight moved like the wind and read signs in every shift of air, among other mysterious abilities. Plausibly, the warrior had scented the flames long before his slumbering comrades could.

I flattened my lips, miffed to see Aire helping Rhys off the ground. The reek of the king's burned flesh permeated my senses. Ancestors born of fire. Assumptions that he was impervious. Bullshit. The man had erupted like a volcano the moment those sparks had landed on his tacky mantle.

Aire lugged Rhys across the grass, balancing the king's limping form. They paused abreast of me and the queen, so that Rhys's glower dashed between us. He alternated between seething in agony and spitting venom my way. "Mark my words, you parasitic fuck! I shall make you weep for this!"

They trundled toward the castle, where the infirmary would treat Rhys's wounds. Thunder slapped the sky. Lighting sheared through the clouds. The effect illuminated Avalea's expression, which transformed from distress to anger, then finally resignation.

Fuck. I knew that look. 'Twas the same disapproving frown a certain princess wore whenever she was forced to perform an inconvenient duty, usually regarding a certain troublemaker who refused to stop breaking laws.

Footfalls pounded across the pasture. I counted a dozen guards likely carrying buckets of water and hoses.

With a heavy sigh, I offered my wrists to the queen and waited for the manacles.

5

Poet

Hours later, I paced the dungeon cell like a panther. Chains jostled around my wrists and ankles, the latter restraints scuffing my expensive leather boots. These guards understood the extent of my agility and knew better than to keep any limbs free. As for my mouth, they'd had no choice but to leave that unhampered. To their dismay, the queen had ordered them not to gag me.

Stalking from one end of the cage to the other, my movements disturbed the rushes, creating a serpentine noise that echoed through the dungeon. Years of mildew had soaked into the exposed root walls, producing a stink that caused my nose to crinkle, the putrid scent darkening my mood further. To this inhumanity, the laws of our continent subjected human beings. My molars ground to the point where I dismissed thoughts of Rhys receiving medical care he didn't deserve. I would deal with him later.

In the meantime, there were more important grievances to keep in mind. Aptly, my neighbors reminded me of that. Unlike the insulated brick cells in the noble prison, which afforded prisoners a semblance of privacy, only bars separated each cubicle here. Within them, one of the captives—a man with pale, sagging skin—chewed on the door railing of his cage, his efforts threatening to whittle down a few teeth, whilst another skeletal prisoner with bright coral irises hunkered in the corner of her own cell. The inhabitants coughed, muttered to themselves, or shivered in their cots, each sound louder than it should have been in this cavernous shithole.

Instead of tossing me into the jail wing reserved for high-ranking residents, the guards had locked me in with the mad. Specifically, the ones Rhys had brought from Summer, from his trade agreement with Briar. Nay, not criminals but slaves. To that end, there was nothing I could do to change their fates unless I behaved and served my time like a good anarchist.

Men and women armed with halberds kept a wide berth from my chamber. Unaware of the reason behind my imprisonment, they cast me furtive glances. Rather typical of most people dealing with the Court Jester and certainly wise of them.

The guards split up, dividing themselves between the dungeon's entrance and the far end of the cavity. They glanced inside the cubicles with pretentious disgust, as if they were saints keeping watch on abominations. So much for charitable, benevolent Autumn. The rushes, latrines, and barred windows emitting a modicum of fresh air didn't absolve this Season from being as much of an asshole as Spring, Summer, or Winter.

Twilight filtered through the window, moon rays slashing past the bars. Another cursed hour until dawn. Not long ago, the thunder and lightning had ceased.

I halted at one end of the compartment and twisted, my back hitting the wall. The irons clanked as I slid to the ground and reclined, steeping one leg and draping a wrist over my knee.

As if synchronized, the hinges squeaked. The noise reverberated from the stairway, followed by insistent footsteps. At fucking last.

A curvy figure turned the corner, sweeping into the dungeon like a mighty ship and stalling outside my cell. Rust-red hair coiled atop her head, slate gray cashmere fell around her frame, and drop earrings swung from her ears. Despite the regal attire, Queen Avalea appeared anything but composed. Rather, that glare told me just how pissed off I'd made her. For I was well acquainted with that look, albeit from someone else.

Avalea nodded to the guards. One of them pulled a lever outside the cage, which caused partitions forged of metal to disengage and roll along the sides of my cubicle. They glided over rails to form thick, makeshift walls that flanked my cell, enclosing me from my neighbors.

Nifty, indeed. And necessary, seeing as Her Majesty looked ready to rip my head off. Or at least shout until my ears bled. This way, our conversation would be muffled, and no one would hear or see us.

The door swung open. The queen marched inside.

I stayed where I was, casually slumping against the wall, with my open coat and shirt blackened at the edges from where the flames had eaten the fabric. I stank of smoke, blood, and malice. And aye, the manacles had officially ruined my fucking boots.

The longer we stared at each other, the heavier the silence grew. In the maple pasture, whilst the night watch had clamped me in irons, I'd voiced only one concern. To which the queen had assured me that Nicu was still dreaming soundly, secure in his bed with the ladies and unaware of the havoc I'd wreaked.

With that settled, I now felt free to indulge in a healthy dose of fury and sarcasm. "Evening, Your Majesty," I drawled, flicking my fingers around the cell. "I'd offer you a chair, but they ran out."

"If I were you," Avalea warned, her nostrils flaring, "I would hold that silver tongue, or I shall be forced to color it red."

"If were you, I would choose a more effective threat. I'm rather fond of that shade."

"Have you any idea what I've been dealing with up there? Rhys is in an uproar. Only a miracle prevented his bellows from flooding this castle and advertising what happened. To say nothing of how the court will react tomorrow when they learn the Summer King was presumably struck by lightning and nearly burned to death. I shall have an inquisition on my hands, which will require careful orchestration to keep you out of the discussion. The residents are agitated as it is, and it shall be worse if the broader public gets wind of your killing spree."

"I'd hardly call it a spree."

"Tell that to the ruler of our greatest enemy nation," she snapped. "All the while, Rhys demands no less than a hundred gallons of your blood, your head displayed on a pike, and your liver on his trophy shelf."

"Pity he's bluffing and won't get what he wants. In any case, I'm astounded that he didn't ask for my cock. Or better yet, my brain. Two valuable assets he lacks in spades."

"Condemnation, Poet! That is beside the point!"

I leaned forward, my shadow slicing across the floor. "'Tis *exactly* the point," I snarled. "That Royal toddler is throwing a tantrum now, but it will pass. Publicizing my actions and calling for my execution won't work to his advantage. First, bitching openly about the Court Jester flogging his ass makes Rhys look weak. Second, a beheading is too easy. He wants me to suffer slowly, and he'll add the princess to that mix when she returns."

Avalea swallowed, grief compromising her voice. "If she returns."

"When," I enunciated like the honed point of a knife. "*When* she returns."

The queen didn't object, though she didn't nod in agreement either. Not because she didn't wish for her daughter to come home, but for another reason. One I understood well.

She agonized over Briar's safety. With tensions rising at court, the notorious princess who'd caused such anarchy would have a target on her back. That was the reason Avalea had sanctioned the banishment in the first place, to keep her daughter out of harm's way.

And yet. Although the queen feared getting her hopes up, she had been exhausting her efforts, searching for a safe way to bring Briar home.

The queen wasn't the only one. I'd been doing my part alongside her. What's more, I felt the same dilemma to the marrow of my bones.

The problem was Briar could be in just as much danger outside of the castle. No one was smarter than my thorn, but whilst she possessed intelligence and some weaponry skills, I hadn't had time to fully train her. Though it was a minor comfort to know Eliot and Cadence had gone with Briar, I wasn't satisfied. The thought of anyone hurting her, anyone touching her, injected my veins with boiling water.

Perceptively, Avalea watched those savage thoughts cross my features. At length, she rubbed her arms, glanced around the dank cell, and observed the open window. "You must be cold."

"I prefer the term hot blooded." For obvious reasons, I jutted my chin to the door, beyond which the mad languished. "However, if you'd like to worry about someone's comfort, preoccupy yourself with them, not me. I hear that's a Royal's job."

The queen stiffened. "You have some nerve."

"I have more than that."

"Not in my house."

I quirked an eyebrow. "Am I wrong?"

Avalea faltered. Shame and responsibility corroded her features like acid and leached the well-fed color from her complexion.

Dammit. What I'd said had been right, but I hadn't needed to be harsh. True enough, the Season's bullshit reeked like in any other nation, except it was concealed under an even denser layer of excrement, which they liked to excuse by calling it charity.

My queen and princess were the exceptions, acknowledging the shortcomings of this kingdom. But with centuries of tradition and three other courts against us, we needed allies. And more than that, we needed time. Avalea and Briar had been risking their lives for our cause—for born souls—to the point where her daughter had been disinherited and evicted from the castle. Who the devil was I to ridicule this woman?

Condensation dripped from a crack in the ceiling. Indeed, it was cold here. Whereas I'd been too fueled to notice, which meant I was no less guilty than Avalea. We'd been too wrapped up in our own demons to remember those who had it far worse, who lived in a perpetual nightmare. They were the ones we meant to fight for.

Avalea sighed. "You're here at Rhys's private request."

I scoffed. "He has predictable taste."

It hardly insulted me to be placed with the mad. The greater offense was Summer's assumption that I *should* be offended by present company. More than having a front-row seat to my execution—public disembowelment, slow castration, buckets of wine splashed onto my wardrobe—Rhys falsely believed entombing the Court Jester with Summer's mad was the lowest he could bring me. Mayhap it also served as a reminder of where he thought my princess belonged.

My canines flashed. Because of him, Autumn assumed Briar had lost her mind. Behind my and Avalea's back, they'd been calling her "The Mad Princess." Oh, but the motherfucker would pay for that.

The queen's expression smoothed out like a plate of metal. "Nevertheless, you're here because of your own actions. A rampage against the king. A path of blood and fire. Considering how you tore into a fleet of my soldiers, to stop Briar from fleeing the castle three days ago, I suppose I should be grateful you didn't leave a dozen massacred Summer knights trailing behind you."

"The night is young," I reminded her. "But while I'm capable and motivated, I'm also not stupid."

"Many would say that attacking a monarch equates to attacking an entire nation."

"One would be wrong. A single body is easier to conceal than a dozen. For their sakes, Rhys's unsuspecting security detail stayed out of my way. Otherwise, we'd be having a different conversation."

"All right, I'm done talking in circles. You've made it clear tonight—"

"Just tonight?"

"Seasons," she groused. "*Numerous times* you've made it clear that you can rip any Royal or court to shreds with your bare hands, but that's not your leading strength. From where I stand, that strength has abandoned you in favor of self-destruction."

I tilted my head. "In other words, I need to control myself."

"At minimum. Your skill for manipulation is wanting, jester."

The manacles shook as I launched to my feet. "Count how many fucks I give."

"For mercy's sake, Poet. Enough with the alpha glower," Avalea demanded as I resumed pacing. "This is not you. Currently, yours are not the shrewd words of the man my daughter set her heart on the chopping block for."

I halted with my back to her. Now we were getting to it. She blamed me for Briar's banishment. Well, she wasn't the only one. It appeared we were both letting our demons get the better of us tonight.

But aye. Avalea was right.

Not without Briar.

In the maple pasture, she had mouthed that plea. Like a reflex, the entreaty loosened my muscles. For all that Briar had unleashed on the king in the courtyard mere days ago, and for all that she'd like to see him tortured by me, she wouldn't want it to happen like this. Not so sloppily.

I flattened my palms against the nearest wall and leaned in. My shoulders tensed as Avalea's words reached me from behind. "This is not how she would do it. And it's most assuredly not what she'd expect from you."

"Wrong," I murmured. "She knows to what lengths I'd go. I burned a king tonight, yet that's the least of my ambitions. I would scorch this world for my princess."

Avalea fell momentarily silent, approval and censure clashing in her voice. "I have only ever wanted someone to love her the way you do. Yet Briar also believes in something larger than herself. To her, a worthy ruler would not want the world to suffer purely for her own survival."

Another thing she wasn't telling me that I already knew. My thorn would seek to annihilate the enemy differently—cleverly. As we'd done before. Together.

Tonight, I had let rage and loss get the better of my tact. I twisted, set my back against the wall, and crossed my shackled arms.

"Apparently, I've been a prick."

Avalea's mouth twitched. "Do jesters always exaggerate?"

"Only if they're vain."

"You have behaved foolishly."

"Come now. Don't sugarcoat it."

She waved that off. "If you wish to work off your guilt, compose some private verse about your infraction and then rewrite it one hundred times."

I slanted my head and gave her a look of mock confusion. "Who said I was sorry?"

It depended on which part we were talking about. But when Avalea pursed her lips, exasperated by the play on words, I yielded and inclined my head. "Apologies, Your Majesty."

Mollified, the woman nodded. The cashmere gown swished as she approached and paused several steps from me. "Do what she cherishes most about you. Sharpen your tongue, and use that as your default. If you don't, the anguish will build inside you until it combusts."

I evaded her gaze. Everything she said made sense and would have been my own line of thinking, had I been thinking rationally at all.

"What I did to Rhys," I prompted, lightning my tone. "Is anger the only emotion it made you feel?"

When I glanced back, Avalea compressed her lips, withholding a grin. A tired laugh escaped us. However, the noise got lost among the sound of a cage door groaning shut and iron keys jangling.

I quieted my voice. "Despite the lack of witnesses, you're right. I imagine my incarceration on the same evening Summer was torched will cause talk, not to mention my presence at that very event. I can't wait to hear the public reason you've drafted for these shackles I'm wearing. More importantly, I hope the lie makes me look good."

Likewise, the queen lowered her tone. "You were having a time-sensitive meeting with me this evening, and we arrived on the scene together. At which point, you made an unfavorable comment about Rhys's injuries, and I sought to rectify your attitude for the night. That will show I'm an impartial sovereign who respects the

Summer King, thus the ruse will keep you alive. And I grant, you have a point about Rhys; he'll go along with the charade."

Naturally, he would. As I'd said, far be it from his pride to admit the Court Jester is the reason he currently resembles a slice of toast. However much Rhys would like to see me eviscerated at dawn, it won't be at the expense of his reputation. Nay, he'll seek compensation by other unknown means.

"About the particulars of the 'accident,'" Avalea began. "That will require another gambit. I assume you have that bit plotted out?"

I pretended to give it thought. "The King of Summer took a night walk and ended up in the wrong place, at the wrong time. Lightning struck the illustrious maple under which he'd been standing. Hence, he went up in flames." I wiggled my crimson-stained fingers. "Etcetera, etcetera."

"An elaborate falsehood," Avalea concluded. "I would inquire how you fabricated the fire. But considering the parcels of Summer tinder Rhys brought to kindle the flames in his suite, I can guess."

As with every Season, nature had its lethal side. In this court, spontaneous combustion wasn't among such disasters. That form of dark, organic magic belonged to Summer, and because Rhys compulsively preferred to outfit his chambers with special tinder from his nation rather than simply use Autumn kindling, I'd developed a case of sticky fingers. Swiping what I'd needed in advance had made the task of creating a pyre much easier, Summer tinder and Autumn lightning having a rather conductive relationship.

Ultimately, the court would scarcely link the incident to me, the queen, or anyone else with a presumed motive. It had been a simple case of the elements. Again, no one ever questioned the will of nature.

"As for witnesses, there are none I'm worried about," I intoned.

"None that you're aware of," Avalea contested. "Kings don't venture outdoors unmanned."

"I imagine Rhys gave explicit orders for his guards to fuck off and leave him alone," I dismissed. "He's not known to be merciful when disobeyed. Of course to prevent any curious nobles or resistant soldiers from intercepting, rumors about his penchant for punishment might have been embellished."

"And just who is responsible for those rumors?"

Slowly, a smirk dove across my face.

Avalea concealed another grin. "Convenient."

"Poor Rhys was already in the pasture, blessedly unaware of his near demise. At which point, nature took over and got in the way. So you do see; I'm a livid jester who's been reckless, but not so reckless as to compromise myself or anyone who matters. I have a son to protect, after all. A princess, as well."

Avalea had been studying me, impressed. But then sadness weighed down her face. "When will you stop doing that?"

My eyebrows pinched together. "Be more specific. The list is long."

"You haven't spoken her name once."

My joints tightened, the crusted wall dug into my back, and a muscle ticked in my jaw. At length, I recovered, but only just. "Rhys was looking for something in the pasture."

Before Avalea could insist that I acknowledge her comment, I forged ahead and recounted how I'd followed the king, saw Rhys trace one of the tree trunks, and watched him fondle the surface in anticipation.

Awareness dawned across the queen's countenance. "He was searching for the tunnels."

Fuck. The tunnels.

Like every castle, Autumn's fortress had secret passages embedded into its walls, outlets for its residents to escape during a siege. Except those channels were confidential, privy only to a select few.

The queen's brow furrowed. "But how would he know about the tunnels?"

Oh, I could fucking guess. I gave the woman a meaningful look until her eyes broadened. "The Masters."

It had to be. Ancestors of those so-called elite crafters had drafted and constructed the castle's passages, then likely passed down the knowledge to their successors. Briar had said as much when she'd explained the guild's history. As traitorous spies working for Rhys, naturally they had reported the tunnels' existence to Summer.

Avalea glanced away in thought. "But then, Summer would already know where to locate them. He wouldn't have to search."

"In which case, I'll amend. He knew where they were but sought to verify it."

"You think he's planning to enter the castle undetected."

"I know he is," I said. "Sometime in the future when he's not supposed to be here. The question is, to what end?"

"Nicu," she fretted, the name claiming my full attention. "Will he try—"

"Not a fucking chance," I growled.

Never mind that Rhys wouldn't get within a hundred paces of my son. I'd gobble the king alive before then. But Summer wouldn't try for Nicu. The bigot would consider it beneath him to attack the same vulnerable spot twice, especially if that vulnerable spot were a so-called simpleton child. Summer wouldn't risk failing and suffering the humiliation for a second time.

That said, I refused to discount Rhys's ability to strike somewhere fragile. He knew his enemies each had something to lose, and he'd find a way to abuse that. 'Tis what I would do.

"This doesn't make sense," Avalea stressed. "Briar is gone; he separated the two of you. There's nothing left to gain by trespassing."

"The princess is alive. Her jester is alive," I rebutted. "Rhys probably suspects his victory is temporary and aims to rectify that. Or he just likes beating a dead horse."

"Then whatever he's plotting, perhaps you've already intercepted him. If not, he can't be intending anything immediate, what with Summer's impending departure alongside Spring."

That stood to reason. In addition to Summer, Spring presently resided in a guest suite. Basil and Fatima had arrived for Reaper's Fest, having been invited by Autumn as a gesture of truce after how Briar and I had betrayed them. But in the wake of bloodshed at the courtyard, the annual revels had been postponed, for who knew how long. Thus, both Seasons would be departing over the next few days.

"We'll find out Summer's plan," Avalea determined. "In the meantime, I'll have the troops seal off the tunnels."

I shook my head. "Keep them open. Have soldiers patrol from a distance." My voice lowered another octave. "You don't catch a hound by removing the bone."

Avalea exhaled. "Very well. But unearthing and subsequently thwarting Rhys's intentions shall work only if you keep your thirst for vengeance in check."

Sigh. The sacrifices one had to make. "At your service, Majesty."

Matter of fact, I welcomed the request with open arms. A jester was more cunning than I'd been. A jester would have attacked from a finely honed angle. Whilst my feelings for a certain princess had elevated my temper, the sharpest attack didn't come from a blade. Frying Rhys to a strip of bacon would have been delightful, but wielding my tongue like a whip would achieve an even greater pleasure.

Avalea bowed her head in farewell, indicating I'd be here a while. For appearance's sake and Rhys's benefit.

My words delayed her at the door. "I … can't say her name."

The truth revealed itself like a chink, like something dislodged and unlikely to mend. It plagued me with a longing so violent, I marveled at my ability to stand upright. To say nothing of how my throat clotted.

Attempting to quell the panic was a futile effort. Bandits, assassins, and rioters were the tamest obstacles my princess had to worry about out there. In The Dark Seasons, we worshiped and feared almighty nature for a good reason. It was one thing to fight humans, but that didn't mean they were the most dangerous things in this world.

Silently, the queen absorbed my confession. She cast me another glance over her shoulder, her eyes watering. On impulse, the woman rushed across the cell to cup my jaw, the way Old Jinny used to. Then she was gone, the door wincing behind her.

I collapsed into the facade, my fists shaking and the irons clanking. If I said the princess's name, I would shatter like glass. Nay, I would only say it when I got what I wanted.

I will find you.

I'd mouthed that promise before she turned on her horse and fled. And if the princess was anything, she was astute. She knew her jester kept his word.

I would find her. And when I did, I would claim her like I never had before.

So long as she stayed alive.

My gaze locked onto a blazing torch bracketed against the opposite wall, the flames whisking about like locks of her hair. She had to be safe. If she wasn't, I would feel it.

6

Briar

If he was not safe, I would know it.

No matter how far, how fast, and how long I galloped from the castle, I would feel such a threat. It would consume me like a sixth sense. And if that happened, I would not be able to keep going.

Gusts of air shoved from my horse's snout, and the mare's solid body quaked beneath me, muscles revolving and hooves stamping into the earth. Miles and landmarks flew by in a mural, from rushing rapids to crusted timber and plaster taverns, from the deep mossy caves of forgotten faeries to brimming pumpkin patches, to sheets of fog capable of disorienting a person, to bulbous root traps, to soaring trees with fox and stag features carved into the bark like ancient monuments. I leaned deeper into my ride and whispered encouragements to the horse. All the while, my features pinched in concentration, and my gaze focused ahead.

Always ahead. Never back.

Dear Seasons. Do not look back.

With my two companions beside me, I shot forward as I had for three days. I kept moving, kept riding. If he were no longer breathing, this would not be possible.

So I knew. My jester was alive.

As was I. For now, at least. But how I wished I could tell him, reassure him, protect him.

Leaves blazed with color from the branches, the trees so vibrant it looked as though the world were on fire. Eliot and Cadence's own horses panted on either side of me. I kicked my mount into full speed, and our trio launched forward in tandem, spearing like arrows through the wilderness.

Silhouettes with metallic antlers, phosphorescent tails, and long tusks swept in and out of my vision. With the roaming fauna so close, we could not stop yet. Not in this territory, where wild things lurked in the condensed shrubbery.

My jester would warn as much.

With every league, the environment changed. Mist clung to the boughs, and thickets of leaves shifted hues, from rich shades to moodier ones.

My loose hair flew behind me like a flaming torch, something his eyes always loved to follow. But what was he staring at right now? What was he thinking of?

Perhaps something red. And perhaps something that burned.

My friends and I broke past the most feral terrain, then took a rest. Although we'd made camp every night, each respite had been fleeting. After dividing tasks for the evening and then splitting apart, I swung off my horse and guided the mare to a creek where she could graze and drink.

"Brave girl," I said, patting her down. "Once I'm done foraging for our supper, I promise to splash some water on you. If only one of us can enjoy a proper bath—"

But my tongue paused, the next words forgotten. As I glanced at my naked wrist, dismay ensnared my lungs. I had tied my scarlet ribbon securely to that wrist, yet not securely enough.

Because it was gone.

7

Briar

"No," I hissed, frantically patting myself down. The ribbon might have only just slipped and landed someplace close. My skirt pocket, perhaps. Or the toe of my boot. Yet grappling every stitch of my clothing yielded nothing.

My chest siphoned air, and perspiration rolled down my spine beneath the emerald cotton dress. Whipping around, I skewered my gaze past toadstools and gnarled undergrowth. I scanned every offshoot and creeper, seeking a glimpse of red.

When had I last seen it? When had I last checked the knot?

How far *back*?

Stumbling around, I yanked aside loose shrubbery. Swiftly, panic escalated to hysteria.

"No!" I shrieked loud enough to wake every dormant predator in a mile radius. "No, no, no!"

It was the only thing I had left of him. It was the only thing that tethered us now.

Crashing onto my knees, I crawled across the forest floor, brittle crimson leaves cracking under my weight. My palms mowed through woodland debris, searching, rummaging, ransacking the wild.

I would need to backtrack. I would need to retrace my steps.

Just then, another sound of alarm tore through the woods. "Briar!" an urgent male voice roared from leagues away. "Briar!"

At that moment, the hedges rustled. A male figure blasted into view, his furious blue eyes flashing and a garrote fixed in his grip. Eliot froze, arrested in place and momentarily dumbstruck, his expression slackening at the sight of me. "Briar?"

"It must be here," I gasped in a frenzy. "It has to be here!"

Realization loosened his features. Turning away, I kept hunting. In the same instant, my friend must have noticed the ribbon's absence because a thud resounded through the wilderness, signaling he'd discarded his weapon.

However, I did not glance up to check. I continued scrambling amid pebbles and chunks of dirt, even while Eliot called out my name again.

Please. *Please.*

I felt my eyes glaze over. I thrust my hand toward another patch of stocky bracken—when a set of fingers blocked me. Instantly, I stopped. Hovering before my eyes, a cord of scarlet fabric lay draped across my friend's digits.

Oxygen emptied from my lungs. I blinked at the ribbon, then took it in my shaky fingers.

Poet.

His name teetered on my lips. Yet I compressed my mouth, holding the name inside me, refusing to let it out. If I uttered that name, I would collapse.

Swallowing, I caressed the bracelet and took care to wrap it around my wrist. As I finished the double knot, a broad shadow materialized over the ground. I craned my head and watched Eliot hunker before me, golden waves falling around his face, stubble shadowing his jaw, and tenderness flooding his pupils.

I opened my mouth to speak, to apologize for scaring him, but nothing came out. Instead, Eliot cupped my jaw, telling me I didn't need to utter a word.

"I'm here," he whispered.

Whimpering, I hurled myself at him. My friend caught me and strapped his bulky arms around my trembling form, tucking me hard against his chest. The steady beat of his heart synched with mine as dry sobs heaved from my body.

"It's all right," he murmured gruffly. "Everything is okay."

No, it was not okay. Nothing about this was okay.

His thumbs brushed my cheeks as I inched back. Our foreheads fell together, resting there until another warm body pressed into my other side. The floral aroma of Cadence's perfume lulled my senses as she circled her arms around me and Eliot. Lost in the moment, neither of us had heard the lady approach. Briefly, I beheld Cadence's visage in the huddle. Evergreen hair to match her eyes and a rare, sympathetic expression.

Twisting, she leaned her chin atop my shoulder and wove her fingers with Eliot's, the three of us cocooning ourselves into one. And this ... this part was okay.

Much later, as eventide veiled the woodland in a deep blue hue, I stared into a blaze while absently stroking the bracelet. Kindling fizzled and split, the flames tossing sparks into the air. Fire could be such a destructive thing—deadly yet enchanting, hypnotic and stunning to behold.

Get near, and it warmed you. Get too close, and it hurt.

Goodness. Melodrama. I was beginning to think and sound like *him*. Despite myself, my lips tilted into a sad smile.

We are a tale for campfires. That is all. That is—

"Everything," I uttered, the words as thin as the tendrils of smoke rising from the timbers.

Yearning squeezed my heart, a wistful moment there and gone. It seemed I hadn't stopped aching since I left the castle. I should have grown used to it, but I never would.

Perched on a log, I wrapped my arms around my knees. Like this, I pretended my touch was his embrace, my fingers his hands. Keeping me upright. Making me burn with need. Like this, I remembered and counted every flame that had existed between us.

A candle he'd once refused me. A fireplace in his suite, where he first slid his bare cock against my damp core, giving me that first erotic introduction to sex. A hundred fires that had burned while he made me come around him. A tale for campfires.

Whether we would experience that privilege again ...

Whether he was all right, faring well, thinking of me ...

Whether his son was safe and happy ...

And Mother. And so many others I could not be there for, would never get to serve, to build a future with.

Cursed tears rimmed my lashes. I sucked them up, then straightened and pretended to be fussing with a loose eyelash as a male silhouette approached. Eliot hiked through the underbrush, his broad physique knocked the offshoots around, and he lowered himself beside me on the log. His palms cradled a mug of tea, threads of steam carrying the scents of apples and Autumn spices.

Silently, Eliot extended the mug. I blinked at the offering, then at his features. A perceptive but gentle grin slanted across his face. "Your favorite," he said.

We had funds, but traveling inconspicuously meant supply stops were rare, which made every ounce of tea precious. Not once in the past three days had my best friend poured a cup for himself, whereas Cadence and I had moaned and groaned in relief with each sip.

My tongue felt parched. As nightfall pushed a chill through the trees, the aromatic liquid tugged at me.

I glanced away. "I am not thirsty."

"You sure?" Eliot tempted. "It's mighty nippy tonight."

"I'm not cold either."

"Such a bullshitter."

My head swerved toward him. "I have Autumn in my veins—"

"So you've reminded me. Numerous times."

"—and I do not require creature comforts. As a citizen of this nation, I can handle the weather. It would take more than a breeze to incapacitate me."

"Briar." Eliot gave me a knowing look, a cloud of chilly air puffing from his mouth. "You don't need to overthink every decision. It's only a cup of tea. Just take the fucking thing and say thank you." I studied his expression. The intention hidden there. The desire to take care of me. My frown loosened, and I gave him a chagrined smile while accepting the mug. "Thank you."

As I tipped back the vessel, balmy liquid doused my palate with familiar flavors. I sighed, relaxing into this small comfort.

Nestling the cup in my hands, I watched as Eliot squatted beside the pit and fed it additional kindling. Firelight sketched the lute tattoo along the side of his neck, the design contorting with his movements and the muscles under his sweater rippling. My friend was blessed with a toned body, but he'd grown more rugged since we last saw each other in Spring. The coarse jaw and longer blond waves, which he'd tied into a bun behind his skull, suited him. In a departure from his customarily groomed appearance, dirt now streaked his fitted clothes, and muck caked his boots. He wore this look well.

Additionally, the garrote he'd set beside the pit had grown on me. "Your technique is improving."

The log shuddered under Eliot's weight as he returned to his seat beside me. A wry grin titled his lips, neither vain, nor self-effacing. "Coming from you, I'll take the compliment gladly, even if I didn't actually use the thing."

"But your stance and the way you handled the weapon," I vouched. "You did so without thinking, as if it was second nature."

"Where you're concerned, my friend? It's always second nature." I laced our fingers together. "I adore you for that. And the feeling is mutual."

Eliot lifted my hand and kissed my knuckles. Releasing me, he twined an arm around my shoulders and tucked me into his side. "I'm sorry I didn't get there quick enough to find the ribbon before you freaked out."

I rested my head in the crook of his neck. "Never be sorry for what you cannot control."

"I'll tell you what," he confided. "Weaponry is as hard as learning to play a lute, which took most of my life. Not that I would choose
between them, and not that anyone's wondering if I would, but I like
the idea of adding ferocity and killer aim to my list of skills, and if
what you're saying is true, I must be an apt pupil." Before continuing
the tangent, he stopped himself and hitched one shoulder. "Or I just
have an ambitious teacher."

Eliot was exaggerating. I had done nothing momentous apart from
schooling him on how to locate his target and strike true. Aim, I had
some experience with.

In any case, I chuckled ruefully. "If I have been strict about practicing, it's only because we're on the run for our lives."

"Yeah. That's a problem," he teased. "Then again, you've always
been an overachiever. Not that I've ever minded, you see. But three
days hence, and I can barely move my arms."

I opened my mouth, intending to respond, when the bushes
shook. A feminine "Shit!" and a subsequent "Fuck!" filtered through
the clearing.

Cadence stomped into view with all the grace of a troll in a ball-
room. Twigs stuck out from her tresses, more creepers snagged on
her fluted skirt, and crud stained the hem. The lady made more noise
than broken dishes. She grunted, spewed profanities that condemned
nature to hell, and then smacked her arm as if an invisible slug had
made itself at home on her sleeve.

"Ugh." Cadence picked her way across a knoll of exposed roots
while shaking out her fingers, as though she'd also touched something
sticky like sap. "I swear, that's the last time I'm peeing in a bush."

I folded my hands in my lap. "I warned you not to stoop near anything resembling flower beds."

"And not to eat apples with green leaves on the stems, not touch
root vegetables or cranberries that aren't ripe, not to pet the eight-
feet-tall deer, not to buy sourdough loaves from peddlers, not to flirt
with passersby—and come on, I'm randy as fuck after nearly half a

week, but I'm hardly shortsighted—not to follow the scent of ginger, and definitely not to wear gowns in dense areas. *Don't, this. Don't, that.* I got it all the first time, Miss Perfect. If I must, I'll hold my bladder until we get to the next village. I'm not interested in beetles crawling up my ass while I'm squatting."

Gallantly, Eliot rose and settled on the ground across from us. That allowed Cadence to drop her backside next to me.

From there, the lady proceeded to sulk at her manicure. "My fucking nails." Without looking, she pointed at me. "And if you value your life, do not lecture me about how I should have clipped them down when we first set out. As if we had time for that."

I clamped my mouth shut. Nonetheless, my features melted into amusement. "Here," I said. "Let me."

Reaching over, I plucked the twigs from her locks, then impulsively tethered them into a fluffy ponytail. Cadence froze in surprise until I finished the job and wiped my hands. After an awkward moment, she fiddled with her hair. "Thanks." But before I could reply, she waved me nearer. "Fine. Turn."

Stunned, I did as she requested. Cadence unraveled my disheveled braid and plaited it anew, recreating the complex weave Mother had taught me. Once the lady was done, she scooted backward. "Perfect."

I traced the braid while gawking at her. Such styles were hardly mastered in Spring.

Cadence read my mind and gave a saucy shrug. "I pay attention."

Long ago, we'd started out as rivals. Regardless, pleasure rippled through me to have the lady with us. In the past, camaraderie between us had been incomprehensible. These days, I felt grateful to be wrong.

Starlight spangled the forest floor. A bronze owl kept vigil overhead, its plumage shimmering. My horse grazed several feet away, along with the two other mounts.

Cadence flitted her fingers toward the pit flames. "I'm no expert, but isn't fire a sure way to get us mauled?"

"Not here," I said. "We call this territory The Vapor Wild. Mist is a constant fixture in Autumn, but here it's so congested, not even flames penetrate the fog. Visibility is limited, so the only way to travel this area is to be educated on the geography. The chances of us being accidently discovered are slim."

"And that's why you're the leader," Eliot praised.

I winced at the word. Thankfully, my friends failed to notice.

Although Cadence's remark was accurate regarding murderers and thieves—open flames might as well be an invitation—the mist protected us from humans and fauna. I'd been putting such knowledge to use with every mile between us and the castle. Oftentimes, the subtleties of this wilderness proved more dangerous than anything else. Merely a few days into our journey, and I'd lost count of how many times research had saved our lives.

"So." Cadence drew her knees to her chest. "What else are we talking about?"

Eliot obliged. "Briar was complimenting my prowess with a weapon."

"Hey." Cadence tossed me a fake glare and indicated the knife at her hip. "What about moi?"

Dutifully, I patted her thigh. "You are a natural with sharp objects and would make a wonderful slayer of innocents."

"Aww. I appreciate that."

"I know you do."

We laughed, but the sound died quickly on my lips. None of this was funny, and I had no right to enjoy myself. We barely had sufficient training, and while I kept a destination in mind, every corner held obstacles and hazards.

To make matters worse, I spotted a line of dried blood seeping through the arm of Eliot's shirt. "You're hurt," I fretted, hastening to search for a cloth.

"Briar, it's fine," he insisted. "It's only a scratch. One of the offshoots got me when I was running to find you."

"You need to clean that," I spoke over his assurances while fumbling to rip my skirt hem, to use as a makeshift bandage. "And you need to dress it. And—"

"Briar," he repeated, his inflection quieting me. "It's fine."

I stalled, feeling the weight of Eliot and Cadence's attention. My best friend was right; it was only a scratch. But out here, it could have been worse. And all because I'd agreed to let him come with me.

As if sensing my thoughts, Eliot murmured across the blaze, "It wasn't your fault, Briar."

I swallowed the lump in my throat. "Which part?"

The born souls locked in Autumn's dungeon, including the maddened ones from Summer who Rhys had used as pawns against me and Poet. The Masters' betrayal and the massacre in the castle's courtyard. The position I'd placed Mother in when she renounced my title. My friends, who risked themselves by joining me on this trek.

The little boy who didn't know if he'd ever see his Briar Patch again. And his father, who'd been forced to watch me leave.

Which part wasn't my fault?

"Everyone near me comes to harm," I said to the fire. "I have brought destruction to Autumn."

"Oh, for shit's sake," Cadence huffed. "You tricked every Royal on this continent; faced off with the King of Summer; weathered the scrutiny of your nation; protected a child from a world of judgment; brought a jester to his knees—in more than one sexy way; rescued him from the Masters, whom you also outsmarted; and led your soldiers to battle against them." She expelled a breath. "Now if you're done lamenting like an opera singer, I'd like to talk about the dinner we've yet to cook."

"Remind me why we brought her," Eliot joked.

"You love me," Cadence declared.

Instead of grinning, I shook my head. "Why did you do it? Why did you choose this?"

Again, the lady fell uncharacteristically silent. After a moment, she feigned interest in the firepit. Trying to affect a casual demeanor, she said, "My whole life, I've been bred to serve rulers, to nurture their beliefs and morals." Distant memories clouded her expression. "But I've never been able to express mine. Not to consider them, much less act on them. Not until I saw another side of Poet."

Giving a start, the lady peeked at me. "Shit. Is it okay if we—"

"It's always okay," I assured her softly.

Mentioning my jester was more than okay. It was essential.

"Like I was saying," Cadence continued. "Not until I saw another side of that delicious man. Not until I met his cute-as-hell son." She glanced at the woodland floor, and her tone grew excessively nonchalant. "And not until I got to know you."

My insides warmed like honey. I would have echoed the sentiment, but that would only have made Cadence squirm and possibly take back what she'd admitted.

All the same, humbleness overwhelmed me. They had betrayed their sovereigns for this cause, had subjected themselves to peril merely to live in exile by my side.

I wrung my hands. "I owe you both—"

"For the last time," Eliot insisted. "You owe us nothing."

"Speak for yourself, hon," Cadence contradicted, then regarded me. "I'd like a new wardrobe when this is over. And that sparkly ruby belt of yours. The one shaped like leaves. I saw you wear it to the welcome feast on your first night in Spring, and I've never been the same since."

I grinned through unshed tears. Then I got a hold of myself and nodded. "Agreed."

"You remember that belt?" Eliot mused at Cadence. "Briar wore it ages ago."

"It's jewelry." Cadence frowned as if Eliot was senseless. "*Royal* jewelry. Of course, I remember it."

Apart from the limited stash of clothing and supplies we'd purchased from various outposts, I didn't have priceless finery with me. Nothing besides my earrings. Be that as it may, Cadence would receive whatever she asked for. Somehow, I would repay her and Eliot, no matter what they said.

That night, we nestled close to one another, our limbs enmeshed under a pile of wool blankets. While Cadence slept, Eliot's nose tapped mine.

Whispering between us, he confided, "I chose this because you're everything to me."

I let those words soak into my skin. "I love you too."

This minstrel was my family, like many others. The comforting thought pulled me into sleep, but the respite was short-lived. I awoke at midnight, ensconced between my friends yet consumed by a bone-deep ache. A loss that couldn't be filled.

However thankful I felt to have them with me, I would only ever rest peacefully in the arms of one person. I imagined his strong body strapped around mine and replayed his voice in my head, his timbre reciting words to me until I drifted off once more.

8

Briar

By the week's end, the environment changed dramatically. We'd been trotting at a cautious pace when I suddenly yanked on the mare's reins, alerting Cadence and Eliot.

A gasp caught in my throat. My eyes consumed the view as if I'd never beheld color before. Cathedrals of oaks and tupelo trees towered ahead of us, their columns rising into the firmament like spires, the mesh of foliage painting the world in a profusion of shades and tints. Gabled cabins perched in the branches. Stairs entwined the trunks, and a lattice of bridges strung through the boughs, all connected by decks nestled into the heights.

Below, a water well abutted a creek, and pathways shaved through the grass. Farther down, a vacant carriage missing one wheel stood within a lush enclosure. Scarves of mist weaved through, ropy and glistening.

The Lost Treehouses.

Our sanctuary. Yet perhaps our detriment too.

Despite the majestic abundance of color and the rustic cabins looming overhead, a dark haze shrouded the outer terrain, and the trees seemed to be watching us. My fingers tightened on the reins. I recalled the lore of this abandoned realm, excitement and trepidation colliding in my breast. For all their etherealness, fairytales had their ghastly sides. Both existed here. That was why no one ventured to this part of the wild, and although it was a risk, the isolation would protect us.

So long as we respected this land, it would respect us back. The test would be to learn how.

My friends' jaws dropped as they aligned their horses with mine.

"Holy shit," Eliot muttered.

"Seasons," Cadence exclaimed. "What is this place?"

My lips moved, speaking in a hushed tone. "This is our new kingdom."

9

Poet

Flames spread and crawled high, engulfing the castle walls. Brick and glass melted. Maple trees ignited, their canopies blazing like torches. The inferno consumed the castle, smoldering it to cinders. In the destruction's wake, the king's words returned to me.

We created fire.

Screams tore through the haze. Yet not a single body materialized, the chaos invisible to my eyes. From across the distance, I only saw her.

The pyre writhed between us, forming a barrier. But fuck that. For if we burned, the princess and jester would do it together. I broke from my stance and thrashed against the blaze whilst she did the same. As the fire snapped at us like fangs, we treaded heat and smoke, fighting our way to each other.

When only a few inches separated us, she leaped for me. I thrust out my arms, ready to grab the princess. But instead of catching my thorn, something flew from her fingers and landed in mine.

A dozen needles bit my flesh, and a rose rested in my grip. The color bloomed as red as her hair, as scarlet as the ribbons around our wrists, and as crimson as my blood. The barbs pricked my flesh, yet the flower glinted in the firelight, impervious to the blaze. Like a weapon. Like a shield. There were two of us. But only one rose.

My gaze ripped toward the princess, who nodded as the fire swallowed her. Stubborn female, always sacrificing herself. Her name ruptured from my chest, yet no sound came out. She dissolved to ashes whilst I stood there, protected by a single rose that pierced my skin with its very sweet thorns.

The stinging sensation intensified—and broke me from the delirium. My eyes tore open as I launched upright off the bed. My chest pumped oxygen, heavy pants punched from my mouth, and sweat varnished my bare chest. Whipping my head backward, I gawked at the paneled ceiling and waited for my pulse to slow.

Another nightmare. I scrubbed my face with one hand, then grunted as something sharp jabbed the other palm. Glancing down, I found the rose trapped in my death grip. A single thorn had embedded itself in my thumb, a bead of blood trickling from the wound.

The Spring rose I had set on Briar's pillow. My head clicked to reexamine the suite with its balcony and atheneum of bookshelves, home to countless titles and illuminated manuscripts. As if I needed additional proof, the scent of apples wafted from the linens.

I had stumbled here and fallen asleep. That explained why I still wore my leather pants. Had I been in my own chambers, I would have been naked, but swaggering across the hall with my ass and cock in plain view would have violated the Autumn guards' modesty. This wasn't Spring, after all.

Instead, I had stumbled here exhausted, shirtless, and bare-footed. In that state, I'd climbed into her scent and passed out.

My tongue flicked at the bloody droplet rising from my finger, my palate wiping it clean and tasting the mark she'd made on me. I must have snatched the rose in my sleep. Yet the flower showed no sign of having been crushed, its petals flawlessly smooth. Flora lived longer in Spring than in any other Season. With this one, the thorns grew more polished, more honed with age. Not to mention its other fine attributes.

I spun the rose by its stem. "That's why I picked you."

Across the suite, muffled commotion drifted from Briar's wardrobe. My head lanced toward the sound of hectic movements—thuds and some type of weight hitting the floor.

Guards patrolled the Royal wing's foyer. Nevertheless, I'd made sufficient enemies in this court. Moreover, Autumn tended to be more resourceful than the Spring residents who used to show up at my door for bribes or sex.

I slid my fingers to my calf and gripped the hilt of a dagger. The blade flashed as I eased it from the harness. Slithering out of bed, I stalked sideways through the shadows.

Down the passage, the doors to Briar's wardrobe stood open, a refuge where I'd once dressed my princess in an ivory gown, then ripped the sodden thing from her body. Moon beams spotlighted the floor, and the rug cushioned my steps, though I hardly required it. They wouldn't hear me coming.

Pausing at the threshold, I flipped the dagger across my knuckles. My ears picked up more thuds, the sound diminutive and ... small.

The fuck?

I hesitated. But when a tiny male cry penetrated my ears, the dagger dropped from my fingers, and I sprinted into the closet. Atop the dais and surrounded by several full-length mirrors, a runty body squirmed within a pile of cashmere littering the ground. Trussed up in the fabrics, the little sprite shrieked, his body twisting back and forth.

"Nicu," I rasped, landing beside him and yanking away the garments.

From under the mound, a shag of dark brown hair popped into view. My son thrashed in his sleep and peeped like a bird caught in a net. He slapped at my chest as I hunched over and framed his damp, tear-streaked cheeks.

"Nicu, love," I urged. "Nicu, hush."

My son's eyes flipped open, the green of his irises so bright they doused the room in color. Wheezing, he shook against my grasp. Confusion and terror bloated his pupils as he struggled to register what was happening.

"Shh, shh, shh," I whispered in a rush. "It's okay. It's okay, darling."

His body went limp, perspiration splotching his orange robe. That faeish countenance was riveted on mine, clarity and recognition seizing his features.

"Papa," he wailed, flinging himself off the dais.

Nicu hurled his scanty body toward me. At the same time, I caught my son and clasped him to my chest, one arm strapping around his waist and the other cupping the back of his head. Nicu scuttled onto my lap and snatched fistfuls of my hair with surprising strength. His face dove into my neck, fresh sobs wracking his form.

"Hush, my love," I murmured into his ear. "I'm here now. Papa's here."

Nicu whimpered, his words muted against my throat. I rubbed his back until he slumped, his cries thinned to sniffles, and his breathing evened out.

"I want Briar Patch," he mewled, the entreaty puncturing my ribcage. "I tried to free her roots from the soil, but I couldn't."

"You tried to save her?" I interpreted, speaking against his hair.

Nicu wiggled back. With his head ducked, he spoke to my chest. "I thought she was in here and couldn't get out, and that's why she's been gone for so long."

This would make sense if my child were anyone other than Nicu. He didn't have the capacity to grasp distances and locations.

"Nicu," I prompted, unsure if he would comprehend the question. "How did you know where ..."

Tumble could have led Nicu here. My son's wily ferret knew the layout of this castle even better than I did. However, the troublemaking familiar was nowhere in sight, which meant he'd gone exploring.

And when Nicu pointed to the ribbon strung across the ceiling, I remembered. Despite my sleep-induced haze, I should have recalled the streamers Briar and I had installed between our suites. Although he wouldn't have gotten past Aire—there was no way the soldier would have allowed Nicu to scramble in here alone—the knight was on duty with his troops. Whilst Aire glued himself to my son's quarters much of the time, the man couldn't abandon his army entirely.

Aire's absence must have given my son an outlet. Nicu had squeezed past the alternate guards and followed the ribbon trail to Briar's chambers, longing to soothe the ache of her departure.

He didn't understand why the court had made her leave, why the queen hadn't been able to stop it, and why we hadn't gone with Briar. Mostly, he didn't understand why she hadn't come back, and careful explanations did nothing to soothe his pain. Nicu hadn't been the same since, his excitable demeanor wilting with each passing day.

When he'd gotten inside Briar's suite, my son evidently hadn't noticed me in her bed. He'd been distracted, guessing the princess might be stuck in her wardrobe.

I dipped my head toward his bent one. "Indulge me, love. Why did you think she would be trapped here?"

Nicu glanced at the mound of priceless clothing. "I smelled her."

My chest caved. Direction was a problem for my son, but scent carried memories. Like Briar's bed, her fragrance permeated the wardrobe. Nicu had followed the ribbons, then followed the aroma of tart, green apples. He'd rifled among the clothes, his mind betraying him, assuming the princess was somehow inside one of the outfits. Hence, the avalanche of textiles, which he must have eventually fallen asleep in, curling himself in her scent before the nightmare descended.

Like father. Like son.

Nicu wiped an arm across his eyes, but his features crumbled. "I promised Briar Patch that I'd be a hero, so I tried to save her. But I didn't see her anywhere. I checked all of them." He gestured to the coats, gowns, and skirts puddling the floor. "And I dreamed the same thing. Even then, I couldn't free her roots."

I curled my finger under Nicu's chin and gently lifted his head.

"I have nightmares too."

His eyebrows puckered. "But you're Papa."

Meaning, I never got scared. People feared me, not the other way around.

But Nicu didn't know how untrue that was. My son terrified me, as Briar terrified me. Except they did so in an unconditional way.

I chuckled. "Aye, I'm quite the enigmatic ideal. Regardless, I have my fair share of shitty nights."

"Shitty nights," he repeated, nodding. "So we're the same."

"But there's a secret to battling those demons." Nicu scooted closer, committing this to memory, cementing it verbatim, as he did with most dialogue. "The secret trick is this: Just because your mind took you somewhere bad, that doesn't make it true. When we mortals sleep, sometimes we see our wishes, other times our fears. But upon awakening, we get to decide which are real and which are lies. The choice is yours."

I wouldn't ask if he understood this. Despite his challenges, Nicu was smarter and more imaginative than the world gave him credit for.

"You *are* a hero," I told him. "Because you tried. You, my exquisite fae, braved the darkness to help Briar Patch. The attempt is what matters."

As the meaning sank in, my son's eyes softened. Someday, he would be quicker than me, wiser than Briar, and stronger than every nation on this continent. As the princess had said before she left, maybe Nicu would be the one to save us all someday. Whether or not that happened, I would spend my life making sure he believed it was possible.

When he was an infant, reciting verse had been the only way to get my son to fall back asleep. With that in mind, I lowered us onto our sides, so that we faced each other. But instead of a simple poem, I murmured a passage from the princess's favorite series, part of the collection's final book, which she'd been hunting for years to find.

Eventually, I'd located the book and given it to her during our hideout in The Royal Retreat near The Pumpkin Wood. To this day, the volume remained at the house, where we'd left it before all hell broke loose with the Masters.

I remembered one striking passage. The only bit of verse on the pages.

From the sacred wild, she will reign.

In the hidden trees, is her domain ...

Nicu's eyes drifted shut, a peaceful expression slackening his features. I'd never lied to him, and I wouldn't start now. On and off over his life, my son had lost too many people. His mother. Old Jinny. Sometimes his father, whenever I'd left him at the cottage, needing to return to Spring's palace.

And now Briar. But not for long. Wherever she was, I would walk to the end of this earth if it meant reuniting them.

A pile Briar's clothing nestled between us. Nicu balled his hand in mine whilst I mumbled the last lines of verse, my own lids hooding and my body succumbing. Yet before either of us drifted into blessed rest, I cradled his face and hissed, "She will return."

My son's chest rose and fell, and he whispered back, "I know."

He might as well have commanded me to act. Just like another Royal I worshiped.

Alas.

Days became weeks. Weeks became months.

In that time, not a fucking thing. In between raising Nicu; meeting with Avalea about Rhys and the castle's confidential passages; conferencing with the council for a thousand other matters; kissing the court's principled ass; and monitoring the treatment of born souls, in addition to Summer's mad, I stalked every acre and square foot of this complex. I ransacked each shelf and studied every map in the library wing, then scoured the books in Briar's suite. I manipulated conversations in the throne room, stalked courtiers through the halls, and interrogated the Royal advisors.

To say the least—and I never said the least—I did everything short of dismantle this fortress to the last fucking hinge. Only one woman in this bedeviled world could evade the Court Jester with success, get him to run in circles, and drive him out of his bloody mind.

I had told Briar I would find her, but would I? Did she want me to? Only now did I recall one important fact. One crucial nugget from that moment, when I'd mouthed those words to her, just before she left.

I had made that promise. Yet she hadn't responded.

Her fingers sizzled a path to my cock. Blood rushed to the head, coloring my skin a ruddy hue, and the length of my erection broadened. I arched into her palm, groaning as she encircled the column in her grip, a slender thumb rolling over the glistening slit at my crown.

Hectic pants rushed from my lungs. I fisted the sheets, realizing a pair of scarlet ribbons bound my arms to the bedposts. Hissing, I locked my gaze with those steely eyes, the irises brimming with desire.

The princess's naked thighs spread around my waist, her soaked pussy grazing my cock like the worst sort of tease. Holding me fast, she lowered herself, straddling me to the ball sac. The walls of her cunt flared around my erection, coating the flesh in her arousal.

My control snapped. I lunged my hips off the mattress and pitched into her, my dick splitting her folds wider. The princess's spine curved, so far back those locks of red hair brushed my knees. She seized my waist for balance, opening as I charged at her, drawing me deeper, deeper, deeper.

She cried out, the moans desperate as I fucked harder into her. Lying prone beneath the princess, I watched her nude body jostle from the rhythmic brunt of my cock, her hair a messy, fiery curtain on either side of her face. Those eyes pierced through the darkness and glittered with rapture.

On a growl, my lips parted. Her name teetered on the wet edge of my tongue. "Bri—"

My eyes flickered open, a groan humming from my lips. Instead of haunted, this time I awoke on the verge of bliss. Condensation glazed my naked skin, the sheets of my bed tangling around my limbs, and blood rushed to the head of my rigid cock.

I ripped off the covers and panted into the room, lust and longing coursing through my veins. That, and annoyance, which segued to anger. I had pumped my dick to thoughts of her so many times, 'twas a wonder calluses hadn't formed on my palm.

Launching upright, I knifed my fingers through my hair and stared into the darkness. "Where are you, sweeting?" I snarled, the sound coming out furious and lustful.

Summer, a hard nay. Winter, unlikely. Spring, foolish.

Jinny would offer sanctuary, but crossing kingdom lines into a Season from which Briar was outlawed was a recipe for disaster. Autumn had evicted the princess from its castle limits, not its borders. By contrast, Spring indeed had. Defying that order wouldn't sit well with Basil and Fatima, a catastrophe if we wanted to reach a truce with them.

Briar was too smart to be obvious, much less reckless. If I knew my thorn, she felt responsible for the fates of everyone around her. Assuming Briar wouldn't face a Spring trial, she still wouldn't put our campaign in jeopardy. Never mind dragging Eliot and Cadence with her, when both were now considered traitors by their origin Season.

Nor would Briar place Jinny in the position of being an accomplice, no matter how much experience the elder woman had in committing treason—and how few fucks she'd give about the dire consequences.

Nay, Briar's conscience would allow none of this. Hence, she was in Autumn. For this nation flowed through her veins like a life force.

She would go somewhere enshrouded by nature. Somewhere that encompassed the written word. Someplace where no one else would dare to go.

Pride over her ingenuity clashed with several irksome emotions.

My fists curled as I succumbed to a new form of obsession. The more she evaded me, the harsher these impulses became. Oh, but my sweet thorn would pay for making her jester suffer.

When I found her, the princess had better be in one piece. If not, I'd shred whoever had touched her and make them beg for death.

Or if she was all right, I'd direct my vengeance toward her, tie the woman down with a dozen scarlet ribbons, and make her spine curl so far off the mattress, the blood would rush to her head. I would make my latest erotic dream a reality. I'd fuck her so thoroughly, make her come so violently, she would feel me inside her every time she moved. From then on, the princess would never know any other sensation than raw, hot bliss.

Pressure built in my temple. A growl scraped a path up my throat.

But as I held back, denied myself the sound of her name, a thought struck me. I recalled the verse I'd recited for Nicu, the one from Briar's book series. It had been about a ruler falling to ruin, then rising to power. But during the interim, that ruler had bided her time by living amid folkloric trees, forging that place into her own makeshift castle.

From the sacred wild, she will reign.

In the hidden trees, is her domain …

I picked through my memory, going back to the first night on Briar's balcony, shortly before I gave her that earth-shattering climax. My thorn had pointed out the geography of Autumn, citing a place where no one ventured.

A realm born of lore and myth, like the pages of a dark fairytale, akin to the one she loved to read. An enclave with historical significance. An abandoned place.

My heart galloped like a beast. I gripped the blankets and crushed them in my fists.

And then I knew.

I fucking knew where to find her.

Briar

When I was a child, I loved playing hide and seek. The thrill of tucking myself away somewhere. The excitement of nestling into a secret recess. The comfort in knowing I was safe, no matter what niche I stashed myself into. Because my parents would play along and search, I loved the challenge of outsmarting them, reassured that the ones who cared would always find me.

Like the nightly expeditions with Father through the halls, when we used to explore the castle's labyrinthine passages, I relished being lost and then found. For a time, grief had accompanied those memories. But now in this veiled forest, I welcomed the recollections.

Hunched over, with my knees in the dirt, I closed my eyes and let the visions enfold me. Father would insist we seek out every burrow of this landscape. Mother would appreciate the lore and history. Nicu would be awed by the colorful leaves. And …

And the rift expanded from my chest to the edges of my being. Yet I allowed the yearning to overtake me, as it had for the past three months. I surrendered to every vivid sensation that accompanied thoughts of him.

I miss you. I need you.

I cannot control it. I do not wish to.

Come to me. But please stay away.

For him, I would feel the anguish, as much as the desire. For him, I would endure every dark and brilliant emotion in existence. For him, I would wear a thousand scars.

A breeze filtered through the underbrush and rustled a strand of my hair, which had come loose from my braid. Along with rich woodland spices, I inhaled amber and vetiver. The scents that clung to his wardrobe. The masculine essences of sin and wit. Seasons, I drew in those fragrances.

At last, my eyes opened. With renewed spirits, I reinspected my surroundings. Mist weaved through the gnarled branches of oaks and tupelo trees, the columns rising as high as towers, some of them spearing through the clouds. Olive moss filigreed the trunks, and dense awnings of orange, burgundy, and jade leaves shivered overhead.

History claimed that fairytales and fables were first conceived here. Every such ominous or mystical story had its origins in this place. From the grisly to the enchanting, it all began in this woodland. Around every corner, the wild could either be stunning or brutal, trustworthy or conniving.

The Almighty Seasons were the deities of our continent, they had their own inexplicable power and mysterious divinity, and this landscape was no exception. It had a mind of its own, deciding who was allowed to stay and who must be exterminated.

So far, so good. The point was no one ventured to this enclave anymore. Not for centuries, aside from desperate souls or fortune hunters seeking lost magic. I belonged in the former category.

The compact thicket enclosed me in a nest of hedges, with only a small gap to squeeze through. Not ideal, but this patch yielded precious edible stalks—filling, nourishing, and delicious. I'd recognized them during my initial quest here. But while superstition held less sway on me, I kept faith in books, which had stressed one crucial rule about this environment: Nothing appeared as it seemed. Taking heed,

I had tested the stalks before deeming them safe.

A basket rested beside me. Muck caked my fingers as I resumed harvesting.

Later, a breeze whistled through the canopy. Umbrellas of leaves shuddered from the treetops, and dampness permeated the air. I glanced toward the sky, making out a few restless clouds. By eventide, it was going to rain.

My fingers reached out, then froze instinctively, arrested millimeters from the next stem. With my pulse skipping, I recognized the plant I'd almost touched. An herb with a fuzzy head that curled inward.

Willow Dime.

Across the continent, few plants were universal natural resources. This one was among those few and acted as a sleeping draught, particularly helpful during painful medical procedures, during which one was better off unconscious.

The problem was, Willow Dime wasn't a remedy for everyone. In fact, this had been made clear when I met Jinny, having arrived at her cottage with a leenix wound. The woman had nursed the injury until I'd fainted. Although she had suggested Willow Dime to blunt the pain, that option would have killed me quicker than the leenix gash. In my case, merely touching the herb would have fatal consequences.

My wrist shook. Cautiously, I pulled away and swerved toward the edible stalks, knowing that if I turned back, the plant would be gone.

Again, nothing was as it seemed. I doubted the Willow Dime stem had turned up here randomly, however universal. This forest liked to play, to test, and to reward. Only those who earned their place, who could see past the wild's trickery, could stay long enough to discover the beauty.

Although my basket was full, I contemplated reaping a few more stalks. I'd hiked three miles to reach this location, and we could use as many rations as possible in case the weather turned. With that in mind, I prepared to extract another stem from the ground.

Something groaned from behind, the sound reminiscent of splitting bark. I wheeled around, my fingers already poised on the thorn quill stashed in my braid. My eyes jumped across the contorted mesh of branches, seeing neither fauna, nor any humanlike figures. Yet another groan passed through the thicket, this time like wood stretching.

I swiveled the opposite way, trailing the commotion. Trepidation set my heart to racing as my fingers switched from the thorn in my hair to the one strapped around my ankle.

Again nothing. Yet something ...

A shadow swayed across the grass, long and bent at a crooked angle. My eyes swelled wide. I swung my gaze toward the nearest trunk just as the soil broke apart in chucks, and a root heaved itself from the earth. Before me, the oak's branches cracked and snapped like the limbs of a wizened creature bristling in offense.

Leaves darkened to a sooty hue, the tips gleaming. The groaning increased in volume. By Seasons, the visual would have mesmerized me if I hadn't been its objective.

It did not take an expert to guess the brunt of this tree would shatter a human skeleton. The roots alone could bury an army. Yet the oak waited, sizing me up and making its wishes known.

My mind rushed back to everything I'd read and studied about Autumn trees. Never had I witnessed one come to life, but I'd known it was possible. Suddenly, my gaze skittered toward the basket of stalks, and a thought hastened into my mind about cautionary tales and the sovereignty of nature.

This oak was not evil. It was upset.

Humbly suspecting why, I let my hands fall to my sides. Abandoning the stalk I'd been about to harvest, I extended my arms and bowed my head. My chest thumped, heavy pants spewing from my mouth. "I beg your pardon. And I am at your behest."

The roots stalled. The groaning ceased. The oak's majestic size overshadowed me.

I counted a dozen hectic heartbeats before a rush of air sailed through my clothes, akin to a great exhale. Lifting my head, I watched the branches recede and the roots withdraw, sinking back into the soil. The oak's leaves fluttered, as though pleased by my display.

One lesson I'd learned while gathering from The Wandering Fields at the castle was never to take more than I needed from the land. Nature required its own bounty, as did the next harvester who ventured here to feed themself.

A branch unspooled and skated over my fingers, ascended my arm and shoulder, and finally entwined into my hair. By now, my braided bun had loosened. This enabled the bough to weave a strand of tiny golden leaves through the red locks, thus forming a single, thin braid.

Something eased in my chest. Something like gratitude.

I sketched the leaf braid and glanced at the tree, which loomed calmly and regally. I would never kneel for my coronation, but I sensed the experience would feel somewhat like this. Wondrous and profound.

I combed out the remains of my bun, allowing the tresses to fall freely, the single braid dangling among them. I stood and nodded to the oak, my lips rising into a grin. "Thank you."

I returned to our sanctuary in a daze. The forest opened and spread itself wide like an amphitheater, oaks and tupelos standing tall, some with hollow chambers carved into the bases, the circumferences able to house armies.

In the heights, winding stairs and gabled cabins with shutters clustered together. Bridges connected the trees, and decks encircled the columns. Up close, one would see peeling paint, rickety planks in grave need of repair, and scaffolding netted in cobwebs. Still, the rustic ambience provided a much-welcome distraction. From the scent of woodsmoke in a nearby firepit, to a candle flickering from one of the treehouse windows, to the vegetable garden I'd planted on the ground level beside the water well, this realm alleviated my homesickness.

Well. It helped half of the time, at least.

Despite the dark legends about this place, I admired the old maj-esty and ruggedness that coalesced here. The arena of timbers and treehouses resembled a castle of the wild, wrought strictly of nature. Even the exposed joints and hardware had all been forged of wood. A true forest stronghold.

Hitching the basket over my shoulder, I climbed one of the stair-cases strewn around a tupelo trunk. My pulse was racing by the time I reached the lowest level, thirty feet above the ground.

"Oh goodie," a feminine voice announced sarcastically. "You didn't die."

I gave a start, having barely stepped onto the platform when Cadence pranced toward me out of nowhere. The lady's swanlike form was outfitted in a dusty cotton gown, and she'd piled those verdant locks messily atop her head. Propping both hands on her hips, she glowered at me. "Eliot was worried sick."

No, he was not. I had returned earlier than promised, from a place I'd been to numerous times. "It isn't sunset yet," I reminded her. "I am hardly late."

"Tell that to him." The lady knocked her head toward one of the larger decks where Eliot practiced with his garrote, my friend's bare torso rippling as he brandished the weapon, his lute tattoo visible even from here.

After a second, Cadence whistled. "Damn," she detoured, admir-ing the bulk of muscles and tanned skin. "I'd fuck that." But before I could level her with a censorious look, the lady batted her lashes my way. "If he'd let me."

I rolled my eyes. "Eliot does not favor women."

"So what?" Cadence asked, evidently being serious and remind-ing me that some Spring citizens did not shy away from experimen-tation. "You might as well be siblings, right? You know the bloke. Is there any chance he'd do it for kicks?"

"Feel free to predict my answer."

Cadence sighed. "My loss."

The lady's origins sat plainly on her face. Despite his physical attributes, Eliot wasn't her type. Though at this juncture, that did not matter. After three months of chastity, Cadence longed for intimate contact.

I empathized with this feeling. Except only one man could ever stoke the heat between my thighs. I wished I could say Autumn modesty had supplied me with a greater measure of resilience against that hunger. However, I would be lying to myself.

Day and night, I thirsted for someone who wasn't here. He had spoiled me, destroyed me for anyone else. Now that the jester had shown me such a degree of pleasure, it simmered in my veins constantly. Every moment segued back to those green eyes and that devious smirk. Even in the busiest moments, I could not stop thinking about that man. Nor did I wish to stop.

"Anyway," Cadence dismissed. "I had to insist the bloke grab a weapon, to preoccupy himself from brooding over your whereabouts."

At the onset, Eliot had grown obsessively protective, never letting me venture from the treehouses alone. But over time, as I'd proven myself capable amid my own Season, he had relaxed. I may have also forced him to calm down, having made a habit of leaving at dawn, before he woke up.

Today was an exception. I'd left later than usual.

As for Cadence, I contemplated how quickly she had materialized upon my arrival. Especially when the vast network of trees and cabins stretched into the distance. She could have been a million places other than this platform, which overlooked the unmarked path leading to and from our private makeshift kingdom.

I stared at her. "And you simply happened to be in this area when I got back?"

"A coincidence." Cadence shrugged, avoiding my raised eyebrows. "It's not like I was looking out for you." Her own brows dipped together. "Everything go okay out there? You seem frazzled."

My mouth opened, then closed promptly. I wanted to share what had happened, but one thing kept me from imparting the story.

Instead, I nodded. "All went well." To illustrate, I lifted the basket loaded with stalks. "We have dinner."

Cadence brightened and snatched the vessel. "I'll get the firepit going." Before departing, the female noticed my leaf braid and flicked it with her finger. "Huh. Cute."

As she walked away, Eliot noticed me and slung the cords of his garrote across the backs of his shoulders. Sauntering to the nearest railing, he gripped its ledge and yelled across the forty paces between us. *"Be wary to believe milady's bullshit,"* the minstrel sang in exaggeration, his tenor ringing through the air, as if performing the lyrics to a ballad. *"Lo, in your absence she hath been suffering a conniption fit."*

"Okay, fuck both of you," Cadence groused as she pranced across an abutting bridge. "I deny everything!"

Eliot threw me an entertained look. I grinned back at him before retreating.

Across two suspensions lined in old lanterns, and up another winding flight of steps, I emerged on a deck surrounding an oak treehouse. The cabin's front stoop protruded from the trunk, the home merged into the bark, and dormer windows jutted from the second story. Climbing the front steps, I stepped through the arched door and collapsed.

My spine hit the facade. Sliding to the ground, I folded one hand over my mouth, concealing a multitude of sounds.

Astonishment. Reverence. Yearning.

Sealed inside the room, I sketched the garland in my hair and marveled once more at its presence. It would have been easy to tell Cadence and Eliot how I'd earned this token from the forest, yet I hadn't wanted to share it. Like every singular moment that had amounted over the past months, I stored this miracle with the rest, saving it for one person.

My thoughts strayed from the forest episode to other cravings. As I pictured his features, my skin pebbled, and my limbs shook.

I wish I could tell you what happened.

I wish you had seen it.

I wish you were here.

That night, my body trembled for a different reason. A hushed moan tripped from my tongue, sneaking out like a filthy secret before I could stop it. As I writhed atop the mattress, the noise echoed in the dark bedroom. Any louder, and the sounds would spill from the open window.

My friends kept their own cabins on neighboring levels, these walls were thick, and the brewing clouds rumbled. They would not hear me. Yet I sank my teeth into my lower lip until I tasted the salt of my own blood.

Always, he affected me this way. Mere thoughts caused me to bleed and my body to quiver with such ferocity that my bones might snap. And how I enjoyed the torment.

The headboard thumped gently against the wall, in tandem to the motions of my hand. With my legs splayed, I arched my fingers into the wet slot of my pussy and probed rhythmically. My walls spread around my digits, which pistoned in and out, the pace sinuous.

I rolled my wrist over my clit, the friction throwing electric currents across my skin. With each pass, the kernel inflated. My crease spilled more fluid, the ache in my cunt building, so that I soaked my hand to the knuckles.

Sweat dripped between my breasts, my nipples erect and pointing to the beamed ceiling. My heels kicked the quilt to the floor. I curled my spine off the bed and clamped my mouth shut, lest the moans should expand into a scream.

His voice drenched me. His words seared my flesh.

I let the memories seduce me into a frenzy. Frustration, loneliness, pain, and desire converged in the slit of my thighs. My backside rocked into the bed, granting me momentum as I lurched my fingers deeper into my folds. The muscles of my pussy contracted, bringing me closer to an eclipse.

My head dissolved into a fantasy. His wicked hand slid over my pumping one. Conniving fingers covered the backs of my palms, the forbidden touch wracking me with shivers. I turned onto my side and drew my knees into my chest, the better to pitch higher, deeper still. From behind, a hot, decadent voice blew against the shell of my ear. "What have we here," the jester murmured. "An heiress all by herself?"

A traitorous whimper escaped my lips, which turned into a gasp as his tongue dragged over the ledge of my ear. Tingles scattered to the edges of my being. My thighs stretched farther, my nipples toughened to the point of agony, and my pussy soaked the mattress.

I worked myself quicker, my fingers shoving into the private flesh. He hovered over me, his shadow draping across my body, those clover eyes glittering as he watched. I felt his gaze like a caress, yet I denied myself another moan.

"Ah, ah, ah," he purred. "None of that, willful princess. Let me hear how your sweet cunt feels."

"I can't," I wheezed. "I cannot without you."

"Aye, my thorn. You can." His molten voice poured down my nape. "Shout for me."

Flames licked a path up my skin. The flanks of my pussy twitched. An orgasm rushed up my throat, and the shape of his name surged across my tongue.

Helpless, I twisted my head over my shoulder, eager to meet his lips.

But instead of that shameless mouth, my lips brushed cotton. The contact struck my senses like a bucket of ice water. My eyes flapped open and landed on the pillow, which occupied the bed's vacant side.

My chest constricted. The heat between my legs receded, and my hand ceased its movements, slickness from my aching pussy coating my fingers. I gaped at the pillow as if I shouldn't be surprised, all the while my pulse struggled to catch up.

I blinked through the lust-fueled haze. The cabin materialized, the furnishings glossed in a midnight sheen. Across from me, an unlit brick hearth embedded into the wall, with a short tapestry hanging above the mantel. Candle sconces framed a dresser and mirror, and a trunk stood at the bed's foot.

My eyebrows slammed together. Fantasies did not turn into reality. At some point, I had neglected to remember that.

Sitting upright, I removed my fingers from the gap in my thighs. Warmth flooded my cheeks. Seasons, I had been on the verge of shrieking. Eliot or Cadence might not have heard a few moans, but a full-bodied onslaught would have inundated this settlement.

Under my nightgown, my breasts hung heavily. The rift in my thighs still buzzed with need, and my limbs still quavered. No matter how often this happened, the blaze rarely died quickly.

Despite the cozy interior, the cabin seemed to shrink. From beyond the window panes, blessed fresh air called to me.

With a defeated sigh, I swung my legs over the edge. Crossing barefooted across the room, I drew a flannel shawl over my shoulders and padded downstairs to the front door. Plaiting my hair would take too long, and it would camouflage the oak braid, neither of which I preferred tonight.

What I needed was a walk. The rain was coming. But with my flesh still burning, perhaps that was a good thing.

And if I got soaked, it did not matter. No one would see me.

Briar

The leaves shook like brilliantly colored shingles, their radiance illuminating the paths. For a while, I wandered the bridges and overpasses. Sometimes, I lingered at a vista point and gazed into the distance, as if able to see beyond the dense canopies.

Then I kept going, musing about the people who had once lived here. Not that all of them had been human during that ancient era.

I debated how to restore and preserve this haven, to return it to its former glory. If I did not have a plot against Summer to enact, and a crusade for born souls to embark on, I might have embraced such a project.

Something hard and round pushed into the sole of my boot. Squatting, I picked the nut off the ground and contemplated its shell. Legend spoke of several acorns that granted a dark sort of magic. According to the lore, they could be anywhere, in any territory of Autumn. And one must know what to look for.

Nothing about this acorn appeared unique. Shaking my head, I pitched the nut to the ground, then a droplet hit my wrist. I glanced through the slender notches between the trees, where gray clouds bunched together and emitted a thin drizzle. Soon after, that drizzle intensified into a shower. Rain sliced through the leaves and patted the treehouse rooftops.

Despite the walk and brisk climate, my skin refused to cool from the earlier fantasy. Hoping to amend the situation, I trekked to another lookout point, this one more exposed to the sky. Wrestling off my boots and shrugging off my shawl, I craned my head to the downpour. Then I did something Autumn Royals never attempted in polite society. I spread my arms wide and let the deluge have its way with me.

Rain splattered my hair and drenched the strands. Sheets of water seeped through the nightgown, rendering the fabric translucent and plastering the gauzy material to my body. Droplets licked down my throat, breasts, and hips.

A princess conducted herself properly. A princess always presented herself groomed and tidy.

A princess did not exhibit herself like this. A princess did not drench herself in public.

But that was fine. No one was around. And I was not a princess any longer.

Even if the tempest failed to snuff out the fire in my veins, I gave myself to the elements. My lips curved into a smile. But when I lowered my head, a flash of red caught my attention. I glanced sideways toward the rich color, expecting to see a vibrant leaf tumbling across the platform.

Instead, my grin faltered, then disappeared altogether. Tied to one of the railings was a length of fabric dyed a rich scarlet.

My heart seized. My arms fell to my sides as I stumbled to the item, rain blurring my vision, so that I questioned what I saw.

Stalling before the object, my breathing grew shallow. Reaching out, my fingers shook violently as they stroked the thin cord. At length, I found my voice.

"She leaves her throne, she leaves her home," I recited in an unsteady voice. *"At night, she roams. The dark, her own."*

The verse broke from my lips, sourced from a long-ago memory. A Spring night when two enemies met in a secluded castle hallway. I thumbed the strip of red. *"Alas, Princess,"* I choked out. *"You're not alone."*

The torrent poured down my face. Even so, I felt the moment it happened, when the first tear surfaced.

My hand clenched the ribbon. His name fell from my lips. "Poet."

12

Briar

My head snapped up. As rain battered my eyelashes, my gaze widened and leaped across the dark expanse. All the while, that single tear rolled down my cheek and blended with the downpour.

Alas, Princess. You're not alone.

No, I was not alone. Because he was here.

My jester was here.

A suffocated noise clotted the back of my throat. Not a sob. Nor a cry. It was something deeper, wrenching from the pit of my stomach, long contained but now rising to the surface. My lips shook, and my chin wobbled.

Still holding the ribbon, I whirled on rickety limbs, swerving this way and that. My wild eyes jumped from a neighboring bridge to a firepit recess, then sprang across other levels. Beyond the immediate area, the deluge blurred most of the treehouses.

Poet.

Mouthing his name, I tore my gaze along the vista. No shadow. No outline. But I felt his presence as I felt the torrent—epic, all-consuming, washing over me.

Although my jester liked to make a spectacle, he held back rather than showing himself. Suddenly, I understood why. Glancing at the soaked ribbon in my grip, I knew. He had promised to find me. Now it was my turn to find him—if I wanted to. The jester had targeted me, but this ribbon wasn't staking its claim. It was giving me a choice.

My heart rammed into my chest, my pulse beating so violently I thought it might snap me in half. He would break me all over again.

I squeezed the ribbon tighter. By Seasons, I had always sensed whenever he was near, could measure his breathing, feel the intensity of his stare. Now I followed that hyperawareness until my gaze landed on another red blot in the distance.

Pebbles danced across my flesh. I beheld the sight like an electric jolt.

Poet.

My fingers yanked, ripping the first ribbon from its post. And then I ran.

Breaking into a sprint, I surged back the way I'd come. Rounding a sharp corner, I flew along a walkway threaded in wet leaves and reached the next ribbon. This one entwined a drooping branch that bobbed under the tempest. I snatched the length of fabric and continued.

My bare feet splashed through puddles. The flimsy material of my nightgown clung to my upper body like an adhesive, but the drenched hem slapped my calves as I darted from one crossway to another. While the rain poured in thick sheets, I catapulted over bridges and past decks.

I pursued the trail, smashing my way through the storm and tracking down the ribbons, each one affixed to a different place. On a treehouse doorknob. On the hinge of a window sash. Around a railing bar. At the end of a bridge. At the beginning of a stairway. I seized every band in my fist, barely pausing for breath.

Here and there, I twisted my head and spun in full circles. My eyes skewered the landscape, searching desperately, hunting furiously.

I will find you.

The wind kicked up, flinging the rain sideways. Yet I did not feel cold. My body heated with exertion as I raced to a set of winding stairs, grasped the railing, and clambered to the next level.

Every part of me went up in flames.

My blood. My heart. My skin. My breath.

More hot tears stung my lashes, threatening to spill. Despite that, my teeth clenched. Damn this jester and his theatrics.

Joy. Anguish. Terror. Hunger.

Everything converged, as turbulent as this storm. Yet I burned through the rain, raged and wept my way through it. In a frenzy, I sped along another overpass, then skittered in place.

The next ribbon flapped from a branch splaying over a lookout point. My free fingers clenched the nearest ledge. Then I followed the panorama, veering my head toward a parallel level.

And my heart stopped.

The wind howled. Half-light crocheted the trees, their boughs whisking about in the tumult. Through that chaos, a tall figure emerged. Rain and moonlight cast his body in a sharp outline, a slash of black that emphasized his height and solid form.

Long ago, I'd watched him step into view like this. Not material-izing from the shadows, as much as sauntering into the light. That's what I'd thought of him then. Some things did not change.

Those eyes cut across the distance like green blades. His wick-ed irises speared through every obstruction, every crossway, every inch separating us. That penetrating stare struck me with the force of lightning, sparking my veins to life.

Poet.

Across the chasm, our gazes clung. We stood beneath the flood, water slicing through our clothes. Suspended in these heights, far above the ground, time ceased to exist.

With another step, the jester came fully into the eventide. That devious face. The slope of his jaw. The hard planes of his body, the arms packed with muscle. Most of all, the way he looked at me.

Agonized. As if he'd just slit his veins open.

Livid. As though I had defied every rule he'd ever made.

Famished. Like he'd been starving for an eternity and just located his prey.

I imagined his pupils marking me. I sensed his knuckles curling, intent on grabbing what was his. I felt the ghost of his touch stoking my blood.

Poet!

I trembled like a rope pulled so tautly, it was about to snap. The choked noise I had been withholding rushed up my throat. Perhaps more than one sound begged for release. Perhaps it was every noise I'd denied myself for months. The cacophony pressed against my lips, fighting to break free.

One second. One held breath.

We stared. Then we broke.

Poet tore from his stance and pounded across the gangplank. At the same time, I burst into another run, hectic pants rushing from my lungs. Vaulting down a short set of stairs and up another, I shot over the platform, arms and legs pumping.

The jester blew toward me like a tornado, his movements destructive. He flipped a stone pedestal table out of the way, sending the object crashing to the ground, the tempest eating up the sound. He bounded over railings instead of going around them, because that would take longer. He threw out his arms, flinging debris and lower branches from his path. More and more of him came into stark relief, from the wet shirt pasted to his torso, to the dark leather pants, to the ferocious expression on his face.

He scorched a path over the planks. I accelerated my pace, rampantly slapping my sodden hair from my face.

Devastated sobs heaved off my tongue. Closer. So much closer. Because now I inhaled the dangerous scents of amber and vetiver.

We cut around the last bend. Not thirty feet away, Poet exploded with movement across the uppermost bridge. From my end, I charged down the platform like a feral thing, craving *this* and *now* and *here.*

His scent. His hands. His mouth.

The jester was on me in less than a second. I hurled myself at him—"Poet!" I cried—just as he snatched me off the ground and wrenched my body against his. We slammed together, crashing into one another with a velocity that knocked the air from my lungs. Heat and strength enveloped me, one arm snaring around my waist like iron, the other hand clamping onto the back of my head and hoisting me into him.

Finally, that terrible sound splintered from my lips. With a possessive snarl, Poet swooped down, his hot mouth catching the noise. His feverish lips seized mine, clamping onto me and devouring my sobs like a ravenous creature. Instantly, he pried apart my mouth, opening me wider and powering us into a furious kiss.

While the sky emptied itself around us, Poet's sinful tongue flexed into me. I gasped against his mouth, with tears streaming down my face. The taste of him assaulted my senses, inundating me with the decadent flavors of wine and spice. The heated clutch of his lips pulled on me, his wet tongue lashing.

I reciprocated, thrusting my lips against his. The contact wrung a pained groan from Poet, his longing matching my own, his pulse smashing into mine.

My fingers ripped through his soaked hair and used the leverage, yanking him deeper. The weight and strength of his mouth wrought another choked noise from my being. My head swam, gravity disappearing from under my feet.

He had come. This was real.

A hundred nights of restraint and silence ruptured through me. I did not merely crack open. I erupted, choking and wracked with tears.

Poet uttered a gruff sound and pried his mouth away. I fell into him at once, my head twisting into his neck, the cries uncontrollable as he gripped me in a steel embrace, holding fast. I felt his own frame radiate, his fingernails digging into my back, the sting pleasurable. Like this, we clung and shook while rain doused the world.

"I'm here," the jester rasped, pulling back and clasping the sides of my face. "I'm here, my thorn."

I nodded into his hands, my cries ebbing as Poet licked the tears, then dipped his head. He plied me with volatile kisses along my jaw, down the sensitive column of my throat, where his mouth latched onto the pulse point and sucked.

I moaned, the sensations overlapping, from heartache to arousal. My head fell back, rain pummeling us both as Poet hummed raggedly and continued sucking my flesh between his teeth, then swabbing my skin with his tongue.

Cupping the back of my head, the jester rushed his mouth along the nook of my jaw and throat, his movements swift and anarchic, as if he had no tolerance for pacing and no patience for sorrow. And neither should I.

This. Was. Real.

I arched into Poet's mouth, my whimpers getting lost in the storm. My nipples pitted into his chest. A hot wet rush puddled in the crease of my pussy, my walls slick and aching.

The jester lifted my gaze to his drugged one, black pupils swallowing those green irises. He must have felt the liquid heat between my thighs or sensed the moment it happened. His savage gaze consumed my features, raking from my mouth to the dark circles of my nipples poking through the drenched nightgown, to the shadow of hair concealing my pussy. Due to my earlier fantasy and the imperative need to cool myself, I had forgone undergarments.

At the expression darkening Poet's gorgeous face, a thrill shimmied through me. Something primitive and absolute reflected in his gaze, followed by another immeasurable emotion.

Finally, he shook his head and groaned, "Briar."

Then his mouth swooped down and snatched mine again. He rammed his lips into me, the rhythm provoking an excruciating throb in my clit. I shoved myself against him, pulling on his hair for balance.

Our tongues pitched together with abandon, the kiss feral and our clothes slipping and sliding together. The contours of Poet's muscles rippled against my breasts, my nipples toughening and scraping his torso. Sparks flared down my spine, so that I scrambled to get closer, because it wasn't enough. Seasons help us, it had never been enough.

I wanted him torn and shouting. I wanted him shattered and helpless. I wanted him needy and begging. I wanted his cock filling my cunt, deeply enough that I would feel him inside me forever. I wanted to rope my legs around him so tightly, no one would be able to pry us apart again.

I wanted his moans. I wanted his screams. I wanted all of him and more, more, more.

I wanted us to burn together.

Poet's hands sliced through my wet hair and shackled the back of my head, locking me in place, the better to devour every sound I made. My mouth rocked under his, our tongues writhing. He licked into me deftly, the tempo urgent. Arousal coated the seam of my thighs, my clit rubbing against the broad stem of his cock.

My nightgown was pasted to my body, impeding my movements. Worse, the barrier of his own clothing prevented me from indulging fully. Every yard felt constrictive.

Grunting, I peeled my lips from his. The jester grumbled in protest, enraged as if I had committed a crime by pulling away. But then a husky noise of approval rumbled from his chest as my fingers grappled the clasps of his shirt. At the same time, Poet seized my hips and urged me backward across the platform.

I caught on and kept pace with him. Satisfied, he let go, braced his fingers on my neckline—and yanked. A gasp catapulted from my throat. The garment split down the middle, shearing to my navel.

We burst into motion, stumbling across the platform while attacking one another, the motions critical as we rid each other of every layer. The top closures of his shirt were already undone, offering a delicious view of his collarbones and upper pectorals. Beneath that, the peaks of his nipples rose through the material, and the chiseled grid of his abdomen contorted, as if he'd been carved from marble.

Impatient, I grasped the closures and gave a harsh jerk. The clasps burst and scattered to the ground, and the fabric shredded, the gap flapping open to reveal that glorious torso. Rivulets raced down his cobbled muscles and rushed into the low waistband of his leather pants.

My fingers itched to sketch every groove. Instead, my hands dove to the buckle of his pants. Meanwhile, the jester multitasked. His head dropped under my jaw, his teeth sank into my neck, and his fingers hooked beneath my nightgown straps and thrust the garment down.

The dainty straps snapped in half and slumped down my arms. The nightgown fell to my waist, and my breasts lurched into view, rain sluicing over the tips of my nipples, the shells darkening.

Poet uttered a gritty noise before scooping one breast in his palm and seizing the nipple between his lips. I cried out into the rain, the sound dire. My head flew backward, a flurry of sensations coursing through my veins, the pleasure so drastic I did not recognize myself.

The heat of his mouth sealed around the bud and sucked. My limbs threatened to give out. Like an untamed creature, I hurried to loosen his belt while enduring the sinuous pulls of his lips.

All the while, we staggered over the bridge. Poet toed off his boots in a rush. I managed to free his belt and whisk it from around his hips. Threads frayed. The wet slap of material resounded in my ears, along with several undomesticated noises grating from the jester's lungs. Together, we stripped our vestments to rags.

Humming, Poet switched to the other breast. With one palm spanning my backside, his free hand bunched the hem of my nightgown and pitched it down my thighs. The strength of his grip tore the muslin, reducing it to scraps and chucking it to the floor.

Shafts of eventide light illuminated my wet breasts and soaked pussy. Poet released my nipple, his forehead bowing to relish the sight. The narrow patch of hair glistened, and my walls clenched under the heat of his gaze.

"Briar," he muttered again, his digits shaking as though holding himself back from touching.

My knees quaked, on the brink of dissolving. I longed to stop time, to watch his eyes feast on me, to savor it. But more than that, I wanted to satisfy my own craving. I yearned for the stiff ridge pushing against his pants.

Poet increased his momentum, steering me across the bridge. I groped the front flaps of his pants, wrenched them apart, and moaned. His cock sprang from the vent, erect and high. The V of his hips sloped to frame the broad head, the skin flushed a ruddy hue, and the slit of his crown emitted a bead of liquid. Poet had been riveted by my pussy, but he hissed as I dashed my fingers from the base of his cock to the tip. The column thickened and rose even higher, and his sac hung heavy. Seasons, even in disarray he was dazzling.

The pulse in my core intensified. The sight of him drenched me.

Our surroundings blurred. Oaks and leaves thrashed against the torrent.

Out of nowhere, my backside hit a facade. Because the sturdy bridge wove through thick branches and extended for fifty feet, we hadn't made it across before Poet rammed me against the ledge. The sides were constructed of slats instead of railings, the facade smooth and vertical enough to support me. We panted against each other's mouths while hustling to get the trousers off, chasing them down his long limbs. Once they hit the ground, Poet punted them aside and homed in on me, just as I lugged him forward.

His arm hitched under my thigh and wrenched it upward, looping my limb over his hip. Rampant, I wiggled closer. Tingles shot across my flesh as my clit abraded the length of his cock, my arousal smearing him.

Whimpering, I coiled into the jester. My breasts mashed into the plate of his chest, and my body vibrated with need. I ripped through his hair, tugged on the roots, and angled his face to mine. "Deeper, Poet."

On a groan, he fitted his waist into the vent of my thighs, splaying me wider. "Farther, Briar," he gritted out.

We obeyed, my legs gaping for his hips and the pommel of his cock probing the seam of my pussy. My walls parted and suctioned around the tip. A disjointed moan tumbled from me as Poet nipped my lower lip and folded his hard body between mine, our muscles shaking with anticipation. The heat from his cock brimmed against my folds, the teasing contact lavishing me with shivers to the point where I might faint.

Pent-up and so long denied, we stood at the edge of the world, at the enclave's topmost bridge, suspended over a void. We did not wait, could not wait, would never wait again.

I needed this now. I had always needed this.

With his cock poised at my opening, the jester veered back and fastened his gaze to mine. Rain struck his body, a powerful gust slashed through his hair, and those orbs glittered.

My hands scrambled from his hair to the taut shape of his buttocks. I clung to the bare swells of skin, bracketing his body against mine and pressing his phallus another inch into my slot. At the contact, a plaintive whine cracked from my lips, and Poet's pupils dilated.

I held his gaze, and a demand surged across my tongue. "Fuck me now." And to be clear, I warned, "Don't you dare be gentle."

The jester hissed. No wicked grin. No naughty reply. I saw him then, at a loss and consumed by the same impulse.

In one slick motion, Poet bolted my hips in place and snapped his waist. His cock lurched between my walls, pitching hard and high.

A shriek broke from my lips. "Oh!"

I clasped him for balance, the impact jolting me upright and knocking the breath from my lungs. My pussy sealed around his cock, taking every inch, encasing him to the seat.

Poet growled, his muscles tensing. We heaved into one another's mouths and thrashed forth. Swiftly, he flexed his cock out of my folds and pounded in again, dislodging another moan from my throat, this one louder. Once more, he slung his hips forward, plying me open with the rounded head.

Seasons. Yes.

How I remembered this. How I'd missed this.

There was no pause. My jester obeyed the command and charged at me. Lost in a frenzy, Poet pumped his cock in and out. He exited fully, only to piston inside over and over, striking a spot that had me chanting into the air.

With every skilled lash of his hips, pleasure scattered from my spine to my toes. He supported the back of my head and hitched my thigh even steeper, the action inflating his bicep while his dexterous movements pinned me into the bridge, the depth of his erection causing my vision to spot.

I hadn't forgotten his size. It was impossible not to recall how long and solid he was. Yet I felt it anew and shouted to the treetops.

Despite the stimulation racking me to the bone, I whined in misery. "Poet, I—"

"Where, Briar?" he husked. "Tell me where."

I swiveled my pelvis to indicate the place that ached. Poet seethed, located the spot, and jabbed his pelvis quicker. And I went wild. His thrusts sharpened, chasing my moans, which clamored through the tempest.

Encouraging him, I squeezed his buttocks, the flesh toned and slick from the rain. With every swipe of his waist, his backside contorted with effort. He fucked so good, so deeply into me.

But not there yet. I needed more of him.

Ambition and greed propelled me to act. With a grunt, I arched into the bridge slats and clenched his ass for balance, then used that to bear down on him. I gyrated my waist, sweeping my pussy over his cock and fucking him back.

Poet's muscles gave. That sexy jaw unhinged, his mouth ajar as a ragged groan toppled out. His fingers dug into me, mashing me closer as he accelerated, hauling his cock in … out … in.

My pussy clamped onto him, wetting his cock. I caught every sleek lunge of that erection and gave in kind, whipping my hips. We collided, our drenched bodies beating out a furious rhythm.

Poet grabbed my other thigh, hoisted it over his waist, and flung his cock deeper, harder, quicker. My cries rang out in tempo. I felt myself leaking, clenching wetly around the jester, my arousal soaking his erection.

My open mouth landed against his. Our breaths crashed together, the same way our bodies did. The rain made everything slippery, enhancing the sensations, my breasts jostling against his pectorals, my legs astride his waist.

The pressure crested. My walls fluttered, small foreshocks rippling through my folds. Yet I buried my teeth into my lower lip, stifling the orgasm because there was more to be had. So much more. On the verge of pleading, I seized Poet's buttocks and squirmed. He read my hectic movements and growled. Still primed inside my pussy, he hefted me off the slat railing, strapped me around him, and stalked to a crescent-shaped bench embedded into the bridge at the halfway point. The bank rested under the only covered section of the platform, the crescent jutting farther over the abyss, with a gabled ceiling bolstered by posts and strewn in leaves.

The jester dropped onto the cushioned seat, where he carefully and agilely twisted me to face away from him, all without pulling his cock from my body. I yelped in shock, stunned by the movement and the wondrous sensations it produced.

Sheets of rain spilled over the awning, creating a wall of water around us. The tip of a thick oak branch extended into the enclosure and weaved along the ceiling. Burgundy leaves dangled like ornaments and trembled from their stems.

Straddling Poet's lap, I sat with my back to his damp chest, both of us dripping all over each other. My buttocks curved into his pelvis, with my limbs sprawled on either side. Yet another newfound position.

Excitement powered through me. My pulse skipped as he captured my hips and jerked me into him. His lips skated over my earlobe, that decadent voice drizzling like black silk, the deep and resonant sound scorching my veins. "Take what's yours and fuck it."

My pussy reacted. The intimate flesh thrummed, pouring from the center of my body and coating his cock. Poet purred, feeling what his words did to me.

I followed that stimulation, gripped his thighs, and ground my hips on his lap. Poet hissed, the noise slicing through the air. It affected me like an intoxicant, emboldening me to row my hips wider—and I keened from how glorious this angle felt, how deeply he breached me. With my mouth hanging open, I coiled into him and bounded my pussy over his cock, my backside stroking his abdomen. Poet's groans sizzled down my vertebrae. His fingernails dug into my hips, encouraging me to scoot back and forth quicker. Seasons, I felt the bulbous head of his erection hitting an exceptional spot.

I cried out, craned my head into his shoulder, and reached backward to grasp his nape. Using his body for stability, I raised myself up and sank on his upright cock in rapid succession. Poet adapted to the rhythm and launched his waist upward, striking me deeper, harder.

Everything slickened. Everywhere hurt in the most wonderful way, so close yet so far out of reach. Every time my body neared a crescendo, Poet switched tempo or assaulted a different notch inside me, prolonging the bliss.

How could torture be this remarkable? How could it ever feel this potent?

Always, he succeeded in this. Never had he failed to startle me.

The jester worked his cock into my cunt, every lash sinuous. In haste, I met his thrusts, bobbing my pussy, my walls spreading around the crown and driving down to the base.

Poet thickened even farther, his girth so broad it expanded my folds and pumped more fluid from my core. Sparks danced across my skin as I galloped into Poet, riding his cock. The cleft of my thighs parted for him, my limbs sprawled wider with each rough slam of his backside, and my tight nipples pitted into the air.

Poet released my hips and leaned back on his palms, allowing me to take control. I bounded forward and backward, dashing my hips on top of him, flaying his cock until his moans grew hoarse.

He took what I gave, letting himself be dominated. I cherished what he offered, stoking the flames. My lips trembled, and I moved with urgency, pursuing his pleasure, frantic to draw every possible sound from us both. And yet the moans escalated and tangled until

I couldn't tell his voice from my own.

As I thrashed my waist, Poet palmed my breasts and pinched my nipples. My being fractured. The volume of my cries escalated, as did my speed.

"Sublime," he crooned into my neck. "Magnificent."

"Painful," I sobbed into the rain. "Unbearable."

"Wrong." Briefly, he snatched my earlobe between his teeth. "You can bear anything, my thorn."

"Not without you."

That response cracked me in half—heartsick and joyous. Poet's frame hitched, as if my response had struck him like a knife. Uttering a profanity, he kicked his waist into my ass, his cock pistoning fast. The jester put his entire weight into the motions, hauling his cock into me until oxygen fled my lungs.

"Nor without you," he echoed, his tone reverent, fierce, and haunted. "Never without you."

I hollered into the storm. "Poet!"

"Briar," he choked out.

Because always, it came back to that. No matter what was said or felt, it was him and me. It was our names on each other's lips, teetering there like a plea.

Poet's hands extended and linked with mine, then lifted them toward the overhead branch. Bracing our arms like that, he affixed our fingers around the suspended offshoot and used it as a buttress. Then my jester flung his hips up into me, his turgid flesh penetrating my cunt at a breakneck pace and robbing me of speech.

I hollered. My pussy melted on him, my skin blazed like kindling, and I coiled so far back, the tips of my hair brushed his groin. Despite the momentum, Poet's serpentine motions were generous—swift and rough, yet sinuous and passionate.

The folds of my pussy convulsed around his cock, my walls gripping and soaking him. We rode each other, surrounded by the torrent, lost to the force of it. Carnal sounds flew into the air, guttural and raw, elemental and real.

I hurled myself into this feeling, gave myself over to it. Nothing else existed outside this dark, torrential corner of the world. No one would ever disarm me as he did.

My jester. My equal.

The one whom I could never escape, never forgot, never forsake, never stop wanting, never surrender. The one I'd been waiting for.

I will find you.

Everywhere. Anywhere.

To the center of this continent. To the ends of this earth.

"I love you," I wept in pleasure. "I love you."

Poet's body flared with heat. A harrowed, hungry noise tore from his throat. I yelped as he pulled his length out of me, twisted my body toward his, and swooped back into my pussy.

I sat astride the jester's cock, face to face with him now. My eyes stumbled across his features and collided with those glittering eyes. The verdant color sliced through the night, his pupils flashed with a thousand emotions, and a severe expression overwhelmed his features.

Droplets ran down Poet's torso and sank to his narrow waist. Every inch of this man's form was toned and packed with muscle. Yet the greatest perfection remained the exquisite snaggletooth that peeked from his lips.

Less than a second had passed before he wordlessly seized my backside and reeled me into him, yanking me into his cock. My mouth fell open, gales of air heaving from me with each circle of his waist. I caught his shoulders for balance as every jolt spread me wider.

Poet's abdomen clenched with the effort. Smatterings of rain trickled from his body and landed on mine. My clit brushed his pelvis, the abrasion causing the tender flesh to swell and throb worse than before.

The jester struck a new depth, sloping his cock and undulating my hips in unison. Seasons, help me. I moaned, sounding afflicted, and held on.

And on. And on.

"Say it again," he husked, though it came out like an entreaty as much as a demand.

My eyelids fluttered, desperate to shut and feel the shape and heat of his cock. Yet I summoned the will to level my gaze with his. "I love you," I chanted. "I miss you, and I want you, and I love you." Poet thickened between my folds. "Again," he implored. "Say it again whilst I fuck you."

"I love you!"

"Again."

Again. Again. Again.

Every time, my voice grew louder, the declaration firmer. Every time, he whipped into me deeper, harder, faster.

I scrambled closer, and his free arm roped around my middle, with the other hand splaying over my buttocks. My breasts swelled against his chest with each panting exhalation. Like this, Poet pitched his bare cock, and I careened into his body.

The wind whistled. Rain smashed into the bridge.

Poet's orbs bonded with mine as he slung my legs over his shoulders, then extended them farther over the railing, so that my calves dangled a hundred leagues into the air. And he slung into me relentlessly, his muscles contracting, so that I felt the brunt of his fucking between my folds.

An unearthly sound ripped from my tongue. Poet yanked me into him, his mouth crashing against mine while his hips belted out a vehement pace. My thighs split, my pussy flooded his length, and my moans tumbled into his mouth.

My jester kissed me, swallowing the noises I made. And I tasted his own growls, the sounds covetous yet possessive.

So long, I had dreamed of this. Even longer, I'd yearned.

We flew into each other, chasing oblivion, long deprived of such bliss. Neither gentle, nor sweet. Neither patient, nor restrained. Yet no less determined, nor less powerful. This loss of control was shameless, reckless, and sinful. This was wild and free, like a scandalous tale for campfires.

That was all. That was everything.

The sacrifice. The waiting. The reward.

For him, I would do it again. For this, I'd surrender my throne a hundred times over.

My folds pulsated. I rushed at Poet, my pussy clamping onto his length, relishing how it twitched inside my walls. I clutched him wetly, sealed my inner flesh around his solid one, and he wrenched me forward sharply, swinging the head of his cock deeply.

His tongue flayed mine, our mouths rocking in cadence to our movements. Embers crackled through my veins. My sobs narrowed, gaining speed as the pleasure mounted, from my clit to my toes.

Poet found a secret spot and attacked. With a vicious hum, the jester pivoted his waist and launched at that narrow place until I was writhing on top of him, with my legs elongated over the bridge's edge. The sensations converged at the apex of my body. I paused, going still and clinging to Poet as heat unspooled through me.

And then I burst. My bones quaked, my cunt squeezed his erection, and I hollered into his mouth. I vibrated on his lap, spasms raking through me as I came around my jester's cock.

Poet groaned his approval. He swallowed the erratic noises I made, as if they tasted of wine.

And then he kept thrusting.

Before I could fully recover, his hips sprinted between my thighs. The impact blasted me with renewed heat, and my lips peeled from his only to unleash another onslaught of cries. I had never been this open, this soaked, yet Poet tilted his cock at an impossible angle and fucked into me, creating another wave of friction.

I broke into movement once more. Only this time, I clasped the back of his head and hunched into him, pressing our foreheads together. My eyes fastened to his, clinging to that magnetic gaze. As he whisked his cock into my pussy, I did not look away, would never look away again.

My moans came out like chipped glass, shattered and stinging. Not because it hurt, but because the way he made love could destroy a person, and the way he fucked could ignite a bonfire. And I wanted him to feel the same thing. I needed him to feel how I loved him. So when I swiveled my hips harshly, Poet's groans intensified, and his face slackened. That sultry voice rustled through my drenched hair. I bucked until I lost all comprehension of anything beyond this enclosure. Eager for more, I rode him into the bench, the tips of my nipples dragging over his chest, my pussy pressing down on his cock until he was bellowing.

We shouted against one another's mouths. Our hips locked and reeled together, colliding over and over. I hollered into the fray, my sobs amplifying and my walls rippling.

Poet lunged his cock into me and hissed, "I love you more."

For a second time, I sprang apart. The orgasm tore through my body, streaks of pleasure multiplying across my flesh. My pussy contracted around Poet's cock at the same time he rammed inside my walls with rapid, shallow thrusts. He struck into me, into me, into me.

At last, his eyes tensed and flashed. My jester paused—then roared into the treetops as his cock jerked, gushing fluid between my folds. He came loudly, the force of it shaking his muscles and unbuckling his jaw. Helpless noises surged from his throat, flooding my ears with the most beautifully chaotic sounds.

How I remembered this. The way he looked when he climaxed.

Poet's muscles gave, shuddering like a fallen tree. His groans melded with my own, the remnants of pleasure taking a long time to ebb. At length, the cacophony tapered, our damp bodies heaved for oxygen, and our mouths slumped together. We collapsed into one another while the echo of rain whooshed into the setting and pattered my toes.

Spent, Poet unhitched my limbs from over the ledge and mashed me against him. In tandem, I threw myself into his frame and wrung my arms around his neck. All the while, his cock remained hard and poised inside me.

Shaking uncontrollably, I buried my face in his throat and crumbled into his embrace. His heartbeat hammered against my own. As the torrent showered around us, my jester carded his fingers into my hair and fingered that single braided lock, where little oak leaves entwined the layers.

Finally, he spoke. His awestruck voice ruptured, as though he'd been holding his breath for ages. "Briar."

At last, the final knot between us unraveled. I lifted my head to grasp his jaw and sweep my lips over his, the corners of my mouth lifting. At once, his chest rumbled, and my grin widened. And then we were chuckling—still moaning but also laughing.

Tucked away in this enclave, I took a deeper breath than I ever had. Exhaling, I whispered low enough that not even the rain could hear. Only the two of us caught the sound of his name as it floated from my lips. "Fenien."

13

Poet

There it was. My true name.

Long ago in Spring, when I first spread this woman around my hips and made her shout, I had whispered the name. The confession had fallen off my tongue like a moan, the temptation impossible to resist.

For safety's sake, I'd spent a lifetime hiding this part of me, concealing the truth behind a mask. Yet without warning, she had ripped off that visor. To that end, confiding in her became an inevitability, as intuitive as drawing in air.

Was it a surprising name? Ill-fitting or underwhelming? I'd once thought so, but coming from her lips now, it took on a different weight. The word ignited from Briar's mouth like the first spark of a flame, like a candle wick bursting to life. A source of heat in this dark world.

A guttural noise ruptured from my lungs and teemed across Briar's mouth. Her breathy exhalations—faint whimpers that illustrated how thoroughly I'd worked her—stirred my cock to life. Blood rushed to the head seconds after reaching its zenith. Her naked body pressed against mine, her breasts quivered, and the warm clamp of her pussy wetted me to the base.

Another perk of our rather enthusiastic reunion was this: Those soft folds hadn't stopped fluttering. Wicked fucking hell, she was still coming.

And Seasons have mercy, I could stay inside this woman for hours. Possibly for several weeks.

She slumped against me, melting into my arms. I relished the whiffs of tart apples and crisp parchment mixed with the fragrances of sweat and sex. She had come so fiercely around my cock that my senses could practically taste her climax.

Soon, I would do that as well, drape my tongue along her slot and snatch that darling little clit between my lips. Indeed, I would do that and more. For there was much lost time to make up for.

Briar's pulse thumped at a rampant pace, and she panted against my mouth. I palmed her ass and scooped her closer, the motion splitting her legs farther around my waist and lodging my cock deeper. The princess gasped, arousal glossing her pupils.

That, and elation. Her irises sparkled like firecrackers. She was happy to see me.

My heart slammed into my chest like a battering ram. Whilst the rain did its worst, pelting the area and soaking the platform, I feasted my eyes on Briar. My fingers sliced through her hair, which framed her face in dark red strands. Her flushed skin made the freckles stand out across her nose. Fuck, I wanted to lick each one.

But even more, I wanted to have a clear view of every detail. Enough with this waterlogged nonsense. I'd seen her in moonlight, against the sheen of a storm. Now I would see her bathed in firelight.

I must look voracious, because her respirations quickened, and that brilliant pulse of hers doubled. We watched each other, our gazes fastening as I slowly withdrew my cock, deliberately prolonging the motion so that she felt every inch.

At the same time, she flexed her cunt and elevated her hips to release me. Her eyelids fanned, and mine grew equally heavy. Fucking her in the rain had been divine, but it had done nothing to satiate us.

In haste, Briar wiggled off my lap and scrambled to her feet. I launched off the bench and reached out to grab her, but she caught my greedy fingers first. Tugging me forward, she uttered, "This way."

Sheets of rain poured over the bridge's canopy. She guided us as we blasted through the wall of water and rushed down the bridge. At one cursed point, she paused and called out over the tumult, "Wait." Then she moved to bend over and collect our discarded garments with her free hand.

At this point, my body was buzzing. After three months of dormancy, I wasn't to be trifled with. Like hell would I allow her to bow that ass in my view without her feeling the consequences.

"Leave them," I growled, pulling Briar upright and hauling her along the bridge.

Of course, a prudent protest called out from behind me. "The clothes—"

"Fuck the clothes."

Briar's laugh filtered through the torrent as I stalked with her through the crossways. However, my feet eventually hesitated, and my eyes tore across the endless network of treehouses, stairs, decks, bridges, balconies, suspensions, and lookout points. The landscape was a marvel, except for one problem. I had no idea where the fuck I was taking us.

Amused, Briar took charge and darted ahead of me, her fingers clinging to mine. "It's not far."

Every few steps, I grunted and spun her to face me. My arms plastered Briar to my frame, and my insatiable mouth swooped down to seize hers. Because the cruel woman parted for my tongue, it took a considerable while to reach her cabin.

I thwacked my palm against the treehouse door. It flew open, rain beating against the floor mat as I swung Briar inside and slammed the partition shut. Insulated in the dark living room, our audible pants filled the interior. I rushed Briar up against the door and pinned her there, our wet bodies slapping together.

An enthusiastic light brimmed in her eyes as I bracketed one arm beside her head and caged her in. She gasped when my other hand spanned her ass, my hips and thick cock wedged her thighs apart, and my torso shoved her into the facade.

My lips crushed hers, engulfing Briar's sigh of delight. I hummed into her mouth, my tongue pitching against her own. Whilst my cock swelled and abraded her sweet cunt, I lapped and caressed each nerve ending, sweeping her into a soul-deep kiss. But when I felt another influx of heat surging from the slit of the princess's legs, I groaned and pried my mouth and tongue from her.

Briar whined and grappled for me, her hands straining for purchase. Nonetheless, my gruff voice stalled her movements. My attention dropped like hot coals to her mouth, and my dick felt the sizzling effect of her gaze.

On a harsh gust of air, I murmured, "I'm going to fuck you all night long."

Briar shivered. Yet instead of basking in that promise, a sudden thought crinkled her eyebrows. Shit. I knew that expression, made a prediction even before she lifted a finger and sketched my jawline. "But first ..."

Dammit all to hell. My aching cock suffered like no cock ever had, especially with the delicate flanks of her pussy pressed against me. But my thorn needed me in a different way now, and my instincts responded. On a tormented growl, I bowed my head in defeat, my muscles vibrating with desire.

I took a moment to calm the bloody fuck down, then lifted my head. Our gazes magnetized, fusing until our breaths evened out. Once certain I wouldn't bite, lick, devour, or so much as nibble, I pulled back and scooped Briar off the floor.

Linking my arms beneath the princess's thighs, I hefted her against me and brushed my nose against hers. With the living room, dining area, and kitchen downstairs, it stood to reason, I'd find the bedroom and bathroom on the second level. I crossed the small dwelling, taking a quick moment to process the plaid-upholstered reading chairs nestled amid bookshelves, along with the tiny herb pots growing on a windowsill.

Hiking up the stairway, I emerged into a loft with a fox tapestry mounted above a fireplace mantel, sconces flanking a mirrored dresser, and a trunk at the bed's foot. Beyond that, it was easy to identify the customized touches Briar had added for herself, like the salvaged fabric she'd turned into curtains, antique book covers prominently displayed atop a peg shelf, and a newly painted footstool holding a vase of flowers.

After collecting a towel from the bathroom, drying us both off, and lighting the sconces, I draped Briar along the bed and climbed in after her, gathering the princess flush against me whilst she tented the linens over our heads. Outside, the storm smacked the windowpanes. Inside, I rolled onto my side and watched candlelight seep through the blankets, illuminating the freckles that sprinkled her nose.

There. Now I could count each delectable one.

For a time, we clasped and stared at one another, soaking in the view. Absently, her fingers etched my face, and my hands scorched a trail over her hips and tailbone. Later, I would massage three months of tension and sadness from her bones, then make love to her so intensely, so fucking luxuriously, she would go hoarse. Until then, I traced every inch of skin like a glutton.

Her voice trembled. "You came for me."

"You led me to you," I husked, thinking of that last book in her most cherished series. "Your infamous heroine fled to an isolated place of folklore." I drizzled my black fingernail down one pert breast, enjoying how her flesh pebbled. "And I know my thorn. It made sense for you to go somewhere reminiscent of that setting, however much you fancy realistic texts over fiction. There's a reason that series was your favorite."

In fact, I'd retrieved the series from the Royal Retreat and brought it with me to surprise her, which I would do once the moment was right. For now, my voice coasted into the darkness. *"From the sacred wild, she will reign."*

"In the hidden trees, is her domain," Briar finished with a smile. "You remembered that part."

"With you, I remember everything. And considering you'd just read that passage to me after a bout of sublime fucking, how could I not? Also, I consider myself well-versed in your every motivation. 'Tis my lifelong goal to become fluent in all things Briar. I'd say I'm doing rather well thus far. Someday, you'll never be able to hide from me, even if you find yourself in the middle of Summer's raging ocean or at the top of some godforsaken alpine in Winter."

"I make one brief statement, and naturally you require a monologue to respond," Briar pretended to admonish. This, despite how her mouth curled upward, fondness softened her tone, and her eyes sparkled.

I repaid her feigned disapproval with a teasing declaration of my own. "Did you honestly expect anything less than excess from me?"

"Your vanity will be pleased to know that oftentimes I keep my expectations rather high regarding your actions. Even then, you exceed them on a routine basis."

"Splendid," I gloated, running my digit up and down that breast. "Look at the pains I took to orchestrate this reunion. I used every good ribbon in my arsenal to make that trail." My lips coiled into a devilish smirk. "The better to see you hunt me down like erotic treasure."

"And here, I thought it was because you were giving me a choice whether to rejoin you."

"That, I was. Your jester was merely embellishing."

Briar imitated a serious expression, playing along with a nod. "Oh, of course."

Her attention dipped from my eyes to my mouth, then coasted down to my waist. Ah, and then to that deviant part which rose under the weight of her gaze. Seasons, she merely had to look at my cock, and all hell broke loose.

I had spent enough time admiring my endowments in a mirror to know what she saw. Sex in the rain had left me as disheveled as a bedsheet, after a night of tossing and turning. My hair was rumpled, and the kohl lining my eyes had become smudged. Yet the messy sight of me had the most intoxicating effect on Briar's features. A virginal shade of pink suffused her cheeks, and the pulse at her neck thudded like bait ready to snare me. To say nothing of how her fingertips lulling over my abdomen drove my impulses to the brink.

Fuck me hard. How the devil had I managed to exist for a second without this woman? If not for the electricity that struck me the moment our gazes collided through the tempest, I'd have called this night a mirage. One, in a string of many over the past months.

My voice roughened, heady from the princess's scent and body temperature. "That said, it wasn't easy to keep myself from tearing across this place and snatching your body the instant you came into view." I circled the tip of my finger around her nipple, my mouth watering as it tightened. "You had me so worked up, I could have demolished this forsaken enclave. As such, I should give my restraint due credit. The things I do for dramatics and grand gestures."

Briar scooted closer, her outtakes growing shallow when my digit rolled over the peak of that nipple. "How …," she uttered, "how did you know … I would be out there?"

My finger stalled. "I didn't."

Her respirations shifted. Those tantalizing breaths paused, as if teetering on a sudden precipice. Urgency claimed her features, the next question vital. I could guess the subject and adored this woman even more for it.

"How is he?" she implored, bunching my hand in hers and pressing them to the breast I'd been fondling. "Tell me everything."

"Nicu is safe," I assured her. "He's under heavy surveillance in our absence, with Aire in charge. Plus, two certain ladies are helping to look after Nicu. Physically, he's well. Alas, emotionally …" I trailed off, recalling the night when I'd found my son having a nightmare in Briar's wardrobe. "He misses you."

Her chin trembled. "I thought of him every moment." She kissed my knuckles and whispered, "As I did you."

My eyes squeezed shut, and I nuzzled her palm as she continued,

"And Mother? Everyone?"

Shit. What to say.

To tell her about the pain and terror Avalea was going through, how the woman suffered in silence, playing the role of a queen first, a parent second, all for the sake of her nation. If any court had done to Nicu what it did to Briar, I would have skinned every resident alive. In this way, Briar's mother had more resilience than I did.

As it was, I hadn't been merciful since Briar left. That was another complicated subject to broach.

I'd never lie to this woman. My willful thorn could weather a thousand storms and fires, but right then smoothing out that wrinkled chin became my priority. She could handle the nitty-gritty of our family later, once she'd slept peacefully in my arms.

But if I wasn't careful, Briar would see through my bullshit. Shaping my words carefully, I said, "Your Mother fears for your return as much as she longs for it."

Briar absorbed my reply, the muscles in her throat contorting. As for the rest, she listened whilst I gave her an abridged version of Autumn's state, answering each question with the tact of a jester who knew better than to insult his princess with artificial pleasantries. From skepticism amid the court and council, to public unrest and the ongoing inhuman treatments of born souls, I gave these parts to Briar candidly. This, she could endure without being primed.

The wind shoved thin branches against the window, vivid leaves gleamed through the darkness outside, and rain pattered the treehouse eaves. Inside, the foundation creaked, the disturbance reminding me how fucking high we were.

Based on what I'd told her, I sensed Briar's mind churning. She had been sated and relaxed moments ago, but now she would hit the ground running, pushing herself beyond the limits. Unless she gave her thoughts a respite, time to process everything, the stress would do more damage than good.

Nay. Not whilst I was here.

I staged an intervention by tracing the single braid entwined in her loose hair, the weave accessorized with miniature golden oak leaves. Her tresses glinted red-gold in the muted light. "I favor this little change. The badlands of Autumn look good on you." Strapping one arm around her middle, I hoisted Briar's naked body forward and cooed, "Now indulge me and share all the ways you've continued to conquer this Season. It appears you've established quite an outpost here. A wild castle of trees, suitable for an unruly heiress."

Over the next hour, Briar told me about her journey. The long and dangerous ride. The wandering butchers and carnivorous fauna she and our friends had managed to avoid. The Lost Treehouses and the wizened oak that bestowed a fragment of itself to her.

It would have been an understatement to admit my jaw had dropped when I first galloped through the mist and saw this place. The sight of cabins suspended countless feet in the air, tucked among a rich tapestry of leaves that glinted like stained glass, had been extraordinary. The vista of decks, winding stairs, bridges, and posts intricately crafted from wood rivaled the talents of Spring's greatest artists.

And yet. All of it had paled in comparison to seeing Briar's red hair and stunning face in the rain.

"The Lost Treehouses are gems," she said, her breath coasting across my lips and her fingers burning a trail along my jaw. "It is a hidden treasure in my land, and yet it's known far and wide. They say it's the birthplace of fairytales, in all their dark and macabre ways." She grinned. "But also in their enchantments and allure. It shows the best and worst of itself, depending on who dares to venture past the treehouse's borders."

I hooked a lock of hair behind her ear. "Yet Sinful Spring is the hub of creativity in The Dark Seasons. One would have assumed that's where this region would exist."

"Not when it comes to stories. Those are universal and thrive everywhere. Your Season may lead our world in verse, epic ballads, dramas, and most fictitious novels, but every nation has its own hold on books and their contents." Briar's fingers skated down the side of my throat. "This enclave was built by craftsfolk—not Masters but misanthropic builders with immense talent, who preferred a life of solitude. They joined forces with those who had magic, back when such beings walked this continent, and lived here until all those cultures died out. As a child, the tales had preoccupied me." Her eyes dropped to my chest. "I was a different person then."

I braced a finger beneath her chin and lifted her gaze to mine. "You wouldn't have fallen for a rakish jester and his son if that were true."

Briar's mouth tipped upward, pride warming her complexion. "Sometimes, I'm wary of this place. Other times, I feel honored that it has allowed me to take refuge here. You must understand the woodland, to be granted this access. In many ways, it's indeed a castle. A fortress of the forest."

"Reestablished by an heiress of Autumn."

Rather than animate her, the compliment cast shadows over Briar's visage. "The only condition for dwellers is to respect this place. Outside of that requirement, I believe The Lost Treehouses would welcome any human, regardless of who they were."

Born souls too. That was what she meant. It would explain the reverent and somber notes in her voice. By comparison, she resented her own castle's inability to accept all people, as this realm would.

Briar had spoken in awe. Yet when she fell quiet, I prodded, "But?"

She gripped the sides of my throat, and her eyes clung to mine. "Nowhere is home without you."

Leaning in, I swept my mouth across hers. "I'm here now, my thorn." Then I jerked back and lifted a brow. "But no scolding or spanking? Does that mean you don't regret my explicit entrance, despite the risks?"

Briar's breath rushed against my lips. "I will never regret having you." She wavered, her words brittle. "But I'm afraid. My actions hurt Nicu. They hurt you and everyone I care for. I could not protect them." That steadfast voice broke as if someone had chopped through it with a hatchet. "I failed."

I seized her cheeks and hissed, "Don't ever fucking say that."

"I lost my father, I lost my kingdom, and I almost lost you. Each time was my fault."

"Hush." My finger braced against her mouth. "You kept my son safe. You kept every born soul in that dungeon from being used as pawns, and innocent citizens from being slaughtered as part of some elaborate scheme to overpower you. You were betrayed, chased, and stabbed.

"Yet here you are, still alive with a beating heart of steel, with elements of this land strewn through your hair. You, my epic sweeting, are like the maples of this kingdom—enduring, born to withstand the elements through the passage of time." I skated my thumb across her cheek and then diced my fingers into her damp hair. "You are Autumn's blade and its shield. I know that determined set of your chin. It has never deserted anyone who matters to her." My hold on her loosened. "Nay. 'Tis I who failed you."

Shock blazed across Briar's pupils. Grimacing, she shook her head. "Poet, no."

"You don't think I blame myself every day for what happened to you? My hatred for Rhys is second nature. But most days, I hate myself more."

"Poet." She grabbed the nape of my neck and pressed her forehead to mine. "You mustn't."

"I know. 'Tis a shame. My vanity is one-of-a-kind." My gaze clung to the princess, the sight of her shredding my words. "I'm sorry, Briar."

"Stop," she demanded. "Sorry for what? You are sin and sacrifice. Your words can make a person bleed more than a weapon. There is nothing to forgive for that."

My neck pumped hard like a rusted thing. Yet Briar's reply resurrected my pretentious side. "Go on," I invited.

A quick chuckle fell from her lips before she sobered. "You are a father who dismantled a nation for your son. You opened a princess to passion and vitality."

"Aye. I did enjoy opening you." Now I gave her an impish grin.

"Deeply, in fact."

She nodded vehemently. "And I expect you to do so for eternity. But more than that, you have given me a strength I didn't know I possessed."

"Ah, but I merely stoked what was already there inside you."

"That doesn't lessen what you've done."

"Nor does the lack of a crown diminish who you are."

Briar gave another crisp nod. "It's settled then." Then the perceptive woman peered at me. "Your turn. What is it you're keeping from me?"

Time for evasion. I rolled my eyes, then flitted my digits. "Rubbish. I'm an angel."

"In devil's clothing."

"Can't I wear both guises? I look rather edible in lace and leather." Unfortunately, Briar merely stared at me until I sighed, "I may have tried to murder Rhys."

The princess's gasp cut through the room. She vaulted off the mattress, the blanket tumbling from our heads as she gaped down at me. Her tits hung heavy and gorgeous, much like her expression.

I slithered upright and gripped her hip, the sheets puddling around our waists. "Jesters never apologize, so don't expect me to. Summer took Autumn from you. Then he took you from me," I growled. "You tend to bring out the ethical as well as the violent in this juggler. If someone so much as gives you a paper cut, my tongue isn't enough. I've developed a habit of shapeshifting from a sinful trickster to a protective alpha. In short, I've been a bad jester, misbehaving in your absence."

It took Briar a moment to find her voice. "As if you have ever conducted yourself otherwise in my company."

"True. My naughtiness is high maintenance."

"Poet."

I grunted. "Inconveniently, the cocksucker is still alive, albeit somewhat misshapen." I wouldn't deny myself the satisfaction of spelling it out. "I set him on fire."

Another intake of air from Briar. I slanted my head, but my tone was anything but remorseful or playful. "Are you vexed with my antics at last?"

Through the shadows, she watched me. In the dim sheen of the room, raindrop silhouettes streaked across her face. She exhaled, a hundred motives and consequences tracking through her mind before she admitted, "Only the part where I wasn't there to help."

The answer hovered between us. Fury and shame etched those words, because she had once lunged at Rhys, hellbent on carving him to pieces after the courtyard bloodshed. I was the one who'd stopped her from taking the shithead's miserable life. Not because I hadn't wanted her to succeed, but because it would have cemented an even worse fate for Briar. One that I'd have reduced the castle to rubble to prevent.

A second later, I saw the change in my thorn. Her features sharpened with conviction, our thoughts coalescing to this: There was a difference between a temptation that empowered versus one that impaired. Slaughtering Rhys quickly and recklessly would have been a quick hit of euphoria, much like a drug—a cheap and short-lived pleasure. When really, this princess and her jester had standards to maintain.

"But we must be smarter than that," Briar said. "We *are* smarter than that." The blankets rustled as she fisted our hands together. "Let us never be like him."

My lips tilted fiendishly. "As you said. We're a clever pair."

"No more wordless retreats."

"No more reckless strikes."

Like an enticement, the princess licked her lips. "When we do this, we burn him the cunning way. Slowly and methodically."

I slid my arm around Briar's waist and hauled her on top of me, her ass landing in my lap and her thighs splaying around my hips. "A game of fire against fire," I husked. "It would be my pleasure, Highness."

She winced and cast her head from side to side. "I am no longer—"

"You will *always* be *that*," I ground out. "You were born to make history, not be erased from it."

To silence any more protests, my mouth lunged and snatched the crook of her neck. A stunned cry sprang from Briar's tongue. Her luscious body arched, her tits swelling into my torso as the next words dripped from my tongue like liquid satin. "My thorn." I plastered her to me and dined on her pulse point, sucking it between my teeth, only pulling away to utter, "My equal."

Then I dove in again, licking and biting her neck whilst she held on for dear life. "My obsession." I palmed her ass and sketched my canines along her collarbones until her joints shook. "My love." Like a drunken man, I dragged my gaze to hers and swore, "My princess" before seizing her mouth.

My tongue flexed into her, lapping at her moans. Molten heat leaked from her pussy and soaked the head of my cock. I thickened instantly, the top broadening and the stem rising so high that my flesh strained between us.

With a growl, I peeled myself back and seethed against her lips. "Mine."

"Yours," she echoed, another moan curling from her when I nudged my hard crown between her folds, the motion coaxing more arousal from the slit. Over her whines, I purred, "Did you miss me, Sweet Thorn?"

"Seasons," she sobbed. "Yes."

"How much?" I commanded, prodding her walls inch by inch, the tip siphoning like a tease. "Show me how badly it hurt."

Rain smashed an errant rhythm against the glass panes. Inside, the temperature rose as I continued to pry open her cunt with lazy beats of my cock. Briar cried out, strapping her naked body around mine and gently swiveling her waist on me.

I groaned. "How I've craved you," I crooned before running my tongue up her throat. "Were it not for my son, I would have lost my mind." My head bowed to her tits, and I flicked my tongue over one nipple. "Unable to eat, nor sleep, nor think."

Briar keened, rolling her pussy over my cock and sinking a little deeper but not fully. We had already done that, fucked swift and hard. Next, I would draw this out until she was begging for it.

I sucked on that nipple, swatting my tongue over the peak. Briar's walls contorted, and needy sounds dropped from her lungs. "Please."

Aye. Good little princess.

Blood rushed to my sac, tightening my balls. My head lifted, and I hissed over her lips, "You soothed my nightmares and inflamed my dreams. Every time I gripped my cock, I heard the echo of your moan." With a quick kiss, I hummed, "Oh, the corrupt things I plan to make you feel. All the ways I mean to punish you for leaving me."

Briar writhed on my lap. With her hair a tangled mess, she sprawled her limbs around me like an offering.

I'm going to fuck you all night long.

Recalling what I'd said when we first blasted into the house, her mouth burned across my lips. "Then do it. Keep your promise."

14

Briar

oet's eyes flashed. Those irises pierced the darkness like green blades, as if everything we'd done outside had scarcely counted, barely sated him. I knew this feeling, the elemental need for him.

A molten noise oozed from the jester's throat, the sound pouring through me like caramel. He gripped my bare buttocks, yanked me into him, and snared my mouth with his. I sighed and twined my arms around his whipcord shoulders, bracing myself to take the brunt of his kiss. Poet's tongue glided across the seam of my lips, coaxing me to part for him. The instant I opened myself, his tongue flexed in and lapped at every nerve-ending I possessed. I whimpered, savoring the familiar taste of wine and decadence.

Poet crushed me to him, my breasts flattening against the sculpted muscles of his torso. His sinful heartbeat slammed into mine. He gripped the back of my head, fastening me in place, all the harder for his tongue to claim me.

Our mouths folded, sealing together. Harsh respirations rushed from our lungs, blood surged to my pussy, and my thoughts fogged.

Poet's tongue dashed into me, licking and curling like a devious thing. I keened, my hips reeling on his lap, the blanket slipping from around our waists. My clit skidded against the solid width of his cock, the sensation inebriating.

Poet had always been a thorough kisser, deep and penetrating. Because he put his entire body into the kiss, I felt his mouth in every fiber of my being. The effect sent flurries across my scalp and turned my knees to jelly. Under the strength of his jaw, I dissolved.

The jester kissed as though it was the first and the last time. Passionate. Possessive. He molded his mouth to my own, the rhythmic tug drawing me into a fever dream.

My tongue quavered against his, catching each of his licks. Ambitious for more, I dove my fingers into the messy layers of his hair and pulled on the roots. I grasped harder than I had meant to, the force of it surprising me, yet I felt the smug grin slide across Poet's mouth. He liked to feel this—the princess demanding her jester's services.

And he obliged. His body lunged forward, smashing us together, and his lips gripped me. That mouth seized my tongue and sucked until I was chanting from the back of my throat.

Another thing I remembered so well. This man never took me delicately, as if I was breakable. Even when it was slow and languid, he slayed me with vigor and stamina. My jester fucked and kissed as if I were indestructible—able to take it all, to endure anything. In each touch and caress and climax, we were of equal power, as durable as any fortress. That was how it felt to join with him.

So when Poet's mouth softened, and his tongue swatted at a more gradual pace, my heart leaped. Tears brimmed my eyelids. This foolish world had tried to sever our bond, but it hadn't succeeded. How utterly it had failed.

A sob escaped me, the muffled noise spilling into the room. Triggered by the sound, Poet hummed tenderly. He banded his arms around my middle and twisted, veering me into the bed. The ceiling flipped, and my back hit the mattress, the blankets falling to the ground.

My thighs split around the width of his hips, with my legs hitched on either side of his taut, naked backside. Bracketing his upper frame, Poet hovered over my body. Black smudges of kohl lined his eyes, which glittered as he looked down at me.

His cock braced along my slit, heavy and hot. The sight and feel of him drenched me, so that I melted onto his crown. Poet's eyelids hooded, yet his muscles tensed, holding back.

Instead of giving in, he hunched forward and ran the tip of his tongue over the shell of my ear. Then he whispered, "Don't move, Highness. Or this jester will make you regret it."

Goosebumps plied my skin. "What are you—"

His finger pressed against my mouth. "And no complaining."

But when I let out a displeased grunt, he responded with a throaty chuckle. "Obstinate heiress."

Quicker than I could process, the jester rose from the bed, the motion sinuous. I had barely uttered another protest when he bled into the shadows and stalked away. The toned muscles of Poet's rear contorted with his movements, the view stalling my tongue. Seasons above, those dimples.

He sauntered downstairs. However, before the jester vanished, he turned his head slightly and placed a digit to his mouth, reminding me. Not a word, nor a movement. If I defied this rule, he would know. Even without being here to witness it, this man would know.

I heard the front door open, the clamor of rain blasting through the cabin before the partition shut again. He was going outside? For what? My brows furrowed, anticipation clashing with irritation. I lay sprawled on the bed, riled up by his insolence and the sight of his buttocks, now so far out of reach. The scoundrel had just left me here, with my legs spread and my core throbbing.

What would he do if I disobeyed? The notion inspired a tiny thrill to ripple across my skin.

Turning up my chin, I ground my elbows into the mattress and scooted myself closer to the headboard railing. A small rebellion, but enough to provoke him. With my theatrical jester, it rarely took much.

My lips curved. Then my smile dropped as the door opened and shut once more. The click of a deadbolt caused me to jolt, palpitations jumping into my throat. For some reason, that noise had sounded intentional and decisive. Final, like a jester approaching his target.

The sound of rustling filtered through the treehouse, followed by the wet flap of a bundle. He must have collected our discarded clothing. Yet that could not be the only reason, not when I'd been laid out like a banquet. Poet would never dismiss that in favor of tidying up.

No. He'd ventured outdoors for something more.

Suddenly, I could not decide whether it had been clever or folly not to heed the jester's warning. Footsteps thumped up the stairs. I squirmed, then forced myself to be still when he emerged like an incubus.

The spectacle robbed me of breath. He stood there, dripping and ethereal, with rivulets streaming from his collarbones to his navel. Shadows threaded across Poet's face and body, meticulously accentuating the smooth and hard parts.

The chiseled countenance. The gleaming pupils.

That athletic frame, hewn from rocks. That smooth plate of skin and sinew.

The tall body of a dancer, the feline agility of an acrobat, the serpentine reflexes of a viper, and the whipcord form of an assassin. Someday, he might kill me purely from the pleasure. Or we might vanquish each other at the same time.

Muscles stacked across Poet's abdomen, and his cock lifted high from between the narrow slopes of his hips. The pome flushed. The stem glistened with arousal, the way it would once it pitched between my folds.

The view proved too remarkable to be real. My lips pursed; curse this man's vanity. No one should be permitted to look like him, though my jester would disagree and call himself entitled.

Nonetheless, a selfish impulse overtook my thoughts. This man belonged to me. He was mine, and mine alone.

Poet's gaze skewered through the room and torched a path across my body. His orbs engulfed me, from my toes to my face, before landing on the seam between my thighs. He traced every inch of my cunt like a fanatic, as if I was the one who could not be real. The magnitude of his attention turned me into a soaking mess, warmth heating my folds as well as my cheeks.

The pulse in my core intensified. From the patch of hair at my center, the crest of nerves projected like evidence of my desire. That, and the slickness leaking from me.

"Heavenly," he murmured. "You are a goddess of Autumn."

My skin flushed anew. No one had ever spoken to me this way. Even after all the things that had left his mouth, I hadn't grown used to this. "I do not know how to take such compliments."

"Aye, you do. Shall I remind you?"

I opened my mouth to … truly, I couldn't fathom what I intended to say. In any event, words fled me the moment Poet noted my change in position on the bed. His eyes simmered, those irises the color of mischief. He tsked, his impertinent tongue clicking. "Misbehaving already, my thorn?" The corner of his mouth crooked. "How proud you make me."

Equal pride thrust through me. However, I cautioned myself not to underestimate that indulgent expression. This jester meant to seek retribution.

Again, it had either been clever or folly of me. Clever, because I wanted him to overwhelm me with pleasure. Folly, because he would prolong the ecstasy to the point where it became torturous. We had played such games before, but the experiences always felt novel, and the outcomes were often unpredictable.

Yet not once had I regretted it. Thus, I restrained a grin and elevated my chin higher.

Accepting that challenge, Poet swaggered toward me. My gaze traveled from his naughty countenance and stumbled across the red ribbons in his grip. So he'd gone outside for them, yet not only that. I registered another item among the scarlet bands. Something tapered, not long enough to be a rod, nor small enough to be a candle.

My heart skipped another beat. Nervousness and temptation sizzled across my flesh. "What is that?"

Poet's mouth merely tipped sideways. Instead of responding, he halted at the footboard and set the objects on the trunk fronting the bed. "I'd like you to keep those sumptuous legs spread and that edible pussy open for me." Plucking one of the ribbons, he stretched it horizontally. "Unfortunately you insist on flouting my rules," he said while contemplating the rain-dampened cord. "Let's make sure it doesn't happen again, shall we?" Patiently, he linked the fabric around my ankle, knotted the band over the footboard post, and tugged.

I gasped, my muscles tensing while he moved to the opposite ankle, splaying me wider. Casually, the jester stalked to the headboard and performed the same actions, fastening me with more ribbons to the posts. My chest rose and fell, but I did not tell him to stop, for I trusted this man with my soul.

Poet returned to the end of the mattress, where he leaned forward and bracketed his palms on either side of my scissored calves. "Comfortable, sweeting?"

My nerves fluttered. It was all I could do to nod.

"Excellent. Though you will tell me if you're displeased. Do so, and I'll unbind you the second you request it. Until then, do you promise to behave like a well-mannered princess?"

Another antsy smile threatened to break through. I licked my lips for his benefit. "Only if you promise to accommodate your lady's every whim."

"As you wish. I'm going to make you feel everything you've been longing for." Then his impish expression darkened. "Eyes closed, Your Highness."

My insides flipped. This reminded me of a night in Spring, when he'd brushed a feathery item over my skin, rallying my body to life and shocking me with stimulation. A cloth had concealed my vision back then, but tonight, the jester simply relied on my compliance.

Dutifully, I let my eyelids drift shut. Instinctively, I stretched my limbs outward, exposing my wet folds to his gaze.

An intake of breath sifted through the bedroom. "Ruthless, indeed." His timbre husked, "Wider, love."

I complied, fanning my limbs apart. To which he murmured, "Fucking perfection."

Desire pooled low in my stomach. "It's brazen to see myself as flawless. I've been taught to consider it the height of frivolity."

"Perhaps, but that doesn't change what I see."

"I would much rather be humble than perfect. It is the Autumn way."

"And yet, you enjoyed the compliment. Little liar, for I see it in the blush coloring your lovely tits and the shift in your breathing."

"That is lust, not ego."

"Aye," he intoned, so that I felt his gaze on my cunt. "I see that too."

After a moment, I shook my head and admitted, "And I like how you see me."

Because however much I stood by what I'd said, Poet defined perfection in a less conventional, unpardonable way, and he knew how to make such endearments attractive. I sensed it in his voice, how he characterized perfection not as someone without faults but simply a person who was true. And how that someone captivated him.

I did not need to be perfect for this world, nor for this man. Rather, he made me feel real, honest, and exposed—and more radiant because of it. With him, I did not need to pretend or resist, much less fear the unknown.

And so, I opened my body. "I trust you."

A gritty noise escaped Poet's mouth, seeming to come from a deeply entrenched place. The bed sank under his weight as he positioned himself between the gap in my thighs, his proximity a heady experience, as if the room had grown humid.

Perspiration beaded in my palms. In my mind's eye, I saw him kneeling—wet, naked, and erect.

Butterflies fluttered through me, expectation scattering to the very edges of my psyche. Poet remained still, perhaps observing me. His quiet attention seemed to amplify everything my body did, every way it reacted. It magnified the sound of my gulp and intensified the pulse in my clit. Restlessness mounted as I waited, unaware of where he would touch me first, what he would do with that long apparatus.

"Ah, ah, ah," he scolded when I squirmed, the motions pulling on the ribbons. Leaning over, his fingers caressed my wrists, relaxing them.

My muscles uncoiled from his touch, then loosened fully as those hands wandered down my forearms, then continued to my biceps and shoulders. His digits branded me with heat, torching a path to my breasts and nipples, followed by my ribs and navel. I sighed and gave in to the scattering of sensations, my skin yielding to his ministrations.

"There we go," he encouraged. "So pliant."

Nonetheless, this man knew the extent of his skills and used them to the fullest. His pace slowed, delaying every so often, drawing out the moment just before reaching the next sensitive area.

My flesh prickled. Each nerve ending fired in anticipation, in whichever part of my body he pursued. Whenever the jester stalled, it caused me to vibrate and grow more sensitive.

As Poet dragged his palms over my hips, I pictured those black enameled nails glinting. From there, he stroked my knees, easing them even farther apart. At length, I whimpered as his fingers brushed along my inner thighs, massaging the flesh lightly, like the most criminal of teases.

Finally, the mattress dipped. Poet hunkered forward, his hair grazing my skin. I gasped, feeling his head burrow into my core. Hot breath ghosted over my pussy and skimmed my clit, the effect saturating me.

Poet planted a soft kiss against my folds. My respirations hitched at the contact, and my core pounded with need. I braced myself for the unholy sensation of his tongue. Yet instead, the jester reeled himself away on a groan, then snuck backward.

Straightening between my legs, he whispered in a voice made of leather and silk, "Preserve your energy, sweeting."

... *all night long.*

Just then, something smooth coasted up my inner thigh. My eyebrows furrowed, and an exhalation snagged in my throat. The object extended a considerable number of inches, not as short as a quill, nor as long as a pole. Yet it bore a similar rodlike shape, and despite the solid exterior, its touch was soft.

Poet traced my flesh with the item, sweeping it into the vent of my limbs. As it neared my cleft, I grasped the ribbons, my fingers wrapping around the fabric. This reaction caused the headboard to thump gently into the wall.

My respirations grew rough and erratic. Whatever it was, Poet was trailing the item toward my pussy. To my astonishment, arousal seeped from my body, and I felt the urge to expand my limbs until I no longer could.

Then it happened. A rounded surface made contact with my slit, its tip polished and rigid. A small yelp jumped off my tongue. In reflex, my rear bucked off the sheets, my feet jerking on their own ribbons, which only snared me firmer in place.

Poet halted the object. His mouth skated across my knee and whispered, "Yield, my thorn."

His voice coaxed my frame back into the mattress, which earned me a hum of approval. With my body fully sprawled, the jester slowly rowed the object up and down my slot, his pace languid. All at once, a stunning type of pressure built, creating a pleasurable friction against the intimate flesh. A noise of appreciation curled from my lips, and my waist moved off its own volition, jutting toward the apparatus.

My jester rasped something under his breath and responded in kind. He swept the tip back and forth along my entrance, each time getting closer to my swollen clit. I whined and coiled, my knees falling wider, as if that might bring my pussy nearer to the rod.

It felt like ... its shape reminded me of ...

"Oh," I keened, a bolt of pleasure streaking through my walls when

Poet circled the object, using its peak to sketch the oval of my opening. Seasons, the stimulation throttled my body. Tingles spread over my scalp, and my pussy dripped as I writhed into the item.

And then I realized what it felt like, what its shape emulated. I thought of Poet's cock, the broad head and slit at the top, the thick length, and hard width. The item in his grip was … was supposed to be a …

My memory strayed to the pleasure vault in Spring, then the sex trinkets stored in Poet's wardrobe. He had used one on me before, but not like this.

Nonetheless, I liked it. Seasons help me, I liked it very much.

With my jester, what should feel sordid and vulgar never did. Rather, it felt innate and authentic. In his embrace, intimacy was playful and joyous, sensual and uninhibited, sexy and beautiful. They were the most genuine, most potent, most empowering emotions I'd ever known.

There was no place for embarrassment or repentance. To the contrary, it would be shameful to deny this.

Another moan shook from my mouth. I hoisted my hips toward the object, warmth cresting between my folds. I wanted it inside me, like I wanted him inside me, penetrating so deeply, so good.

Poet muttered another incomprehensible obscenity and skimmed the head up to my clit. He etched around the distended flesh, then feathered it over the apex. And I lost my faculties.

A gravely cry toppled out of me, followed by another, then another with each pass atop the stud. My pussy ached terribly, seeping freely now. The ribbons gripped my hands and ankles as I vaulted against the toy.

Poet alternated between swabbing my clit and tracing my cleft until I was sobbing. The disjointed noises spurred him on. At last, he took pity and pushed forward, using the tip to probe me.

My folds expanded, flaring for the object. With shallow jabs, the jester thrust the rod in and out, siphoning just so. Each time the shaft went a bit deeper, my pussy spread a tad wider, and my cries escalated.

I dug my heels into the mattress and took over, using the leverage to burrow down. A great moan vaulted from my throat as I straddled the object and sank around it fully. The solid length pistoned into me, and my soaked walls clutched its thick shape.

Then I began to ride it. My hips bobbed with abandon, wetness smothering the toy. Tied down, I relied on my lower body, pumping myself over and over.

"Good, Your Highness," Poet urged. "Very good. Play with it. Fuck it as you'd like to fuck me."

Emboldened, I lapped my core against the tool. My eyes continued to squeeze shut, darkness engulfing my vision, the sensations more extravagant because of it. I clamped around the rod and swayed on top of it. All the while, Poet stroked the item into me, his tempo gradual.

My blood spiraled, about to relinquish control of itself. The orgasm mounted, shoving me toward a precipice. Yet I resisted, my hands fisting the ribbons.

Poet sought the opposite. Using his best efforts, he shifted the object, hitting a narrow spot that never failed to disarm me. With every thrust, he encouraged me to let go, to release myself on the tool, to come all over it. Foreshocks rippled through my veins, small climaxes threatening to obliterate me.

However, I longed for more. I yearned for him.

Always, him.

I whipped my head back and forth. My eyes flew open and landed on Poet's features, his expression gripped by awe.

The carved ridges of his body radiated with heat. The muscles contracted with every heaving outtake of air. He could have been a deity in his former life, except there was more. Purple welts looped under his eyes, as if he hadn't slept in months, and a shadow of stubble lingered across his jaw.

Only then did I register these details, the sight clogging my throat. I wiggled until he translated my movements and hunched forward, enough for my tethered hand to cup the side of his face. "Oh, Poet."

Gone was the sinful rake intent on seducing his princess. Now his eyebrows crimped, pain slashing through his face. He twisted his head, bringing his jaw into sharp relief as he nuzzled my hand.

"Not alone," I pleaded. "Not without you."

We had done that for far too long already. This wasn't only about me, nor only about him. This moment, this night, was all us.

Poet lightly bit my wrist, then returned his gaze to mine. Those eyes glinted, reflecting my own desire, some manner of primal instinct consuming us both.

Uttering a haggard "Fuck," he withdrew the object from between my thighs. My gaze caught a flicker of the long shaft, shaped like an erection. Yet it bore little comparison to Poet's size as he tossed the item to the ground, untied the footboard ribbons, and hefted my lower half off the bed.

He rose on his knees, taking my limbs with him. Aligning my legs vertically and flush against his torso, he braced my ankles on his shoulders, seized my hips, and stared down. Those eyes tacked me to the bed, binding me more than the ribbons.

He watched my countenance, his expression smoldering. This man beheld me as if I was the very earth, the foundation beneath him.

I understood this feeling. Only one emotion could topple and rebuild kingdoms. In the jester's arms, that emotion filled me to the brim.

This was why I had opened my eyes. This was why I'd wanted him instead of the fantasy.

In the pleat of my thighs, Poet's cock lifted high, primed and poised. That length and ruddy hue consumed my attention, along with the droplet of cum rising from the slit.

Capturing his gaze, I rolled my pussy along the stem of his cock, saturating his crown, which swelled in response. His frame quaked, and his eyes sank into mine as he positioned himself.

"Briar," he panted. "Wicked hell."

Then he swung his hips, and his cock pivoted into me. The head splayed my pussy and stroked deeply. I shrieked in pleasure, my mouth ajar at the depth of his erection. Poet groaned in tandem, the reverent sound showering over me.

Despite the haze, we watched one another. Poet slung his hips back and forth, his backside working, launching his cock. My pussy clung to him, wetting him from the crown to the sac as he slowly pitched in and out. His waist pumped, the roof of his phallus opened me, persuaded my body to spill on him.

I grappled the ribbons and beat my own hips with his, our waists locking. With my legs upright, Poet struck another new angle, another new place that vanquished all expectations. I wept aloud, and he growled, whisking his cock into the damp clutch of my body.

Never once did our gazes stray. They remained fixed on one another, savoring each moan, every shift in expression. Nothing concealed or hidden.

No mask. No crown.

Only fire. That, and happiness. For too long, we had been deprived of this.

Fuck me sweetly. Make love to me hard.

I remembered. How I remembered.

The jester circled his hips, leisurely slinging his cock inside me. We had unleashed in the rain, then we devoured each other in this room. Now we worshiped.

Poet banded one hand around my ankle, spanned my buttocks with the other, and gently flung his waist into me. I keened, my clit thrumming and my pussy smearing him to the seat.

My expression must look as drunken as his, everything in me disintegrating into pleasure. So deep. So long. We made love so patiently, it hurt.

The jester pursued every sound I could possibly utter. I progressed from sighs, to whimpers, to moans. Eventually, I was gawking at him and shouting.

Poet hissed, and his pupils infiltrated the darkness. My feverish reaction elated him, so that he increased momentum by another fraction. His reflexes kicked in, and he angled his himself steeper, the steady lash of his cock penetrating me to the hilt. His width broadened, sloping through my walls, and I wailed with each stroke.

"That's it, Princess," he crooned. "Tighten for me."

"Closer," I begged. "Deeper."

Poet seethed, released my legs, and descended on me. He landed between my thighs, splitting them around his waist. Then he grabbed the ribbons and bound his own wrists with mine, tying us together.

Like this, we sprang at one another, slick and slippery. And so very, eternally slow.

The jester ground his hips into me, steering his cock and plying my folds. Our mouths hung open, my moans colliding with his roars as we beat our pelvises together. One of the ribbons tore from around my foot, enabling me to link it over his thumping waist.

Moonlight splashed across the floor. Hours must have passed, and in that time, Poet had not let up. Nor had I, though several times he twisted his hips and lunged his cock in a way that prompted me to nearly faint.

My voice grew hoarse. My nipples toughened and pitted into his chest. My clit bloated, rubbing the column of his erection.

All night long must have happened, though I could no longer recognize the world outside. Only the change in light warned me. Yet I did not care if minutes or days or weeks had passed.

Poet kept a measured pace, his waist snapping. The headboard and footboard rocked, but the ribbons did not chafe or constrain. We clasped our fingers and held fast—held on.

And on. And on.

Shadows sketched Poet's abdomen, which clenched with effort as he bolstered himself above and lunged into me. Pleasure crackled between my walls, small convulsions vibrating through me. On the brink of nirvana, I made a grievous noise, my pussy clenching and seeping on him.

"Poet, come with me. Come with me," I repeated desperately.

White hot liquid surged through my legs. As it did, Poet growled and accelerated his hips, his cock pumping, hitting that spot. I tensed, shrieking and unraveling, my pussy contracting around him while he continued the onslaught.

My breasts arched into his torso, and he watched me dissipate into a million pieces. I came so hard, my throat stung. Then Poet slammed into me once, twice, three times more before stalling his buttocks. His cock twitched, and a hot rush of fluid gushed into me. The jester's features cramped, then collapsed, a bellow ripping from his lungs as he came seconds later.

"Briar!" he hollered.

Our fingers clasped, the ribbons mooring us to one another. His cock shuddered, my pussy gripping him hard, both of us spasming in unison. Even while the climax ruptured through us, while we were still locked in free fall, Poet's mouth crashed atop mine, and he spoke.

"Please, Briar," my jester choked out in a whisper. "Please don't leave me again."

I shook my head, my breathing ragged as I made a similar entreaty. "Please don't let me go."

Because I missed you. And I need you. And I want you. And I crave you. But also, I love you.

We nodded against one another. Still moaning, our lips slanted and melted together as though sharing a vow.

15

Briar

Fingers stroked the side of my face, gently nudging me from a dream state. My eyelashes fanned open. Opaque furnishings trembled into focus, a warm patina spilling through the windows and laminating the bedroom so that every surface resembled aged brass. I lay on my stomach, the bed and pillows cushioning my limp muscles, and the quilt barely covering my backside. As I twisted my head toward those wandering digits, a sleepy yawn curled from my throat, then my lips raised at the sight that greeted me.

Poet lounged on his side, naked with his broad pectorals and tight nipples exposed. The blanket slumped just below two steep hipbones and scarcely covered the base of his cock. He watched me back, his features cast in a sheen of daylight. Layers of dark hair hung around his face, the tousled mess accentuating the sharpness of his jaw and chin. Never mind how those clover irises danced with color or how that sculpted chest flexed with each intake. Goodness, this man.

Elation fluttered in my flesh. Other pertinent cravings roused the blood between my thighs. Inwardly, I berated myself to regain some composure and come up for a proper dose of air. It had been a long and relentless night, wrought from more positions than I could count.

Him, hovering above. Me, astride his waist.

Him, from behind. Me, on all fours.

Him, pumping around my lips. Me, straddling his mouth.

On the bed. On the floor.

Atop the windowsill. Against the wall.

Had we been alone in this enclave, I suspected we wouldn't leave this cabin for several days more.

Poet's digits sketched my temple, then quested to my ear, which he rubbed between his thumb and forefinger like a trinket. Or a treasure. Delighted shivers rushed up my skin, and a closed-mouth sigh drifted from my lips as the jester continued to etch my countenance with those dexterous hands.

"Hello," I whispered, happy with exhaustion.

"Hi," he murmured in that husky, drowsy timbre.

I stretched and burrowed into Poet's touch. He traced the length of my body as though he'd been doing so since I fell unconscious at dawn, encased in his arms.

Then again, the realization clicked. My brows furrowed, the space between them wrinkling like paper. "You have not slept."

"Good afternoon to you too," he teased.

"Why have you not slept?"

"Chiding me already? Jesters have rules about that. No lectures before coffee or sex."

"Poet—"

"I didn't want to miss this," he answered plainly, running his knuckles down the edge of my waist to illustrate. The motion tickled as much as it enticed, a combination that shouldn't be humanly possible, were it not for his skills.

Something akin to melted sugar seemed to pour down my limbs. Why must my concerns always come out sounding like admonishments?

I softened my tone and reached out to caress the grooves of his abdomen. "You need rest."

"You're my rest," he assured me, snatching my fingers and dragging them to his pulse. "You hear that? 'Tis evidence of your effect on me."

Relaxed tempo. Strong and steady.

If I revealed my own heartbeat, it would sound much the same. The notion wrung a relieved smile from me, especially when other facets came into clearer view.

The purple shadows under his eyelids were gone. They had vanished at some point last night. As for the slight bristles tracking across his unshaven jaw, I rather enjoyed the unrefined and ruggedly sexy appearance it gave him.

Presently backdropped by the gilded light, this jester should not be of our current world. Rather, he resembled a careless fae of ancient times, in all his disheveled glory, though no less lethal.

Peace filled my lungs to capacity, then whooshed out in a great exhale. We gazed at one another, inebriated with bliss. I had marveled at the mysticism of this place, but Poet's presence turned the treehouse enclave into a paradise. Like our own hidden castle of the wild, where untamed things happened.

I swayed my own fingers over Poet's bare chest, relishing every contour. Feeling as blithe as a Spring citizen, I bent my knees, lifted my calves into the air, and crossed them at the ankles.

A deep masculine noise strummed from Poet's throat. His lips crooked with appreciation and mischief. "Look at you. My reigning thorn. If I didn't know better, I'd say you were gloriously fucked all night, by everything from my fingers, to my tongue, to my cock." When my face suffused with heat, he quirked an eyebrow and gave voice to my private thoughts. "And by some other source as well. Care to confess your sins, Highness?"

That sex toy he'd used on me, after tying my limbs in scarlet ribbons. Although it was nowhere in sight, I imagined the object tucked safely in a drawer after Poet had meticulously cleaned it. He catered to such tools the way he did his wardrobe.

Heat blazed across my cheeks, surely painting my skin in a mortified and wanton shade of pink. With a half-groan, half-laugh, I slapped my palms over my face. "I cannot believe I did that."

The bed shook from Poet's lazy chuckle. "Oh, but you did. Energetically, I might add. Come now," he said, pawing my hands from my face. "None of that. You should be proud, sweeting. Such heights can't be reached without the tenacious will of a princess and the deviant prowess of a juggler."

Playfully, I smacked his bicep. "What perverse miscreant brings a dildo to a romantic reunion?"

"Someone who'll never bore you. Let's not forget I'm of Spring and a man of performance. Likewise, I had extra space in my bag."

"With your addiction to textiles, I very much doubt that."

"Fair enough, but I made room. And what unbiased heiress judges a mere trinket as being perverse rather than sensuous? What Autumn calls debauched, Spring calls intimate. There was nothing hedonistic about what we did."

"Fair point," I teased back. "And I agree."

Like a sly devil, he crawled over me. Like a willing captive, I rolled onto my back and spread my thighs for his weight.

We moved in sync, my legs knitting around his backside and his hips prying me farther apart. With his cock braced against my pussy, he hunched over. "I should congratulate myself on wielding that weapon with finesse."

"You have enough vanity to supply this continent," I pretended to reprimand, arching and moaning as he leaned in and dragged his mouth over the sensitive bridge between my neck and shoulder.

His mirth vibrated against my skin, then darkened into a purr. "I take it you liked our little plaything?"

"Yes," I gusted as he licked my collarbones. "I liked it immensely."

However stunned, I had lost the ability to feel shame for anything we did or anything he brought out of me. I loved it all, wanted it all, needed it all. Like air and water.

Proof of the jester's impact on me was not limited to my pulse. Further evidence manifested in the delicate pulse of my core, the walls of my cunt once again growing damp.

As a pampered soul, the jester knew how to spoil his lovers in kind. He probed my folds with the tip of his cock, the sound of rustling blankets filling the room, along with a collective tremor of leaves outside. But for some reason, the reminder of his many conquests sent an unexpected pang through me. Not out of envy but protectiveness.

On another moan, I veered back and framed his profile. "Why did you pleasure them?" When Poet's gaze sobered in confusion, I slanted my hips, and he took the signal. Easing his cock backward, he pulled back several inches and simply sprawled himself between my legs, holding me as I held him.

"All of those courtiers back in Spring." I shook my head. "Why?"

Poet hesitated, distant memories rising to the forefront. I had broached this subject long before we journeyed to Autumn, far back on a night in his Spring suite. He had explained his motives, but additional details were missing.

I cradled his jaw, heedful to keep my voice low and gentle. "I would never judge you. I just ... I want to understand."

Aside from simply enjoying sex, he'd told me his promiscuity had also sprung from loneliness and the need to release tension. It had stemmed from the pressure of keeping treasonous secrets from the Crown, not to mention the isolation from Nicu.

Yet how had Poet found gratification in people who would spurn his son? Why copulate with his adversaries willingly, much less erotically?

"Fame and acclaim, though not quite the same," Poet rhymed while thumbing the oak leaf braid dangling among my loose hair. "Not every soul in Spring was the enemy. Isn't that what we're crusading for? Cadence. Posy. Vale. Eliot. In Spring, they weren't the enemy."

"That's true," I conceded.

"I chose my playmates carefully, targeting the ones who let certain sympathizing tendencies slip. Otherwise, I picked those whom I wanted to ridicule or strip of secrets. For that was the second motivation. Giving people orgasms tends to loosen tongues, which provides clout, bargaining chips, and leverage. Fucking provided a quick sexual fix, in addition to long-term advantages."

"Yet you still pleasured them," I pointed out.

"I dominated them," he corrected, sweeping his nose against mine before curling his deceptive mouth. "And I pleasured myself." That crafty grin dropped. "I turned them into the truest of fools."

I shuffled, and Poet moved in tandem, comprehending each of my intentions. As I sat up, so did he.

The jester slung me on his lap and tangled my limbs around his hips. In kind, I scraped my fingers through his hair, skirted my knuckles over the stubble, and ran one thumb over the kohl smudged beneath his lower eyelids.

When he sucked in a ragged breath and clenched his eyes shut, my stomach flipped. Tenderness and sorrow overwhelmed my senses as I thought of him targeting people, tempting people, and tricking them. I imagined this man reaping ecstasy from each dalliance and every deception, yet always returning to a cold and empty suite, with no one there waiting, no one who knew his true self. Nobody for him to talk with.

Such was the life of a Royal. But whereas I had Mother, Poet had no family in Spring's castle. For all his popularity, and for the fans and admirers who wanted him, he'd been entirely alone.

I pressed my forehead to his and framed his face. "I'm sorry no one was there to touch you like this."

Another grin dabbed at his lips, this one caught between wistfulness and reverence. "Ah. But there's the problem, sweeting." His eyelids blasted open, flooding me with so much green. I gasped as he jerked me into him and hissed against my mouth, "No one else *could have* touched me like this—"

On that final word, I flung myself into him and clamped my mouth over his. With a growl, Poet responded. He hitched me tighter around his waist and slanted his lips, fusing them to mine. We sucked in oxygen. Our nostrils flared, and his wicked tongue strapped around my own, tugging me into a passionate stupor.

The distended roof of Poet's cock spread my crease, wetting my pussy. I'd barely uttered a moan, scarcely taken a moment to broaden my thighs and sink on his erection when the jester grunted in misery. He inched back with effort, gulping harshly, "You shall ruin me."

"Then why did you stop?" I complained, lost in delirium.

Poet consoled himself by relishing my whine. "Now, now," he panted, sensuously stroking my chin. "We can't have a victory lap without sustenance. If you're going to berate me about sleep, I get to pester you about food. When was the last time you ate?"

"Dinner," I managed to answer. "I last ate at dinner."

"Mmm." He contemplated. "Well, as much as I'd like to feast on your delectable cunt and fuck you as I did for nearly eight hours, I'll make an allowance to postpone that treat for another ten minutes. It's been too long since I had the privilege of tending to my sovereign, and I'm eager to pick up where I left off." His incisors nipped my lower lip. "Hungry, Your Highness?"

Not until Poet posed the question did my stomach lurch. And hadn't I just chastised myself about coming up for air? For mercy's sake.

But how I luxuriated in this moment. The treehouse's languid glow. The silence after the storm. Us, naked and depleted from love-making, and with our hair in disarray.

Sheepish, I grinned and nodded. "Famished."

Poet slid from the bed. I twisted, rewarding myself with a view of his narrow buttocks flexing as he descended the stairs. After a minute, the jester returned with a bowl of sliced apples, bread, and cheese.

Dropping onto the bed with a contented grunt, he leaned into me and flipped an apple slice between his digits. Holding it up, he murmured in a raspy tone, "Open wide."

Pinned to his gaze, I parted my lips and sealed them around the apple. Then I sucked the wedge into my mouth. Tartness burst onto my palate, and I moaned. No Seasonal flavors compared with Autumn's ripest crops. Methodically I chewed, slowing my lips for good measure, the better to kindle Poet's gaze.

Black pupils swallowed his irises as I gulped the fruit down my throat. Licking my lips, I said, "Another."

The request earned me a voracious gaze. Poet tilted his head like a carnivore. "A dangerous request, Princess. But you already know that."

Yes, I did. However, when he provided me with a second morsel, something occurred to me. No birdsong outside. No early hour shafts of light. Instead it was quiet and bright beyond the cabin. Which meant ...

My eyes widened, and I seized Poet's thigh. "Seasons. What time is it?"

The sexual gloss hadn't drained from his gaze, yet a tinge of amusement lifted his features. Instead of feeding me, he set the apple on his tongue and whisked it into his mouth. Chewing, the jester slanted his head in contemplation. His expression became remote, as if concentrating on signals from outside, as though hearing movements I could not.

At length, he fully consumed the apple, the muscles of his throat working. Then a shrewd light banked in his orbs, which slid toward me. "Late enough for others to notice."

Not a second after that prediction, a fist pounded on the front door. "Briar!" a female voice squawked. "Dammit, woman!"

My features went slack. Based on the angles of light outside, it must be well past noon. Eliot and Cadence had planned an early morning trip to an outlying village, to replenish supplies while I stayed behind and tended to the cleaning. We'd perfected this routine, so they wouldn't have knocked before leaving, and the trip usually took a good portion of the day. They must have only recently returned and noticed my absence outside.

In any case, our friends didn't know Poet was here. And I had been swept up in a thousand wondrous emotions, so that I hadn't processed the hour.

I opened my mouth to call out, but Poet pressed a finger to his plush lips. Wiping his hands and rising, he leisurely stepped into a discarded pair of low-slung pants and sauntered downstairs.

I popped out of bed, unable to access my wardrobe quickly enough. Already, I heard the knob twisting under Poet's hand. Wrapping one of the sheets around my body, I hastened halfway down the stairs.

"Briar, I swear!" Cadence quacked. "Are you unwell? Did you eat something rotten? Did a rabid creature bite you?" Another loud knock. "I know it's not a ploy to get out of chores, because you never avoid chores, so you'd better open this door before I start to freak out and break down—"

Poet swung open the door.

And Cadence froze. She stood at the threshold in a dusty gingham dress and apron, with her tresses tethered in an unkempt ponytail. No rouge. No lip color. No jewelry. No finery. Quite possibly, the jester couldn't have picked a less fashionable time to shock her.

Moreover, she'd been thumping on the door with the hilt of her knife. Her grip went lax, the weapon clattering to the deck. The lady's mouth fell ajar, and her eyes ballooned from worry to mortification.

After a speechless minute, she glanced down at her rumpled self, then back at the jester. "Fuck my life," she groaned.

"Afternoon, Cadence sweeting." Leaning casually against the jamb, Poet twirled his finger toward the knife. "I favor that accessory. Much better on you than diamonds."

The compliment achieved what he'd intended. Cadence's embarrassment dissolved, her confidence restored and followed by an open-mouthed gasp of mirth. Yet instead of squealing and tackling the jester like Posy and Vale would do, the lady recovered her moxie. Crossing her arms and feigning a glare, she pursed her lips. "Well, well. It took you long enough, handsome."

Her attention drifted over his shoulder. She found me hovering partway down the stairs, blushing furiously, and clad in nothing but the sheet. Likely, I looked as if I'd walked through a hurricane. Properly fucked, this lady must be thinking, and she would be correct.

Cadence relished my state. Her eyes twinkled with a mixture of relief and triumph, as though catching me in shambles had earned her a medal. "What I wouldn't give to have this moment captured on canvas."

"A large one, I hope," Poet quipped.

"With you? Always a large one."

Despite how my skin baked, I rolled my eyes at the flirtation. The lady simply couldn't restrain herself. Yet something vivid brightened her gaze when she glimpsed me once more, reflecting a pleased sort of kinship that further boosted my spirits.

She was thrilled to see Poet. And she was equally happy for me.

After poking the jester's abdomen, Cadence swiveled away and pranced down the connecting bridge while singing over her shoulder, "It's about bloody time."

Yes. It was most definitely time.

16

Briar

From across the walkway, Eliot strode toward us while breaking into a wide smile that rivaled the sun. On a jovial laugh,
he slapped Poet's hand with both of his, then they tugged
each other into a clasping hug. "I fucking knew it," my friend boasted, drawing back and shifting his beaming gaze between us. "It was
only a matter of time."

I had been savoring the image of them together, one of many
moments I'd envisioned in dreams. However, I crossed my arms
and pretended to scowl through my own grin. "You did not predict
he would show up."

"Well, I was hoping for it," Eliot conceded. "When Cadence and
I returned from the village, I went straight to groom the horses and
didn't notice your absence at first. And well, it's a big-ass enclave,
and sometimes it requires a damn odyssey to locate each other, so
that's no surprise. But the extra stallion grazing near ours was enough
of a hint, considering the saddle bore Poet's insignia.

"I drew the obvious conclusion from there, and before I could
quest to your front door—just to make sure all was well, you see—

Cadence had already beaten me to it. Then she blasted my way to share the news." He rubbed his hands together. "I'd say our reunion is prime inspiration for a ballad."

"This jester can help there," Poet gloated. "Most people are inspired by me."

"Neither of you have changed, then," Eliot joked. "You two are magnetized to each other." He flapped his wrist, as if to amend. "Not like actual elements, if you follow me. But like moths to flames or ... never mind," he chuckled ruefully, then regarded Poet while feigning exasperation. "So what the hell took you so long?"

"I made the same comment when I caught them post-fuckery without a stitch of clothing," Cadence announced, sashaying up to us after having changed into a claret dress with a high slit up the leg.

The outfit caught my attention less than the comment. Nonetheless, my skin roasted for the hundredth discreet time, and I lifted my chin. "We were decent."

"Yes. Decently naked by Spring standards."

Eliot snorted. Poet's lips slanted deeper into a smirk. My frown hardened while Cadence merely winked at me, loosening the chinks in my facade. Despite myself, a dry laugh fell from my mouth.

"Just in time," Cadence said, trotting toward a set of intricately carved stairs roping around an oak trunk. "Who else is starving?"

Poet quirked an eyebrow. "You cook now, do you?"

Glib as ever, the lady flipped a thick lock of hair over her shoulder. "It happens."

Eliot took one step after her, then wheeled back around. "Oh, by the way." Pressing a fist to his mouth and concealing a perceptive grin, he fumbled in his pocket and plucked out a weathered band of scarlet, which he placed in my palm. Tipping into Poet and me, the minstrel whispered, "You dropped this."

My mouth parted as he sauntered away with a smug—and knowing—expression. Dear Seasons. My face detonated with heat.

Before fucking me in the treehouse last night, Poet had stepped outside to gather our wet clothes and the ribbons. Traces of our escapade should have been cleared from the platforms. Yet I jammed the ribbon into the pocket of my spruce-green wool dress and then swiveled to meet the jester's sniggering features.

"Hmm," he said, tapping one finger to the crook of his mouth and assessing my visage. "You're making the official Briar Face. Something on your mind, Princess?"

I scolded under my breath, "You forgot one."

Poet wove his fingers through mine, as he'd done on the way here. As we moved to the stairs, he leaned into me and whispered, "Nay, I didn't."

At once, I melted into a resigned chuckle. Too joyous to mind such embarrassment, I burrowed my face in his shoulder and groaned, "What must he think?"

"Eliot hails from a sinful and rather creative nation," the jester said blandly. "What do you suppose he thinks?"

True. Also as my best friend, Eliot was the last person who would balk at our behavior. Neither him, nor Cadence. And truly, Poet and I had done nothing to be mortified about.

Quickly, the jester muttered into my hair, explaining that he'd left the ribbon as a signal to Eliot and Cadence of his arrival, as well as a request not to disturb us this morning. My best friend must have noticed the ribbon, whereas the lady hadn't. That explained Cadence's appearance at my doorstep earlier versus Eliot, who would have otherwise been concerned why I wasn't up yet.

Regardless, I knew my theatrical jester. His actions hadn't simply been practical. This man could do nothing without making it into a spectacle.

I hooked my free hand around his bicep, shaking him gently. "You rake."

Poet nibbled my earlobe. "You like me rakish."

"I do," I replied. "A lot."

Satisfied, the jester kissed the top of my head and gathered me closer to his side. We migrated to one of the upper elevated decks, below the highest bridge where Poet and I had made love last night.

At the landing, the jester strode ahead to where Eliot was banking a fire in one of the pits.

Cadence took a moment to admire my lover's backside before whirling to meet my disapproving glower. "Oh, stop with that," she huffed. "Everyone knows you own that man's cock as much as his heart. And well done, Highness." Her voice reached a level of coyness I hadn't heard in three months. "Sex on legs, that jester is. Yet he looks thoroughly conquered, and you look as though you've had about fifteen orgasms."

Diverted, I gave the lady a deliberate once-over. In addition to the sumptuous dress, Cadence had brushed her hair, allowing it to hang in loose Spring waves. I compressed my lips, withholding amusement. "And you look as if you wasted no time."

I squared her with a knowing look, which she dismissed. "He's Poet. You think I wasn't going to redeem myself after what he saw twenty minutes ago? Anyway, who cares?" She motioned for me to hurry up and spoke in a confidential tone. "Details, now. I require all the spicy nitty-gritties."

"You are not getting them," I sang while strutting past the lady, restraining myself from laughing at her pout.

Well. Perhaps I would share a crumb or two when next we were alone.

Two crescent-shaped benches embedded into the deck and faced each other across the blazing pit. Around us, a vista of oaks and tupelos catapulted into the sky, their leaves dripping with orange and burgundy shades. In Autumn, the sun descended early, dusk pouring through the mesh of trees.

The world smelled of cedar, vanilla, and woodsmoke. After tucking into wedges of potato and mushroom pie, then washing it down with jugs of water, I curled into Poet's side while Eliot played his lute. The flames sketched my friend's profile, highlighting the ends of his gilded waves, the inked tattoo across his neck, and the tips of his fingers as they plucked the strings. Cadence reclined beside him and stared at the sky, its expanse void of clouds and fog for once.

Poet admired the scenery while intermittently studying me and our companions. I saw our group through his eyes, from the smattering of whiskers on Eliot's own countenance, to several calluses on Cadence's hands, and our collective scars from weapon training and life in the wilderness. Grooming aside, the lines of our faces had tapered into something tougher.

Eliot, in a frayed pullover that clung to his frame. Cadence, in a wrinkled textile and dirt smudging her exposed toes, despite her efforts to groom. Me and Poet, dressed as humbly as we had been at Jinny's cottage.

Eliot had said that Poet and I hadn't changed. It was mostly true and somewhat not. All of us were the same but different. Once, I would have found the notion disturbing, but now a thousand bricks fell from my shoulders. I treasured who we'd all become and trusted what the future would make of us.

After tonight, things would change again. Poet had been direct, keeping me abreast of Autumn, yet he hadn't told me everything. I sensed him withholding something, pacing himself. So I seized the peaceful remnants of this moment, yet another calm before another storm.

As Eliot strummed the final chord, the notes bled into the trees and vanished. We had sat in comfortable silence, but now a heavier quiet lingered between us.

The devious jester. The pragmatic princess. The talkative minstrel. The cavalier lady.

There was no telling who would speak first. Until Cadence clapped her hands together and swooped her gaze to Poet. "Leave nothing out. I'm pining for gossip."

Eliot propped his lute on the ground and remarked wryly, "Gossip before news."

"News before plans," I amended.

"Me before all else," Poet countered.

Everyone broke into low chuckles, though the sounds bore no humor. I had told Poet my side of things, so Eliot and Cadence filled in the rest about our time here. After that, my jester hunched forward and tented his fingers. His open shirt and velvet trousers lacked adornments, which made the abundance of rings gracing his digits stand out.

He gave Eliot and Cadence an abbreviated synopsis of everything he'd told me and answered their questions before setting his gaze on mine. Embers burnished his irises, turning them into green fire. "Autumn needs you, Sweet Thorn."

My heart clenched. I straightened and squeezed my hands in my lap. "What else has happened?"

"Rhys happened." Poet's jaw locked. "The motherfucker was looking for something the night I tried to cremate him. He was strolling through the maple pasture at midnight, running his paws over every tree."

A hiss fled my lungs. "The passages."

My jester inclined his head. "It appears he knows of their existence."

"Passages?" Cadence prodded.

Fury and protectiveness prickled my skin. I struggled to recover while describing to my friends the castle's hidden tunnels, how they'd been constructed centuries ago as escape routes in the event of a siege. There were only two ways to access them, either from panels concealed within the castle halls or doors camouflaged in the surrounding maple trunks. Entry required knowing where, and how firmly, to press one's palm. It was not easy to achieve.

Not all the trees contained such outlets. For the safety of our fortress, few knew of their existence, lest enemies or spies should become privy to their whereabouts.

I held Poet's gaze, the conclusion raising my hackles. "You suspect Rhys is searching for the passages because he means to invade."

"Or something fancier," Poet murmured. "Either way, it's part of a larger scheme having to do with a certain sexy couple and their renegade intentions for equality. He doesn't believe we're out of the picture, even with you gone."

"Considering you tried to fry him like a slab of bacon within days of Briar leaving, I'd say that's a fair assumption," Cadence remarked.

"Considering Autumn's princess is the staunchest woman on the continent, I'd say that doubles it," Eliot added.

Former princess. The urge to correct them pressed against my tongue until I remembered Poet's words from last night.

You were born to make history, not be erased from it.

When our friends questioned how Rhys had learned about the tunnels, my mind whirled. Mother and I knew the passages' locations, as did Poet. In addition to us, Aire possessed this information, as the First Knight and commander of our army.

However, another group of individuals were privy to the secret routes. On that score, my words grew teeth. "The Masters of old built the tunnels."

"Fuck," Eliot muttered, his head dropping forward.

Cadence grunted. "That miserable piece of shit."

The Summer King had recruited Autumn's current guild of Masters to act as informants for him, to spy on my nation. Outraged by the campaign Poet and I were waging for born souls, Rhys had bribed us to end our crusade. In response to our refusal, he threatened to rouse the crafters, to have them commit treason, massacring innocent citizens and scapegoating the maddened prisoners—the ones he'd traded with me—for the crime.

It hadn't worked. The jester and I had outwitted the guild, but the conflict had resulted in bloodshed at the castle. And although the Masters had been slayed, they must have imparted additional valuable intelligence with Rhys prior to that tragedy.

Over generations of elite crafters, privileged knowledge about those outlets had been passed down to every guild successor. As allies, why wouldn't they also share this with the Summer King?

What's more, the subject prompted another likelihood. "Whatever Rhys has in mind, he is not doing it alone," I asserted.

"The Masters' progenies could be helping Rhys now," Cadence offered, glancing at Poet. "Seeing as Briar and you basically mopped the courtyard with their parents' corpses, I'd say they have one hell of a grudge to burn off."

"To top it off, you were planning to change laws about who gets admitted into the guild, making it more inclusive for everyone instead of just passing those ranks on to the Masters' heirs," Eliot added, reciting what I'd told him during our journey here. "The list of motives adds up."

Because Poet had already given me a summary of court news, I briefly pressed my lips together. "It was not them."

Poet reclined, propped one booted foot atop the pit's rim, and slung his arm across the bench, assuming an indolent pose. Yet his voice narrowed like the edge of a dagger. "The Masters' spawn defected to Summer." With that, he shrugged. "Dead parents. Disinheritance of their ranks. A so-called 'mad' princess. And a rival king's promise that no such catastrophes would happen to them in his nation. Not least of all, they probably weren't interested in dying the way their mothers and fathers had. The offer was too good for them to resist."

While redefining the guild would be easier now, their departure signified yet another breakdown in Autumn's system. Through abandonment, the Masters' children had gotten their revenge without risking themselves. All the same, though it should have pained me when Poet delivered this blow last night, it had not affected me in the slightest.

Still, the fact remained. If not the Masters' successors, who was working with Rhys now?

We went over the particulars, theorizing what Summer was planning and with whose help. But most of all, when we should be ready for him.

"Come now, children," Poet said when the rest of us lapsed into silence. "I'll admit this is coming to me late, but take it from Spring. There's only one glorious time the enemy can successfully raid a castle, and it's when people are too drunk and fucked to notice."

I stiffened. "Reaper's Fest."

"Ugh." Cadence lamented. "That asshole's going to spoil a perfectly good party."

Eliot scrubbed his face. "Nothing like a loud, widespread revel to obscure the sound of people screaming. Everyone will mistake it for merriment or public sex."

"In Autumn, I would doubt the latter," I proclaimed. "But otherwise, yes."

According to Poet, Mother had delayed the annual revels and bonfire ball out of respect for the fallen. Along with Summer, the Spring court had departed shortly after the announcement, Basil and Fatima surly and our relations more fraught than they'd been before the king and queen had banished me from their court.

Now with a period of mourning approaching its end, Mother believed it was the optimal time to stage the revels. With tensions running high, levity was the lesser of the two evils. Wait any longer, and it might lead to civil unrest. Nobles and commoners alike were feuding daily. Verbally, at least. Hosting the festivities might dilute the impact before things escalated to violence.

That said, it would be the ideal opportunity for Rhys to act, when everyone was vulnerable. But what exactly he intended was still up for debate. We wouldn't know without prying.

Rage boiled through me. This game wasn't over. Summer would continue to plot against this kingdom, Rhys would further subject born souls to cruelty, and by some manner he now threatened Autumn's stronghold.

Alongside wrath, a premonition crept into my mind. "Rhys would not attach himself to a full-scale rampage," I stated. "Laying siege to a kingdom unprovoked would be seen as a betrayal against the Seasons. It would defy the age-old peace treaty and require each court to take up arms against the perpetrator. To incite a war of that magnitude would be folly. Summer's actions would pull Spring into the conflict. Most importantly, Winter."

Eliot and Cadence shuffled. Poet watched me keenly.

Autumn's forces, Summer could handle. Perhaps Spring as well. But if there was one court that could take down Rhys with a single icy flick of the wrist, it was the glacial court of Winter. That, he would not risk.

"Even volatile Rhys would not squander his forces, much less instigate a continental brawl without being pushed to his limit. That cannot be his objective." I stared at Poet's lethal expression. "There must be more."

"Something less conspicuous that also won't point the finger at him." He glimpsed me sideways through the blazing light and read my expression. "But first, he'll wait to see how long we last apart."

"And what move we make from there," I finished. "How long do we have?"

"I do love the sound of vengeance on your tongue," he cooed, then flattened his tone. "Reaper's Fest is in four weeks."

Four weeks to reclaim my place, vindicate the union between Poet and me, discover Rhys's next move, and burn that man's agenda to the ground before he had the chance to act.

A princess does not retreat.

A princess bides her time, recovers her strength, then rises from the ashes.

That time had come. It wasn't just my fight; it was ours. I wouldn't target Rhys alone.

Poet had waited for me. Then he'd come for me. No matter that I had been stripped of my title and forsaken by the court, we had known better. It hadn't been the end of us, nor our crusade. He'd understood I would never leave with no intention of returning to him, Nicu, or Mother. Or to my home, my people. Eliot, Cadence, and I had survived, trained, and planned for this purpose.

Time to light a match. Time to go home.

"That man will not take action unless he's certain he won't suffer the consequences," I declared to the group. "Not unless he has a guarantee that Spring and Winter will remain on his side."

Across the firelight, Poet and I consulted one another in silence. Then after a moment, I took a fortifying breath. "And not unless we stop him."

Slowly, the jester's mouth tipped upward.

17

Poet

Brilliant, willful woman. How could I not relish the sound of Briar vowing to take back what was hers? Least of all, the sight of those steely irises reflecting nightfall and firelight. She could be an heiress one moment, a temptress the next. Had we been alone, my greedy fingers would have ripped the clothes from the princess's body and fucked her right there, until she was shouting through the woodland. Instead, I forced my cock to behave and gave her a look that promised anarchy later.

Despite our animated sexual history, Briar flushed such an intense red that it rivaled our scarlet bracelets, as well as the blaze thrashing from the pit. Our blood's combined temperature threw a different kind of heat across the deck. I granted, there was a certain enticing perk to fury.

We stared for so long that a lithe shadow moved in my periphery, and someone else cleared their throat in amusement. Briar and I blinked out of the haze, twisting to find Cadence and Eliot gazing our way with the sort of indulgent glee only citizens of my Season could muster.

Damnation. Since when did plotting treason turn me on? Since the moment I'd cornered Briar in a dark Spring castle hall. That was fucking when.

Alas. The minstrel and lady's reverie was short-lived, as was the colorful bloom in Briar's complexion and the lift of my cock. The princess got a hold of herself first, squaring her shoulders whilst I clamped my canines together. Back to the plan, for devil's sake. The rest of the night, we tamed ourselves. Conducting our next move became the main objective—how to ensure Briar's return without it amounting to a public demand for her execution. In which case, I'd be forced to go on a killing spree. We would achieve nothing if we couldn't get her through the front gate, to say nothing of backing the queen into a political corner.

Like me, Avalea would sell her soul for Briar. However, the people might not give either of us that chance. There was no way I'd let the princess near the point of a single blade or arrow, let alone a firing squad of them. Far be it from me to ever undermine this woman. Yet to keep her safe, I would chain Briar to the nearest tree first, a feat worth every curse and scowl she'd throw my way.

We worked around that possibility, scheming through the night, planning tactics carefully and meticulously. After that, our clan spent more hours brushing up on weaponry skills. Eliot and Cadence proved remarkably fast learners with his garrote and her knife, especially since they'd taught themselves a few nifty maneuvers. The minstrel and lady had each previously engaged in love affairs with knights of Spring, which had yielded some combat lessons. Purely for a lark back then, but Eliot and Cadence had remembered the instruction, even if it was given to them whilst naked.

What Eliot lacked in momentum, he made up for in strength. What Cadence lacked in brawn, she made up for in stealth.

We crossed weapons on the ground level, in a clearing between the oaks, routinely switching opponents. Briar and I sparred, her thorn quills against my staff and daggers. We prowled around one another, our feet swishing through the grass.

The second we paused, Briar narrowed her gaze, those freckles shifting in tandem. "Do not hold back."

My sly lips curved. "Don't be gentle," I muttered, reminding her of last night at the colony's highest peak, when she'd whimpered to me. Though internally, I added my own vulgarity to the request.

Don't fucking be gentle.

Her breathing hitched. My own respirations twisted into a growl.

We launched toward each other. And so it went—her meticulous foresight versus my impulsive agility, her concentrated scowl against my exhilarated grin—until sweat drenched my bare torso and trickled down her low neckline, perspiration glazing the swale between her tits. Seasons fucking help me.

Sometime after midnight, Eliot and Cadence retired to their respective cabins, certain to pass out.

Briar and I disarmed in silence. All the whilst, I intended to wreak more havoc on her body—massage her aching muscles, draw us a shower from one of those delightful vista outposts that some ancient genius of a bygone era had installed, and then use my tongue to fuck away the princess's agitation. Even before all that, I considered tossing her over my shoulder and racing up the nearest stairway. Strolling, stalking, striding, or anything considered average speed wouldn't be quick enough.

But before I could snatch her against me, Briar set a palm on my chest. "Walk with me?" she whispered.

The plea worked on my reflexes like a mechanism. I threaded my fingers with hers and dove my free hand into her damp hair, the locks braided into a bun at the nape. "Anywhere," I intoned. "I'll go anywhere with you."

A shy grin wreathed across her face. "Even through a storm?"

"Aye. Typhoon. Monsoon. It doesn't matter."

"Even through a burning building?"

"Even then. Infernos are underrated. Just think of the ambient light."

Her grin widened, then slumped abruptly, folding in on itself.

"Even into a war?"

Looming over her, I snared Briar's chin. "A thousand wars, sweeting."

This whole time, from the firepit to the training session, she hadn't wavered or lost her nerve. Like a well-groomed Royal, Briar had composed herself and performed her role. But with Eliot and Cadence gone, she did what I'd been waiting for her to do. My thorn let go.

On a tremulous sigh, she sank into me. My arms corded around her, cementing Briar in place as she wedged her face into my collarbones. "Will I die tomorrow?" she asked.

My soul caught fire, and I fastened her tighter to my frame. "So long as I live, you will too," I hissed. "There were many times either of us could have died, and it didn't happen, nor did it stop us."

"We do not know if this plan shall work."

"Hush," I dismissed, speaking into her hair. "We'll never know if any plot will work. Yet I like to think we have a decent track record."

"Jesters are too confident for their own good."

"That's because you spoil my ego," I quipped. "'Tis all your fault."

Briar chuckled, but the mirth segued into a frightened noise. "Our last plan ended in bloodshed."

"But with you standing and Nicu safe," I reminded her.

She nodded, melting further as I cradled her. We said no more about it, and when her outtakes grew steady again, I whipped off my coat and draped it over her shoulders. "Come now, Highness," I murmured. "You promised me a walk."

The distraction worked. Armed with a purpose, Briar nestled into the coat and accepted my hand. We hiked into the treetops and navigated a labyrinth of bridges, platforms, and cabins tucked into the branches. Deep rich shades filtered through the darkness, pouring vibrant shafts of light across the planks and railings. Below, a noble stag with brass antlers strutted through the colony. Above, dewy cobwebs glistened like nets from the boughs. Although Briar played guide, I clasped her fingers and walked slightly ahead like a shield.

In the half-light, the trees brought another memory to the surface. I recalled that little stripling who'd worked for the Masters—the girl who'd called herself Somebody. Despite keeping most of her face concealed beneath that oversized cloak, I had noted the grainy patterns in her skin, reminiscent of bark.

After the courtyard battle, Somebody never returned, her whereabouts now a mystery. As I'd said to Briar back then, if we saw her again, that would be the girl's choice.

Briar grew more animated. Along one of the gangways, she twisted and rested her back against the railing. "Since childhood, I've always wanted to see this place. Under different circumstances, of course."

"Is that so?" I mused, gripping the banister on either side of Briar's hips and caging her in. "You mean, you never planned on being a scandalous, felonious heiress? What a shame."

Fondly, she shook her head. "Insolent devil. I think you're controversial enough for the both of us."

"Now you're just being generous."

"And you are not being remotely humble."

I curled my nose in distaste. "Perish the thought."

She glanced up, marveling. "This is the first time I've beheld the wonders of this timberland. I thought I knew everything about Autumn. Yet reading about the kingdom, touring it on occasion, and harvesting only got me so far. I've never interacted with the wild this way. Not beyond the castle boundaries." Briar extended an arm overhead and strained her fingers toward the leaves. "Perhaps I needed to be banished," she wondered. "If only to become a tangible part of my home."

"Perhaps," I said absently, riveted by her.

Out of nowhere, Briar gasped. The noise snagged my attention from her profile, my head craning toward the source. One of the twigs—almighty Seasons—stretched toward her like a finger.

We froze, staring as the offshoot brushed the tip of her digit. "If I didn't know better," I began, then raised an eyebrow. "And really, the knave in me rarely knows better, but I'd say it's reacting to your speech."

Briar tilted her head. Her throat pumped as though swallowing a lump of rocks. "It has been a long time since I felt like I've earned something, rather than believing I've ruined it. But since leaving the castle—with the oak tree plaiting its leaves in my hair and now this—the former has eclipsed the latter."

The princess lowered her voice, her tone secretive whilst she spoke to the branch. "I've come here later in life than I should have, and purely for refuge. I sought and took what you would give me. When truly, I should have considered what I could give you. So humbly, I extend my gratitude and beg your pardon. Thank you for your protection. And I swear by my Royal oath, I will honor you as you have honored me."

After a moment, the twig curled around her finger. When it did, Briar smiled.

"Sweet Thorn," I muttered, then leaned in from behind and ghosted my breath into her ear. "If you ever needed proof of who you are—" my lips slanted, "—you have it now."

Her spine lifted. I sensed her committing those words and this moment to memory.

In the final hours before dawn, my body screamed for hers, eager to make Briar come repeatedly until the sun rose. Instead, her joints loosened to putty not long after, and her eyelids fluttered with exhaustion. Lo, the desire to give her more than an orgasm—or a dozen—exceeded other cravings. In the treehouse, I stripped the princess down, washed us both in the shower, and gifted her the final book in her series, which she hugged to her chest. After reading a chapter together, I nested Briar under the blankets and fell unconscious to the rhythm of her sleep.

The following morning, I fucked my princess deeply into the mattress. With her ass tipped upward and curled into my pelvis, and my cock pistoning into her slick cunt from behind, and our shouts hitting the roof, I made sure the first thing she felt at dawn was our bodies locked and a climax launching from her throat.

Before we left the colony, Briar penned a note and tied it to the branch from last night. This missive was intended for the enclave's next guest, whoever that might be. "It might help them," was all she said.

Always instinctively looking out for her people. That was my princess.

We armed ourselves, packed the essentials, and mounted our rides whilst leaden clouds floated through the firmament. The four of us savored one more prolonged view of The Lost Treehouses, then kicked the horses into a gallop.

Aye, poets tended to exaggerate for the sake of it. Be that as it may, the journey passed in seconds and decades. Shockingly, it was less eventful than it had been getting there, for myself as well as their party. The stab-happy criminals, lethal crops, and rabid animals were nowhere in sight, the days and nights flying behind us in a montage.

Cadence kept up the banter, Eliot played for us at night, and I recited a few graphic verses to liven things up. To no avail. The closer we got to our destination, the quieter Briar became.

Indeed, the only time she made noise was when I pressed her against the trees at night, far from our various encampments, and fucked my cock into the wet clutch of her pussy. Lovemaking, in addition to the moments when I succeed in getting a laugh from her, became the exceptions.

Finally, the forest receded, giving way to a panorama of wheat and corn beneath a dome of stars. The Wandering Fields sprawled across the hills, stalks burnished and swaying in the breeze. The lower town's steepled roofs clustered together, and the statuesque maples rose into the sky. Laced in thickets of fog, the brown masonry and flat towers of the castle materialized, its bronze pennants slapping the wind.

Halting our horses on the brick road leading through the fields, we studied the fortress. Cadence slanted her evergreen head. "I know it's supposed to resemble a grand library, but maybe next time, paint the castle in a more cheerful color."

"Rose gold," Eliot joked mildly. "Like my soul."

"I rather fancy the brown," I boasted. "The contrast brings out my eyes."

In a perfect world, we would have chuckled. Sadly, even jesters as skilled as I had their off days.

A tendril of red hair feathered Briar's cheek. Her voice drifted across our group. "Orange," she whispered, gazing at the stronghold. "Happy Orange."

Nicu's favorite color. As my son's face manifested from the princess's answer, my black heart exploded. The princess would make it inside. She would reunite with him if I had to dismember every soldier on duty.

We tethered the horses at the forest border and drew handsewn garments from our packs. One of the advantages of Spring. Our culture got creative with attire, and not merely for role-play kinks. As a nation of artistry, our court excelled in performance as well as sin and sex.

Whilst making camp last night, we'd gone to work on scraps of old abandoned clothing from the treehouses, fashioning them until they resembled lower ranking councilors' robes. Nonetheless, I sulked at the bland, unembellished panels of suede, each yard the color of fresh turds.

"If anyone cares to stay on my good side, you'll never bring this up after today," I warned.

"Says the man who'd look good wearing mud," Cadence remarked while tying a belt around her waist.

Briar fastened the toggle closures that scaled my chest. Despite herself, she repressed a sudden grin. "You do realize she's right."

The lady could be right about anything as long as it alleviated Briar's anxiety. Matter of fact …

The princess expelled a breath as I hauled her into me. "You do realize you'll be taking this off me later."

"Then stop complaining, brat."

"At your service, Princess." I brushed a hot path across her lips. "Also, I've worn mud for you before."

The first kiss. That Spring meadow. All the fucking gunk covering us. Seasons, I'd never loved dirt so much in my life.

We crossed into The Wandering Fields on foot. Briar led the way, her pace confident, having done this countless times. No need to worry about being consumed by delirium and getting lost here forever, for the fields only trapped dwellers whose intentions were malevolent. That alone should work in our favor before the court. The first part of the plan. To have the fields—paragons of nature and the Seasons—vouch for Briar's character.

My mouth twitched because the more ground we covered, the surer the princess's footfalls grew. Her pace increased, the castle's prospect trampling her fear. Based on the woman's straight shoulders, I would call it mettle.

Without stopping, Briar grasped one of the stalks. She raced her fingers up the kernels, collecting the batch in her palm and dropping them into the pocket of her wool trousers beneath the robe.

Beyond the fringed horizon of corn tassels and wheat beards, the castle's silhouette loomed higher, its crenelations like bared teeth and its chimneys coughing smoke. We emerged from the fields unscathed, though I kept a grip on my staff, with a dozen blades also tucked beneath my outfit.

Despite the disguises, Briar had issued a demand. Should our group encounter a hostile welcome, we'd aim to incapacitate rather than kill. The last thing she needed was Autumn's blood on her hands, in which case the people would call for a death sentence.

I'd stab myself before letting that happen. Though my restraint would last only if no one touched her.

In any event, my boots slowed at one point. My gaze scrolled across the ramparts, unable to locate a single outline. We had timed the night watch's rotation, but still. To find no one up there was odd. Moreover, improbable.

Deftly, I maneuvered in front of Briar. At this late hour, the lower town was easy, the denizens retiring early in Prudent Autumn. And although navigating the alleys without getting gutted or fucked was far less likely than in Spring or Summer, I took zero chances.

The maple pasture came next. Copper and red foxes darted through the grove, their frothy tails swishing and titian eyes glittering like cut gems. Otherwise, all was silent and vacant.

Yet the moment we located the right tree with its camouflaged entrance, Briar stalled. "No."

In unison, the three of us whirled toward her just as the princess yanked off the fabricated robe. This revealed a long knit shirt and those slender trousers tucked into her boots. She unbound her hair, the red tresses cascading around her shoulders like a red flag. "No. I won't."

"Won't fucking what?" I snatched her shoulders, ceasing her motions. "Briar—"

"I will not hide."

"This isn't hiding. It's the fucking opposite."

Briar inched back and folded her palms over my tense knuckles. "In the treehouse enclave, when that leaf clung to my finger, you said it proved who I was. I must remember that and show myself authentically to Autumn. We value honesty here." My thorn's chin raised, her gaze lingering on my frantic one. "Poet, I won't enter my house in disguise, like a criminal. I will enter with my head high, like a ruler."

My teeth flashed, but she draped her fingers gently over my mouth, silencing a hundred obscenities and protests. Her eyes tracked my own, awareness softening those irises from sterling to mercury. "You won't lose me again. I promise."

With a groan, I seized Briar's mouth, devouring the noise that curled from her throat. My lips spread hers, my tongue dashing inside her. We barely had time for me to swipe against her once, twice more, before I wrenched myself back. "Impossible woman," I grunted against her lips. "Such an impossible woman."

A feminine huff interrupted. "So either this gets pornographic for my sake, or we keep moving," Cadence drawled, wiggling out of her own councilor's robe, which had been layered over a flouncy shirt and pants. "I've been living in squalor among marsupials and insects for three solid months, and I don't have all day to commit treason, so—"

Briar dragged herself from me and flung her arms around the lady, shocking her into silence. Cadence's arms extended midair, stilted and frozen. Nevertheless, the princess drew her in tightly. "Thank you."

The words held the weight of more than today. As Briar pulled back, Cadence fought to speak. Eventually, the lady collected herself and nodded awkwardly.

Briar and Eliot threw themselves at each other next. I glanced away to give the pair a moment, grateful their friendship had remained intact after what happened in Spring.

Afterward, Briar spread her fingers and pressed them against a constellation of minuscule knots in the maple trunk. With a dusty grunt, a rift cracked in the facade, and a door swung inward. Briar and I had once passed through a similar threshold in The Forbidden Burrow, to meet with the Masters.

Remembering that time, I swerved in front of her. "Jesters first."

Because much as I fancied the notion of watching her skulk ahead of me, with her ass outlined in those luscious trousers, her life took precedence over my baser instincts. Ignoring Briar's objection, I flipped out a dagger, braced the staff, and sauntered down the steps. The rest of them trailed in my wake, each of us dumping our disguises on the tunnel's brick floor.

Darkness enveloped the conduit. The serpentine cavity dug into the earth, roots threaded into the walls, and the dank scent of soil coated the air.

An eternity later, the ground sloped upward to another hidden door. My shoulder bumped open the partition, and we spilled into a compact lawn. I identified this sector of the troops' dormitories and training grounds, the latter vacant and banked in torchlight.

Now then. Arriving in what could be deemed the worst possible location had been intentional. But what hadn't been part of the plan was for us to take one cautious step—then to halt as dozens of weapons leaped from the shadows.

18

Briar

They surrounded us. My kingdom, this court, and its soldiers. They fenced us in like felons, outcasts, and traitors. My home did not welcome me. Rather, it sought to take me prisoner.

Beams of starlight dripped onto the lawn. The wind whipped through the high grass as a legion of armed bodies lunged from every corner, bronze mantles whisking around the knights' chainmail. A cacophony of ringing steel, drawn fletching, and clanking iron filled the air. Axes, archery, halberds, hammers, sickles, saw blades, and swords braced toward our group.

Most of them aimed at me. The army brandished their weaponry at my chest, where my heart drummed. Intricate braids embellished their hair, and their faces reflected a myriad of emotions.

Scorn. Betrayal. Distrust. Astonishment. Resentment.

And uncertainty. Also, confusion. Even remorse.

The latter came from a handful, at least. These men and women had banished their princess, but they had never struck a weapon toward her, never threatened her life.

Half of me shattered like porcelain. The other half bled with yearning.

On a deadly growl, Poet moved. With the speed of a phantom, he swerved in front of me, blocking my form from every blade, the tips hovering centimeters from his chest. Yet that didn't prevent him from windmilling his staff and bracing it overhead with one hand, then flipping his dagger with the other.

Members of the troop jolted in place, the jester's motions too swift for them to react quickly enough. However fiercely trained, few of them matched Poet's agility. Yet not only was it an uneven fight, but several knights fixed their axes at Eliot and Cadence, both of whom had drawn their own weapons. The garrote's cord strained between my friend's grip, and Cadence's wrist shook as she extended her knife.

In the time it took to suck in a breath, manacles clattered from behind. One of the warriors launched my way, the bite of iron seizing around my wrist. That was as far as he got before another male figure tore into motion. Like a squall, the jester blasted through the troop, followed by a loud blow and the crunch of bone. The man apprehending me yowled, his body blasting sideways as if shot from a cannon. He catapulted into the air, twisted at an inhuman angle, and crashed to the ground.

And then Poet was on them. He spun, his dagger flying and nailing one of the warriors to a post. At the same time, he rotated his staff and smashed it against someone else's skull.

Mayhem ensued. The troop broke into action.

Eliot shouted my name, then snapped on the handles of his garrote. Cadence screamed, ducked an arm, and jabbed her knife in reflex.

Blood spurted from someone's throat. More crimson sprayed through the air.

The scene trapped me like quicksand, pulling me into the past. The courtyard. The dismembered bodies. The goldsmith driving a knife into my gut. The court sneering at me with disgust. The king's triumphant look.

Poet's elastic movements defied gravity. He might as well have transformed into a panther, swerving and springing into the air. The staff spun like a propeller, like an extension of him, until he became nothing but a blur of arms and limbs. His legs scissored and cuffed an assailant who bellowed in pain.

An arrow sliced Poet's way. Before the warning cry could rip from my lungs, he whirled toward the projectile, having expected it. The staff caught the arrow midair and knocked it off course.

Never halting, the jester either impaled or split in half anyone who got near me. One by one, he took them down, blood seeping into his clothes and slickening his knuckles. But for each body that fell, another appeared, swarming him. It would take a sliver of movement, and any of those weapons would shear through him like a knife to butter.

Red exploded in my vision, sweat bridged across my throat, and protectiveness surged up my fingers. With one arm shackled, mobility was limited. Using my free hand, I ripped a thorn quill from my braid and hurled it toward Poet's next attacker, then wheeled and dispatched another to a knight gaining on Eliot.

Suddenly, another male voice swooped into the fray. A muscled body seemed to take flight, spearing through with the velocity of a raptor. Twin broadswords flared from the man's arms like a wingspan and diced through the frenzy.

Ashy hair. Angular face. Eyes as blue as a twilit sky.

Aire.

Relief washed through my veins. The First Knight lanced through his comrades, defending Poet and my friends. "Cease!" he commanded the legion in a gruff voice. "Stand fast!"

Half of them staggered from Aire's orders. The rest either disobeyed or hadn't heard.

My respite was fleeting as the knight landed back-to-back with Poet, both shearing through the mass—yet about to be consumed by it, nonetheless. My temperature rose. If the army touched my jester or friends, I would slay the warriors.

A vignette flashed through my head. The crown I had sent plunging over the tower rampart and the vow I'd made to myself, how a princess forged her own crown. Likewise, I recalled all the other pledges I'd made in my life.

These warriors were still my kin, still my roots. And by some measure of grace, I summoned the will to aim without severing arteries. Adrenaline fired through me, all the while I recalled my oath to this nation, to every soul who deserved to live freely. Clinging to that, I aimed to injure, not to kill.

Compassion. Mercy. Empathy.

That was Autumn. That was what we must strive for.

I thought of the wheat kernels in my pocket. And I remembered why I'd collected them.

Thrashing bodies packed the lawn. I scanned the area for a clear spot and sprinted toward a small dais at the yard's border. The manacles dragged behind me, so that I grunted and hobbled with effort. Whirling to face the skirmish, I dug into my trouser pocket and yanked out the wheat kernels.

My voice launched into the sky, uprooting from the pit of my stomach. "Honest Autumn!" I roared, then flung out my arm and released the kernels into the wind.

The grains scattered and sailed like a pennant. Moonlight illuminated the sheen of every pod and seized the crowd's attention.

The knights drew back, their weapons stalling. Their gazes followed the wheat seeds, which soared beyond the training lawn and shrank into the horizon. At once, the attention of every fighter transferred to me.

The magic of The Wandering Fields was not lost on a single witness. If my intentions—if Poet's, Eliot's, or Cadence's intentions—were not honorable, we wouldn't be standing here. The fields would have led us astray and trapped us inside, and we'd have never emerged.

I had collected the kernels for this reason. Releasing them provided evidence of where we'd passed through. If these warriors must acknowledge anything, it had to be this.

Weary, reluctant gazes stared back. Bruised and lacerated, they braced themselves.

From across the distance, Poet's gaze latched to mine. Scrapes marred his face, and his shirt was splattered in blood. But he was alive … beautifully alive. As were Eliot and Cadence, each of them battered and heaving for breath.

Aire loomed beside Poet, his features reflecting pride as he inclined his head. "Your Highness, we shall hear your words."

Protests burst from the troop and overlapped across the yard. The words "Mad Princess" cluttered the lawn.

"She's a traitor," they said.

"She's a sympathizer," they rioted.

One of them shouted, "They died because of you!"

The Masters. They died because of me.

Poet stalked my way, lest anyone should try to accost me. Looming close, he snarled at them, with Eliot and Cadence joining in. But Aire held up his palm and yelled, "She did not kill the Masters! I have sworn so before, and I shall swear it again. I was there to bear witness. They attacked first, and their leader Vex attempted to assassinate Her Highness."

In my absence, he must have defended me along with Poet and Mother. Up until now though, that defense had fallen on ignorant ears.

Tonight, the army reconsidered this testimonial. Not all the soldiers had been present during the courtyard carnage. Of the ones that were, only Aire had survived. As their leader, the most trusted warrior of this nation, and a man known for his intuitive nature—which rivaled that of a seer—Aire's word traveled across the legion, ringing with authority.

Seizing upon their stunned silence, the knight continued, "Briar of Autumn reveres her soldiers. In The Shadow Orchard, she honored Merit's death in the custom of our people. 'May Autumn keep you warm,'" he quoted. "With the fabric of her own gown, she cleaned his blood. With grief, she set a maple leaf upon his head. I saw this!"

"As did I," Poet hollered. "Is that not the mark of a genuine soul?"

Murmurs flowed through the troop. Commonly, Royals did not prostrate themselves and tarnish their priceless garments to bathe a subject's wounds. But I had. Merit had deserved my homage and more. It had been the least I owed any soldier of this nation. Truly, I would do that and beyond for these people, for my kin, for my home.

Poet had said he would sacrifice this continent for me. And while I loved him for that, I respectfully disagreed with one part.

A princess would never put herself before others.

A princess would sacrifice herself to save this world.

A ruler did not divide her people. A ruler united them.

That was the mark of a true leader.

Our plan had been to arrive near the troops' quarters and appeal to them first. In this court, the fealty of a soldier held more ground than the council's approval. If there was one group I needed most on my side, it was these fighters. If I had them, I had a chance with the nobles, whose support could eventually spread to the rest of the kingdom.

The Masters may have constructed this nation. The council may supervise it. The Crown may lead and represent it. But these soldiers protected Autumn, defended it with their lives. Their blood had watered the soil for generations. How could I not yearn for their acceptance first and foremost?

If this had been Spring, Summer, or Winter, perhaps my display wouldn't have sufficed. But this was Autumn. Benevolent and charitable. Although the crowd hedged, they also listened.

I kept my head aloft. "Beloved Autumn. I have returned with the promise of loyalty and the hope of your forgiveness. I place no hierarchy on my people and never have. *Every* citizen is equal in my eyes, and while you may not approve, I swear to you." Setting a palm to my breast, I let my voice take flight. "As Autumn is my blood, I will defend this kingdom and serve this court as I always have—with care and dedication. The harvest fields have let me pass. Your First Knight has spoken. Now it's up to you. I'm at your behest and humbly beg your allegiance."

Morally constructed. Properly addressed. Respectfully delivered.

But not enough. I saw it in their creased expressions and furrowed brows. The soldiers would not be easily won with a formal speech.

My gaze flickered to Poet, who bowed his head a fraction. *Words are stronger than weapons. Bewitch them, Highness.*

I paraphrased under my breath, quoting the jester from a Spring day long ago, in a secluded cottage when we finally stopped being enemies. "Fools believe glory can be found at the tip of a sword, rather than the tip of one's tongue."

Yes. That.

Thus, I sank to my knees. The genuflection received an instant response, stunned noises rising from under the knights' breaths. No Royal of lineage and breeding had ever prostrated themselves for their army. Yet I had never claimed to be a superior being, and I would never consider myself one.

I was not merely a princess of tradition. I was a princess of the people.

Fate had brought me into this life. But my actions permitted me to stay in it.

Bloodlines had granted me a throne. However, I would not sit back and reap the rewards like an entitlement. Always, I sought to earn what I had, because the citizens gave me that honor.

Autumn did not belong to me. I belonged to Autumn.

And above all, this kingdom valued honesty.

It grew so quiet one could hear a length of straw hit the ground. The blood-soaked grass swayed in the breeze, fog girdled the castle towers, the great maples rose to the same heights, and the distant fields shone beneath the star-flecked sky.

With one wrist shackled and the other free, I drew words from a deeply buried place. One by one, my eyes trained on every face, starting with Poet. "I treasure you," I said, my voice as raw as an open wound.

Glimpsing my friends and the knights, I continued. My words grew muscle and a heartbeat. "We are not very different. We have our loves, our fears, and our doubts. Many days, I was frightened to be a ruler. Other times, I felt humbled. And other days—" I grinned sadly, "—other days, I was grateful. Not for my throne, its power, or its riches. The privilege came from serving Autumn's majestic trees, its roaming fauna, and its misty skies.

"I've farmed and harvested among you not to validate myself, but to give myself to this land, to nurture it, as it nurtures us." My throat swelled, yet my voice steadied as I spoke to each warrior. "I can recite the lore from memory, identify every seed and crop, and navigate these roads without a map." I thought of the oak leaves strewn in my hair, a blessing from The Lost Treehouses. "But only in my absence have I fully bonded with this land, and it has embraced me in kind. The Autumn wild has taught me how little I know and how much there is yet to learn."

The manacles clanked from my arm. "I am not perfect, but I am genuine. I have made mistakes, and it won't be the last time, which terrifies me. Yet if Autumn is a nation of honesty, then I return to you stripped, exposed, and at your behest. More than a sovereign, I am your servant."

Finally, my gaze circled back to Poet. Eternally, it began and ended with him.

"I will always do what I believe is right for this Season and for you. If you trust that, stand with me."

The jester's mouth tipped upward, and his lips moved. *Bravo.*

My own mouth cracked into a tired grin, which collapsed as Aire stepped forward. The man punched his fist to his chest and kneeled before the dais. And then it happened.

A female soldier followed in his wake, aligning herself with the First Knight. Then came another, and another, and another. In succession, the soldiers lowered themselves, with their attention fixed on me. Murmurs filtered across the troops, building like a wave. "Your Highness," they chorused at intervals, the words hushed but earnest.

Aire's head slanted my way. "Rise, Princess. Be our champion."

Tears breached the corners of my eyes. Slowly and hazily, I gained my feet, the chains clunking from my wrist. My attention stumbled across the lawn, privately thanking every face. Then I blinked, realizing more knights and troops had joined them, flooding the lawn to capacity. At some point, the entire army had turned up to hear my speech.

Not only that, but additional witnesses had arrived. Several slack-jawed members of the court and council idled on the fringes.

I gawked at the congregation, immobile despite the sound of keys jangling. Someone approached my periphery. The iron shackles at my wrist shuddered, broke open, and struck the dais. At the sound, I twisted to find Poet standing beside me, the key in his grip. He must have accepted it from one of the soldiers.

Pinning our gazes together, the jester flippantly tossed the key over his shoulder, reverence and admiration glinting in his irises. Yet at once, his attention jumped across the lawn and landed on something behind me. Instantly, those pupils exploded with light.

I veered in that direction, my gaze stumbling across a pair of figures who watched from the sideline. At once, my breath caught. The world vanished, and my pulse thudded loudly in my ears.

That little faeish face. Those wide green eyes.

Nicu sat frozen in Mother's arms as she held him against her chest, with his scanty limbs strapped around her hips. She held the child like he was her own. Their gazes clung to mine from across the yard, their mouths parted as if spotting a mirage—something that might disappear if they got too close.

Mother feasted on me, her stricken eyes glistening. Whereas the child's orbs swelled with joy.

His name fluttered like a plume from my tongue. "Nicu."

I was too far away for him to hear, yet he read my lips. That was all it took for the boy to believe what he saw. He squirmed against Mother's hold, his voice breaking free. "Briar Patch!"

That did it. On a whimper, I tore from my stupor and flew across the grass.

Mother released Nicu to the ground, and the child scrambled my way on legs as thin as spindles, his speed quicker than it should be for his age. The distance receded. Our surroundings dissipated. And then we collided.

I threw myself to the ground and opened my arms just as Nicu hurled himself at me. The impact knocked me backward. My body hit the grass as the child strung his limbs around me, and I clutched him so tightly, his heart rapped against my own. Like this, we slumped beneath a maple tree, rolling back and forth.

Shaking. Crying. Laughing.

The fragrances of sweet milk and sunshine flooded my senses. I combed through his hair and chuckled as he kissed my ear, my chin, my forehead. Swiftly, Nicu wiggled back and started chattering as we sat up. "You have Autumn in your hair," he chirped, playing with the gold leaves woven in my braid. "I thought you were in the closet, but you're here."

The chink in his voice betrayed pain and sadness. I cupped his face and whispered, "Yes, I'm here. And I'm not leaving again."

Nicu knitted himself into me, and I squeezed him back until a shadow cut in. Carefully, I untangled myself from Nicu, who recognized his father and dashed toward the jester. "Papa!"

Grinning, Poet hoisted his son into the air and murmured something that made Nicu chortle. I savored the view, then swung to Mother. Rising, I absorbed the sight of that rusted red hair trussed up and gleaming with gems. The curvaceous form, so regal and poised until moments ago. She merely stared, her eyes latching to me, her body tensing as if about to spring apart like a coil.

"Mother," I whispered, unable to quell my nerves. When she made no reply, I rushed ahead. "I'm so sorry. I know it was a risk, but I had to. This is my duty, and I could not simply sit and wait for ... well, you heard everything," I guessed, figuring she and Nicu must have witnessed the whole speech.

Aware of our audience, I struggled to collect myself, folding my hands in front of me. "I'm aware it won't be easy or that I'll be accepted readily, but the knights' support will absolve me to a degree." I counted off my fingers, all the while Mother shook her head. "With the soldiers on my side, there won't be a need for arrest. As for regaining my title, it might take time, despite how the troops addressed me. And there's the matter of Summer, but I think we can forge a plan if—"

With a sob, Mother threw her arms around me. Her body slammed against mine as she crushed me to her, a riot of sensations scattering through my being, her embrace enveloping me like a blanket and flooding me with warmth. "Briar," she croaked. "My Briar."

After a moment, I surrendered to her. "Mother."

This time, I inhaled the scents of cinnamon and misty mornings. The essence of her and Father. The smells of home.

As we pulled back, I opened my mouth to continue. Mother chuckled through her tears and patted my face, the motions quieting me. "Later," she insisted. "Come inside."

Eliot and Cadence approached. Seconds later, the doors leading from the armory and soldiers' dormitories burst open. Two ladies spilled out in a whirlwind of violet organza, ivory linen, and squeals that could slice through concrete. Posy and Vale blasted forward, hysterical shouts splitting their mouths open.

"Oh my Seasons, oh gods, oh shit!" Posy bleated. "Briar!"

"Dammit, finally!" Vale choked out.

Poignancy overwhelmed me. Half-gasping, half-weeping, I stumbled backward as Posy crashed into me while Vale jumped on Cadence. We teetered from side to side, our hug expanding between the four of us, then five when the ladies yanked Eliot into the embrace.

As we disbanded, I caught Aire's attention. He rose with his brethren, and despite his fixed expression—often determined to appear serious—the man's eyes flickered with exaltation. Immediately, he tried and failed to smother the evidence with a distinguished frown.

Members of the initial troop were beaten and bloody yet thankfully alive. For today, at least. That was the best all of us could hope for. From across the yard, the First Knight gave me a devout nod, from one leader to another. And again, that brief glint returned to his eyes.

A tall shadow appeared to my left. Poet sauntered up to me while balancing Nicu in one arm, the boy's head resting in the crook of his father's neck. The look on the jester's face promised a million ecstasies and infractions to come, the pair of us about to cause more trouble. Albeit this time, we were ready to set the world on fire.

By Seasons, it felt as if I had been gone a thousand years. Also, it felt as though I'd never left.

With his other hand, Poet captured my fingers. Skating his devious lips across my knuckles, he murmured against my skin, "Welcome back, my sweeting."

19

Poet

At dawn, we stood before the threshold. Avalea, Briar, and me, each of us contemplating the doors to the library wing's council room. Books lined the inset panels, patterned rugs cushioned the floor, and the distant sound of pages turning filtered through the repository.

The moment we'd stepped into the castle, Briar and I had reveled in private time with her mother and Nicu, mainly listening to my son's stories and answering his questions about Briar's "adventure." And after that, we tucked in my son and passed out for the remaining hours before sunrise, knowing what awaited us in the morning.

Guards flanked the entrance, their attention fixed ahead. Yet I scrutinized the faint twitching of their jaws and the restless flashing in their eyes. Clearly, they were eavesdropping. They wanted to glance at us, to judge the defamatory couple who kept raising hell in their nation and getting away with it.

The women beside me sensed this as well. Intentionally, they nodded toward the guards, who faltered before awkwardly training their attention elsewhere.

Unlike other monarchs of this continent, these two Royals showed their servants respect, plus a genuine desire to earn that respect. See the value in a ruler not by how they treated their equals, but how they treated their subjects. That was Briar and her mother.

Avalea clasped her daughter's hand. "Courage, my dear," she said, attempting to sound nonchalant. "It's only a nation of millions."

"Two million, two-hundred thousand, and thirty-three souls," Briar whispered. "Give or take."

"A small audience," I remarked. "Enough for us to handle."

Avalea swerved and framed Briar's face. "No matter what happens, I'm proud of you."

The princess gripped her mother's fingers. "As I am of you."

Smiling, the queen regarded me with wry admiration. "Relentless man. You have my utmost gratitude."

For finding Briar. For bringing her back.

I inclined my head. "I appreciate your commendation, but it wasn't me." Jutting my head toward the princess, I remarked, "This one brought herself back."

Briar's eyes snapped to mine, those gray orbs glittering. "Smart answer."

The queen's mouth split into a grin. "Excellent answer."

"But you're also wrong," my thorn admonished me fondly. "We brought each other back."

Those words set me aflame like a match. We stared at one another until Avalea shifted, jostling us out of the spell. She winked, then wheeled toward the threshold. "Shall we?"

That, we shall. Like a fucking magnum opus.

Avalea had chosen a regal sapphire frock. Briar radiated grace in a hazel silk gown paired with chandelier earrings. For myself, I'd shaved until my jaw felt as smooth as marble, then painted the edges of one eye in spidery whorls and selected a fitted coat of ebony damask that made me look as though I'd been resurrected by a reaper.

Aligning ourselves side by side, we formed a unit. Curvaceous, honed, and brilliant to behold. Much like a weapon.

The doors flapped open. The advisors rose, their movements stunted as we entered.

Avalea glided into the wainscoted room like a naval ship ready to do battle against an armada. Briar stepped inside as though prepared to dominate an inquisition, with her shoulders squared. I sauntered behind them, my mouth caught between a smirk and a snarl. The former, relishing the princess's return. The latter, a protective alpha tendency that had sparked from the moment I met her.

Our footfalls resounded in the quiet space. Briefly, my thorn's gaze swept across the book-lined shelves and the bronze leaf inlaid across the floor. Nostalgia brimmed in her pupils before her attention settled on the advisors and cemented with purpose, plus a hefty dose of modesty for their benefit. We'd plotted this, for the committee needed to see their heiress humble.

Avalea sailed past the men and women who bowed and chorused, "Your Majesty."

As the queen took her place at the table's head, Briar covertly reached behind. My fingers caught hers, our digits brushing, the contact electrifying my skin and sending a heady buzz through my head.

I leaned forward, my voice draping like satin across her nape. "Sharp as a thorn."

Her conspiratorial whisper injected a hot rush through my veins. "Clever as a fox."

Awkwardly, the council tipped their heads our way. I swaggered in, the very picture of reincarnated triumph, with a dash of depravity for good measure. Inside though, my blood simmered, primed to extinguish any figure who so much as frowned in Briar's direction.

Echoes of "Jester" resounded from the ensemble's mouths, then a moment of indecision flooded the space as they fumbled over how to address Briar. Despite the troops' acknowledgment, the prospect of greeting her by rank fled the advisors' tongues.

Yet like a gracious Royal, Briar took the initiative. She curtsied and said, "Your Excellencies. It's my honest pleasure."

Stated with the perfect balance of esteem, authority, and discretion. Collectively, the members seized the opportunity with relief and ducked their heads. "Daughter of Autumn," they replied, stunted but with a gratified light as they reappraised her.

Not Princess. Not Highness.

Still, it was a start. Somehow, we'd find a way for Briar to regain her title.

In the meantime, we took our seats and started causing a shit-load of trouble.

Over the following hours, we dove headfirst into matters of priority, including the public's response to Briar and how best to reintroduce her to the court, all of whom had been casting her glances that ranged from resentful, to admiring, to uncertain. According to reports and basic common sense, the castle residents stood divided on what to do about her, how to react, and what to believe.

It came down to pacing. Every court session and soiree needed to be navigated skillfully, to bridge the gap between kinship and leadership.

Briar held her ground during the conference, her words gaining momentum and confidence as time passed. For my part, I behaved. Except when provoked to sarcasm or mild death threats regarding the subject of potential assassins who might act against the Crown.

We listened to everyone's contributions, then took charge with Avalea about the solutions. Regardless, it hadn't slipped our notice that a handful of members refrained from talking at all. Now that they'd recovered from Briar's appearance, misgivings lingered amid some.

Each time one of them gave her a dubious look, a hiss rolled up my throat. My fingers strapped around the stem of my chalice and squeezed, since it was better than going for the person's neck. With Briar and Nicu's fates at stake, not to mention the future liberty of every born soul in The Dark Seasons, committing another felony wasn't an option.

Also, I might be overreacting. 'Twas second nature when it came to my son and my thorn.

After the council adjourned, the queen retired with us to the same private room where Rhys had blackmailed me and Briar. History volumes lined the walls, wingback chairs bordered a coffee table near the fire, and thankfully Summer's stench had vacated the premises.

There, we summoned additional members into our huddle. Aire, Eliot, Cadence, Posy, and Vale strode into the room. In hushed tones, we debated confidential problems, starting with the bane of my existence.

"Rhys," I nearly gagged.

Our group theorized about Summer's intentions regarding the secret tunnels, including potential allies who might be serving him. On that score, the most obvious suspects were the castle residents.

The council? Not bloody likely. I'd spent enough time with them to conclude their flustered quirks and ethical mannerisms were legitimate rather than bullshit.

As for the nobles? More plausible.

"What about Rhys's spies in Spring?" Avalea broached. "And in Winter?"

"Feasibly, those spies are still dispatched across the continent," Briar stated. "Rhys may have no conflict with those courts, but he also has no reason to dismantle his informants. Not if Spring and Winter remain unaware of the betrayal."

"It could be leverage against Summer," Cadence suggested, waving her palm in the air. "Blackmail on you worked for him. Why not give the man a taste of his assholery?"

From his end of the room, Aire frowned. "Blackmail would make us no better than him."

"Besides, he'll see it coming," Posy said. "Sometimes people like to assume everyone else is capable of the same manipulation."

"In which case, he'll have a contingency plan," Vale added.

"In stories, the pricks always do," Eliot remarked. "Not that this is a book, but archetypes come from somewhere real."

Briar studied the flames. "We have no evidence. Nonetheless, not telling Spring and Winter puts us in a guilty predicament. We are bound by oath to inform them. Imparting this information is the right thing to do. Otherwise, our silence makes us traitors as much as Rhys."

"Pacing, sweetings," I reminded them. "Without proof, Rhys will twist whatever accusation we throw at him." I plucked an unlit candle from the mantel and flipped the taper between my fingers. "He requires a precarious balancing act. One that fucks with his short fuse, so he gets clumsy. In the meantime, predict your combatant's next three moves before you make one."

Everybody agreed. We maintained that if Rhys acted, it would be during Reaper's Fest. This, provided he felt confident of success.

That afternoon, we indulged in more time with Nicu. However, by early evening, the mood turned from blissful to tragic.

Beneath the earth, the landscape changed. The abundance of foliage vanished, replaced by a hellish pit void of light and color. Here, it was enough to convince even the most optimistic soul those things didn't exist.

The dungeon reeked of several stenches, from mildew in the rushes to the ammonia of old piss. The bare minimum, a few meager comforts such as latrines and high but shallow windows admitting fresh air between the bars, did nothing to forgive Autumn for its crimes. Any semblance of the Season's renowned compassion and benevolence disappeared, reducing Autumn's reputation to a grand farce.

At best, it was a distortion of the truth, meant for only public consumption. At worst, it was a denial of the Season's real nature.

Recently, I had spent a brief vacation here, enjoying the amenities after Rhys's death had nearly become a reality. Prior to that epic failure, my son had languished in a shithole like this. The difference was that atrocity had occurred in Spring, a nightmare also provoked by the Summer King.

My boot heels thumped against the bricks as I stalked beside

Briar. Her eyes shimmered, not with tears but flames, the mounted torches reflecting in her pupils as she beheld the prisoners. Behind cages, they hunched in corners or stared into space.

With her jaw set, the princess rounded on the guards. Her clipped voice could have sheared through iron. "The provisions we ordered," she reminded them. "The food, water, and blankets. Are these people receiving them?"

One of the wardens purpled, disconcertment suffusing his flabby face. It could have been from Briar's question or her use of the word "people."

"Yes, Your Hig... Daughter of Autumn," he corrected. "We've been supplying them as requested before—" Again, the man cut himself off from referring to her banishment, prior to which Briar had instructed the guards to provide the born souls with the necessities all humans deserved.

The man's eyes clicked over to me, his complexion turning ashen at the deadly look I gave him. He swerved back to the princess and tried for a second time. "We've been tending to the prisoners."

Bull. Shit.

I'd maintained Briar's request whilst she was away, making sure every inhabitant received proper nourishment and sanitary linens. Yet apparently the wardens had stopped carrying out those orders from the moment I'd left to find the princess in The Lost Treehouses.

Either that, or these guards had sought out loopholes. In which case, food could mean scraps. Drink could mean muddy water. And blankets could mean coarse rags infested with insects.

Coming from a skilled tongue, words became malleable, capable of being shaped like clay. Unfortunately for this fuckwit, he didn't know an effective lie from an ejaculation.

Briar's eyebrows shot up. Her features sharpened on the man, her silence drawing the same conclusion and letting him know it. "I suppose Poet and I shall need to increase the frequency of our visits. Expect us here more often and our visits unannounced."

I stepped from the shadows and into the firelight, emerging beside Briar. My boot sole crushed an errant twig, producing a loud snap that sounded like a cracked bone. The noise echoed off the dungeon's blood-stained walls.

We stared at the man until he bowed and shuffled backward, along with the rest of the guards. At which point, the princess and I broke apart to check on the captives. The dungeon had expanded in capacity, housing additional born souls as well as the maddened ones from Summer.

We requested the provisions these wardens had been too negligent to dish out. With the help of a servant, Briar and I passed out flasks of fresh water and baskets of meat, cheese, fruit, and bread. Several prisoners sat listless, their glazed eyes uninvested in the offerings, having lost the will to believe it would make a difference.

Approaching a few angry but rare exceptions, I loomed over the princess, my fingers resting on my dagger as she attempted to communicate. They scarcely responded beyond glaring, repeating her words, or staring back with cool detachment.

Amid the lucid and more welcoming souls, we swabbed their wounds, doled out clean bedding, and murmured hopeful words. Still they didn't respond, other than to devour chunks of sourdough and guzzle from the flasks.

The princess took her time at each cubicle, but I sensed her urgency, the eagerness to reach a particular compartment. At length, Briar neared a cell where a young woman hunkered over a mound of dirt. She must have swept the mess from the corners of her cell, creating enough of a pile to work with.

Crossing her legs, the female leaned forward to flatten out the granules with her palm, then glided one finger through the filth and drew something there. Despite the torches mounted to the walls, my view was limited.

The young woman had to be around Briar's age. She wore a moth-eaten shirt and grain-sack hose cut off at her thighs, with threads coming loose from the hem. Muck caked her fingernails and blackened her bare feet like soot, and matted hair hung in waves to her shoulders.

The scent of salt, reminiscent of an ocean floor, wafted from her. And from what I could tell, the female's complexion was lovely, deep olive and burnished like a bronze coin. 'Twas as if she'd spent her life on an island, drenched in the sun's rays.

Now I remembered. Briar had interacted with this captive before and mentioned her again after the courtyard battle, when the princess ventured here for the last time. She'd told me about it, had talked about the drawing.

Briar had also developed a fleeting kinship with this prisoner and hated to leave her down here. She'd loathed abandoning any of them. As for my brief stint in this jail, I hadn't been located close to the female. And during my subsequent visits, she'd routinely kept her head down, signaling no desire for company or comfort. Otherwise, I'd have engaged.

"I'd be wary of that one," another guard cautioned from across the lane. "That creature has got fangs."

Briar ignored them. I stood close by, watching as the princess knelt, her profile mustering a grin. "Hello again."

At the sound of her voice, the woman paused. Her finger froze, arrested in the soil. Yet instead of dismissing the princess this time, the prisoner swerved toward Briar, the motion blasting us with light. A pair of golden eyes burned through the darkness like explosives. Almighty Seasons, the irises hardly seemed authentic. They blazed so intensely, they might as well be combustible.

She didn't smile, but she didn't have to. Those eyes glimmered at the princess, then registered me. Hesitating, the woman swiveled toward the lump of dirt and resumed sketching.

Disappointment sagged Briar's face. I lowered myself beside her, my gaze returning to the drawing, each line meticulously illustrated. To the untrained eye, the etching made no sense. But to a Spring native, its artistry was striking. Words appeared to be camouflaged within an unknown shape, which proved harder to determine, which made it even more impressive. Especially when I noticed a certain element about the text.

Inspecting the sketch, I raised an eyebrow. "You fancy poetry."

The woman's fingers stalled. Yet she didn't reply to my guess.

"Or mayhap it's not verse," I ventured again. "Then perhaps something with lyrics."

At that, she surged back into motion and continued working on the draft.

Very well. Some type of song hidden within an image.

I murmured, "My son has taught me that some words are meant only for the ones who understand them, for the people who can protect such words from the wrong eyes. Likewise, certain artworks have the same fate."

Once more, the woman stopped. Her head lifted a fraction to listen.

I softened my tone. "It appears we each have tales to keep safe."

Perhaps it was because I hadn't asked, hadn't pushed her to explain the drawing and corresponding lyrics, nor to describe what they meant. But after a moment's indecision, the female scooted backward, scarcely an inch but enough for me and Briar to view the image closer.

We accepted the invitation and craned our necks. "Transcendent," I mused. "In Spring, we believe artists don't merely choose their creations. Rather, the creation chooses the artist. We become its fateful steward, entrusted with its mysteries." My lips slanted. "I find it a rather fetching thought."

The young woman swallowed, then her gaze tipped in our direction. Through that knotted curtain of hair, vitality brimmed in her features, a passionate and almost fanciful temperament. Her expression gripped me like an ocean current—fierce, vigorous, and with a depth one couldn't see unless they dared to go further.

She mouthed something. Briar frowned and exchanged a puzzled glance with me before realization hit. The woman couldn't speak.

Understanding our inability to read her mouth, the female swiped her drawing from the dirt pile, clearing out the lines and then writing on the surface. I hunkered next to Briar as we scanned the letters.

You're back.

Briar regarded the woman. "Yes," she whispered. "I have returned."

"We're both here for you," I murmured. "If you'll allow it."

After a tense moment, the woman's lips tilted. The motion drew my attention to her neck, where a sequence of black sunburst tattoos encircled the skin like a collar. Briar recognized them at the same time, her furrowed brow indicating she hadn't noticed these markings before, likely because the woman had kept to the shadows until now.

The captive patted her chest. Then she mouthed the next word slowly, doing so a few times until we comprehended. *"Flare."*

Flare. That was her name.

In the shadows, I inclined my head. "Poet, at your service."

The princess rested her palm on her own breast. "I'm Briar."

One of the guards stomped closer, his leery gaze tracking Flare's movements, as if observing a feral animal. His approach snipped the moment in half like a cord. The woman's grin dropped, her eyes threw fire his way, and the faintest sound of a growl curled from her throat. Turning back to the dirt pile, Flare withdrew into herself.

Fucking interloper. Briar and I glowered at the numbskull with such menace that he retreated, presumably out of range from her scowl and my tongue.

Good luck with that. Moreover, if he or any other brutes fucked with this woman—with any born soul—we would end them.

That night, I found the princess standing at her balcony, over-looking the panorama of harvest fields. Plant boxes overflowing with cattails projected from the rim, the stems swaying in the breeze.

Because of what she'd seen down there, Briar's muscles strained beneath her pleated blouse, which was wrinkled and haphazardly tucked into a wide, belted skirt. Her fingers gripped the ledge, guilt and sorrow emanating off her like static.

Sauntering behind Briar in an open shirt, loose pants, and bare feet, I corded my arms around her middle. Brushing my lips over her crown, I spoke into her hair. "Let go."

At once, the princess's body unraveled. With a bereaved sigh, she twisted and fell into me, wringing herself around my waist. I pulled her against my chest, our heartbeats thumping with rage. Like this, I held her for an eternity, until both of us could breathe again.

And after that first day back, time passed with the force of a wind-storm. Apart from fucking between dusk and dawn, soaking up precious hours with Nicu and the queen, and visiting born souls in the dungeon, the steadfast princess and cunning jester resumed their performance from before her banishment. Only now we changed course, powering through to restore the princess's title, recoup widespread acclaim, win the court's endorsement, and unravel the truth behind Rhys's actions on the night I'd tried to rotisserie him.

At every assembly and dinner, we braved the people's scrutiny, aiming to flip their intolerances inside-out by means of Briar's intelligence and my wit. Not to mention, my sex appeal. Putting it mildly, it had worked in the past. Attraction often did, however much people denied it.

We added Reaper's Fest, weapon training with Aire and his troops, the treatment of born souls, and raising a son to the ever-growing mountain of entanglements. Unspooling a black widow's web would have been simpler, were Briar and I not equipped for the magnitude of intricacies that came at us daily. Half of which were self-inflict-ed, since we weren't about to stop pushing buttons, albeit tactfully and gradually.

At night, once my son was tucked in, Briar and I would regroup alone to whisper tactics, drawbacks, and advantages.

The two of us. Always the two of us, at the beginning and end.

Poet

The sound of a log splitting nudged me from sleep. But it was the knowledge of who rested next to me that fully roused my senses, including the rascal hardening like a pole between my hips.

A drowsy groan rumbled from my chest as I reached out to claim Briar. For although we'd plastered ourselves to each other after the third orgasm, she'd wiggled too far away from me sometime during the night. Unconsciously, of course. No mortal ever disentangled themselves from this jester on purpose.

That aside, the mattress was big enough to accommodate an orgy, plus a dozen different positions I hadn't yet sprung on her. I was nothing, if not flexible. In any case, it wouldn't be difficult for Briar to shift from me whilst sleeping.

Armed with several naughty, decadent, obscene, and downright lecherous ideas of how to awaken the princess—which involved a multitude of erogenous zones—my hand extended to grasp a bare hip or thigh.

Fie and fuck. My digits found only a bundle of quilts instead, the pile void of her warmth. Blearily, my eyes peeled open to find the princess's side of the bed empty.

Unacceptable. Twisting in all my naked splendor, I sprawled onto my back and bracketed my elbows on the mattress. Rising partway off the bed, I scanned my suite, from the gold mirror above the fireplace, to the bookshelf filled with sonnets and erotica, to the deep green accents and silk pillows. Eventide filtered through the stained glass window, and the hearth blazed. One of the stumps had broken in two, sparks flitting over the grate. That accounted for the disturbance that had initially woken me.

Best of all, this: Our clothing littered the floor in the most sumptuous trail.

Yet no princess in sight. Leave it to this ambitious woman to leap into action before fully basking in the afterglow. Likely, I would find her trussed up in a robe and tucked away with a stack of books or seated at her desk, pouring over ledgers and notes on the court's current state.

This, at past midnight. That, according to the timepiece on my mantel—a product of Winter, forged by their engineers.

Ah, my stubborn workaholic heiress. With a groan, I flopped onto the quilt and crossed my arms over my eyes in delicious misery, because let's not forget I was a man of verse. We excelled in dramatics.

But then, I shifted upright. Hunching over, I draped my arms over my upturned knees, a thought occurring to me. At once, my lips slanted. I knew where to find my thorn.

Stepping into a pair of loose pants, I padded barefoot from the bedroom and crossed the sitting area, then sauntered into the bath chamber where a door led to an adjourning suite. Migrating through the smaller assortment of quarters, I paused just inside the nursery's bedroom.

At the threshold, I leaned one shoulder against the frame. And there, I watched them.

In my son's bed, Briar and Nicu lay curled up like a pair of intertwined ribbons, with Tumble coiled like a furry snail between them.

The night sky cast the trio in pearlescent light, their breaths rose and fell in tandem, and their exhalations floated through the space. The final book in Briar's series lay tucked in the crook of her arm, signaling they must have snuck in an extra chapter.

Fuck it all, witnessing this private sight was like taking a sledge-hammer to the chest. Each night since our return, Nicu had been riled up more spectacularly than a firework, blowing through his energy until bedtime. But whilst I'd love for the princess and him to indulge for as long as they wished, Nicu had suffered from poor sleep in Briar's absence. He couldn't afford more deprivation.

Routinely, it took several recitations of verse to get Nicu into bed, then another handful for him to fall asleep, then yet another tug-of-war to coax Briar from the room before my son could wake up again. But no sooner did I put a temporary pause on lovemaking tonight, than Briar had scurried back to Nicu's side. And no sooner did I re-cline into the doorframe than her eyelids flapped open, and her gaze drifted to mine, landing there without pause.

Locating me in the doorway, she lifted her mouth into a lazy, peaceful grin. It would shift into a pragmatic, ambitious frown of concentration by the next morning. But for now, I consumed the view. Propping one elbow and resting her temple against her palm, the princess watched me.

At my inquiring brow, a bashful flush painted her cheeks. Briar returned her attention to Nicu's sleeping face and whispered, "I just want to look at him."

"Get used to it," I intoned. "'Tis a perpetual instinct amid parents."

"Parents," she echoed in a trance whilst tucking a lock behind his ear, which had a slightly pointed tip. 'Twas yet another facet of his faeish appearance and one of my favorites. "Is that what I am? A parent?"

"If you'd like," I responded, my voice rough and sounding rather drunk, her question intoxicating my senses. Blood surged to my neth-er regions—another eternal reflex regarding this woman—although my swollen dick had already deflated prior to entering Nicu's room.

The last thing I needed was to explain that mystery to my son, on the rare chance he should wake up.

Nonetheless, Briar's words threatened to resurrect the problem.

"If I'd like," she repeated quietly, as though I'd tempted her with forbidden magic. Glimpsing me in the doorway, Briar's wistful expression cleared in favor of something even more devoted. "He must decide."

When Nicu was ready and comfortable. During a heated fight with me, months ago in the castle's pear orchard, Briar had nearly referred to herself as Nicu's mother. She'd cut herself off at the last second, but the word had lingered in the air between us, seducing me on the spot.

Be that as it may, Briar set aside her own wishes. She wanted Nicu to determine their relationship, to choose whether to call her his mother.

Damn this woman. I shook my head, unable to fathom how she'd come into being.

"Careful, Highness," I husked. "Any more of this perfection, and my cock will cease to behave."

"Shush," Briar hissed whilst bolting upright and placing a finger to her lips, a scandalized blush setting fire to her freckles. "He's right here."

"And I'm right *here*," I flirted, amused and more experienced in Nicu's sleeping habits. It would take an explosion to pull him from dreams.

Besides, that flush wasn't purely out of discretion. When I first swaggered in here, I'd seen how Briar's gaze had gone molten, traveling down my torso, to my navel, to the low waistline of my pants, which exposed the V of my hips.

I crossed my arms and let my velveteen voice ooze into the room. "Who said you could sneak off without my permission, Princess?"

Her flustered expression intensified. "He did," she confided, nudging her chin at Nicu. "As a matter of fact, this fae commands attention even in his sleep. I could not help myself, unable to stay away."

"Ah," I mused. "The true ruler of our court."

Briar's grin faltered, reflecting hope and doubt. Successors didn't have to be blood related, much less born into the line. Though it was preferred, alternatives existed in The Dark Seasons. Royals had the liberty to appoint whomever they wished, provided the heir or heiress suited the role. From there, the selection required council and military approval. If not a birthright, the decision had to be unanimous.

We were fighting for rights like this, for every human. But even if Nicu had a chance of winning that approval in the future, that didn't mean it was his destiny. Briar would designate him someday—if it became possible, if Nicu could handle such a life, and if he embodied the role of leader.

Most importantly, if he wanted that fate. And provided our crusade triumphed in that timeframe, which was less likely. What we planned might take generations. There was no telling if we'd see that day come to fruition, or if we would simply be the spark that fueled the centuries ahead.

"Papa," Nicu's small voice drifted into the chamber. "Briar Patch."

Our heads dove toward my son, whose eyes remained closed. Only half-awake, he mumbled, "Are we going castle faring now?"

"He means 'exploring'," I explained when Nicu fell back into slumber.

"Oh." Briar's face softened. "I once told him about exploring these halls at night with my father. He must remember the conversation."

"Nicu remembers everything," I reminded her.

Briar nodded. "With his condition, do you think it would be possible? To do that without him getting lost?"

"You once took Nicu into The Wandering Fields without leading him astray."

"That was different," she said, recalling that day. "Our intentions were pure, so the fields wouldn't have entrapped us. Also, I'd chosen a row with a dead end. The wings, levels, and towers of this castle are another matter entirely."

"I think you two are a force to be reckoned with. Try and let anything stop you."

Reassured, Briar contemplated. "I would like to do that with him. If there's a way." Then she brightened. "Wait."

Scooting from the bed, Briar bunched the blankets around my son. Then she shuffled toward me on quick limbs, grabbing my wrist and dragging me from Nicu's bedroom. She ushered us from the nursery and through the foyer hall. Hastening past the guards who pretended not to notice, Briar urged me into her suite and shut the doors.

At her sudden enthusiasm, low chuckles rolled from the back of my throat. "My, my, my. So eager," I purred as we climbed the athenaeum stairs to her study loft. "What ambition does to your sex drive."

"Not that." Briar whirled, smacking my arm as we reached the landing. "Expand your mind for once tonight."

"Perish the thought," I snarled playfully from behind, seizing the waist of her nightgown with one hand and sliding the strap down her shoulder with the other.

The princess's censorious huff dissolved into a moan, her head flinging backward as my lips snatched her neck and sucked. Wringing her arms up and across my nape, I burrowed in. My tongue lashed at her skin, pausing once to mumble, "I plan on expanding your mind, your thighs, and your pretty cunt several times over before the sun is up."

"Which is in three hours—" Her protest tapered into a whimper as I licked and snacked on her flesh. "Oh, curse your tongue." On a breathy grunt, Briar pried herself away, her pupils not yet glazed enough for me to do permanent damage. "If you keep touching me to the point of distraction, I shall not forgive you. Focus and make haste, jester."

She planted a consolatory peck on my mouth, then tugged me to her desk. Throwing herself into the chair, Briar moved with purpose. In quick succession, she lit a candle, then selected a quill and a leaflet of parchment.

Almighty Seasons, she was right. From the moment I saw this princess again, months of repression had resulted in a perpetual cockstand, and I'd metamorphosed into a demon-lover with cravings that would put a fucking incubus out of business. Not that I was apologizing for this, but shit.

Chagrined, I scrubbed my face and forced myself to concentrate. It wasn't as difficult as I had predicted once I registered the markings Briar sketched onto the paper. It was a rendering of the Royal wing, followed by additional sections of the castle, each one furnished with lines that connected throughout.

Swiftly, I identified the delineations. My chest warmed at the sight of cords weaving through the blueprint.

"Well, well," I marveled, grasping the back of Briar's chair and leaning over her. "Those look familiar."

"I should like to think so," she said proudly and defiantly, twisting to drop another kiss on the side of my throat before continuing her work. "I'm stealing your idea."

To the contrary, she'd already done that when we first arrived in Autumn from Spring. Briar had ordered ribbons strung through the Royal wing for Nicu to follow. But this time, she'd extended them across the stronghold, only excluding the areas where it was risky or dangerous to go. It would give my son the chance to explore with Briar, albeit with precautions in mind, in case they got separated.

"I'm home," Briar confided to me. "So let this be the first task achieved."

The first task achieved. Although we'd been meeting with the council on a regular basis, those conferences had revolved around discussions and decisions. And whilst we'd been socially engaged with the court, it was still limited to the exchange of words, with hopeful intentions.

But a change that would take effect sooner rather than later? That was different. Out of a hundred accomplishments having to do with the court, the next guild of Masters, or a certain Summer fart at large, Briar intended for this moment to yield the first tangible result.

For the next hour, I hovered over the princess. Planting my palms on the tabletop, on either side of Briar, I collaborated and provided suggestions to help direct Nicu. As the sun pitched over the fields outside, the map came to life.

Finally, Briar released a contented sigh and set down the quill. Carefully, she blew on the parchment and held it aloft for my appraisal.

"Approved," I murmured.

"Agreed," she said.

Then she set aside the map and retired the quill. Anticipatory silence followed, in which I stared over the princess's shoulder, mesmerized by her profile with its resilient features and tender expression. She was proud of this rendering, proud to do this for Nicu, and fucking proud to know him.

And in that second, every part of me—every ounce of blood, every thought, and every beat of my pulse—converged to one place. Two words took shape in that place, forming on my lips and then surging off my tongue in a whisper. "Marry me."

21

Poet

Briar sucked in a breath and swerved toward me. Rather than widen in shock, her eyes glistened. We had agreed to keep things as they were—enemies who'd become lovers. Naught but a jester and princess, reigning together without sharing a crown or throne.

Yet at some point, between finding her sleeping beside my son and sketching this draft for him, I'd changed my fucking mind. And it appeared, so had she.

The princess's throat worked. "I thought you didn't want to be a king."

"Tsk, tsk," I said, kneeling. "Who said anything about being a king?"

Stunned, she breathed, "More riddles."

"Supremacy isn't my calling. Kingdoms deserve passionate rulers to lead them, whereas I'm a jester."

"And I love who you are. I don't need you to be anyone else."

"Yet ..." I skimmed the backs of my fingernails across her chin. "I can be your husband without being a monarch. We've broken rules before. This is merely another. In fact, we might as well have stopped keeping count at this point." My digits etched every freckle down her neck. "You know how in ancient cultures, the lovers performed no ceremony?"

"I read about it once," Briar said. "They simply found a place that was meaningful to them."

"And there they made a promise, traded a token, and fucked until dawn," I summarized. "That's how the human mates cemented their bond. It wasn't meant for others to bear witness. Only them."

"No ceremony?" she tried to joke, her voice clogging. "You?"

"It's remotely possible," I quipped. "This is between you and me, a sacred bond meant solely for us. You be the ruler, I'll be the trickster, and let us show the world there's no difference between those ranks." My hands scaled through the flames of her red hair. "Your thoughts are my thoughts. Your touch is my touch. Your pain is my pain. Your bliss is my bliss. Your life is my life." I cupped the back of her scalp. "I don't give a fuck about being a king. What I want is to be your ally and equal in every sense. Most of all, I'll be wholly, utterly, completely yours."

"Poet."

"And I want you to be mine."

Mine. The word filled my mouth. Half-benediction, half-growl.

Briar shuffled closer and rested her forehead against my own, and whilst I braced myself for something akin to reason, for this woman to talk sense into me, for her to gently reject what I'd laid bare, the princess did what she always had. She surprised the shit out of me.

Speaking in a faint, secretive tone, Briar uttered, "Yes." And when I blinked, flabbergasted, a small chuckle escaped her. "Yes, Poet."

My tongue stalled. Had I known this would happen, I'd have staged a spectacle, replete with all the fuss she'd have deemed excessive. Candlelight. Stringed instruments. Ambience in a more lavish location, preferably with a selection of surfaces upon which to spread her naked afterward. Certainly, I'd have dressed better and prepared a speech, likely in verse.

I hadn't intended to blurt out a proposal whilst we occupied her desk in nothing but filmy, wrinkled nightclothes. By Seasons, I hadn't bargained for any of this. But where the Autumn Princess was concerned, nothing had ever gone according to plan.

Briar nodded. "Yes," she repeated. "When this is over."

When the chaos was over, and we came out on the other side unscathed. When we didn't need to rely on deceit and elaborate schemes. When everyone else had the chance to live freely, so would we.

Then. Oh, and then ...

My thorn had chosen wisely. We would do this when the time was right. For this woman, I would wait an eternity.

"Aye," I agreed with a slanted grin. "Considering how picky I am, that shall give me time to splurge on a ring."

Instead of beaming, Briar's expression grew vehement. She raised her wrist, tethered with the scarlet ribbon. "I do not need a ring."

Wicked. Hell.

My hands snatched Briar's hips and hauled her off the chair. The princess gasped as I swept my arm across the desk, the remaining contents crashing to the floor. In seconds, I dropped her lovely ass on the desk, then stalked into the vent between her legs.

As I did, my palms followed. They rucked the nightgown's hem to her hips, then grabbed her thighs and scissored them apart. The jolting motion splayed the princess open, exposing the delectably pink flesh at the nexus of her body. Briar's cunt spread, those pretty folds framed by a patch of hair and her clitoris swelling under my gaze.

Her walls seeped with arousal, the tight passage deep and dark. My fucking mouth watered, my tongue as wet as her pussy.

Based on Briar's visible reaction, I must look deadly. Her pulse thumped in her throat, and that sweet kernel bloating from her core seemed to throb as well. Bashfulness suffused her complexion, enhancing her freckles like morsels to feast upon. I could dine on this woman's body and never be satiated.

With a growl, I charged at her. My waist shoved into the gap of her thighs with such momentum, the desk shuddered. Briar slipped backward, but we both broke her fall. Her hands swung behind her, palms flattening on the surface just as I slung my arm around her middle, bracing the princess before she ended up sprawled on the surface. Oh, that would come eventually. Only not yet, for I needed her upright to start, the better to take the brunt of my cock.

Elation and lust replaced Briar's coyness, the effect brightening her features. I launched into the princess. My hips spanned between hers, and we moved in unison, panting as our hands reached low between us and tore at the closures of my pants.

In one swift and hectic motion, we ripped apart the flaps. My cock sprang free, the stem hard and high, as though it had been welded that way. The ruddy skin thickened, my balls hung heavy, and the slit across my pome leaked with a blot of cum.

"Careful, jester," Briar cautioned whilst using her heels to push my waistband farther down, until half of my ass rose from the fabric. "Control your strength before something breaks. This desk is an antique."

"Perish the thought," I rasped, snatching the straps of her nightgown. "Are you suggesting I can't fuck you with precision?" I shoved the garment down her biceps, her resplendent tits popping from the fabric, those nipples puckering into the cool air. "You should know by now what a flexible jester can achieve—"

Yet my words were cut short, a ragged noise grating from my throat as Briar's fingers draped around the base of my cock and gripped. "True," she acknowledged whilst siphoning my erection, inflating the veins. "Except I also know how animated your lovemaking can be."

I seized her chin between my thumb and forefinger. "Is that a challenge?"

As if contemplating, she swiped her thumb over the line in my crown, smearing the bead of liquid. Only when I seethed did those sterling irises glitter with defiance. "Yes," she said against my mouth.

My cock jumped. Well, well. So be it.

A growl catapulted from my lungs and hit the ceiling. With one arm still shackled around her waist, I hauled the princess against me, splitting her thighs so far that her legs flopped apart, and her feet planted on the drawers. And in one sinister move, I whipped my hips upward.

My cock pried her drenched folds wide. The tight flanks of her pussy clenched, sucking me in as I pitched to the hilt.

Briar's yelp bolted through the room. Her body snapped backward in an arch, and her hair flooded the desk's surface like a red river. The noise she'd made cemented into a moan, then another as I whisked my pelvis in and out, the head of my cock striking a compact little place inside her.

Circling my lower body, I plied into the princess, her cunt soaking me to the brim. Seasons, she dripped onto my sac. I lurched my cock, jutting deeply, wanting her to smother my flesh with her arousal.

Briar sobbed in pleasure, her whimpers punctuated by each jab of my waist. She palmed my ass, which contorted with effort over the sagging waistband, and anchored the other hand behind her. The princess's body bowed like a spring, jolting to the impact of my pistoning hips.

Groaning, I hunched over her, forcing us at a steeper angle. Grasping the desk's edge for leverage, I hauled my cock into her. Her tits bounced against my chest, and she steepled her knees high, to take the force of my hips. Almighty hell, her pussy sealed around me like a vise, the inner muscles fluttering.

Without warning, the princess twisted and flipped us over. My back hit the furnishing, and she scrambled onto the tabletop, batting at me to do the same. Sprawling myself over the surface, I howled as Briar straddled and rode my cock on her desk.

With her nightgown fluttering around us and her cunt astride my dick, she clamped onto me so fitfully that spots danced in my vision. Renewed, I used every muscle, every joint to vault her upward, fucking into her thoroughly.

Briar dug her palms into the surface and ground her hips, beating her cunt over my cock, matching every pass. The desk quaked, more innocent objects fell off the edge, and a ripping noise cut through the cacophony of moans as her nightgown tore.

Indeed, something did break. But it wasn't only my fault.

With a fiendish smirk, I lanced into Briar. My cock expanded and spread her lips around me, the magnitude bumping her forward and backward.

Briar's free hand found purchase at the tabletop's rim. She clung to me, taking every slam of my cock, the pleats of her cunt hot, slick, and wetting from the roof to the seat.

My growls collided with her cries until both tangled. Blood rushed from my sac to my slit.

We pumped into one another, staring, gazing. My mouth hung ajar, and my features scrunched in the most blissful pain. I groaned and held back, pitching into her until that darling pussy began to ripple.

Briar's lips fell apart, then a prolonged cry splintered from her throat. Her pussy came, the walls undulating around my cock.

Ah. Not all the way, sweeting.

I hummed, snatched her hips, and drew her above my mouth, broadening her thighs atop the desk. Like this, she fucking drizzled onto my lips. I went at her again, pelting my tongue against her clit until a second climax joined the first.

Then again. And fucking again.

Only when Briar's folds squeezed my cock in the third orgasm did the release consume me. With a deep, resonant growl, I pitched my crown, and she swatted her hips on mine. The length of my flesh twitched until those spots from earlier burst.

My body locked, my cock jolting as it gushed into Briar. I bellowed against the underside of her chin, my pleasure overlapping with hers, so that I couldn't tell which of us screamed louder.

And over the next weeks, so it went.

Frequently.

22

Poet

"On your knees," I rasped.

The princess's reply seared across my lips. "Be careful what you ask of a Royal."

In an ornate, zigzagging stairwell entombed in darkness, she pressed me against the mahogany wall, slid down my frame, and sank to her knees. Eventide poured a faint violet haze across the steps. Dressed in a sable black leather jacket dress, Briar stooped to the ground, and I felt her palms sizzle along my ribs and waist.

"Here?" she inquired, her voice echoing as she rushed her fingers over my abdomen.

"Aye," I gritted out, my muscles flexing under her touch.

"And here?" she wondered, altering her voice to sound like a virgin, innocent and chaste as though she were one of my former targets. "Pray tell? Is this where I should touch, Sir?"

"It is, Princess," I hissed whilst she sketched her hands over my ass. "How obliging of my sovereign."

"I'm glad to meet with your approval." Daintily, Briar's palms traced my hip bones, then dipped to the rigid bulge of my cock. "Oh," she pretended to gasp. "What about here?"

A half-laugh, half-groan fled my being. "Indeed. There."

"And may I taste it?" she begged like a maiden. "Please?"

I barely had the sense to recite the alphabet, much less to nod. This, as if she could see the gesture through the darkness. Nonetheless, the princess knew.

My groan turned into a hiss, the noise slithering down the chute as her fingers plucked the closures open. The hollow chamber amplified our breathing, and the looming shadows intensified every sensation. Briar's hot breath coasted over my cock, which strained from my leather pants. The weight of it rested heavily against my pelvis, as stiff as cement.

And then another noise sheared from my mouth as Briar's wet lips sealed around the tip. "Fuck," I muttered, the word multiplying down the tunnel.

We'd been returning from one of the confidential passages, the better to unearth Rhys's plan. The channel had proven secure, with no recent signs of disturbance.

Via the stairwell on the way back, Briar had stopped walking. Her exhalations had grown rough and shallow, and so forth.

Now her mouth strapped around my cock, sucking me into her. The soaked cavern of her lips pursed and drew on me, consuming the column down to the base, where my balls tightened. Ragged groans emptied from my lungs as her head bobbed, tugging on me, wetting me. Unable to see a thing only magnified the sensitivity, the effect like firecrackers down my spine.

With a growl, I seized her head but kept still, letting her work me over. Briar hummed around my cock, the vibration threatening to buckle my knees. Her tongue dragged up to the broad head and lapped over the slit.

I seethed, my head thumping against the wall. Fuck, almighty. She would pay for this.

"What is it like with a man?" Briar asked whilst settled on a tufted stool in my wardrobe. Through the vanity mirror's reflection, I paused from lining my eyes in kohl. With a quirk of one eyebrow, I set down the makeup brush and leaned back in an elegant sprawl, my silk robe slipping open to reveal my torso, the better to impress her.

"My, my," I mused. "Go on. You have my undivided attention."

Briar strayed from my abdomen to my face. She wore a tweed wool corset over a blouse, pairing the set with a contrasting patterned wool skirt, looking every bit the scholar. Struggling to remain formal, she cleared her throat and folded her hands primly in her lap. "I would never presume. But if I may inquire?"

"You can ask me anything," I told her quietly.

Pleasure stole across her face. "That is perhaps the most attractive thing you have ever said to me."

"I certainly hope not. It wasn't an enticement. 'Tis merely the truth."

She fought to withhold a grin, then swerved her eyes toward the rug as if it just became more fascinating than my half-dressed splendor. 'Twas rather cute how she feigned nonchalance by shrugging one shoulder. "Is it the same as being with a woman?"

"Ah. To that, it would be foolhardy to speak on behalf of everyone whose tastes vary," I said through the mirror. "But for myself, no. It was distinct with every lover, as it was different with every position, and with every temperament. Yet making love to you ..." My voice deepened. "That's in a class of its own, sweeting."

The makings of another flustered smile pushed against her lips, which she fought to contain in the most endearing way. This woman had weathered the scorn and judgment of two kingdoms, deceived a dais full of Royals, endured humiliation in Spring during the Lark's Night carnival, outsmarted the Masters, survived a stabbing, suffered banishment twice, and then marched right back into Autumn to deliver a speech that had brought an army to its knees.

She had tricked a jester into losing his heart, making him the target instead of the other way around. She'd won the devotion of my son. She had faced a nation more than once with her head high.

Yet. Despite all the mayhem we'd caused, all the sinful walls we'd broken down, and all the ways in which I'd made this princess come, she still ducked that same head and blushed when it came to sexuality, fuckery, and kinkery.

After a moment, she murmured, "But do you ever miss being with men?"

Apparently, I needed to make it clear. "The only things I've ever missed were Nicu and you."

My eyes tracked the direction of her slender finger as it glided along the ledge of her seat. "But if you could feel that again … feel being with a man … would you?"

For a second, territoriality fired down my arms, prompting my knuckles to curl. Before Briar, I'd enjoyed my share of multiple conquests at once. Indeed, I had enough experience there to fill an anthology. Yet the mere thought of sharing the princess with another male set my canines on edge.

Regardless, if she expressed a sincere desire for it, I'd indulge her. However much I would love to slay the interloper, I'd set aside the predatory impulse for her sake.

But a threesome wasn't what she'd meant. Practice had taught me how to interpret gestures, tones of voice, and subtext in my partners. Even more, my history with this princess had given me plenty of insight, to the point where I anticipated her cravings as though they were my own.

I knew what she wanted.

Although I hadn't moved, I made sure she felt my gaze like a caress. "Mmm," I mused. "How interested are you in finding out?"

The sight of her fingernail digging into her seat cushion made my cock rise. But when she opened her mouth, I intoned, "Eyes on me, Highness."

Nothing like a princess who hated being called out on her timidity. Slowly, her gaze leveled on mine. "Very much interested."

With relish, I would accommodate her.

Without a word, I rose from the chair. Turning her way, I crooked my finger twice, then pointed down to the spot before me.

Briar gained her feet and migrated across the wardrobe. When she stopped an inch from me, I leaned in. "Left side. Third drawer from the top."

Then I watched, my cock lifting as Briar followed my directions, approaching the drawer and pulling it open. An arsenal of trinkets and toys rested in velvet cases. She examined the choices, taking my silence as an invitation to pick her pleasure. As usual with a woman who made zero decisions without consulting a pro-con list, this took a bit.

My lips quirked when she finally plucked an object from the collection. Quite a long one, in fact. Ever the ambitious, overachieving princess.

In addition to the toy, Briar wisely collected a small bottle of lubricant. Her steps grew in confidence as she returned to me, focusing on my expression, which had to be voracious by now. When her breasts scraped lightly over my torso, my respirations faltered.

"How do you want me?" I whispered.

Briar considered the wardrobe, sweeping her gaze over the alcoves packed with racks of clothing. She indicated the three-way mirror mounted on a dais, its layout similar to her own closet. "Put your hands on the glass."

She was forgetting something, which was fine. Pinning her with an indulgent look, I peeled off the robe, letting the vestment pool to the floor before going to work on the trousers. Once the closures slipped open, I made a show of stripping the pants down my hips.

My feverish cock rose from the gap, hard and hot to the touch. Already, the head bloated, and the veins stood out.

Divesting myself of the trousers, I kicked them aside, luxuriating in the princess's rapt gaze. Then I turned and sauntered to the dais. There, I planted my palms on the central mirror's frame, my body on display.

In the glass's reflection, Briar followed behind me, her proximity radiating down my spine. After a beat, the sensations scattered across my flesh. The tip of the pleasure tool coasted along my vertebrae, then over the swells of my ass.

"I don't know what to do," Briar husked.

I responded gruffly, her admission injecting blood to my groin. "I'll help you."

And so, I did. In low, sensuous tones, I instructed on how to wield the toy, where to spread me wide, and how deeply to penetrate my opening. No surprise, my studious heiress was a quick learner.

Briar dipped her fingers between my ass and smeared me in silken oil, then she set one hand on my hip and aligned herself flush with my back, the points of her breasts grazing my skin. Like this, she held on—close and connected, as if to feel the same stimulation. Angling the tip, the princess sloped the object between my swells, its girth splitting me open.

I groaned, remembering this feeling. Tilting my ass, I gave a gentle pump, sinking the tool farther into me, pleasure crackling across my muscles.

Briar caught on, sifting the makeshift dick deeper and deeper with each pass. I bowed my head forward, bent steeper, and undulated my buttocks, my moans in tempo to every beat of the object.

A small whimper dropped from her lips. "You're beautiful like this," she praised.

I was beautiful in all ways, but the naughty reply died on my tongue. A hiss came out instead, and my back arched as she probed me to the hilt.

Aye. Fuck.

In the mirror, we watched each other, watched Briar fuck me from behind, watched my cock twitch, and watched it bead with cum when her free hand wrapped around the stem. Fractured noises filled the wardrobe—her moans and my growls—as she worked me from both ends, siphoning my erection in her fingers and hoisting the toy in and out of my ass.

The princess entered and withdrew, increasing her depth and

swinging out to the crest. All the whilst, I swiveled my waist, meeting her thrusts.

Was it different with a man? Aye.

Was it different with this woman? More than with anyone.

She made it hurt exquisitely. She pierced deeper, longer, harder. She fucked so good, I felt it in my scalp.

Her arm cranked in my periphery. Her panting exhalations struck my spine.

My palms shoved against the mirror, tingles rushed across my cock, and a broken roar scrolled up my throat. Damn this princess yet again. For the first time in my sinful life, I wouldn't last long.

My fucking turn.

In a moonlit row of wheat stalks, I made love to her hard. The fields shivered, the tall reeds flanking us. Walled in, Briar's knees and palms imprinted into the checkered blanket. She hunkered on all fours and bucked in front of me, with her bare ass spreading for my cock.

Taffeta and leather were discarded across the soil. Daggers and thorn quills littered the tract. The princess's naked shadow jostled over the ground and blended with mine whilst I bent over her.

"Soften your muscles, sweeting," I whispered against the shell of her ear.

The princess nodded and loosened her joints. It had taken more than one previous romp to prepare her for me. Despite hinting at this after our delightful session in my closet, she was nervous. Yet that changed as I massaged the jitters from Briar and teased her body into submission.

My lips grazed her spine. My mouth planted sensuous kisses across her shoulders. My tongue licked into the hollow of her neck.

As I traced the princess's nipples, she whimpered. When I sketched her crease, she became pliant and delirious. And so ready for her jester.

Brushing my solid cock over the split in her buttocks, I murmured, "Do you trust me?"

She gasped, circling that luscious bottom and seeking friction. "I always trust you."

A hum danced up my throat. Such a beautiful answer.

I rubbed Briar's passage with the same satiny oil she'd used on me, then coaxed her backside into the air. With my palms framing her hips and my knees digging into the ground, I marveled at the sight of this woman, her body splayed and stunning.

My cock ached, upright and poised. From behind, I rolled the hard flesh up between her thighs, fitting myself inside that tight hole.

Briar's light cry turned into a heavy moan. Whereas I struggled to contain my growl, to slide fully into her anus without exploding into movement. Wicked hell, but this woman felt divine.

Because we had practiced, it required merely a few passes to seat my cock. From there, it required only few whisks of my ass to make her writhe.

Tonight, I took more and gave more. Palming the space between her jaw and throat, I pulled the princess's head into me and kneaded her clit with the other hand. She groaned in startled rapture, the noise reverberating down the fields.

And whilst plying the warm grip of Briar's opening, I rasped into her shoulder, the sound rumbling from my chest. The echoes twisted together and ruptured into the void, getting lost in the dark landscape.

Briar bowed upward and gripped the blanket. Her freckled ass bent into my waist, her pussy leaking and her body jolting to the steady rhythm of my cock.

As I buried myself and punted into her, shrieks catapulted from the princess's throat. By Seasons, I made that happen, made her feel this way, made her come with abandon.

Every touch, every outtake, every drop of arousal was mine. Thusly, I claimed what belonged to me, what I bled for, and what she offered.

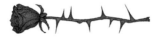

"Here?" I purred as my fingers ghosted over Briar's ankle.

Shivers danced up her calves. In the firelight, her tongue dragged over her lips, and her head shifted, indicating she was trying to see through the cloth bound over her eyes. "Yes," she answered, her voice a blend of shyness and intrigue.

Grinning, I praised the heiress with a brush of my mouth against her ankle. It wasn't the first time I'd used one of my favorite gadgets to trifle with her. We'd done so in Spring, when I introduced the princess to the erotic pleasures of touching, savoring the view as she discovered the places that set her aflame.

Merely a beginning. For I had yet to penetrate deeper, unraveling her to the sensuous core.

Briar reclined across her four-poster bed, offering herself and welcoming the ministrations of my hands. Like a sexual tutor, I alternated between exploring the tantalizing regions of her body and massaging the knots of stress from her muscles, loosening the princess until she melted into the mattress. From there, my palms torched a path over her shins, behind her knees, and to her inner thighs.

"And here?" I murmured, playing the role of instructor. "Answer swiftly, Highness. Say it, or I'll stop."

Her voice became faint. Ever the apt pupil, she replied, "Yes."

"Yes, what?"

"Yes, my jester."

My mouth tilted. So responsive and obedient.

Her body strained toward my hands, pink mottled her breasts, and her nipples toughened like pellets. Naked, she extended her arms and limbs, exhibiting every curve and dip. Her pussy swelled, fluid dripping from the slim crease.

Perdition, but she was marvelous. I responded with another teasing kiss, this time to her thighs. Whenever we identified another spot that ignited Briar's blood, I rewarded her with a sweep of my mouth or a lap of my tongue.

Sighs, moans, and whines drifted from her, the noises feathery. Nervous curiosity mingled with those sounds. She arched keenly into the stroke of my palms, the skim of my knuckles, and the flick of my fingers.

This woman, who loathed relinquishing control. This woman, who used to spurn the unknown, unfamiliar, and unpredictable. This woman trusted me.

Like hell would I take that for granted. Addicted and obsessed, I serviced her with more touches over her hips, encircling her tits, and swirling around her nipples.

My tongue licked those pretty disks, bit into the soft skin of her throat, and sucked gently on her earlobe.

And here?

Yes, Jester.

And here?

Yes. There.

Enough with the fingers. Time for something a bit more experimental. Moving too quickly for Briar to process, I leaned toward the nightstand, plucked a certain rose from its vase, and returned to her.

"What about here?" I crooned, hovering over the princess and dragging the petals down her stomach.

At the softness, Briar sucked in a breath. Still, the heiress trusted the jester. Briar's mouth parted, absorbing the teasing sensation as I skated the rose over her cunt.

And over. And over.

Another tremulous moan floated through the room. "Yes."

Satisfied, I lowered my head and kissed her wet folds as if it was her mouth, fusing my lips to her pussy and flicking my tongue into the narrow passage.

Briar gave a cry and grabbed my hair, then released a plaintive sound as I pulled back. Alas, she should know better. I wouldn't eat her so soon after our game of role-play had begun.

Moreover, I had sworn to make her pay for that stunt she'd pulled in the stairwell, when she swallowed my cock amid pitch darkness, then again when she fucked into my ass with that dildo, thus driving me to the brink within seconds.

Now I exacted my retribution on both accounts. And with vigor.

Briar strained to peek past the cloth. I watched, amused as the well-trained princess schooled herself not to ask questions, although I could tell she wanted to know about the flower.

"Ah, ah, ah," I lectured, my tone stern. "None of that, Highness. Listen to your mentor."

The princess yielded. Her pussy flushed, clenching and seeping arousal as I traced her walls, the delicate hollow of her entrance, and the crest of her clit with the petals. Every so often, I lightly etched her with the barest tip of a thorn. It would be easy to draw blood, and I sensed she could guess which flower I used on her, yet Briar never flinched. She knew this vital fact: I would let her prick me with a thousand thorns before I so much as scratched this woman with one of my own.

For that reason, I brushed her pussy in a sinuous tempo, tapping her clit with the rose petals until she tensed. Her mouth hung open, and a cry splintered from her lips. "Oh, Seasons!"

With a jolt, she came long and perfectly, the cleft of her thighs rippling, the muscles spasming and shaking like a leaf. Slickness poured from her, seeped into the petals and thorns, and smeared the stem down to my fingers.

Unable to resist, I mopped her climax from the rose with my tongue, the taste exquisite. To say my cock didn't grow to the point of torturous, merely by watching this woman come wetly against the flower's barest touch, was an understatement.

Her mussed hair lay strewn across the linens in glorious splashes of red, and pleasure soaked her clit and folds. Still consumed by the orgasm, Briar panted as I removed the cloth from her eyes. Quickly, the princess's glazed pupils swept from me to the rose perched in my fingers.

"Such an obedient Royal," I complimented. "Did you enjoy yourself?"

"Yes, my jester," she said, recovering her breath. "Thank you."

"Nay. Never thank your tutor."

"Apologies," Briar amended dutifully, still playing along. "Where did you get that rose? I have been meaning to ask."

When she first came home, Briar had discovered the flower on her nightstand and thanked me, assuming it to be a homecoming gift. It was impossible to find such flora here, yet my princess understood by now not to underestimate the treasures I could locate for her. All the same, I hadn't had an opportunity to share more fetching details until now.

I contemplated the blossom, admiring its ripe color. "'Tis a special rose from Spring. I may have stolen it from Basil and Fatima's greeting bouquet when they turned up for Reaper's Fest."

When Briar remained silent and waiting, I glanced at her. We sat upright on the bed, my pant-clad legs having intertwined with her naked limbs at some point.

Juggling the stem between my fingers, I avoided the thorns whilst flipping the flower right side up. "I left it waiting for you, when you were away. At first, I set it on your pillow. However, I feared a servant would assume it needed to be discarded whilst cleaning."

I ran the petals across Briar's cheek. "Such species are rare, and this one possesses a singular magic. I thought it suited you rather well."

Briar accepted the rose with a grateful smile. Still flushed from the pleasure I'd wrought, she inhaled the flower's perfume. "What magic?"

"Its petals are able to withstand the passage of time without wilting." My lips quirked. "And its thorns are impervious to fire."

23

Poet

Briar and Nicu chuckled as they dashed down the corridor ahead of me. Midnight dripped cobalt blue through the halls. The patrol averted their gazes whilst the princess and my son traipsed from one room to the next, one passage to the other. With the ribbon installations completed, Briar did what she'd been eager to do.

She took my son on an exploration of the castle. I trusted my thorn and wanted these times to be for them alone. But with unknown threats in our midst, we couldn't risk it.

Tumble draped himself across Nicu's shoulders but then lost patience. The moment my son placed the restless ferret on the ground, Tumble scampered ahead, galloping beside Nicu's feet.

Briar and my son's whispers trickled from the mezzanines to the towers. Their fingers clasped, and their voices blended, symphonic to my ears. I brought up the rear, grinning at the trio—heiress, child, and familiar—their outlines forming shadow puppets against the walls.

Nicu's gaze flitted across a corner and paused on a nondescript crack in the wainscoting. Trotting over to it, he traced the line and said, "It's like a ribbon."

Something for him to follow. For a moment, Briar assessed the crevice, doubtless thinking to have it fixed later. Not wanting my son to get ideas of trailing random apertures in the corridors, I distracted him by pointing out my own shadow reflected against the passage. And then we kept going.

At dawn, I left Briar to tuck Nicu into bed, intent on giving them more time together after so long apart. As I shut the nursery door behind me, Aire approached to relieve the guards patrolling Nicu's chambers. The soldier marched forward in a sleeveless number that exposed a trail of raptor tattoos taking flight up his right arm, which he usually kept hidden beneath long sleeves. The man's ashy hair was unkempt, and his dark blue eyes squinted against the harsh light pooling through the corridor windows.

At his nod, the guards departed. It wasn't unusual for the First Knight to show up an hour early in his rotation. He and my son had established a bond. Except today, Aire's excessive punctuality had less to do with Nicu and more to do with those bloodshot eyes.

To witness the honorable, upstanding, morose knight suffering from a hangover warranted a page in the history books. I slouched one shoulder against the mahogany frame and burdened the man with an animated look.

Seeing me waiting to harass him, that surly exterior deepened into a grimace. He said nothing, which was typical. Not to mention, the man had become well-acquainted with my lack of filter.

"Hmm," I mused at his present state. "This is new."

Aire grumbled and flapped his palm in dismissal. "Do not start."

"You're appealing to the wrong egotist, sweeting. I notice and criticize everything about a person's appearance."

"I wish you wouldn't."

"How seldom those words have been spoken to me," I replied. "Yet how often."

"Riddles," the man grunted as he switched places with me, his stance firm despite the dregs of alcohol lacing his veins. The man might have acted out of character last night, but one wouldn't notice based solely on the warrior's posture. His broadswords could take down an army with his eyes closed and ears plugged. It was the only reason I didn't ram my knuckles into Aire's face for thinking to guard Nicu in this condition.

"By the way, how dare you engage in devilry without me," I scolded.

"It was not devilry," Aire defended, aghast. "It was a lapse in judgment."

"I should say, considering I didn't get an invitation. 'Tis no revel without a jester to steal everyone's attention from you."

Another grunt. "Reaper's Fest is upon us," he said, by way of an explanation.

Ah. The revels were approaching, in which the most humble and prudent of Seasons abandoned inhibitions for the night. That explained the military getting a head start on the festivities, as more than one party was already planned regarding the main event.

I scanned the navy blue raptors soaring up his arm, which matched the shade of his irises. Because I'd never asked about them before, I remarked, "Drunk or otherwise, I never took you for a fan of accessorizing."

"I am not," was all the knight said.

I sighed. "One day, some brash and unexpected troublemaker is going to make you crack a smile that lasts longer than three seconds, and I'll be there to watch it happen. You'll be so fucking obsessed, you'll beg them to keep ruining your life." My lips tilted. "Trust me, I have experience."

At the reference to Briar, the knight's sour puss turned bleak. In the beginning, her return had demonstrated the only proof that this man possessed a cheerful bone in his body. The princess, my son, and I were the rare beings who didn't require a crowbar to pry the soldier's lips into a grin, if only temporarily.

On that score, every mention of Briar had brought a jovial light to Aire's pupils. Until roughly one minute ago.

My eyes narrowed. "You knew we were coming that night. "

Aire wavered. The soldier rarely took pleasure in expressing his cryptic ability to anticipate things before they happened, nor his knack for seeing beyond a person's veneer. After a reluctant moment, he nodded. "I felt you coming."

That clarified why the parapets had been uninhabited when we'd passed into the castle. What's more, the alarm horn hadn't blown from the tower.

Aire confessed how he'd orchestrated that. A hyperawareness woke him from slumber, signaling to the knight that we were heading to the stronghold. To prevent an ambush, he'd instructed the night watch to shift rotation.

However, Aire hadn't gotten to the full army in time. At some point, a small company of soldiers had spotted us and positioned themselves before their leader could prevent it. From there, the resulting chaos had alerted the remaining troops.

Moving on, I sketched the man's features for hints of another premonition. Routinely, the dutiful set of his jaw and that ominous, introspective glaze in his eyes were dead giveaways. Sensing Briar at the helm of his thoughts, my humor died a quick death, and my voice tapered. "Say it."

Aire contemplated the vista of maples outside the window, the leaves drenched in maroon. And shit, the knight's fingers settled on the hilt of a broadsword anchored to his hips. "I do not know." He glanced back at me, his demeanor grim. "But it's been too easy."

I felt that answer in my fists. The same hunch had been plaguing me now that Briar had been home for a while.

My thorn had delivered a speech worthy of deities. That hard-won display in the training yard had earned the princess widespread support from the troops. In turn, that had gained Briar admittance to the castle and spared her from retribution.

But whilst the knights' allegiance went the distance, influencing the nobles to reconsider Briar's position, the deceitful part was this:

No one had protested.

Win the knights. Win the court. Win the people.

That was the order.

Nonetheless, it should take time for us to redeem ourselves fully in the court's eyes, to salvage and regain their acceptance, much less their enthusiasm. And whilst some of the courtiers would redirect their loyalties to Briar, it stood to reason that many would still give voice to their objections.

Yet nothing so far. Benevolent Autumn or not, Briar's reception had been too quiet, too tame for my sanity. I didn't give a shit what Season this was. People were civil and innocent until something pissed them off or insulted their orderly world views.

The princess, the queen, and I had acknowledged this in private. Unsurprisingly, Aire confirmed this sense of foreboding.

Between Rhys and the court, we could cherry pick from our enemies. We needed to be doubly prepared for anything, including another storm to follow this period of calm.

The hackles across my arms rose. Indeed, it had been too fucking easy.

Candles pulsed with flames along the banquet table. Throughout the dining hall, nobles feasted on pheasant pies and baked pears, the diners conversing among themselves, sips of hard cider unraveling their tongues. For once, not a single attendant cast Briar or me a skeptical, hesitant, or intrigued glance.

After two weeks, tensions had relaxed enough for Avalea to enjoy a congenial chat with the courtiers at her end of the table. And at the other side, Eliot strummed his lute for guests, taking requests from Vale, Posy, and Cadence. The court had grown used to the ever-expanding presence of Spring, despite the scandal of it and the rumored grudge it caused our former sovereigns.

Briar attempted to concentrate on the music, as well as her friends' conversation. However, another sight distracted her. Sitting adjacent to the princess, I lounged with Nicu in my lap and muttered verse into his ear, which encouraged him to eat servings of food instead of fixating on the crowd.

Slowly, we'd been introducing him to these feasts, getting him used to the sensory overload so that he wouldn't jump on strangers. In turn, it gave the court a chance to grow accustomed to my son, to see him as someone other than a so-called fool.

A long archway frothing with foliage curved over the table, leaves dripping from the trellis. As I pointed out to Nicu the extravagant dishes situated amid brass tapers, I sensed Briar's admiring gaze. My attention cut to hers, fastening on the princess to the point that heat stole up her throat, the column of skin ornamented with a dainty choker.

Desire swelled her pupils, so that I became hyperaware of the vine motif painted around my lashes and the low brocade neckline of my shirt. The garment split down to my navel, with rows of necklaces dangling in the gap of my torso.

Briar wasn't the only one admiring my attributes, nor my penchant for graphic fashion. Pun very much intended, a host of female and male gazes ogled me against their wills. Yet my thorn was the only admirer I gave a shit about.

The square neck of her bodice pumped with oxygen. The mercury of her irises glinted, more so with my son present. So this woman found my fatherly devotion sexy, did she? I'd dine on that aphrodisiac later, once Nicu was asleep.

In the meantime, her teeth sank into that plush lower lip. My incisors ached to finish the job.

At one point, Briar cleared her throat and rubbed her neckline absently. But then she did it again. Blinking, the princess shook her head and snatched her chalice, taking a deep drag of wine.

I would have fetishized this display. However, her ruddy skin gave me pause. I knew the difference between an aroused blush and patchy outbreaks. My eyes scanned her features, then landed on a red splotch branding her chin, the sight akin to a welt.

Like a bad omen, my gut clenched. Quickly, I stabbed a wedge of apple and jammed the prong into my mouth, chewing the fruit to a pulp. Tartness doused in nutmeg melted into my palate. Nothing out of the ordinary.

Until the aftertaste materialized. An herbal zest assaulted my senses. I'd been too immersed in Briar earlier to recognize the flavor. But I did now, for the universal ingredient spanned every Season, down to Jinny's own cache of remedies.

Standard poison would have been too easy, too commonplace for the food tasters to detect. By contrast, something generally harmless wouldn't be cause for alarm. Unless for instance, it was something Briar had an allergy to.

The ladies and Eliot noticed, their lively expressions creasing in confusion, then in worry. From across the table, Avalea noticed the same effects mottling Briar's skin. The queen was already rising from her chair and opening her mouth, all of them registering what I saw in half a second.

It happened like most deadly things. Gradually, then instantly.

My eyes sliced toward Briar's plate, laden with the sumptuous fare of Autumn, like a clever disguise. Another terrible noise clotted Briar's throat, as if she had a rash, which she tried to clear by coughing, unaware of the cause.

The room shrank. Terror seized my breath. Blood rushed to my head just as the princess plucked her fork off the table.

"Briar!" I growled. Tearing Nicu off my lap and setting him on the ground, I slammed to my feet and lunged across the table. "Briar, nay!"

Jesters moved fast. But never that fast.

In any case, too late. The princess had started eating a while ago.

My warning bellowed through the hall as she slipped the fork into her mouth and swallowed. An instant later, Briar frowned in bafflement, right before a stream of blood spurted from her lips.

24

Briar

Scarlet. The color spread everywhere, spraying the plates and brass chalices. Geysers of red squirted across the table linens and stained my twill bodice, the rich pigment seeping like paint into the fabric. It spread, unfurling across my chest and dribbling from the tips of my fingers.

The shade of a ribbon. The hue of a rose.

The taste of fire.

It hit me after the color did. The acrid flavor of something charred invaded my palate, blackened and bitter. My tongue ignited like tinder, as though someone had doused it in oil and then lit a match. An inferno erupted in my stomach and launched up my throat, traveling as if fueled by dry brush.

I wobbled from my chair, then slipped forward, my palms slamming onto the table to break my fall. The room dimmed, obscuring every shape.

Blistering pain seized my lips, so that when they parted, nothing came out. Cries built in my mouth, thrashing to break free. Yet nothing happened, my vocal cords unable to produce noise.

But that did not matter. Because everyone else made noise for me. Screams resounded in my ears, the sounds of upheaval flooding the hall. Bellows, breaking dishes, booted feet charging my way. My name blasted across the table. People shrieked at a thousand different octaves, in a thousand different accents, and referred to me in a thousand different guises.

"Briar!"

"Daughter!"

"Princess!"

The clamor reminded me of those moments when Mother and I would present ourselves before the people, when she would stand beside me on a terrace overlooking the citizens. Countless faces would peer up and holler, cheering until the combined uproar flooded the kingdom.

Except those receptions had been joyous. This one was not. To the contrary, the combustion was turbulent, frantic, and smothering.

I could not breathe. Clasping my neck, I hacked and wheezed for air. Hot pokers stabbed my throat, scarlet continued to pour from me and splatter my hands, and the taste of scalded flesh assaulted my tongue.

Amid the pandemonium, a child screeched and then began sobbing. "Briar Patch!"

Louder still, a familiar male voice roared, "Briar!"

That voice. I knew that voice.

As honed as a dagger. As priceless as silk.

Usually that timbre was suave, smooth, and sensual. Not tonight. On this eventide, it shook the rafters. In a flash of movement, too swift to be human, the source of that male tone manifested inches from me.

Powerful hands caught my body before I collapsed. The scents of amber and vetiver swept into my nostrils. Strong arms banded around my waist, preventing me from falling, a sense of safety dulling some of the agony.

"Get him out of here!" that voice commanded to a group of female silhouettes, one of whom snatched a tiny, squirming shape off the floor. As the woman raced from the hall with the little figure—the wailing child—more shadows dashed in and out of my vision.

The world spun as my feet left the ground. Those strong arms scooped me up and clutched me against a wall of muscle. I levitated for a moment, then slumped into that solid chest, its rampant heartbeat pounding against my cheek.

My arms and legs flopped like useless things. Briefly, irritation eclipsed pain. I did not care for being useless; damnation, I could walk!

But when I twisted to break free, fire lashed through my limbs. I shuddered, inhaling whiffs of his skin, his clothes, and his panting breath. All at once, the jester's grip on me alleviated my qualms.

Safe. With him, I was safe.

But it hurt. It hurt so badly.

My head dropped onto his chest, and suddenly we were moving, bolting across the room. Doors whipped open. He moved like a hurricane, tearing through anything and anyone that got in our path. Shouts pursued us, along with a dozen footfalls.

"Briar," he repeated, the word slippery on his tongue, laced with panic. "I've got you, love. I've got you. Stay with me, Sweet Thorn."

With him grasping me so tightly, where else would I go? Where else would I care to be?

Nowhere. Never.

My savior charged ahead for what felt like miles. At once, the walls shrank, flooding us in darkness.

Despite his pleas, the jester held me as if I'd evaporate in his arms. Scared that he might be right, I dug my nails into his shoulders. Yet my energy waned, the flames engulfing me and mixing with the aftertaste of blood.

Blood as red as scarlet. The color was as rich as something else that escaped my memory. A vague object that nonetheless mattered dearly to me.

Something precious.

At last, the flames died. Heat drained from my body.

But as it did, another sensation took over, freezing me to the bone. Sudden chills gripped my joints, leaching warmth from all the places that had once scorched my skin, the frost penetrating me from brow to foot.

Where I was hot before, my body now shook for a new reason. My flesh stung as if encapsulated in a block of ice.

Cold. Everything was so cold.

Visions floated before me like dust motes. Red ribbons encircling my wrists. Wheat swaying in the breeze. Crowns tumbling from the ledge of a castle and smashing into a million gold pieces. The branch of an oak tree. Rose thorns on fire but never wilting.

At one point, I flailed. Desperate to reach those images and touch them, to catch them before they disappeared, I thrashed against a mountain of blankets.

Fingers snagged my arms, gently but firmly. They tried to steady my movements, tried to compose me.

With a grunt, I whipped my arm into the air. Whoever it was, my palm cracked against their face with a loud thwack. Then my eyes rolled back, darkness swallowing me in its maw.

As I twisted and turned, images shifted, crystallizing a little more. Fingers strumming a lute. Hands tucking quilts beneath my chin. The platinum gray of Father's eyes and the rusty red tresses of my Mother.

Her voice filtered in, congested with unshed tears. "I'm here, my dear." Soft hands combed through my hair. "I'm here."

Another tenor followed, this one boyish and childlike. He sang a song, his tone like a metallic bell.

After that, more words and speeches unfolded, each one begging me to fight, to wake up.

Please, Briar. Don't leave us.

Eventually, unfamiliar inflections emerged. Muffled tones strayed to me in fragments, one of them brisk and formal but compassionate. Every urgent question and cautious answer overlapped, some of them growing in pitch.

"Fever. Chills."

"She's burning up."

"Quite a strong will."

"It should have killed her by now."

"No one is able to endure this much ..."

"She needs ... purge the infection ..."

"Stockpile of antidotes ... appears to have been tampered with ..."

"Nothing we can do ... we must contact ... appeal for help."

"She will die—"

That last declaration was cut off, replaced by the sound of someone gagging. I blinked toward the commotion, toward the blots of movement, where a tall male figure had another slender form pinned high against a facade, a single inflated arm trapping the latter, whose limbs flapped.

More figures swarmed the first, urging him to "calm down." As my mouth opened, another wave of black consumed me.

Time lost all meaning. It lost all shape and substance.

But whenever I stirred, he was there. More than any other sound, that male timbre whispered, keeping me afloat. Always there. Never leaving. Each stroke of his voice felt like a caress, and the contact of his fingers as they clutched my own felt like a promise, his constant proximity akin to a shield or a shadow.

Protective. Eternal.

His tears splashed onto my knuckles. Caught between begging and crying, he murmured many things. Lilting rhymes, passionate entreaties, secret promises.

"Come back to me, Highness."

"Be stubborn, sweeting."

"I love you, my thorn."

Conviction and yearning pressed against the backs of my eyelids. I wanted so terribly to respond. But when I tried to answer, my tongue failed us both.

25

Briar

lankets cocooned my limbs. Soft drafts of air winnowed past me, the breeze caressing my cracked lips. Words piled in my throat, aching to be set free. Then all at once, a single utterance broke through, shattering the barrier of silence.

"Fenien," I mumbled, the name echoing as lightly as a plume.

My eyes fanned open, my vision instantly consumed by him. The jester lay slumped in a chair angled beside the bed, and his head was flopped back in unconsciousness. His fingers tangled with mine, black nails meticulously lacquered. Morning light burnished the carved ridges of his profile, laminating him in ochre.

Molten liquid flowed into my chest. I might be dying, and this could be a hallucination. Or I might be dead already, the sight of him an illusionary consequence of the afterlife, like a cruel trick. Regardless, the image erased any lingering traces of pain. The flames had died, as had the cold.

Only one sensation remained, one emotion having to do with this man. His chest rose and fell in sleep, the grooves of his muscles exposed beneath the open shirt and embellished with rows of necklaces.

So he was real, and I was alive. Even dreams could not measure up to the reality of this view.

Such an impeccably disheveled mess. So glorious.

My equal. My jester.

"My Poet," I breathed.

As if struck by a mallet, Poet jolted awake. His eyelids flew open, those irises flooding the room in a spectrum of green, reminiscent of bottled glass. His head whipped in my direction, and he shot forward to hunch over me.

Relief washed the haggard expression from Poet's features. "Briar," he hissed, squeezing my fingers with one hand and clasping the side of my face with the other. A whimper curled from my lips as his shaky mouth captured mine. I grabbed his own face and spread my lips, opening for the urgent flicks of his tongue, the kiss equally sweet and ardent.

Unable to keep still, Poet veered back and planted kisses over my jaw, my cheeks, my forehead, my eyelids, and my chin. "Wicked hellish fuck, Briar."

On a reassured sigh, I arched into him. Poet misinterpreted the motion and pulled back, releasing my mouth, heedful of overwhelming me.

After a moment's recovery, I licked my lips only to discover they were as cracked and brittle as bark. "What ... where are ... who ..."

Despite his subdued tears, the jester's expression alighted, twisting with mirth. "Barely cognizant but already requesting the facts." He cocked his head, haunted but amused. "You are a unique creature."

"I am no creature."

"Aye, but you are." His thumb stroked my cheekbone. "Only someone with an unearthly willpower could have survived the last three days."

I lunged halfway off the bed, the exclamation shooting from my mouth. "Three days?!"

"Hush," he intoned, urging me back down.

"I am no creature," I repeated, exhaustion mellowing my tone

227

as I reclined against a mountain of pillows. "And I will not hush."

"I'd expect nothing short of defiance, but it was worth a try."

"For three days, I've been incapacitated?"

"Seasons eternal." Laughter boomed from Poet's mouth as he threw back his head. "The healthy scowl on your face. Woman, only you would express outrage at being rendered unproductive whilst on the brink of death."

I watched as he migrated from the chair to the bed, then proceeded to fluff the pillows and anchor my back. Silence descended but for the rustle of my childhood quilt—strewn over my lap—and the caw of a falcon from outside. After inventorying the details of my suite, from the music box on my nightstand to random stacks of books, I resumed studying the jester. He concentrated on the pillows far too much for my peace of mind, his attention fixating on the task.

My eyes trailed Poet's every gesture, and I registered each unspoken word. Because it was rare for him to keep things from me, I puckered my brows. This man was not distracting me from the truth, so much as distracting himself, purely to contain his wrath.

Sarcasm, mockery, and flirtation were Poet's coping mechanisms. Yet he was employing none of those tactics, as though they wouldn't work for him. Not this time.

Then I remembered. The lingering zest of herbs. The bitterness of burned foliage and smoke, combined with the flavors of spiced pears and savory game.

My octave lowered. "They tried to poison me."

Poet froze, then his gaze cut to mine. "Aye," he ground out, his mouth twitching with a hint of pride. "Emphasis on the word *tried*."

To feel surprised would be ludicrous. What Royal did not live with this threat daily? Yet it had only taken one instant, one bite to incapacitate me.

Scooting forward, I moved to loop my hair behind my ears. My fingers encountered a thick weave, skillfully managed. It might have been Mother, but the self-congratulatory look on Poet's face as he admired the plaiting told me it wasn't. "You braided it," I marveled.

Poet gave me a slanted grin. "Let no one say the Princess of Autumn never looks her best."

My heart broke. Scrambling onto his lap, I straddled Poet's waist, grabbed his face, and tugged him to me.

He reacted at once, launching forward and seizing my mouth. We gasped, emitting slices of air in between kisses, until he shuffled back. Reading my expression, the jester nodded to himself and stood, extending his palm.

Grateful, I set my fingers in his and let him guide me to the athenaeum. Books packed the built-in shelves, perfuming the room with the smells of old parchment and vellum. My illuminated manuscript collection glinted in the daylight, and the final book in my favorite series finally stood beside the other installments.

Poet hadn't chosen this area merely because it was closest to the bedroom, therefore easier on my energy. Yes, there was that. But the ambience was my haven, bringing me a level of comfort he'd predicted I would need.

By the time we reached the plush wingback chairs, I felt winded. Poet reclined in one of the seats and settled me on his thighs, twisting my body to face him. One of his palms landed on my hip, cupping me there. Even the lightest of touches simultaneously wracked me with heat and anchored me to the earth, solid and secure.

I traced his jaw. "Tell me."

Fresh rage kindled in Poet's eyes. "What do you remember?"

The dinner. The lovely vision of Nicu sitting on Poet's lap. The baked pears and platters of pheasant pies soaked in an herb sauce. The forkful, the blood, and the shouts.

Then Poet's arms, which had caught me before I'd fallen. Then a child's petrified screams, which had shredded through the room.

"Seasons," I gasped, scrambling to get off his lap. "Nicu saw what happened! I must go to him. I need to—"

The jester ushered me once more onto his thighs. "What you need is to stay put."

"But he must be distraught."

"Something rather close to it." Poet's voice took on a honed edge before softening. "Currently, Nicu is in one of the courtyards with his ferret familiar, several Spring ladies, and your esteemed minstrel, all of whom are trying to cheer him up. But he'll fare much better once he sees you.

"Matter of fact, we've likely been overheard by now, what with your outburst and my laugh. 'Tis only a matter of minutes before Aire and the guards report that you've awakened. Which means we have limited time before the clan rushes in here, starting with your frantic mother. Everyone has been rotating, barging in on Avalea and me."

Despite the complaint, Poet spoke fondly. In that regard, I'd heard voices on and off while scarcely conscious. Among others, it had always cycled back to Mother's soothing tone and Poet's silken whisper. Their nearness. Their touches. My unfaltering family, who had stayed by my side for three days.

Moreover, when I'd uttered his name—Poet, not Fenien—the intonation had been as faint as a breeze. It would have been easier to hear the curtains flutter, yet the name had summoned him instantaneously from slumber. The jester had made himself a permanent fixture in this suite, to the point where the barest whisper had alerted him.

On that score, his present ensemble seemed familiar. Hadn't he been wearing the same open shirt and necklace assortment during dinner?

My chest constricted as I traced the edge of his shirt. "You have not changed your clothes."

"I know." Poet pinched his collar and feigned disappointment. "'Tis a frightful thing to see me wear the same garment twice. Quite the waste of an enviable wardrobe, tailored for a specimen such as myself."

How I wished we could simply tease one another, filling the room with nothing but banter, followed by moans. "Was anyone else harmed?"

"Nay." The piercing edge to Poet's reply could have minced stone. "You were the target."

I revisited that moment, from the first bite to the last. Taste testers would have detected basic poison, the fatal ingredient too concentrated to mask itself. However, my would-be killers had been smarter, choosing a form of contamination more difficult to catch.

"Willow Dime," I said.

Poet twined an errant thread of my hair around his finger. "Whoever it was, they mixed it into everyone's dish, knowing it would affect you in a much harsher way than the rest of us."

"Rather shrewd," I observed.

Willow Dime had a subtle flavor, which needed to be consumed raw for it to come through. Ironically, it was the one herb that dulled even more when heated, its essence diminishing to the point of blandness.

The only reason Poet had been able to distinguish the herb was because of his upbringing. Jinny kept bundles of Willow Dime in her cottage. The jester had tasted it often enough while growing up, the remedy having been essential whenever he wounded himself during acrobatic training. Hence, he'd recognized the danger seconds before it was too late.

In any event, the kitchen staff knew of my allergy. Not only was Willow Dime uninspiring to any cook, but it was also too risky; the most skilled testers wouldn't have been able to root out the herb's presence. Therefore, the servants wouldn't have included it unless one of them wanted me dead.

But based on the look crossing Poet's face, they'd proven themselves innocent of duplicity.

"You haven't found the culprit," I assumed.

The jester's nostrils flared. "Even if we had, it would have been impossible to identify the body later. I'd have made sure of that."

Shivers racked my flesh. I believed him. Touch the jester's family, and there would be no limit to the person's suffering.

I combed through Poet's disheveled hair. "But I didn't die." To illustrate the point, I glanced sideways across the suite, focusing on the bedroom, where my nightstand held a single rose. Then I swerved back to the jester. "Remember? Some thorns are impervious to fire."

I had meant it figuratively, but Poet's mouth slanted. "True. Matter of fact, if you absorb the thorns' essence, the rose will protect you from the flames. The effect doesn't last forever but long enough to create a temporary shield. That dark magic extends to you and everything you keep close." He tapped my lips. "Anyway, you're not allowed to die first. Certainly not before you marry me."

"Oh, and rob you of the chance to dress up?" I teased, folding my arms around his neck. "Of course not."

With a tired chuckle, Poet noticed something from the corner of his eye. As he captured my wrist, we discovered the scarlet bracelet had come loose. Carefully, he adjusted the cord, tying it as securely as his own.

"Better now," the jester husked before returning my arm to its original position, folding it around him.

Like this, he snatched my mouth in a brief but penetrating kiss. My toes curled, his embrace warmed me down my soles, and the gentle flick of his tongue pulled a sigh from my throat.

On a groan, Poet hummed against my lips. "I've never known someone with your strength of will. The Court Physician made the same comment."

Perhaps. That aside, my memory recalled bits and pieces of that conference. I'd been partially awake, listening to the hazy discussion and viewing the obscure silhouettes in my suite. At one point, the physician had said something that produced a rather violent response.

I squared Poet with a knowing look. "And what precisely did he say to make you strangle him?"

Fresh anger creased the jester's face. "Ah, that," he said without mirth. "There is one slight hiccup. It appears your infirmary had a cache of antidotes to allergic reactions of this magnitude. Unfortunately, our unidentified motherfucker got to them prior to the feast."

"Always pay attention to your props," I recited.

Poet nodded. "'Tis the rule every treasonous jester lives by."

"If I'm not mistaken, you are the only treasonous jester."

"Correct. So many ways in which I'm one-of-a-kind. Take care of this rare being, Princess. For I can't be replaced."

I tried to smile. "I know that."

He attempted to grin back, but it came out like a grimace. "Your mother and I conducted an inquisition with the council, questioned the court in its entirety, and conducted a search of the castle down to the last skeleton in the last closet. There's no suspect or trace of the attacker." His intonation darkened. "Rest assured, I made certain everyone answered truthfully."

Again, I did not doubt that. Few could match Poet's tongue, much less endure it. "Then perhaps they're not residing in the castle," I guessed. "Which means they had an outlet to get in and leave quickly."

"Mayhap something like a tunnel few people know about?" Poet suggested.

I nodded. "Which also means this person is connected to Rhys. Or it could be a faction of people like the Masters. In hindsight, he wouldn't operate with only one individual. Certainly, a lone assassin would have an easier time avoiding notice, but Rhys is arrogant and excessive; he prefers a disposable entourage. For the attempted poisoning, perhaps one or two people were picked from a larger gang."

"And maybe the king's not waiting for Reaper's Fest, after all. Either that, or he changed course," Poet added. "An opportunity presented itself, so Rhys took a chance. He knew that if it didn't work, he could try again during the revels." The jester rubbed a finger over his lower lip. "Yet despite how thoroughly I interrogated everyone, we can't fully rule out the courtiers. Outside of this castle, who knows you have an allergy?"

A rhetorical question. Poet knew the answer. Only my closest allies, the kitchen staff, and the Royals of this continent were aware of my susceptibility to Willow Dime.

The former two groups all resided in this fortress. The latter did not.

It was a fair point. Like all the Season monarchs, Rhys was privy to my vulnerability. He must have equipped his stooges with this confidential information. And since he likely had more than a few traitors working for him, they could be spread out, within and beyond the castle.

"You're saying we could be surrounded," I hypothesized.

"I'm saying anything is plausible. If they live off the castle grounds, they would have needed to accomplish two feats. One, avoid The Wandering Fields, seeing as their intentions weren't exactly honorable; the harvest fields would have sensed that and crushed them before they made it through. Two, get past tunnel security.

"But if they dwell inside the castle, neither are an issue. In which case, committing Royal murder becomes more doable. Plain and simple, except they left no tracks. And again, my investigation alongside your mother yielded no potential offenders.

"Then again, it takes time for people to fuck up. I've worn the guise of a traitor, so I know what it means to perform in one. Whether they're here or beyond these walls—"

"We'll find them," I finished. "So if the antidote stores were compromised, how am I alive?"

The jester's gaze relaxed. "I'd say an otherworldly combination of your stubbornness, plus a dash of something creative." Pointing to the bedroom, he indicated a small glass bottle I hadn't noticed earlier, which stood on the nightstand beside the rose vase. Sage blossoms swam in a profusion of clear, effervescent liquid, the vessel's half-empty contents indicating I must have ingested a portion of it already.

Poet produced a note from his pocket, whipping it aloft between his index and middle fingers. Forest green petals embedded into the wax seal, and the parchment smelled of wildflowers and berries.

"Jinny," I exhaled.

A wily grin crooked the jester's lips. "A raptor delivered it last night. I ground one of the rose thorns and added it to her mixture, per the woman's instructions. As I said, the thorns' essence resists the effects of fire, which alleviated your pain. The other ingredients in Jinny's remedy did the rest." He offered me the note. "She sent three. This one is yours."

The elder woman had been doing this routinely, sending tidings to each of us. Yet I hadn't feasted my eyes on one of her letters in the months since my disinheritance.

After breaking the wax seal, I let my gaze fly across the contents. Jinny's handwriting was as brisk as her grit, but the words filled me with wistfulness.

Spring's flora has the most nefarious poisons. Summer's heat makes for pestilence. Winter's got cures for both.

But remember this, Miss Briar Patch. None of them have empathy. Autumn is where you truly heal.

Hold that knobby chin high, and take care of my boys. And for shit's sake, keep swallowing them bundleberries.

Yours, Jinny

Laughter skipped from my mouth. My chest lightened. Jinny knew how to combat Willow Dime's effects, lest it should be consumed by someone with a susceptibility like me.

Poet explained that he'd sent a raptor to carry his message. The elderly woman who'd raised him had responded quickly, parceling a remedy with the avian.

However, tension still lingered in the jester's expression. Royals were raised to be aware that all solutions either came at a hefty price or with a time limit.

"I'm still in danger," I concluded.

Poet's jaw ticked. "Aye, Sweet Thorn. You are."

My fingers grew clammy, but I held fast to the jester as he explained. The rose thorn and restorative from Jinny were enough to dilute the Willow Dime, mitigating but not flushing it out completely. It was a temporary fix, not the solution. The woman's generous concoction would stave off the ramifications for a while. But not forever.

"You'll feel better," Poet imparted. "Only to suddenly, out of nowhere …"

As he trailed off, I weathered a splash of fear. This, followed by something stronger, braver. "We need a true antidote," I said.

"More like a process than an antidote," he shared. "According to Jinny and the Court Physician, what you need requires treatment administered by someone who knows how to do it efficiently. The procedure is otherwise risky. You might call it critical, if not administered by an expert hand—someone familiar with such deadly symptoms." Poet's voice turned purposeful. "Both are on their way."

An antidote. An expert hand.

If both were coming, that should be good news. Poet's expression indicated it was. But again, I thought of that hefty price.

What was this costing? Who was coming?

Then I knew. Only one court had the skill to cure the most fatal of ailments. And only one Royal was a master at it.

One cruel heir. One cold prince.

Winter.

26

Briar

ot him," I demanded, shaking my head. "Not Winter."

Poet scrubbed his face. "'Tis already done, sweeting. Without his help, I risk losing you. That's a dealbreaker." "You don't know what he's like."

The jester leaned back and stared at me, waiting for more. Outside, leaves shook against the morning breeze, producing an audible shiver through the courtyards. I hesitated, then glanced away, focusing on Poet's ribbon bracelet.

It was unfair to judge a person I'd only encountered once. Likewise, it was wrong to interpret rumors and hearsay as truth, especially as a Royal. And if recent events had taught me anything, one couldn't know the true heart of a ruler without peeling back the layers. I knew what it was like to be condemned, and so I weighed my thoughts as judiciously as possible, all the while recalling that one incident. That one time I'd met the Prince of Winter.

"I was fifteen the only time he came to Autumn," I told Poet. "Jeryn was sixteen, yet a mere glance from him had chilled my blood. His silence spoke volumes, and those austere features intimidated anyone who braved his stare. But more than anything, I remember the lifelessness in his eyes, like a barren landscape. I failed to register any emotions from him, which never surfaced even when ..." I cringed, then lifted my gaze to the jester. "I saw him disembowel a man."

Poet's face cinched. "I'd ask whether it was self-defense," he prompted, reading my features. "But I have eyes."

"There was a public execution. As guests, Winter attended, including Queen Silvia and Doria's heir."

"The Queens of Winter brought a child to witness a fucking death sentence?"

"No, they did not. They objected, but the prince insisted on being there. Even then, he was known to have a frigid constitution, and they rarely denied him.

"Mother never wanted me present when I was young either. But on this day, our nation required it for our guests' sake. Although I averted my gaze, the prince did not. And afterward, he requested the organs. Right there, in front of everyone."

Thinking back, I grimaced. "Mother could not refuse our visitors. So we watched this future monarch, who was not yet a man, dismember the prisoner without batting an eye. The blood streaming from Jeryn's fingers did not faze him, but the worst part was the convict was still miraculously alive. We hadn't realized it until he made a noise.

"Yet the prince kept cutting, kept sawing through until the man was truly dead. In the end, I was clinging to Mother while the prince was still clinging to his blade."

"Fucking hell," the jester swore.

I recuperated from the story. "I understand Winter's help will save my life. I do," I conceded. "But I don't like this, Poet. We represent everything that man hates. If he would disembowel a condemned noble at that age, what is he capable of as a grown man? And against people he scorns? With my title stripped and my loyalties in question, Jeryn of Winter would no more save me than Rhys would. So what is the prince getting out of helping us?"

"The same thing every ruler gets when trading with another nation," Poet answered. "Natural resources. It wasn't difficult to offer him valuable Autumn provisions for Winter's scientists and physicians, in exchange for his assistance." Yet the jester's eyebrows lifted. "At least, that's what he's getting on the surface. But aye, we're on the same page. However beholden I am to him for your survival, I'm guessing this heir will require something more than sourdough grain as compensation when he gets here."

I nodded. "The question is what."

"And if we're willing to relinquish it." Poet's lips twitched with mischief and mayhem. "Or if this princess and jester will have to make things difficult for the poor sod."

"We cannot underestimate him. Summer is aggressive, and Rhys's temper can make him fight clumsily once we find his weak spot."

"To that, we shall."

"But by contrast, the Winter court is unflappable, with the queens being the only exceptions to this rule. If what the continent says about the prince is true, then he's as cold and vicious as most of his nation. He'll have no vulnerabilities."

"Everyone has vulnerabilities," the jester countered. "So long as they're human."

I deliberated. "And if he's not human?"

Not in the otherworldly sense. Rather, in terms of the prince's conscience.

Unlike his Queen grandaunts, the Prince of Winter was reputed to be cruel, to a villainous degree. His supreme intelligence and mastery of medicine aside, reports of Jeryn's loathing for born souls was only matched by the man's obsession with the brutal ways in which he treated them. Terms such as "experimentation" and "torture" had been publicized amid the kingdoms. And while this was hardly surprising given Winter's culture of science, I could not shake the feeling that Winter's future king took those practices even further, to a harrowing level.

Seasons forgive me for denouncing someone just as my own nation had denounced me. I took stock in facts rather than premonitions.

Yet if the nettling dread inside me came to fruition, Poet and I might be dealing with a Royal far more destructive than Rhys.

Poet coiled the oak braid of my hair around his finger. "If he's not human, we'll make him regret that choice."

I leaned into his touch. "It appears our list of targets, obstacles, and threats is expanding." With a sigh, I swiped my head from side to side. "Rising public tensions, our attempts to redeem ourselves in the court's eyes, Summer's cryptic agenda regarding the castle's secret passages, preparing for all contingencies during Reaper's Fest, the assassination attempt on my life, and now this. Winter's intervention."

"Rubbish," Poet murmured against my cheek. "We've talked about this more than once. You're a princess, and I'm a juggler. We have experience in multitasking."

A short laugh slipped from my mouth. "I wish I had your stamina."

His expression became severe. "You do."

The magnitude of his stare drained the unease from me. I trained my eyes on the jester, the sight of him infusing my veins.

Ambition and something fiercer brimmed hotly in his pupils. I knew that look, felt it in the nexus between my thighs. My heart rate doubled as he slowly released the red tendril of hair from around his finger, the motion like an enticement.

"In case you need proof," Poet whispered, "allow me to show you."

Guiding me from the chair, he gently hoisted my weight off the ground and strode to the suite's exit with my limbs hooked over his waist. My eyes widened, yet my tongue failed to protest when Poet crossed from my chambers to his.

The knights standing post gawked for two reasons. One, I was alive. Two, I lacked appropriate attire and was plastered to my lover's chest. Blessedly, the nightgown hanging from me flared at the waist, so that it cascaded instead of bunching to expose my thighs. Also, my stiffening nipples were concealed by the plate of Poet's torso.

I buried my face in the jester's neck, half-scandalized, half-mirthful. Perhaps the near-death experience had made me bolder. Or perhaps the aghast looks of the soldiers were simply too funny.

Poet rested his forehead against mine while addressing the guards. "One word," he cautioned. "One word about this, one single utterance to anyone in this court, and I shall know." As a knight hastily opened the door to Poet's suite, the jester added, "Unless my son is in crisis or the castle catches fire, we're not to be disturbed until the princess says so. Only then may you alert everyone of Her Highness's recovery and admit visitors. Disobey this command at your own risk, sweetings."

The speechless guards bowed as Poet closed the door. I smacked his thick bicep while he stalked us across his chambers. "You are impossible."

"You're eternal," he replied, nuzzling the spot under my jaw.

Never mind scolding him. My blood heated at the contact of his lips, which stroked and licked every sensitive crook between my shoulder and neck. Oxygen rushed from my lungs, a string of sighs trailing in its wake.

I clung to Poet, my head falling backward as he lapped and kissed, plying me with tingles. Only when my ears picked up the sounds of a handle twisting, followed by sprinkling water, did my eyes flutter open.

We stood in Poet's bathroom. Or rather, one of the inlaid sections of his bathroom.

The opulent space featured dark soapstone walls reminiscent of a luxurious cave, antique fixtures with rich patinas that contrasted with modern details like a floor to ceiling mirror, plus a central shower with several spouts that rained like fountains. From the sides and overhead, the shower sprayed water, the deluge splattering the tiles.

Steam fogged the room, humid tendrils curling into the air. A spiced fragrance saturated my lungs.

Not bothering to divest us of our clothing, Poet carried me deeper into the mist. My gasp bounced off the walls as the water struck my skin. Warmth raced down my body, turning my nightgown and Poet's shirt into filmy layers.

My erect nipples poked through the fabric, and the dark patch of hair concealing my pussy showed beneath the garment. The jester's eyes flashed green as they scrolled over my form. His expression could have set a cauldron to boiling, and his muscles flexed under the wet shirt, his own nipples two hard disks and the grid of his abdomen clenching through the drenched material.

Then another kind of wetness dripped from me, the slot of my legs pooling with arousal. The temperature building in my pussy must be radiating into Poet's groin, because his cock swelled. The rigid length primed against my clit, inciting a throb within my folds. By Seasons, the friction stole what little oxygen I had left.

My mouth hung open in anticipation. I expected the jester to lift my nightgown, unbuckle his pants, and stroke that cock into me.

Instead, he pressed my spine against a tiled wall, between a pair of showerheads. Then he carefully lowered me to the ground. Seeing my confused expression, Poet traced his teeth up the shell of my ear. "Grab the spouts and don't let go."

I did as he bade, groping the nozzles flanking me. Satisfied, Poet fenced in my body and proceeded to kiss every inch of my flesh. Lazily and sensuously, he dragged that wicked mouth down my throat, between my collarbones, and lower to my bodice. Sinking to his knees, he scooped one breast in his palm and strapped his mouth around the nipple.

I cried out, my head swerving backward. While the shower submerged us from numerous angles, the hot cavern of Poet's lips sealed around the pointed tip and sucked, hauling on my breast through the fabric. My fingers choked the fixtures, and I squirmed against the wall, my pussy clenching and growing slicker.

Humming against my nipple, Poet switched and attacked the other disk. As he did, the jester palmed the backs of my calves, then grazed my thighs, his trajectory throwing shockwaves over my flesh. At last, his hands snuck under the nightgown, where he cupped my naked backside and tacked me deeper into the wall, preventing me from thrashing.

And when he released my nipple to glance up, I knew what this man had meant by showing me. In his grave expression, I saw it. This wasn't about him. He'd been powerless to heal me himself, but he could help me recover. That infinite look on his face—love, passion, reverence, possession, and kinship—sealed the gash in my chest. As if bonded, everything he felt coursed through me as well, these feelings requited beyond anything I'd ever known.

He hadn't lost me. Nor had I lost him.

From a hook in the wall, Poet retrieved a cloth. After lathering it with an aromatic bar of soap, he reached under the nightgown and dragged the material over my pussy, bathing my aching folds. I whimpered, unable to resist rolling my waist against the textile, the gentle abrasion stunning.

With his free hand, the jester raised the hem of my garment and mashed it against my hip. He watched foam build over my crease, suds running down my thighs while he cleaned me. His pupils dilated as he concentrated on the task, the tempo of his movements drawing moans from my mouth, each one quaking into the balmy air.

Belts of steam surrounded us, water dashed everywhere, the torrent drowning our clothes and hair. Everything grew hotter, heavier, headier. Was there no end to what this man could do to me? If I did not die from treasonous acts, I might just perish from his touch.

Or perhaps I underestimated what I could withstand. Perhaps that was this man's point.

Poet circled the cloth over my clit and rowed it along my seam. Desperate for more, I swiveled my pussy into the cloth, chasing the stimulation. No matter how much I longed to, I kept my grasp on the nozzles and ground my folds into the fabric. The rush of sensations depleted me of air, exhalations rupturing from my lips, my cries resounding through the bathroom.

Poet made a gritty sound of approval. Yet his motions were tender and gradual, and I matched them. Together, we drew out the minutes, prolonging the euphoria until I was delirious.

He rubbed the cloth, meeting my rhythm. My pussy leaked onto the textile, my arousal mingling with the suds. The sleekness of it only made the motions more slippery, juxtaposing with the cloth's texture.

I whined under Poet's ministrations, the crescendo accumulating in the rift between my limbs. Yet somehow, I resisted. He'd intended to show me, and so I yielded to the calm juts of his wrist. Taking over fully, he worked me into a frenzy, swiping my cunt until I could take it no longer, until I needed more, needed all of it.

Sensing that, Poet obliged. He withdrew the cloth and angled a nozzle in my direction, spritzing my folds and rinsing the foam. The splash patted my clit, tapping the stud just so, overwhelming me anew. Fresh sobs poured from my lungs, because this felt unreal.

The gentle pressure struck my clit, then dipped into my opening, then returned to the kernel inflating from my body. This happened over and over and over. Engulfed in a flurry of sensation, I chanted into the humid air, and Poet heard me.

Deftly, he angled the valve deeper, targeting me and striking true. I moaned, wailed, and then fell momentarily silent. My muscles seized as pleasure gushed from my pussy to the rest of my body.

I came with a hard moan. The noise shot from my mouth and flooded the sweltering room.

No sooner had my climax rushed into the atmosphere than Poet's mouth descended. On a groan, his lips caught my pussy. His tongue rode back and forth across my groove, lapping the arousal and drawing more from me.

My moans had no time to dissolve. Instead, they began all over again.

Poet sketched my core, licking and probing my entrance apart with slow strokes. Stirred once more, I cried to the ceiling. The reverberations were frayed yet resilient. Because yes, I had stamina.

He pitched one of my thighs over his shoulder and sucked on my private flesh, pumping his tongue farther on each pass. Then his head bobbed, the vigor of his jaw reaching higher. The flat of his tongue pitched inside my walls, flicking against places that prompted me to scream.

I could not help surrendering one hand from the faucet to seize

Poet's hair. My fingers crushed the roots. It must have stung him, because he winced, yet his own sultry growl vibrated against my pussy.

Heat scorched my skin. The throb in my clit pounded like a pulse.

Poet's tongue flexed up my slot, swirled around the peg of skin, and then he snatched the whole thing in his mouth. And he proceeded to tug. Teasingly, terribly, tenderly.

Plugging my clit between his lips, Poet drew on me. The tip of his tongue laved the crest with swift little licks. The moment I uttered a pleading noise, he sucked firmer, and firmer, and firmer.

"Oh, gods," I wept.

Rivulets pelted us. Water sloshed across the tile floor. The mirror across the room fogged, reducing our reflections to puddles.

Poet resumed siphoning between my folds. My pussy dripped onto his tongue, soaking his palate just as the shower soaked us. Amid this humidity, he swallowed my arousal whole.

My cries narrowed to a single holler. Again, my joints braced and released. I convulsed, my cunt pulsating around Poet's tongue as I sprang apart. To the marrow of my bones, I came for a second time, the walls insulating every shriek of pleasure.

It took a long time before my cries ebbed and my limbs buckled. Even then, Poet lapped at me, consuming my climax to the final drop.

At which point, my other hand let go of the pipe. When my palms found purchase on his cheeks, the jester caught on. He released my sensitive clit, surged to his feet, hooked onto my gown straps, and stripped the sodden garment from my frame. In turn, I inched the shirt over his head, baring all that exquisitely carved flesh to my view.

His pants went next, each yard collecting on the wet floor. The feverish crown of his cock bloated and darkened, the tight slit leaking cum and his sac hot to the touch. Every distended inch looked painful and felt glorious against my fingers.

Yes, he'd wanted this to be about me, but it never had been. It was about us. Eternally, it began and ended that way.

Naked and drenched, Poet hauled my thigh over his waist and rasped, "Care to be fucked by my cock, Princess?"

My plea came out in a whimper. "I do."

"And can you take it?"

"I can."

"And will you last?"

"I will."

With a hiss, the jester pitched his cock between the pleats of my pussy, spreading me wide. I jolted upward on a moan, clasped his face, and bore my mouth down on him. Tremulous sounds rushed from my lips into his, and I tasted his growls, our tongues entwining while his waist swiveled, fucking deeply into me.

Even more moderately than the last two orgasms, Poet's hard flesh pistoned slower, slower, slower. Each leisurely swipe of his wet cock wrought a sob from me, which he consumed with relish. By the time I came for a third bout, my heart threatened to explode, and my voice grew hoarse from shouting.

True to his word, this man proved just how much stamina I had.

Afterward, he toweled us dry, dressed me in a linen robe, and brushed my hair. And soon, the warmth of family and friends packed the suite, beginning with Mother and Nicu.

While I was sick, Poet had sought to avoid frightening his son. He'd told Nicu the episode was an accident, due to a plate of spoiled food. Although the child believed him, and further relaxed when I vouched for the fib, it took some time to fully reassure Nicu.

With his spirits restored, the boy snuggled against me for the rest of the day. His presence, along with Mother's and our clan, revived my strength.

Surely, I needed it. Because three days later, Winter arrived.

Poet

Ice. It was the first thing that came to mind when the queue of black carriages skated down the brick path toward the main courtyard. A dome of eventide stars chipped at the sky like shards of glass. Beneath that spectacle, a fleet of stags and moose pulled a line of vehicles, each fauna statuesque and frothing with fur around their cloven hooves. With those antlers curved inward like spoons and ending in spiked tips, the creatures alone could impale an army.

A procession of steel wheels ground into the earth, imprinting layers of sleet in the vehicles' wake and freezing a path to Autumn's castle like permafrost. The trail shaved across the bricks like a trap, so translucent it would be easy to miss up close. Anyone clumsy enough to disregard where they were going would trip and snap their neck.

Leaning forward, I bent my forearms and rested them on the balcony's ledge. "Well, well," I said with a raised eye, staring down at the scene. "With an entrance like that, one would think he's trying to outdo me."

At my side, Briar gripped the railing. "First, that is impossible.

Second—" she wavered, as if more troubled by this next vital fact, "he does not care about impressing anyone."

"You say that like it's going to be a problem."

"Most would agree."

I straightened and turned to the princess. "We aren't most."

Briar's frown caved into a small grin. She wore a walnut and black gown, with the tight, ribbed bodice and sheer sleeve cuffs accented in antique gold. The skirt split to reveal fitted leggings and supple boots beneath, the modestly high heels stabbing the floor.

The princess had pinned up her hair in a sequence of intricate but loose braids, though that single plaited lock with its diminutive oak leaves remained the focal point, braced by the rest of her tresses. Ebony earrings swung from her earlobes and matched a heavy pendant glinting between her collarbones.

"Prim and elegant, yet fierce," I assessed, sliding my arm around her waist. "With plenty of space to hide sharp things."

Her mouth compressed to withhold another smile. "You may search for them later."

That, I would. Plucking every concealed thorn quill from her outfit would be as enticing as stripping the rest of that sumptuous fabric from her body.

Later. So long as hell didn't freeze over in Winter's proximity.

With a critical eye, Briar studied my obsidian coat etched in a fine trim of silver. "You're aiming to antagonize him, I see."

Silver was Winter's color. It would have been more docile of me to choose a different shade, except for one thing. "I'm a jester," I told her simply before crooking my arm. "Shall we?"

Minutes later, we strode down the corridor to the throne room with our entourage guarded by Aire. At the halfway point, Avalea and her own retinue joined us, both companies blending without halting. Our trio matched one another's steps as we crossed halls and mezzanines, the echoes of chainmail and broadswords clanging behind us.

The second Briar's recovery was reported, Avalea and Nicu had flown into the suite. Yet tonight, the cloud Her Majesty had been floating on deflated, trepidation eclipsing parental joy. 'Twas effortless to gauge why.

However, there was more. The queen seemed on edge in a way that suggested several past catastrophes. Namely, the courtyard battle and Briar's banishment.

I chalked it up to uncertainty and did a head count of the daggers stashed in my coat and pants. It wasn't that we were ungrateful for Winter's help in saving Briar's life. With my blood and breath, I would be eternally indebted to the prince for that.

'Twas more that we couldn't say what his true price would be. And if Winter was the only Season capable of making Rhys shit himself, there was no telling how much worse that payment would be compared to Summer's wrath.

This turn of events could lead to an alliance. Or it could drop another enemy in our laps.

"Measure your words and speak plainly," Briar reminded me, summarizing the tactics we'd agreed on earlier. "He will not respond to veiled mockery or riddles."

"If he responds at all," Avalea added, a bronze crown glinting from her head. "The man is colder than the sleet his carriages poured across our newly renovated brick paths. Though I'll thank Winter for thawing that mess before he leaves."

"Doesn't know how to interpret subtext, is that it?" I asked. "Hardly a challenge for us."

"Oh, he can interpret it," Briar confided. "He just won't engage. It's not artifice or disguised words that we should worry about from the prince. It's his candor."

"Even that's a ploy, Sweet Thorn. Everyone hides something," I replied blandly. "Some merely do it in plain sight."

The carriages would take a while to cycle through the barbican and unload in the courtyard. Customarily, we should have been outside to welcome a visiting Season. Be that as it may, Winter's culture rejected ceremonies, preferring throne room receptions instead.

This meant we should have had at least ten minutes to arrange ourselves before our guest stepped into the room—if not for a discovery. The sentinels idled at the entrance, with their complexions blanched and their movements stunted as if someone had recently run them through a meat grinder.

Our group slowed. We swapped glances, then stalked past the guards, who hastened to open the doors. Although we should have been announced, the sentinels seemed to have misplaced their tongues.

The lapse provided ample time for a baritone voice to chill the room. "You're late."

Standing at the throne room's center—nay, fuck *standing* since *towering* was a more accurate description—was a shadowed figure. The human tower loomed with his back to us, his yeti-sized frame hitting six-feet, four-inches. Two of those inches exceeded my own height, to say absolute shit about his width. The man seemed to be growing muscles out of his ass, as if he'd spent his childhood carving icebergs instead of building sandcastles.

An avalanche of dark blue hair hung past his shoulder blades. Beneath a floor-length coat lined in bristling fur, boots toed with steel spikes covered his feet.

I couldn't see what the hell this prince was doing with his hands, but if my kinetic instincts had to guess, he'd linked his thumbs into his front pockets. That accounted for the way his open coat flared around his upper body. With the Royal's head bent forward, it seemed as if he'd voiced an observation rather than a complaint.

You're late.

My gaze slitted. Calculation or not, it was still an insult.

So we were doing this, were we? I'd start off easy, then. Before the queen or princess could reply, my tongue flicked out a pellet. "So eager to see us," I commented to the prince's back. "Yet evidently you've forgotten the term *grand entrance*."

From the way my tenor had swatted the air like a jeweled whip, most would have winced. Or at the very least, stiffened. Whereas the prince merely lifted his head slowly.

Really fucking slowly. And then—with the patience of an immortal—he turned his profile to the side. His eyelids lowered as though evaluating my voice and how much it was worth in pints of blood.

Apart from that, only his angular jaw showed from behind the mane of blue hair. Regardless, it didn't take a jester to catch the polished threat in his response. "And evidently you've forgotten the phrase, *speak when you're spoken to.*"

This, plus the misdemeanor of addressing him informally. Funny, that. "On the contrary," I remarked. "I've heard that rule as often as I've heard the words, *Evening, Your Majesty and Highness.*" The mockery I'd promised to restrain died, my words flattening. "*'Tis glorious seeing you again.*"

Next to me, Avalea's sigh drifted through the room.

From my other side, Briar muttered under her breath, "Poet."

But the prince heard her. His frame clicked in awareness, the prickly fur collar rustling. "Leave us," he announced impassively.

At the threshold, the knights waited for Avalea's nod, then retreated into the corridor. As the last one to go, Aire swerved his glower from the prince's back and leveled his attention on me and Briar, the First Knight's pinched features reflecting offense. A jester's unpredictable filter was one thing, yet for a Royal to greet another Royal offhandedly smacked of superiority. However grumpy, an invisible halo tended to float above Aire's head, so this breach in protocol flouted every decorous precedent he lived by.

By the time the doors shut, the prince had returned his gaze to the vacant dais.

The incessant silence grated on my nerves. "Alone at last," I said. "Perhaps now—"

The prince turned, the motion bringing his features into severe relief. Abruptly, several lines of excellent sarcasm went numb on my lips.

Motherfuck me. I'd expected icicle-shaped cheekbones, ivory skin worthy of dire wolf lore, and a deep voice that sounded as if he'd swallowed a bear for dinner. Indeed, there was that and more. Matter of fact, this might be the first time the sight of someone—other than Briar and Nicu—left me speechless.

Prince Jeryn wasn't merely an heir of Winter. He *was* Winter incarnate, with crystalline irises that could give his victims frostbite down to the balls. The crescents beneath each orb were naturally pigmented in faint smudges of blue that matched his hair, whereas his eyebrows and lashes were a deathly black.

A cleft practically sliced his chin in half, a blade handle projected from a sheath at his waist, and a vial that reminded me of a glass fang hung from a low chain around his neck. Some type of clear liquid filled the pendant, which signified his renowned obsession with science and medicine.

In the lingering quiet, this fucker dissected us with an expression that could sterilize a fire-breathing dragon. Many called me provocative. Even more called me sexy. But the world would say Winter's heir was frightening, as beautifully fatal as a blizzard.

If I didn't know my thorn, jealousy would have curled my digits into fists. But a quick glance at Briar confirmed my thoughts. Rather than attraction, her features sharpened on the prince as if remembering the day she'd watched him gut a prisoner years ago. All at the ripe age of sixteen.

"Your Majesty," the prince acknowledged, clipping his head toward Avalea.

Then to me, Jeryn cast a brow one inch higher, his pupils anatomizing my figure from head to toe. Damn, but my thorn hadn't been exaggerating. I'd ask what cult had sucked out his soul, but Winter was Winter for a reason, and he embodied the Season to its fullest potential.

Another way of putting it was this: Whatever he hid, this man did it well.

I decided to fuck with that theory and matched his unflinching stare. I'd see his intimidation and raise him a dose of my own. However, I tamped down the urge to go further. We needed his help, just as he wanted whatever the fuck he wanted from us.

Nonetheless, Jeryn's features never wavered. We stayed this way, at an impasse until he transferred his attention to the princess. Again, the man's countenance remained unchanged.

Moreover, he offered no title or bow. Not a fucking ounce of acknowledgement. The bastard regarded Briar like a gnat—a nuisance he was being forced to deal with rather than an actual threat, much less an equal.

"Your Highness," she broached with squared shoulders. "It has been ages. Autumn thanks you for coming."

Unfazed by the speech, Jeryn withdrew his blade. "Come here."

My growl hit the roof. I stepped in front of the princess, but Winter merely tossed me a vapid look whilst speaking to Avalea. "I suggest you leash your jester."

Briar wedged herself past me. Setting a palm on my elbow, she muttered, "He won't hurt me."

"You intend to cure my daughter here," Avalea balked. "Sire, we have an infirmary."

For a split second, the prince's mouth twitched in dark amusement, as if Autumn were just that naive. Instead of answering, he allowed his silence to speak for itself. Apparently, Winter could minister to a person anywhere.

Cementing my glare to his, I prowled farther aside for Briar to approach him. Whilst the princess stepped forward, Jeryn shifted his knife; the honed shape resembled a scalpel, only much bigger. Several slits embedded into the handle, indicating a cache of additional blades tucked within.

Thumbing the hilt's cap, the prince unfastened some type of compartment, from which he extracted a thin, damp cloth. After wiping the blade's edge, and then disinfecting his fingers, Jeryn instructed, "Open your mouth."

Fuck it all, but another savage noise rushed up my throat. Though this one, I contained.

Briar complied. After stuffing the cloth back into the hilt, Jeryn angled the knife's tip, which flashed as he used its leverage to ease her lips apart. "Slowly," he cautioned her.

At which point, his eyes tapered and studied the composition of her mouth. That concentrated gaze seemed to penetrate Briar past her fucking tonsils. Whatever he saw, the man's expression remained neutral—until his eyes stalled on something.

The space between Jeryn's eyebrows creased. "A dosage this strong should have killed you quickly."

"That was the point," I remarked.

Almost. The prince almost rolled his eyes.

And how the fuck could he tell the dosage's strength purely by sight? Either Winter citizens were manufactured in a laboratory rather than physically conceived, or they were descendants of warlocks, and the history books forgot to tell the rest of us.

Ignoring my statement, Jeryn reached into the inner panel of his coat and fished out a small bottle with a puckered top. Swirling the contents, his motions grew efficiently quicker. A droplet landed on Briar's tongue, and when she swallowed, her neck illuminated like a constellation. Jeryn's eyes probed her deeper, then he sought a particular spot on her tongue. "If you move, this will get messy."

Swiftly, he pricked the knife's tip into her flesh. Briar winced as blood trickled to the surface. The prince switched to another bottle and carefully administered a single bead to the place where he'd jabbed her, the black liquid smoking as it seeped into her palate.

Jeryn waited, then stored the liquid back into his coat. "Done."

Oxygen blasted from my lungs. Avalea sighed in relief.

The spotlight radiating from Briar's mouth faded. She inched backward and rubbed the nape of her neck. "I'm grateful for your assistance, Sire."

"Careful speaking too soon," Jeryn replied, shoving the knife into its sheath and again omitting Briar's rank. "Winter is here to correct your mistake, not seek your gratitude." He gave the princess a candid look. "Make sure the error doesn't happen again."

How rapidly moods changed. He'd given us all of three seconds to appreciate him before fucking up.

Avalea uttered something to the prince, her tone reproachful. Though with my eardrums pounding, I failed to catch the queen's reply. The man was implying that whilst Briar would survive the allergy poisoning, it wouldn't have happened if she'd been vigilant. And because her presumed incompetence had forced Winter here, Jeryn wouldn't be so generous with his assistance a second time.

My words grew teeth. "If I'm not mistaken, Winter is supposed to be a nation of wisdom. You might want to exercise that intelligence before I'm tempted to respond in a visceral way."

Annoyance flickered across Jeryn's features, there and gone before I could commit the phenomenon to memory and use it later to bribe him. "And if I'm not mistaken," he replied, "you're a jester who should have left the room a while ago."

"Aww. I hate to break it to you, but that won't stop you from thinking about me."

His eyes thinned. "I'll put it a simpler way. This is a meeting of Royals."

"Then do your intestines a favor and acknowledge every Royal present."

So much for not engaging. The man stalked three steps forward. "I'd advise you to proceed with caution, licensed fool. I can easily reverse the effects of my remedy, to an excruciating degree." He canted his head, a callous light banking in his pupils, as if he got off on the concept of torture. "Would you care to witness the essence of true pain?"

I sauntered up to the prince, halting inches from him. "You'll need to give a more creative answer than that."

"Whereas you'll need corrective surgery in another moment," he drew out.

"Oh, but you misunderstand again. 'Tis not me you should be worried about." I knocked my head to Briar. "'Tis her, you're underestimating. For a start, she has a name."

"Does she," the prince observed, dicing his attention toward the princess. "It's a shame she hasn't lived up to it."

I hissed, and Avalea opened her mouth to intervene, but her daughter's voice cut in. "And *she* is standing right here," Briar rebuked. "I am a princess, your host, and your patient. And I would thank you to remember that."

Instinctively, her eyes captured mine. But instead of privately scowling and reprimanding me for having yet another alpha relapse, a gleam of understanding flashed across her face—right before a riot of screams tore through the room.

The four of us broke into motion just as Aire blew past the doors with his broadswords unsheathed. Our group rushed to the window, beyond which flames engulfed a section of the maple pasture. There, a dead body was affixed to a tent of kindling, the corpse blazing just as Rhys's body had when I tried to murder him.

Only this was different. For this burning body didn't belong to the Summer King.

28

Briar

Gasps of distress tore through the pasture. We raced across
the grass and then staggered in place, a thick wall of smoke
barreling into us.

Mother's lips parted, her eyes glazing with shock. "Dear gods."

Our friends had arrived shortly before us. Posy and Vale clasped
hands as they beheld the scene. Cadence and Eliot stared in speechless horror.

Aire grimaced and pointed one of his swords at the troops.
"Disband!" he shouted, ordering them to stalk the area, lest the
perpetrator was nearby.

The stench of charred flesh singed my nostrils and watered my
eyes. Amid the tumult, my joints gave, and I stumbled backward into
Poet. The jester caught my shoulders, steadying me while hissing an
oath under his breath.

"Seasons al-fucking-mighty," he uttered, ripping out a dagger,
flipping it between his fingers, and bracing the hilt. At the same
time, he yanked me harder into his chest, slinging one strong arm
across my midriff.

The murderer could still be here. Of course, Poet would react instinctively, priming to protect me.

Nonetheless, he did not block my view. The jester knew me well enough by now, accessing my thoughts like his own.

A princess does not look away.

This had happened before in The Shadow Orchard, when the Masters forced an innocent child to sever the head from one of my soldiers. As I had back then, I straightened on shaky limbs, needing to see the extent of this nightmare.

I locked my gaze on the blackened mass, its form attached to the pyre. The corpse slumped like a mound of smoldering coal. Orange sizzled across numerous parts of the body, the flesh too incinerated to be recognizable.

Bending my arm, I covered my nose and mouth. Then I stepped out of Poet's grasp and shuffled toward the victim.

"Princess," one of the knights warned.

"No," I protested in a daze.

Yet another soldier tried. "Your Highness."

"Leave her," commanded the jester.

The outbreak of noise faded, the court falling into horrified silence while I stumbled closer to the scene. Amid the stench, cinders flitted into the air. The army had extinguished the fire before we'd arrived, yet heat seeped through my clothes.

The agony this person must have felt. The screams we hadn't heard, because we'd been too far away, a world away from their suffering.

My chin trembled as I reached the corpse. Their features had been reduced to a flaky pulp, so that I could not discern their expression. I stared, my heart grieving for this unknown soul. No sooner did I mourn than the pain tightened into something harder, harsher.

Panicked, we had checked on Nicu before coming here. Even so, I'd already known—prayed, prayed, prayed—it wasn't him. The body belonged to an adult, not a child.

Still, it was *someone*. In another two decades, the person *could* be him.

Rancor churned in my gut, which intensified as a towering shadow materialized beside me. Adding insult to injury, a mane of dark blue hair filled my peripheral vision. I had forgotten about Winter.

Despite the hideous display, the prince's baritone filled the void. "This is a born fool."

My head swiveled toward Jeryn's granite profile. By Seasons, he observed the victim's remains without so much as a wince. Not an ounce of emotion compromised that arctic visage, his indifference making my skin crawl.

Then his words struck me. The victim was a born soul.

"How do you know?" I prompted while other silhouettes joined us, including Poet, my mother, and our friends.

In response, the Winter Prince tilted his head to further study the corpse. The spiked toe of his boot extended to nudge the person's stomach, their skin flaking to ash at the contact. When it did, Jeryn knelt and grabbed the same area none-too-gently, collecting more specks and sprinkling them into the air.

Poet snarled at the man, and my lips curled in abhorrence. Of all the disrespectful, contemptible acts. Yet the prince kept scrutinizing the body like an experiment, nothing more than a specimen beneath a microscope.

I rounded fully toward him and fought to keep my tone civil. "In our nation, it is customary not to defile the dead."

Jeryn merely flicked his eyes at me and then cut away, as if my comment were as inconsequential as the buzzing of a fly. A minor distraction. Based on the expressions of Mother and my friends, if I didn't punch him first, they would.

To say nothing of the jester. Poet's muscles tensed, his tongue—if not his dagger—about to flay the man.

At that precious moment, the prince's voice pointed out, "The womb is shrunken and frail, particularly near the uterus." Wiping his hands as though they were filthy, Jeryn rose. "Summer trades with Winter for preventatives to keep the born from procreating in their cells and infesting the Season with their spawn. It's a permanent solution that renders the recipient infertile for life and helps control Summer's captive population." He jerked his chin to the victim. "A womb this slight on a grown fool means they were given a dosage."

With precision, Jeryn clicked his head in our direction. The black ice of his pupils settled on me, then Poet, then Mother. "The last time I checked, Autumn doesn't possess this drug."

No, we certainly did not. The potent mixture of which Jeryn spoke had been customized and commissioned by Summer from Winter's scientists.

Autumn would never commit such an atrocity. And because this nation didn't render its prisoners infertile, the components stacked up. One of the mad. The prince's assessment meant the deceased had been one of the mad.

Summer's mad, to be exact. They were the only people from Rhys's kingdom living here.

I swept my attention to the body as murmurs filtered around me. Among them, Mother's furious voice addressed one of the guards. "Who did this?"

Aire stepped in to respond. "That is unknown, Your Majesty. I didn't sense anyone's presence. Thus far, the routes to and from the dungeons are clear, and the troops found no signs of entry or exit." He measured his words, the weight of them clear. "It is as if they've vanished."

Vanished. Which implied they'd used a passage not likely to be spotted. I traded confidential glances with Poet.

The secret tunnels. The ones Rhys had been searching for in this area.

Because the late Masters had shared their knowledge with Rhys, the king could have directed these new butchers to the dungeons. Summer must have instructed the agents on how to evade the guards, then gave them tools to breach the cells.

That repulsive excuse for a monarch. So he wasn't waiting purely for Reaper's Fest.

Whomever he'd sent to do his filthy work had failed to kill me. But they'd succeeded in maiming one of the innocent people the jester and I were campaigning to liberate. Our actions may save the born someday. Until then, our choices endangered them too.

If the murderers targeted a born soul, it could be a warning or an act of retribution for my return. Either way, this had been done by whoever poisoned me.

"Search the castle inside and out," I heard Mother instruct Aire. "I want every square inch inspected, each resident interviewed, and every sentinel questioned." Her orders carried across the pasture to the troops. "There is a saboteur at large. A slayer in our midst who has already committed two atrocities. Find them."

"They won't," I whispered to myself, redirecting my gaze to the dead body. "They won't find them."

Provided the enemies didn't live in the castle, and assuming they'd used one of the tunnels, they were long gone. For now, at least.

Aire and his brethren departed to fulfill Mother's orders. While courtiers murmured to one another, our friends attempted to dilute rising accusations from getting out of hand, and Mother delivered more instructions to additional guards.

I thought of Merit, the soldier we'd lost. I thought of the born souls Rhys had tried to use as scapegoats for his own deception. I thought of the Masters, who'd sacrificed themselves for their version of the so-called greater good.

I thought of Nicu, who could have been the target of this wretched crime.

The montage compiled as I caught sight of the prince. It was not my imagination when I noticed him flicking a speck of ash from his sleeve. I balled my hands into fists, then forced them to relax.

Winter had a remedy for such wounds, an ointment that dissolved layers of burned flesh and acted as a balm, thus alleviating the sufferer to a considerable degree. It was too late to help the soul, but it was not too late to mend their skin. We could minister that salve to the deceased, repairing their body while offering some measure of comfort in the afterlife, before we brought the person to the crypt, where they would lie until their burial. This way, they could rest in peace.

Taking advantage of this private moment, I aligned myself with Poet, then approached the prince. "Sire," I petitioned. "The charred flesh. Autumn humbly asks that you remove it."

Only then did the man turn from examining the body, acknowledging me at last. His black eyebrows rose, offering the first sign of an actual visceral reaction. However, it was not a look of surprise. Rather, it was the imperious countenance of a ruler who considered the request absurd.

"What for?" he murmured.

"Are you fucking joking?" Poet seethed.

In tandem, my nostrils flared. "What for?" I repeated, appalled and gesturing at the evidence. "Look at what's been done. Do you not see the problem?"

Jeryn gave the question due consideration. While appraising the corpse, his face might as well have been carved from a glacier. After a notable amount of time, he answered, "Yes." Then that merciless, cold-blooded gaze sliced our way. "The problem is they should have finished the job."

My breath stalled. Revulsion climbed up my spine. Beside me, Poet growled, barely able to stop himself from mincing the Royal to pieces. The only thing preventing him was me, because committing another treasonous act would not serve us.

Across the way, Eliot and my ladies glowered at Winter, having overheard the most crucial part. The bit where Jeryn had stated the body should have been fully burned to cinders.

Unfazed by our reactions, the detestable prince turned. He sauntered off, his imposing form breaking through a cloud of smoke.

My hands thwacked against the double doors, the partitions blowing open as I marched into the Crown suite, the hem of my gown snapping around my legs. "Barbarous," I hissed, my fists balling while Mother followed me inside. "Who would do this?" Halting at a window overlooking a squash garden, I stormed around to face her. "And never mind this continent's prejudice. What Royal besides Rhys would react that way?"

Mother bobbed her flat palm in the air, endeavoring to calm my temper. Once I clamped my lips together, she nodded for the guards to shut the doors and then crossed over to me.

For a moment, Mother visibly replayed the incident, one hand covering her mouth, the other fixed on her hip. She'd been alive for longer and witnessed things I never had. People had killed before in Autumn, and it was certainly not the first time assassins had targeted the Crown in the last hundred years. And because of our crusade for equality, I had anticipated us being tested, the pacifistic heart of this nation being challenged in a way it hadn't before. At least, not since the age of ancients.

But foreseeing these horrors and witnessing them come to fruition were different matters. Since the moment I'd returned from Spring, this court had been ravished with hatred, death, and such violence that rivaled Summer.

Merit's murder. Betrayal by the Masters. The courtyard battle and Rhys's accusations against my capacity to lead. My subsequent banishment. Our scrimmage against the soldiers when I came back. The poisoned dinner, which Nicu had witnessed. And now, an innocent prisoner had been torched.

All of this, coupled with rising conflicts amid the citizenry. All of this, because they didn't trust their princess or support her beliefs.

Rhys had done more than recruiting the Masters against us. He had undermined the public's faith in me and their growing esteem for Poet. In its place, the Summer King had planted seeds of doubt, which were sprouting faster than we could chop them down.

This burning was no isolated incident. In some way, Rhys had engineered this, prompting his new cult to act. If we did not catch the culprits or find a way to expose Summer, such atrocities would not end but only become more grotesque, spreading from the castle to the outlying villages and towns.

Poet and I had concluded as much without trading a single word. It had taken a mere look from across the ashes.

Mother hardly needed me to voice these thoughts. As a monarch with decades of experience, she perceived every gesture and action a person took.

Nodding to herself, Mother recuperated and uncovered her mouth. "Whoever attacked that captive—" she cupped my cheek, "—and you, they must have access to the secret tunnels. More than one passage, to be sure."

"Poet and I drew that conclusion as well, after I recovered," I told her. "Though we haven't ruled out any castle residents. For all we know, this gang could be divided. As to the rest, we're missing a vital piece. And after that flagrant display in the pasture, we cannot discount Winter's own agenda. Jeryn did not come to heal me out of the goodness of his heart, particularly when he appears to have misplaced that organ in the first place."

At the mention of him, Mother's face creased. More than loathing, apprehension cinched her features, her mind whirling with unspoken thoughts. And that was before she began fidgeting.

My mother never fidgeted. Not even under duress. Something else was wrong.

I frowned. "Mother?"

"Where's Poet?" she blurted, yet another thing this woman rarely did.

"He's with Nicu," I drew out, confounded. "You were there."

Yes. She was with us when Poet and I had checked for a second time on his son. We'd left them together, so Poet could watch over the boy. The jester would join us soon, yet apparently not soon enough for Mother, who started pacing like a lioness.

Unnerved, she gusted out, "I was hoping to speak with both of you."

"Mother," I insisted. "What is it?"

All at once, she halted. Then she grasped my hands, urging us across the suite to the fireplace, where she lowered us onto a settee.

Glancing at our threaded fingers, Mother mused, "Your father was better at advising you."

"That is not true," I objected. "You were equals."

"Yes, well." She spoke to our joined hands. "I'm not about to insult you by rattling off platitudes. And so I must simply come out with it."

Something cold splashed through my stomach. "Please do."

She had been speaking more to herself than me. Like the fidgeting and pacing, I could count on one hand the number of times Mother had ever done that.

Also, during only one other time had she looked this afflicted. Back when she'd had no choice but to disinherit and evict her daughter.

Awareness dawned on me. She knew what Winter wanted. In fact, the remorse blasting across her face signified that she'd already entertained some type of negotiation. And she'd done so not only without my knowledge, but without Poet's.

It must have been when I was sick, while the jester remained by my bedside. No other window of time made sense.

Mother lifted her gaze as though it weighed a thousand pounds. "There's been an arrangement." But when she fell silent again, I pulled back to sketch her features, foreboding plaguing me anew. "Mother," I pressed. "What did you do?"

At last, she met my eyes. "I gave Winter what he values."

Knowing Jeryn and the rest of this continent, the answer came quickly. In Spring during the Peace Talks, the Dark Seasons had signed an amendment regarding the trade of born souls. I had used that to my advantage, to bring Nicu and Poet to Autumn.

Fools, and all that they are, shall be bound to their new Season.

As the amendment's clause invaded my memory, nausea roiled in my stomach. The implication struck like a mallet, knocking my senses off kilter. Treachery, repugnance, and anarchy flooded my voice. The reply shot from me like one of my thorn quills.

"No," I hissed. "Mother, no."

She winced. "Dearest, I had to."

"You gave him people."

"I gave him Summer's prisoners."

"You gave him *people*."

"And for that, I saved my daughter," she defended under her breath. "For that, Jeryn of Winter traveled a vast distance to cure a denounced princess who represents everything he despises. For that, he is here. For that, you will survive."

The twenty prisoners I'd negotiated from Summer.

Nineteen, I corrected privately. Nineteen prisoners, now that one had burned to death.

Mother gave the rest of them to Winter, the court known to conduct brutal experiments on born souls. Reputedly, Prince Jeryn led those procedures. Summer had the largest population of maddened captives, and Winter valued that beyond wealth. For the second time, the trade amendment of the Fools Decree had been enacted—by Autumn.

And Flare. That woman in the dungeon, who couldn't be much older than I was. The kind female with golden eyes and a fierce expression, who repeatedly sketched the same cluster of words into a pile of dirt. The one whose gaze had alighted when she saw me and Poet, who had finally entrusted us with her name.

She belonged to Winter now. I had checked in on the prisoners earlier, relieved to see Flare hadn't been the one who'd gone up in flames. I had envisioned a hopeful future for her, only now to discover which heathen would claim her next.

"You gave him Flare," I uttered. "You gave her to him."

Mother's initial confusion gave way to realization. "You're on first name terms with the inmates."

"Did you expect anything less from me?"

Her face transformed, a gleam of pride straying across her eyes. "Never," she said. "It's what your father would have done."

Father's memory eased some of the tightness in my chest. Yet only marginally. Poet and I had learned the names of every prisoner, and while some had been hostile, most were not. If anything, tonight proved the prisoners weren't nearly as vicious as the free-roaming courtiers who claimed to be sanctimonious.

Various hues of brown and taupe outfitted the suite, from the foliage wallpaper to the velvet pillows. Sage green accents lent a bit of softness to the space. Mounted above the chunky, heavily carved fireplace mantel was an oil painting of a copper fox amid brilliant trees.

I stared at the artwork for a long time. "I'm aware of how much Winter values test subjects. But are born souls so valuable that Jeryn would choose experimentation over letting an anarchistic princess die? Or does he not take threat of our campaign seriously?"

"Perhaps both," came Mother's voice from beside me. "The prince is candid to an astringent degree, yet he is not known to explain himself. He is methodical in a way that would impress Poet, if the jester didn't rightly despise him. But if there's a greater reason why Jeryn accepted this transaction, none of us will discover it. What Winter doesn't want you to know, you won't."

A sad smile coaxed my lips upward. "You are forgetting who I'm bonded with."

I swerved from the painting and found Mother struggling to muster a grin. In truth, I would have abstained from receiving Jeryn's medical help, had I known the cost. Yet I would never express that to Mother or Poet, because I knew what they'd say.

"We must prevent him," I pushed instead.

Mother shook her head. "The contract is binding, and we cannot afford to offend Winter. Silvia and Doria are not the issue, but their heir is another matter. If you think Rhys is a problem, you don't want to make an enemy of Jeryn."

Try as I might, I could not keep the scathing tone from my voice. "Yes, I remember his last visit quite well. It appears he has not changed."

"He will find a means to sway his grandaunts without them realizing it," Avalea cautioned. "In turn, you might end up condemning this nation, including every other born soul—including Nicu—for the sake of nineteen."

"But there must be some way out of it."

Yet again, anxiety dominated Mother's countenance. "Hear me out," she prompted, her inflection strained as if prying the speech from her ribcage. "This is your choice, but hear me out."

My choice. The way she'd emphasized that. Based on The Dark Seasons' history of negotiation between Royals and noble families, I knew where she was going. I'd been bred to know it. Nonetheless, Mother and Father had never been the types to consider it—unless they became desperate.

Venom coated my response. "I won't do it," I seethed, enunciating every word. "I will *never* do it."

"I've not given you the details yet," she implored as I launched from the seat and marched to the fireplace. "Briar, please. Don't turn away."

At the mantel, I whipped toward her. "Do I look like a whore and a bigot?" With each word, my octave escalated to a high-pitched shriek. "Or are you seriously, earnestly, morally suggesting a marriage of convenience to that vile *fucking monster?*"

"Of course not!" Mother swore, rising from the settee and pressing her palms together as though in prayer. "I would sooner sell myself than see you eternally pledged to that man. I'm not implying marriage; I'm talking about a false engagement. A passing deception."

"I am taken," I reminded her, tormented and refusing to believe she'd forgotten that. "I am in love. I am already engaged."

Poet and I had been waiting for a peaceful time to tell her. Instantly, Mother's expression transformed, shifting from anguish to tenderness. Blessedly, her elated features eased the pressure on my chest. She loved Poet and Nicu like her own flesh and blood.

"Oh, my dear," she said, rushing to me and clasping my face.

But when a flash of resignation betrayed her features shortly thereafter, I inched backward. "No one else exists for me but Poet. What you're laying out is impossible," I stressed. "I couldn't begin to pretend—"

"For the public," she clarified. "Only for the public's eyes would you pretend."

"Why?" I clipped. "Why would you entertain this?"

"It would be temporary. It's a means to pacify our nation before the tension amounts to bloodshed. Look what's already happened." Mother's voice steadied. "You know what's required to lead, the sacrifices a ruler must make, the struggle to balance our duties as monarchs with our principles as human beings. The latter doesn't always find an equilibrium. Most often, they're conflicted, where we must choose between doing the right thing, the loving thing, and the smart thing. Passions don't always outweigh protection."

She was not telling me anything I didn't already know. Not that it mattered when I had made a vow. I'd chosen my jester, willing to face this continent in defense of our union because it was worth it.

Interpreting the look on my face, Mother heaved a breath. "A courtship, then," she advocated. "If not an engagement, a courtship."

"I've already been declared mad," I argued. "This would also portray me as indecisive."

"It will prove you're putting the kingdom first over your desire," she countered, lowering her voice because the guards were outside. "The prince will break it off."

"Poet and I are working to prove our strength as a couple. This will negate the headway we've regained amid the ranks."

"Or the people will see you in a more hopeful light, and they will trust you and Poet again, even after Winter ends the charade. I suspect the prince will agree to this stunt, provided we bargain well. Not people this time," she said when I opened my mouth. "But we'll offer him a vast extent of our natural resources. Winter has been hankering for those damn apples you used against the Masters. Apparently, they make viable ingredients for medical research, and we've never traded them before."

"Mother! To stake Winter's reputation like this, crops will not suffice. You *know* it won't." I pointed to the floor, my finger stabbing the air. "I do not agree with this. Neither will Poet. He'll slit Winter's throat before that fiend gets within twenty feet of me."

"Dearest, what do you want me to say? What would you have us do?"

I clamped onto her arm. "We have the knights' fealty. Reports indicate a percentage of the citizenry is coming around. It's not everyone, but it's a start. Between the three of us, we can elevate our plan to reach those who would see us dethroned."

"We do not have time to orchestrate another plan," Mother pressed. "Not after everything that's happened. The people are stewing, alternating between doubting you and disputing with one another. Yes, tales of you and Poet are winning over some, but now the public is becoming divided on the matter. And with Rhys's followers targeting the Crown and born souls, it will only serve to rile the denizens further, which could very well be Summer's objective.

"Briar, be sensible. At this rate, we could have a brawl on our hands by morning. We must act immediately to mollify the people. A courtship with Winter will show your willingness to restore balance to this nation, to maintain peace with the Seasons rather than defying them at every turn."

Mother's visage twisted, as though she hated what she was about to say. "If you can't do this, what chance do you have with greater negotiations? How will you lead an army, should you need to? This is the least of what you'll be expected to do. After everything you and Poet have been through for this campaign, I shouldn't have to remind you of that."

I growled, another protest launching up my throat when Mother clasped the back of my nape and drew our foreheads together. "Daughter. I swear on my honor, I would never hurt you, nor Poet or Nicu. They are part of our family now, and I adore them. But you must show some form of allegiance with Winter, or our hopes may not see the light of day. If Poet cares about your future together, and if he cares about this crusade, he will play along. Give him that credit."

Denial solidified like a stone in my chest, and the polished floor felt too hard beneath my boot soles. I could not refute her points.

Knowing my jester, he would not either.

Mother was right. The role of a monarch could be painful, even gruesome. And I could not blame her. At this juncture, it behooved any ruler to consider such a course of action.

However, I was not any ruler. History and tradition ended with me. I'd broken my crown, and I would not allow yet another sovereign to break me. Even if I went along with some type of farce, it would be of my own design. I'd make sure of that.

No. I would not court the prince. Not in the way Mother proposed.

My voice sprouted thorns. "Poet is the only match. If the prince must be solicited, we'll do it together. On our own terms."

Rebellion must have shown across my face, because Mother blinked. As her gaze studied mine, perception eclipsed resignation. "You have a different plan. In the span of three seconds, you've devised a different plan."

"I might have," I told her. "I've redefined what it means to be a princess. I'll redefine the very meaning of allegiance. Not a betrothal, but a collaboration."

Mother stared. Then her expression crumbled, and she gripped my hands once more, a stream of words pouring from her lips. "Forgive me," she beseeched. "I almost lost you. Twice, I almost lost you. And …"

I raised our fingers, balled them into a single fist, and held it between us. "It's okay."

It was. I had been separated from Mother, then poisoned in front of her. Of course, she would consider anything to keep her daughter alive and safe.

"We are all fools in some way. Me included." Her mouth lifted into a marveling grin. "I beg your pardon for not having anticipated any other response."

"The most conniving jester on this continent knows what it's like to wear a mask and perform for his audience, as does the most steadfast princess in The Dark Seasons," I affirmed. "We are skilled deceivers."

"Then use that power," Mother encouraged. "By Seasons, if there's another way out of this, wield that strength like a weapon." As if to imbue me with fortitude, she uttered, "Fool them all, dearest."

Fool them all. That, Poet and I could do.

But to accomplish it required a dangerous proposition. To defeat one villain, we'd have to join forces with another.

29

Poet

My dagger cut through the distance and punctured a figure's stomach. Pivoting and scissoring into the air, I executed a backhanded toss and sent another blade flying. This one speared into the figure's throat, piercing its larynx before shooting through the opposite side, the weapon's tip protruding from the back.

My muscles burned, but scarcely hot enough. Refusing to pause for breath, I vaulted into a series of twists and ducks across a network of suspended beams lined in barbs. Gliding through like smoke and leaping onto an upper platform that swayed from side to side, I whipped out the next dagger and let it fly, striking my adversary between the eyes. The weapon speared the skull clean through and pinned it to a wood-plank wall, which marked a dead end.

The obstruction materialized so quickly, I staggered in place at the stable edge of the crossway. Around me, numerous suspensions with serrated railings and swinging impediments comprised the training course, meant to test a fighter's balance, dexterity, and aim. The main target drooped in front of me, its form stapled to the partition and signifying I'd successfully completed the track.

More than that, it appeared. I'd depleted myself of every blade and pulverized every vital organ the mannequin possessed.

Wind blew through the practice yard. The lawn was vacant for a good reason. Only a fool would be out here, on planks raised high off the ground, training in this weather.

My lungs siphoned oxygen, my chest pounded, and sweat drenched my bare skin. The mannequin slumped against the wall, its burlap face void of expression and sand trickling from the wounds like fake blood. I had a fine imagination, pictured the face before me, and wasn't nearly done with him.

Yanking my dagger from the target's skull, I juggled the hilt and lashed out of my arm, slicing its face horizontally. The satisfaction was short-lived. Too many parts of its body remained unscathed, so that I slashed through the mannequin's husk, from its hip, to its wrists, to its invisible mouth. Flipping the blade in my fingers, I slammed the tip through the figure's heart.

That miserable, useless, fucking heart.

Guttural sounds launched from my tongue. Over and over, I thrust the dagger through. The burlap fibers split. More sand gushed from its body, and my thoughts spiraled as that imaginary face became clearer.

Dropping the blade, I smashed my fist into the husk, clear through to the wood facade. Then again, and again, and again. Putting my whole weight into it, I rammed my knuckles into the enemy's face, pain exploding in my hand and fluid oozing from the gashes. The sound of splintering wood and a howling wind funneled through my ears, and my joints felt as though they were being roasted on an open flame, yet my arm refused to stop. Not giving a wicked fuck, I hammered into the lifeless figure, the wall behind it cracking.

I cranked my arm back—and a set of fingers caught my bicep. With a grunt, I veered. My attention locked onto Aire's, those solemn blue orbs reflecting my own glazed pupils. He'd scaled the training platform from the opposite end, where a set of rungs led to this suspension, situated nearby in case some tenderfoot novice got stuck or impaled.

Concern wrung across the knight's face. The wind tousled his hair, and though he didn't glance at the destruction behind me, the soldier didn't need to. I saw it on his face, the damage I'd done, the lengths to which I had gone.

I gazed over my shoulder to what was left of the mannequin. Its face had been whittled down to a pulp of fabric, the whole thing ripped open and no longer resembling a human being. Behind my target, the wall had caved in, wood shavings hanging lopsided. I had punched my way through, crimson leaking down my knuckles.

Expelling a breath, I returned my gaze to Aire. "'Tis exactly what it looks like."

The man watched me in troubled silence. "This is not how you shall triumph."

"Nay. But I get a kick out of spectacles, and I tend to exaggerate my actions. Hence, it felt good to pretend. Ever done that?"

"No," Aire merely replied. "Poet—"

"Fear not." I gestured to the wreckage of the training course. "This was merely child's play. If I meant serious business, this platform wouldn't be standing any longer. As for the mannequin, it's not as if I was slaying the actual king this time. Or the prince, for that matter. Not even the miserable fucks who slayed an innocent tonight."

With the rest of the court, donning a mask was easy. By contrast, this knight's perceptive gaze visibly peeled a layer from my exterior. "Except it wasn't the king, the prince, or the murderers you were punishing."

Shit. He needed to stop doing that. Frankly, I wasn't in the mood to be transparent. "I'd quit while I was ahead," I warned.

The knight gave me a look that testified how much he doubted that. "It was not your fault, Poet."

To which, I grinned without humor. "Which part?"

My son's nightmares. Briar's banishment, then her poisoning.

Every born soul I still hadn't freed from the hell in which they lived. The incinerated victim in the maple pasture, their life reduced to ashes before I could prevent it.

Tally all my errors, all the ways in which people had suffered because I hadn't intervened fast enough, and all the ways it affected Briar, and all the ways my failures endangered Nicu. Not counting friends like Aire, Eliot, Cadence, Posy, and Vale. Itemize my mistakes, and scribes could fill an omnibus.

So. Which fucking part wasn't my fault?

The soldier studied my expression and floundered. "I have spoken out of turn," he grunted. "Apologies, Sir."

"Poet," I corrected. "I'm pissed off at the world, but I'd like to say we're kin."

Aire blinked. His gruff features relaxed enough for a hint of pride to show through, shortly before he cleared his throat. Nodding, he said, "Then permit me to say, Her Highness is also my kin."

"Her Highness," I quoted him. "Whereas I've been hearing the titles 'Daughter of Autumn' or 'The Mad Princess' bandied about. It appears most people would disagree with you there."

"I am not most people."

"I should hope so. My standards for friendship are high."

"Your standards for everything are high."

"Meh." I flitted my fingers. "You say that like it's a flaw."

Aire glanced at the remote harvest fields, then back to me. "I have sworn an oath. The princess is still my sovereign, and I will continue to serve her, as will the troops. I'm glad to repeat how she has won them over fully."

The corners of my mouth tipped upward. "Another thing we have in common."

A congenial light flashed across his face before it melted into awareness. In that moment, I saw what he sensed. Beyond the bracket of his shoulder, a slender figure materialized several feet behind him from the same set of rungs, her hair a red lantern amid eventide's indigo sky.

Attentive, the First Knight inclined his head to me and then bowed for Briar. Her eyes swerved from mine to his, and she offered him a solemn but companionable grin before dipping her head, acknowledging the soldier in kind. They'd reached that zenith where allies became kindreds, fewer words needing to be spoken.

As Aire stalked off into a shawl of wind, the plates of his armor glinted like dragon scales, iridescent against the dark backdrop. Nicu had been right, for the man oftentimes resembled a winged creature. However, only a modicum of my attention remained on him, and only to anticipate the soldier leaving me alone with my next visitor.

Routinely, this woman did that. She made everyone vanish, even if they were standing beside me.

Beneath a vault of stars, Briar stood with her fingers nestled into the pockets of a mantle that hung loosely off her shoulders, with a hood cascading behind her. The cold air brushed her cheeks, and ornamental beads dotted the braided bun knotted to one side of her nape. The princess had changed into a less formal outfit than the one she'd modeled when we greeted the Winter prick.

Comfort clothes. That meant she needed to talk quickly and quietly.

No matter. This female could wear strings of wire and still take me captive. Matter of fact, that ensemble sounded rather appealing.

Like a reflex, my mouth slanted at the sight of her. "Evening, beautiful. Out here alone with an armed jester? That's asking for a lovely amount of trouble."

Despite the flirtation, she charged my way and cupped my face. "Are you all right?"

Fuck. Why had I bothered trying? She knew me better, might have even witnessed my rampage against the mannequin.

Guilt, wrath, and concern eroded on my tongue. "I'm much more invested in how you're feeling."

"You needn't worry about me."

"But that's my lifelong calling. Haven't you heard? We're inextricably linked."

"None of this was your doing," Briar insisted.

My eyes closed. The vision of a burned body flitted before my eyes, as it must have been doing to her. My jaw hardened, then collapsed against her touch.

Opening my eyes, I focused on Briar's face. "Nor was it yours."

Sweet resignation sagged her features, then her gaze slipped to my crimson knuckles. "You're injured," she fretted, pulling back and stroking the blood-clotted joints.

"Merely a few stings," I dismissed. "As you can see, the training course had it worse. And so long as it wasn't my face, I'm not bothered."

Seeing the injury wasn't vital, she nodded absently. I watched her mind churn, a stack of words piling behind her lips. Those gray irises darted across the lawn, as if searching for a way to continue.

My voice deepened and caressed the air. "Look at me, sweeting." And when she dragged her gaze to mine, I stepped nearer. "What is it?"

"We must act quicker," she ventured, then shook her head at whatever blasphemous thought entered her mind. "Mother proposed something. A way to use Winter as an advantage against Summer." Her eyes sought my own. "But I refused to do it."

It took me a second. A mere second to weigh those words.

Based on Briar's expression and a history of political maneuvers, it didn't take a genius to guess what subject Avalea had broached, especially after tonight. As the implication struck, my blood's temperature spiked. Red flooded my vision, and a possessive hiss struck like a whip from my tongue.

My fingers snatched Briar's hips and yanked her against my naked chest. "Like fuck is he coming near you."

"I know," she rushed out, her voice wrought of steel and her fingers locking into the hair at the back of my scalp.

"Do you?" I asked, capturing her chin between my thumb and forefinger. "Do you know how much you belong to me?"

"As much as you belong to me."

"Then this had better be the last time we entertain this subject." If not, I would carve the flesh from the prince's bones.

I used to be good at hiding unbridled emotions. Hatred. Malice.

Disgust. It had been effortless to conceal my deceptions and wage clever war against my enemies.

Until this princess. She'd shredded through that facade long ago.

"Agreed," Briar said, her palms flanking my profile. "Mother understands that now." The princess's lips curved as she etched them over my mouth. "I told her. And she's elated for us."

The emphasis coaxed my jaw to relax. Briar had told her mother about my proposal and her daughter's reply.

I let out a gruff chuckle. "How could she not be thrilled by the prospect of having a jester in the family? I hear we make things more interesting."

Briar's swift grin melted into a sigh. "The earlier part of our discussion was a lapse any ruler would eventually come to."

"And she was acting for her child, who'd nearly died," I acknowledged. "I might have some empathy for that."

"So an alternative. It turns out we need Winter, but there's another way to make that happen."

My head cocked, and my thumb languidly grazed her hip. "I'm all ears."

"More than that, I hope," she urged. "Autumn will need your tongue."

To that, my lips crooked, and I whispered naughtily, "She has it."

Together, we schemed. A courtship, much less an engagement, would have been a commonplace tactic. To boot, it wouldn't have seemed genuine to Summer or Autumn.

To convince The Dark Seasons, our deception had to be more subtle.

By no means did this erase the shit Jeryn had said in the pasture. If anything, it made him a new target in my eyes. However, other matters took precedence.

Summer first. We would deal with Winter later.

Karma tasted sweetly addictive on my tongue, like melted sugar mixed with alcohol. To fuck with Rhys's ego, we'd have to pursue Jeryn. It would be suicidal for any Season to dabble against Winter.

With this sort of advantage at our disposal, the Summer King would piss himself.

"This plan will prevent Rhys from attacking," Briar confided. "Not wishing to involve Winter, he may not attack at all. He may very well stand down."

"Best case scenario," I said. "Though, we'd be asking Winter to stake its position."

"Which means whatever we bargain, it had best be worthwhile to him."

My eyes tapered with mischief. "There is the matter of Rhys's spies being spread across the continent. We've been meaning to have a chat with Spring and Winter about that."

That was the initial reason we hadn't used this knowledge as an ultimatum against Rhys. Leveraging the details instead of informing Spring and Winter would have destroyed us in the long-term. Also, as Aire and Briar's moral compasses had reminded our clan, it was the right thing to do.

Not that I often prescribed to such motivations. As the morally gray player in this group, I left ethics to the knight and princess.

Torch posts and maple leaves illuminated the dark atmosphere. Our shadows extended across the ground. If one were to look, they would find two silhouettes blending.

"If we do this, it will build trust," Briar predicted. "But as far as making a pact, there's no assurance Jeryn will loosen the reins entirely."

"Sometimes, all we have is a leap of faith." I ghosted my mouth across hers. "We'll simply have to be ready for a chess game."

"Would you say we're up for that?"

A sly grin broadened my lips. I'd been tracking Jeryn's every move and gesture, including the minutiae that tended to catch his attention. "Wear that cunning little silver dress tucked in your closet," I suggested. "The prince favors silver."

30

Poet

He filled the dungeon to capacity. Firelight reflected the bristles of his fur collar, giving the illusion that small needles grew from his body.

For fuck's sake. In this dank atmosphere—in any atmosphere besides the tundra from whence he came—how did the man stand it in that coat?

I marveled for only so long, my attention returning to the prince's colossal height. Whereas I stood statuesque, he was a fortress capable of surpassing an oak tree. 'Twas a miracle that dark blue head didn't slam into the root-laced ceiling and cause a migraine.

I hated to admit it, but *prince* was too frivolous a title for him. The fucker embodied the term *future king*.

That didn't stop me and Briar from targeting him as we paced down the cavity. No surprise, we'd been informed of his whereabouts among the incarcerated and suffering. Jeryn's profile was as tapered as a spire, his gaze unruffled whilst examining the prisoners like booty.

Or like specimens. Another hideous bit of news the princess had imparted to me. Her mother had traded Summer's mad with Winter, in exchange for Jeryn leaching the poisonous residue from Briar's blood. I would have verbally ripped into the queen for this, were her actions untenable. The trade had saved Briar.

As he stalked along the corridor and appraised the captives one by one, I sensed the prince's morbid thoughts.

Which of these people warranted experimentation? Which were expendable?

How loudly would they scream?

My molars ground together. The closer we came, the uglier those intentions got as they radiated from him. And because Jeryn's expression hadn't wavered, naturally I began to wonder if he possessed the ability to blink.

But then, he proved me wrong.

Winter's gaze did a double take. He stalled in his tracks, his eyes landing on one of the occupants languishing in their cell. When I counted the number of cages, a growl skidded up my throat. At the same time, Briar seized my arm, recognizing the figure sequestered in that cubicle.

As usual, the woman hunched over a mound of dirt, scribbling to her heart's content. Except then her finger halted, sensing an intruder. Or rather, a predator.

Flare's head whipped up, her flaming irises colliding with a set of chilled ones. Anybody else would have staggered from either of those stares.

One of fire. One of ice.

Yet neither combatant flinched. Although Jeryn's expression betrayed no outward reaction, a flicker of intense focus gripped his face, captured as if by a snare. Whereas Flare glowered, hurling every emotion in existence his way.

The prince's concentration dipped to the collar of sunburst tattoos encircling her neck. For an instant, his lips tightened. "Who marked you?"

Not the question I had expected. Nor had Flare.

She hesitated. Then she gave him a defiant look whilst batting her hair to shroud the markings.

Evidently, the man was accustomed to getting prompt answers. When Flare denied him that, Jeryn's nostrils flared. He opened his mouth, but then something else drew his gaze. Glimpsing the contents sketched into the lump of dirt, the prince tilted his head.

Without looking away, he waved over a guard and jutted his cleft chin toward the pile. "Sweep away this filth."

Shit. The second he issued that command, a gritty noise rumbled from Flare's chest. She popped onto her knees, grabbed a handful of dirt, and cranked her arm backward.

"I would not try it, little beast," the prince cautioned, his voice like a razor's edge—smooth, polished, and capable of slitting an artery.

The difference between this motherfucker and Rhys was paramount. Unlike Summer, Winter didn't raise his voice. Because he didn't need to. The man perfected a cool, calm, and fatal tone that raised the hairs along my forearms.

Shouting wasn't his power. Quiet was, for it sliced into a person like a deep incision.

The prince and prisoner's gazes magnetized. No matter that we could simply overrule Jeryn's order. No matter that we could procure more soil for Flare, which we'd learned she preferred over drawing tools. From her perspective, if she heeded the man's warning, the dirt in her cell would be swept clean.

This may not seem like a severe consequence to a free person. But to a captive deprived of the only tangible means to express herself and mentally escape this hellhole, the threat amounted to war. Take what mattered to her, and she would take back.

It happened in the span of seconds. Briar and I broke into motion, hustling down the conduit.

Protective of her territory, Flare charged to the grille. She cannoned her arm through the bars and nabbed the only thing potentially valuable to the prince. Swiping Jeryn's fang-shaped vial necklace, the force of her grasp ripped the cord. Jumping backward, Flare put her entire frame into flinging the necklace against the bars.

Although Winter glass didn't shatter easily, the impact produced a crack. Fluid dripped from the vial and seeped into the rushes. Thankfully, no toxic scent invaded the dungeon. But whatever the pendant had contained, it was important to the prince. To say nothing of the keepsake itself.

For the first time, Jeryn's composure snapped. An aggrieved expression twisted his face. Right before he lunged.

With a corrosive hiss, the man moved faster than I would have given him credit for. And because the woman had underestimated how far he could reach, she didn't see it coming. The prince's hand vaulted past the rail, snatched the back of her waist, and hauled her flush against the door.

Flare grunted, squirming to break away as his digits burrowed into her scalp. "That was quite the fucking mistake," he spat into her face.

The woman hurled her fingernails toward Jeryn's countenance, intending to peel off his skin. In response, Winter's scalpel knife appeared from nowhere, the hilt trapped in his fist. Before he could spear through her, my hand clamped onto his wrist, our forearms striking the grille. Iron shuddered from the impact, the sound echoing down the cellblock.

Both captor and captive halted. Flare's pupils dulled, the blaze snuffing out as she recognized us.

Jeryn registered my hold on his arm. His features folded, logic returning as his grip on her loosened. At the same time he released Flare, the prince's free hand seized the necklace from her.

Flare staggered back with a scowl. Once she was a safe distance from him, I let go of Winter.

Still, it took some time for Jeryn to dice his gaze from her to me. "You're either foolish or suicidal to interfere with my property."

"How dare you," Briar seethed. "You will not touch her again, nor any of these people. They may be your prisoners, but they are still on Autumn soil."

Jeryn's attention slithered from me to the princess. He surveyed

Briar's appearance, from the loosely braided bun at her nape to the silver, strappy gown. She'd donned the color of his court, the silhouette glittered with a thousand dainty chains like armor, and the skirt hissed with every movement.

The prince hedged. His fingers closed protectively around the fang-shaped vial, then he shoved the keepsake into his coat pocket. "Show me your mouth."

From any other living, breathing, talking entity, this command would have met the point of my dagger. However, he'd made such a request once already.

Briar parted her lips. Once she did, the prince vacated his position by Flare's cage. He stalked up to the princess, balanced his finger beneath her chin, and angled her mouth to the torchlight, his gaze dissecting every crevice.

"Much better," he said, lowering his hand. "You have a strong constitution."

After what had just happened, Briar merely nodded. Whereas I summoned every remaining ounce of self-control. "That'll be the last time you set a finger on Her Highness. Or anyone down here, for that matter."

To which Jeryn merely cut an eyebrow my way. "You mistake me for someone who gives a fuck about your savior instincts."

"Amusing. Who said anything about me needing your approval?" But clearly, Jeryn was used to squashing his opponent with a simple look, whereas I volleyed, "You know, I thought princes were supposed to be intimidating."

"And I thought jugglers were supposed to be perceptive," he contended. "We are both mistaken."

"Oh, I'm quite perceptive. Try me."

"No," was all he replied.

I seized on that trap. "Which could either mean it's not worth your effort or you don't dare to. It may be the former, but not replying at all means you're still leaving the latter up for debate."

To that riddle, he sliced his attention to Briar. "Must we do this?"

"Converse? I'm afraid so," she clipped. "Poet and I have the queen's blessing to approach you on Autumn's behalf."

Jeryn pared his eyes at her. His silence indicated that Briar should speak her mind before he lost interest and carelessly strode away.

Her face pinched. The shift in her freckles signified she was about to stray from our plan, if only to voice a pertinent thought. Not only due to the incident with Flare, but also the burned body he'd refused to heal. "Being a ruler might grant you the power to reject those you deem unworthy. But as a doctor, you have sworn an oath."

"I have sworn that oath to human beings," Jeryn stated blandly. "Not to living plagues."

"Too close to home?" I wondered.

For some reason, the prince's eyes ticked toward Flare's cell. In response, the woman's golden irises sizzled. She moved in front of the dirt mound where she'd drawn her sketch.

So many ways to interpret the demand he'd made about that pile. *Sweep away this filth* had sounded as though he was referring to both Flare and the muck. Mayhap the mess insulted his tidy sensibilities, though a hunch told me it was more than that.

Consequently, they were off to a dangerous start. In which case, Jeryn's intentions upon returning to Winter didn't bode well for Flare.

Realizing that he'd been focused on her for too long, the prince wrenched his gaze back to us. "Give me a reason to keep listening."

Briar obliged. "You have stalkers."

"Though considering your charming disposition, I can't imagine why," I scoffed.

"There are spies in your midst," the princess clarified, lowering her voice so the guards wouldn't overhear. "Summer has informants stationed within Winter's borders." As Jeryn's brows stapled together, Briar seized on that rare opportunity to catch him off guard. "Rhys indicated as much to us. He has been monitoring every Season, including our own, and has been for some time."

Whilst the information solidified in the prince's mind, his features darkened. Even then, he didn't blink.

But he did start moving. After trailing his eyes downward and back toward Flare's cage, the prince broke into motion. The fur-lined coat slapped his calves, and his shadow cloaked the walls. Accelerating past us, he prowled down the corridor, silently expecting his companions to follow.

Whilst I loathed trailing in anyone's wake, I made an exception. Taking Briar's hand, I migrated with her from the dungeon. After too many flights of winding brick steps, and through too many passages, we emerged onto the parapet walks.

Clouds stretched over The Wandering Fields like shredded cotton. Celestials burned with white light.

Alongside Autumn sentinels, a wolf pack of Winter soldiers patrolled the vicinity, including a woman with frothy white hair and a split complexion. One half of her visage was pale, the other a lunar grey. The opulent plates of the female's attire outranked that of her comrades, thus identifying her as the First Knight.

Collectively, the troops' cloaks were woven of frost. And amid crossbows and blades with variously shaped tips, the soldiers' baldrics housed throwing stars. The weapons twitched as the men and women noticed us coming, and they bowed to Jeryn with looks of deference.

Nevertheless, their prince focused on only one figure. He strode across the platform, heading toward a Winter soldier idling near the ledge. Without pausing, Jeryn unsheathed the knife affixed to his hip. And before the knight could bow, Jeryn was on the man.

The scalpel-shaped weapon punctured the warrior's side like a blade to pudding. The knight howled, buckling to the ground whilst the prince sank with him.

Briar gasped, her palm shooting to her mouth. Seething, I whipped her against me and snaked my arm around her middle. My free hand dropped to the hilt of my dagger, and we froze whilst the prince went to work.

Bracing on his knees, with his profile devoid of remorse, Jeryn studied the man. Then he twisted the blade and leisurely cut a path through the knight's stomach, the weapon shearing through as if the armor was made of tinfoil.

"What do you know?" Jeryn murmured calmly.

But when his victim only bellowed in pain, the prince moved the scalpel upward. Blood spurted from the knight's mouth, crimson staining his teeth as they flashed in agony.

It became all too fucking clear. This man knew something about the spies in Winter, and the prince wasn't merely stabbing him for information. Known for his medical prowess, Jeryn was gutting an organ from the knight's stomach.

"Take your time," the prince invited, digging deeper and slower. "I'm patient."

Briar's chest heaved in shock. I ripped my dagger from its harness.

At the same time, the Winter knight gargled one word. "Scholars."

To which Jeryn nodded. "Much better."

Done and done. Yet instead of releasing the man, the satanic prince made it worse. He plunged farther, globs of crimson leaking from the soldier's gash, which expanded along with every screech of anguish.

"Stop!" Briar cried over the knight's howls. "Stop this!"

Jeryn ignored her. He continued skewering the warrior like a side of beef, until a hint of gooey flesh poked through the crater, the makings of his spleen peeking into view.

A whistling noise rent the air. The soldier grunted, tensed, and slumped to the bricks. His visage went slack, death fogging his eyes.

A sharp object protruded from between his brows. Briar's thorn quill had penetrated the man's skull, ending him quickly.

My head whisked down to where her arm lowered, then swerved toward Jeryn, who turned in her direction. Like a panther, I stalked in front of the princess, my grip still on the dagger.

"Sorry about that," I said innocently, wiggling my free fingers to demonstrate. "My hand slipped."

In the background, a handful of Autumn guards stood immobile, their expressions ranging from haggard to petrified. By contrast, the female First Knight and her Winter brethren scrutinized the dead soldier in offense, having swiftly comprehended some type of grave infraction against their sovereign.

Jeryn, on the other hand, looked more than insulted. Pissed off might be accurate. Or rather, defensive.

Recalling how he'd cradled his pendant after Flare broke it, I beheld the same protectiveness sneaking across his countenance now. Yet it vanished too rapidly to process.

Prolonging the movements, Jeryn rose to his full height, the steel tips of his boots flashing. Blood splattered his open fur coat. Jerking his head, the prince whipped strands of hair from his face, and he regarded us like pests—cumbersome, if not lethal.

If he only knew how close I'd been to launching the dagger into his throat. Briar's own reflexes had been what stopped me. She'd simply gotten there first, though her aim had been of the compassionate sort.

Unlike Rhys, Jeryn was no volatile idiot who let fury override his logic. The cerebral prince knew better than to swallow my bullshit.

He strode up to us, his gaze carving into me. "Your Autumn mercy treads a fine line."

"You don't say," I parried. "Lucky for me, I'm an acrobat."

"You suspected that man of disloyalty," Briar muttered, horrified by the puddle of blood fifteen feet from us.

Her conclusion made sense. This prince excelled where his counterpart didn't. Instead of acting impulsively like Summer, Winter observed deliberately. To that end, Jeryn must make a shrewd habit of watching his subjects at court.

Briar's assumption about the knight's limited knowledge had also been accurate. Few mortals could have endured that much torture and still held back if they possessed additional information. In any case, Rhys must have recruited some group of academics to shovel his shit in Winter.

"You knew and said nothing." Accusation laced Jeryn's baritone voice. "Refusing to divulge information is grounds for conflict between Seasons." He slanted his head, those crystalline eyes sparkling with hostility. "Do you want conflict with Winter?"

"Do you wish to waste time having conflict with Autumn?" Briar argued. "We're telling you now."

In the distance, the harvest fields shivered. The briny reek of blood and the bitterness of charred skin clotted the atmosphere. Along the parapets, crenelations stood out against the night sky like teeth.

Once more, Jeryn showed no sign of astonishment at Rhys's actions. Rather, his countenance reflected only cold malice and something else.

Something guarded.

Aye, he'd already suspected this. But until now, he hadn't been able to confirm it.

Jeryn nodded to his soldiers, who set about collecting the body. The wordless exchange between the knights and their prince signified loyalty. Despite what he'd just done to one of their own, they fathomed why it happened. Their comrade had been withholding treasonous information. And despite the treachery of one warrior, Jeryn maintained eye contract with his troop, the respect between them mutual.

Never mind how he'd gotten wind of the lone soldier's duplicity. It was highly unlikely this Royal would expand on the identities of these spies, mainly because I doubted that he knew enough yet. Otherwise, the man would have walked away by now.

There, we had something valuable to offer. As such, my tongue prepared itself for a match.

"Tell me what you have on these spies in Winter," Jeryn requested. "Tell me what Rhys has told you."

After trading a look with me, Briar said, "We don't know the particulars of Summer's conspiracy in your court. But we managed to root out Autumn's traitors."

Speeches wouldn't work on this bastard. As we'd plotted out earlier, Briar let the answer trail off, prompting Jeryn to fill in the blanks. That sort of glamour, he responded to more.

The implication wedged itself into the space between us. To maintain order among the Seasons, we were obligated to inform the prince. And no matter how he felt about it, that placed Winter in a position of debt.

"You're here to negotiate," Jeryn intoned. After a moment's deliberation—in which a hundred outcomes must have entered and exited his mind—he wiped the bloody knife against his velvet-clad thigh. After shoving the weapon into its case, he strode toward the rampart's edge whilst murmuring, "State your terms."

Gladly. Converging beside the crenelations and away from prying ears, we laid out the bargain, presenting our agenda like a variable to an equation. Briar had lobbied for this method of communication, having vetoed my suggestion for a tinge of embellishment, or at the very least a smidgen of enticement. To my sulking disappointment, the prince favored transparency over ambiguity. Because he wanted things spelled out, it forced me to neuter my vocabulary and speak like a mathematician instead of a trickster.

Discussing Rhys's downfall should have been orgasmic, tantamount to knotting a noose around his neck. Instead, I consoled myself with fantasies of jamming my dagger through the man's gullet and listening to him squeal like a pig when this was over.

Jeryn kept his back to us, with his silhouette bookended between merlons. As he consulted the horizon of wheat fields, the man listened to Briar speak. For my part, I lounged my shoulder blades against one of the brick intervals and interrupted her at the precise moments we'd discussed.

The gambit was this: Winter and Autumn would stage an elaborate deception. We'd fake a united front, showing everyone that our courts had established an affinity for one another. Casual, without need of some arbitrary and random contract, to be more convincing.

Although Briar hated to flout Autumn's tenet of honesty, our actions would protect this nation from whatever else Rhys had planned. Also, it presented a tougher fight. Binding documents held weight, but those were technical and could be amended. Whereas an actual kinship would be more difficult for Summer to dismiss.

Our methods would revolve around pleasure rather than politics.

Our weapons would be revels instead of blades.

For now, at least.

On that score, Briar issued an invitation. "Stay for Reaper's Fest."

"And the revels leading up to it," I added.

Jeryn stiffened, then twisted our way. "This is your deal. For Winter to attend a bonfire ball."

"It's our seduction," I corrected.

"Coercion," Briar amended prudently.

"Whatever." I fluttered my fingers. "Attending the festivities would make a statement and illustrate a show of support. It would tell this kingdom Winter endorses Autumn, its choices, and its sovereigns, including the magnificent creature in our midst. In case you didn't notice, she's the angel on your left, and I'm the devil on your right."

The prince merely grunted, as though he found both archetypes not only ludicrous but insufficient to describe us.

"Autumn hosts two events prior to the holiday," Briar explained, the moon's cast accentuating the chains of her gown. "Both will culminate in the bonfire ball for Reaper's Fest. Attend all three celebrations as our guest. In this way, you will pretend to support us."

Jeryn's gaze narrowed, the better to see in the dark. "Winter has never accepted a social invitation from any Season."

"Queens Silvia and Doria have accepted invitations before," Briar rebutted. "But the heir to Winter's throne has not."

"Do so now," I campaigned. "Acknowledge and engage with us. That alone will sway the public in our favor and help tame the rising tension across Autumn."

"Spring and Summer will attend Reaper's Fest," the princess supplied. "By then, your camaraderie with us will be an established fact, and His Majesty shall witness it for himself."

The night of the courtyard battle, Rhys had feigned a change of heart and declared he wouldn't attend Reaper's Fest. In short, the bitch had been lying; he would show up. Oblivious, the king would emerge from his carriage only to discover Winter on our side.

As the future monarch of the continent's most withdrawn nation, a gesture of cooperation from Jeryn wouldn't be taken lightly. That alone could dissuade Rhys from being a nuisance on Reaper's Fest. Neither he, nor his peons would think to call the bluff.

Nevertheless, this hoax wasn't as easy as it sounded. How frequently people forgot that wars weren't merely fought on battlefields. Some of the deadliest ones took place in ballrooms and throne rooms, with a lash of one's tongue rather than a sword. Masquerading as collaborators would require regality, clever wit, and scare tactics. The grace of a princess, the cunning of a jester, and the candidness of a prince might be the right combination to succeed.

If it worked, chickenshit Rhys would stand down. At least long enough for us to prove he'd colluded with the Masters—to the point of endangering any Autumn citizens who got in their way—and plotted Briar's disinheritance. For that, we'd need more time. Until then, this ploy with Winter would keep my least favorite mongrel on a leash.

Jeryn considered our strategy, one blood-stained hand gripping a merlon, the other wedged into the pocket of his pants. His attention slid to the courtyard, where the Masters had been slaughtered among numerous Autumn knights. There, Summer had declared Briar mad.

Only the towering maple remained now, its trunk rising high. The dome of resplendent leaves reached this level, the branch's lambent colors reminiscent of plumage. At the tree's base, a resident copper fox traipsed across the bricks.

By now, Winter's silence could only mean one thing. If not, he would have said no.

At last, Jeryn addressed the courtyard. "I have a condition."

Splendid. Now for the dubious part.

Briar braced herself. "Name your price. Apart from our family and additional captives, of course."

Here, I whittled my gaze at the prince. From this vantage point, the sharp architecture of his profile illustrated no vested interest. Impressively, his features were a blank canvas. That aside, he knew my eyes were searching for a crawl space through which to penetrate his thoughts, to unravel whatever weakness lurked beneath the surface.

By Seasons. This man was good at freezing people out.

Then he replied. "That little beast with the eyes."

Briar and I tensed. I straightened from the crenelations, and the princess clasped her hands tightly.

Flare. The woman who'd likely sealed her fate by testing Winter's patience.

"I want her locked separately," the prince said in a low register.

My jaw clenched. He was asking us to place Flare in solitary confinement. Essentially, a dealbreaker.

My tongue was prepared to strike when Briar snapped, "We will do no such thing. As I said before, she still resides on Autumn soil."

"Yet the little beast belongs to me," Jeryn replied smoothly.

"Stop calling her that! She's a kind and passionate soul."

A growl scrolled from my lungs. "If you go near her, I'll make you remember it."

The man swerved, his nose about to tap against mine. "If you try stopping me, I'll make it worse."

Meaning, he would rescind on this arrangement. My eyes cut to Briar, who agonized. The young woman's isolation versus a nation's future.

Nicu's future.

I traced the harsh lines of Jeryn's face and saw it at last. For a second, his grip on the merlon tightened. He wanted this request fulfilled. Badly.

But to what end?

Unfortunately for him, making deals with a jester was risky business. If he abused Flare, the princess and I would know. Even before then, we'd prevent him.

Sensing a chink in his facade, I nodded. "She'll be moved," I replied, verbally maneuvering a chess piece into place and aware of the princess's shrewd attention on me.

Aye. Flare would be relocated. We just wouldn't tell the prince where.

Jeryn might as well have been examining me under a microscope. Regardless, he took the bait, inclined his head, and strode away. Yet he stopped as my voice flicked a nugget at him.

"That's your only condition," I mused. "Don't you want something else? Aren't you more worried about Autumn's future actions versus what Summer would do?"

The prince's head clicked over his shoulder. "Get to the point."

Gladly, if Winter insisted on pretending like he hadn't already figured it out. "The captive must be worth a lot to you."

"No Season intimidates Winter." The shadows bisected his features. "And no fool is worth anything."

When he disappeared into the nearest tower stairwell, Briar gained my side. Together, we watched the door shut behind the prince.

"Ruthless," she condemned. "Yet that cannot be his only cost."

My fist flexed around a second dagger, with its hilt concealed under my coat. "It's not."

He'd made clear his feelings about Autumn's campaign for emancipation, doubting it would pose a continental threat and believing we'd fail spectacularly. Therefore, bargaining with us hadn't warranted concern. As for Summer, Jeryn must have concluded that Rhys's messy, hot-headed recklessness was more of a long-term issue.

But that couldn't be the extent of it. Winter could have requested anything from us, so whatever else he sought to gain from this deal, it would take endurance to find out.

From a distance, the prince seemed to be the lesser of two evils. Alas, that was the problem with people who wore masks. For I should know.

Whereas vengeful Summer raged like a tempest, unflappable Winter exuded cold restraint. Not to be obvious, but the only thing worse than a stupid monster like You Know Who was an intelligent one. At this point, there was no predicting which would be more fatal. Whether we'd just made a deal with a greater oppressor than Rhys remained to be seen.

31

Poet

'Twas a good thing the princess and her jester had practice in keeping our enemies close. With that in mind, we strolled into the pear orchard the next evening as one unit.

Long tables stood between rows of trees, baskets held bushels of glowing pears, and strands of poppy-orange lights pulsed from the branches. Cadence, Posy, and Vale sipped flutes of white wine and charmed the council, all in pursuit of stoking our reputation. From a different corner, Eliot and Aire did the same with members of the nobility.

Briar idled beside me, with her fingers looped over my arm and her cognac gown swishing across the ground. The upper half of her locks were plaited and swooped backward to the nape, with the rest of her hair looping through the weave in a makeshift low ponytail, which hung down the dress's backless V.

For this occasion, I'd opted to look mildly disciplined, combining the pampered elegance of an ancient fae with the disheveled audacity of a rogue. A leather vest left my arms bare. But the high neck and bullseye clasps atoned for the potentially perverted exposure of skin. A diamond motif—as close to a typical jester's motley as I would ever get—patterned the vest in shades of raven black and whiskey. Because of that, I toned down the rest with streamlined pants, the sides exhibiting slivers of flesh through nets that ran up the sides.

Very well. Perhaps I hadn't toned it down at all.

On Briar's other side, Jeryn wore an ankle-length navy jacket tailored from priceless wool and trimmed in steel gray thread to match his boot tips. The vestment was sealed shut and clung to the slab of his chest like a straitjacket, and matching navy pants ascended the cliffs of his legs. But for once in his tyrannical life, he'd shrugged off that bristly pelt of a coat, no longer looking as if he was carrying a dead elk on his shoulders.

Don't get me wrong. The fur coat was fabulous in its design, albeit sweltering even in Autumn, not to mention questionable regarding its original source.

From her seat at the banquet table's head, Avalea rose and beckoned us. Horns resounded, the brass noise trumpeting through the air to announce us.

At which point, hundreds of heads swiveled in our direction. After what happened in the maple pasture, the courtiers hadn't had a chance to process Jeryn's arrival. But they fucking processed it now.

"Poet, Court Jester of Autumn."

"Briar, Daughter of Autumn."

"His Highness, Jeryn of the House of Northwall, Heir to Queens Silvia and Doria, Prince of Winter."

Quite a mouthful. No wonder the man rarely said much. Everyone did it for him.

Insulated, dispassionate Winter was known to enter feasts without companions. To do otherwise signified partiality and a bias rarely associated with Jeryn's systematic court. Murmurs and whispers floated across the orchard. Courtiers gawked at our trio, too stunned to maintain neutral expressions. Council members perked up, their capillaries bursting with approval. Eventually, the attendees collapsed to the grass, bowing and curtsying.

The moment they rose, our choreography began. The prince turned to Briar, lifted her free hand in his, and inclined his head. Amplifying his voice, Jeryn expelled two vital words. "Your Highness."

I wouldn't lie to myself. The barest contact between them set my teeth on edge. Not because I didn't trust my thorn. Rather because anyone who touched the princess risked losing their liver.

Nonetheless, the declaration accomplished what we'd expected. It became airborne, commanding everyone's attention and sending a buzz through the grove. Briar played her part, ducking her head as if she'd anticipated no less from her guest. Now that he'd accomplished the first task, she took the initiative and slipped her fingers from his.

Next, Jeryn nodded my way. "Court Jester."

Raising my eyebrow like a question mark, I mirrored the action. "Well met, Winter."

Outwardly, I performed. Inwardly, I restrained myself from decapitating him on the spot. In my periphery, the princess widened her eyes and gave me a private shake of the head, warning me to behave.

With our performance fully executed, Jeryn strode toward Avalea, his gait parting the crowd. Whilst they preoccupied themselves, observing Winter greet their queen at the banquet table, I tossed the princess an insubordinate wink.

She narrowed her eyes. *You fiend.*

My lips slanted into a grin. *You enabler.*

'Twas the princess's fault for bewitching her lover with that dress. If I'd wanted to rip Winter's paws from her, who could blame me?

As the night wore on, we promenaded, mingling with the nobles as we'd perfected before. With each passing hour between meal courses, the changes began. Courtiers eagerly welcomed us into their huddles, expressed relief for Briar's recovery, complimented my fucking outfit, inquired whether I would divert them with verse during the upcoming revels, and commended us on inviting Winter to the festivities.

As for Jeryn, courtiers and council members flew to his side like sheep whilst he circulated with Briar's mother. The residents fawned, welcomed the prince's monosyllabic responses, and endured his superior stare, if only marginally.

Seasons. If I'd thought Aire was brooding, the hard-boiled First Knight was a ray of sunshine compared to this lone wolf. The soldier might have a tedious moral compass that violated my usual standards of corruption. But at least I didn't have to deal with Aire randomly looting stomachs and extracting the vital organs of his troops.

And to be clear, I kept a severe watch on Jeryn. The second he rested a pinky on Briar's head, that pinky would be cleaved from his hand, along with the rest of his most valuable limbs. In addition to those protective instincts, my retinas scorched as Briar switched with Avalea and joined Winter to make a few obligatory rounds.

Elated to see their princess standing in solidarity with a fellow Royal, the residents beamed, flocked, raved, paid verbal tribute, and did everything short of licking the prince's balls and presenting him with a medal. Aye, the set of Briar's jaw told me she wasn't enjoying the proximity to Jeryn, would sooner stab her heel into his shin than get any closer. And the flat set of Winter's mouth illustrated his underlying abhorrence for her values, in addition to this charade.

And yet. Until now, it had been the pair of us dominating this court. Although our clan—Avalea, Aire, Eliot, Cadence, Posy, and Vale—worked the orchard just as well for this campaign, Briar and I had been inseparable during gatherings.

My one consolation came from seeing the people sing Briar's praises at last. Otherwise, envy pricked my spine like sweet thorns. Just as I despised the thought of anyone touching Briar, I also hated the thought of anyone deceiving, wooing, or conspiring with her.

That trickery was *our* game.

Several times, I reminded myself to acknowledge whichever closeted Autumn admirer was drooling at me. Numerous times, I dragged my gaze from Briar and Jeryn to whoever the hell was babbling. Thousands of times, I felt the electricity of her own stare.

By midnight, our eyes collided across the room. Briar's attention spanned my attire, her complexion ripening with a delightful pink hue. She sketched the painted dagger slashing through my left eye as if it were made of licorice, then licked her lips.

The visual mollified my killer instincts, replacing them with a bolt of heat straight to my cock. Then and there, we turned this farce into something more pleasurable, a teasing sort of dance. For if the woman could schmooze alongside a prince, I could retaliate.

And she could react. Thus, the pull intensified between us. It stretched from her end of the grove to mine like a tug-of-war.

We sought one another's attention by conversing with others and exaggerating those interactions. Like this, we engaged in yet another form of the forbidden. Until it became too much, prompting Briar to lower her lashes and fan them in my direction.

Unruly thoughts slinked into my mind. I let those thoughts ignite across my face, then seared my naughty gaze down her dress, openly flinging impure thoughts her way.

Briar's throat contorted. Her freckles stood out like bite-sized pieces of candy. Taking the hint, she excused herself from Winter and wove through the crowd. I watched her slip from the pear orchard like an innocent princess. And like a sinister jester, I gave the woman three fucking minutes before I followed her.

32

Briar

Never catch the Court Jester's attention. And never be alone with him.

That had been my rule eons ago. How often I had broken that rule, how eagerly I'd defied it at every opportunity, and how little I regretted giving in to the temptation. Rather, I chased that impulse, exiting the orchard and returning to the castle, knowing he pursued me.

I marked myself as his target, made myself vulnerable by strolling unattended. At this juncture, I had practice with evading my entourage. The jester had taught me this skill, and then I'd perfected it on my own. Like a well-educated, well-groomed, well-bred princess.

The hem of my gown slashed across the patterned runner, my heels muffled by the textile. Grazing my fingers along a mezzanine railing, I shuffled down a corridor.

Amber flames pulsated from the recesses. All the while, the weight of his shadow lingered behind me. Electric sparks tracked down my vertebrae, heat rippled up my thighs, and a hive of fireflies swarmed my stomach. It felt as though time had rewound itself to that fateful first night when he'd cornered me in a hall of mirrors, back in Spring. Only on this eventide, he wouldn't catch me off guard.

I had lured him on purpose. And that's how I led him to a trap.

While descending a square stairwell, I detected the light thud of his boots. Others would fail to register the sound, because he was just that good at hiding. But I knew. I recognized every noise he made, as if it was my own.

His steps were my steps. His movements were my movements. Like a cord. Like a fated bond.

Quickly, I peeked over my shoulder. The attempt yielded no silhouette, nor a single flash of his outline. Yet he might as well be inches behind me, the weight of his presence like silk unfurling down my spine.

Turning back around, I sank my teeth into my lower lip. This sort of chase had never grown tiresome. Each conflict we embroiled ourselves in only served to enhance the anticipation.

We had crossed many lines. But always, new forbidden ones cropped up for us to defy.

I guided him through the complex and into a subterranean level. At the landing, double doors loomed. An iron plaque of Autumn's coat of arms—bronze leaves, gilded stalks, intersecting axes, and a red fox—ornamented the facade.

Often, I had quested here with Father during our midnight romps in the castle. Poet knew of this place as well, though we'd never been here alone together.

Unlike most restricted areas in the fortress, this one lacked bolts, levers, or padlocks. Individuals without classified admission wouldn't know how to access it. For the rest of us, this threshold required a code.

From behind, I felt the weight of his eyes watching me. His stare brushed every inch of my exposed flesh like a kiss, particularly the nape of my neck, those invisible lips slicing a path along that delicate space. Already, the knave was trying to distract me.

An intricate brick motif extended between me and the doors.

I took the first step, the sole of my heel landing on the right brick, before progressing to the second. Forging ahead, I executed a complicated sequence of steps.

Several lefts and rights. Backwards and forwards. Side to side.

The correct pattern, in the correct order. One mistake would trigger a mechanism. Select the wrong brick, and it would collapse into the ground, then clamp around the intruder's ankle, shackling them while the alarm sounded.

I did not dwell on such worries but moved with confidence, traversing from one plank to the next. As I reached the final brick, the doors reeled open and disappeared into a set of wall slots. From there, I vanished into a treasure trove.

The relic vault spread itself as wide as a cavern, the air dense and permeated with the scents of dust, old vellum, and aged wood. It should have been dark here. Yet the pearlescent light radiating from a glass globe encasing Winter stardust lent visibility to the archives.

Shelves, cabinets, alcoves, and cubicles displayed curios, mementoes, heirlooms, artifacts, and keepsakes of Autumn's history, as well as antiquities from The Dark Seasons. From the pelt of an extinct breed of fox; to bronze feathered armor from ancient times; to Autumn's first illuminated manuscript, its pages scribed with the ink of pulverized gemstones and propped open on a miniature dais. Perhaps the rose Poet had given me would be stored here someday, for others to discover and muse about its significance.

One section housed the Royal jewels, including all the princess crowns, circlets, headbands, and tiaras I'd failed to destroy. Encased behind glass, they glittered like constellations and shimmered like suns. I traced my fingertips along the edge of a crystal leaf headband. It would be easy to destroy the rest of them, to hurl each object from the ramparts, as I had with my gold crown before I was banished.

My fingers curled inward, resisting the temptation.

Then my digits tripped, stalling as the doors slid shut, and boot soles echoed with feline grace through the vault. The rhythmic, predatory noise resounded from around the corner, the sound trickling down my flesh like warm syrup. I'd known he would make it inside without my assistance, before the entrance's timer lapsed. He'd already acquainted himself with this place, and his kinetic abilities rarely failed him.

Locked inside, he was mine now.

With my pulse accelerating, I strolled to the next aisle. My hands skimmed deadly blades of legends past, busts of fabled fauna, and mythical mirrors. Following in my wake, I heard his own fingers etching the items I'd touched. And as he drew nearer, his pursuit stoked the pleat between my thighs.

Cobwebs trembled from the ceiling. My breathing grew slender and shaky as I unclipped my necklace and discarded it on a shelf for him to find, then traipsed into another lane. His masculine chuckle rumbled through the vault, signaling he'd found my token.

I had never done something like this, divested my clothing in such a teasing fashion, purely to goad him. Yet he inspired me. Staggering as it proved to be, my lover awakened these impulses on a frequent basis, cracking them open like a porcelain shell.

It had been the uncivil way he looked at me in the orchard. Jealous. Covetous. Vicious. I'd sensed his reaction as he observed me beside Winter, and I had liked every one of my lover's possessive thoughts.

So why not bait him more? If we must partake in this performance, why not derive a thrill from it?

Next, I skirted into a niche of rolled maps and kicked off my heels. Then I snuck past a rack of priceless coronation robes. Plucking the front laces of my gown, I striped off the garment and hung it beside the collection. After that, the underskirt puddled into a basket.

Each panel of material produced a different husky noise from him. But it was the stockings and garter that unleashed the harshest growl.

I skulked behind a broad ring of tapestries depicting all four Seasons, the artworks surrounding a chaise lounge. By then, I felt winded. Oxygen fled my lungs, my pussy leaked with desire, and my pulse crashed against my chest.

The tapestries quivered. And he appeared.

The Court Jester stalked from the shadows, the back of his hand whipping aside one of the textiles. His tall, sculpted body filled the compact space, the muscles of his arm flexing as he braced the tapestry. His eyes glittered from behind a black mask with a long beak, which he must have collected from the pile of costumes dating back to ancient Reaper's Fests. Through the peek holes, his gaze poured green light into the vault, those irises the very color of envy and mischief.

Poet stood there, blocking my exit. The same way I'd lured him into a sealed room, he now had me cornered.

Yes. We had trapped each other.

That accounted for the upward slant of his mouth beneath the visor. Those illicit lips, loaded with shameless words, which he could unleash at any moment.

I braced myself. Then I changed my mind and stopped waiting.

"I've been expecting you," I confessed.

"Oh?" the jester inquired, still holding the tapestry aloft. "Based on your little breadcrumb trail, I might have thought you were anticipating a different visitor."

Because I knew who he meant, my lips curled. "Never."

"Really? If he weren't ice cold, I'd say the prince was rather hot."

"Yet he's not the person who tempts me. Only one man does that."

"Hmm. Lucky for him, he'll live to see another day. I'd hate to waste such a fetching garter on someone who looks like he's never peeled a scrap of fabric from a conquest's body in his life."

"Rest assured, you've tricked, ruined, and burned me for eternity."

"Such prose," the jester mused. "For your sake, it had better be fact instead of fiction."

The sultry warning oozed from him like liquid silk, imbuing me with power. This man, who could have anyone he wanted, who could verbally pick the lock off a chastity belt, and who took a person's virginity merely by speaking. This man could never be threatened by that monster. Yet even as we made this into a game, I detected a thread of spite in his words. Not because he distrusted me, but for another reason entirely, the notion wetting my undergarments.

I leaned casually against the wall. "Loyal jester. Are we feeling a bit territorial?"

"Cheeky heiress," he taunted back. "Are we feeling boastful?"

"Well, now that you mention it," I mustered. "It's dangerous to be left alone with a princess like me."

Officially prompted, the jester glimpsed my reduction in clothing. His attention scraped down my corset and drawers, the nexus of which had grown damp. Noticing this, his pupils swelled like bottomless pits.

Poet's fingers snapped open, releasing the tapestry, which flopped in place as he sauntered forward. His long legs ate up the distance. Looming over me brought the devil-black kohl lining his orbs into stark relief.

Despite the mask's beak, the jester's mouth was fully exposed and accessible. Therefore, he swept his lips over mine. "'Tis dangerous to be near you *anywhere*," my seducer corrected. "Whether alone or among thousands, be it in a cramped throne room or trapped in a vault—" one of his arms snatched around my waist and jerked me forward, "—you have me in your relentless grasp."

"That's because you're the only one I want." My lips shook against his and dared to bait, "So if you're feeling possessive, I cannot imagine why."

"Forgot how you affect me, is that it?" His arm tightened, fingers burrowing into my hip. "Allow me to remind you."

The room spun, objects and shadows whirling in my vision. In a flash motion, Poet wheeled me away from him, and my back slammed against his chest. I gasped, the maneuver knocking the air from my lungs. For an instant, I had overlooked how quickly and deftly this jester could move. And how creative he could be.

Sliding his digits around the front of my neck, Poet gently but firmly urged my head back, until my scalp pressed into his collarbone. He dipped his jaw, heady exhalations scalding the line of my throat as he spoke against it. "Don't move until I tell you to."

Anticipation shimmied up my inner thighs. Love, lust, and longing coalesced inside me. All three squeezed my heart, roused my blood, and struck the wet rift between my legs.

While facing the tapestries, I felt the first lap of his mouth. Those parted lips gusted heat onto my flesh, then skated along the rim of my throat. And I went limp. Sinking into him, I emitted a string of fluttery noises as Poet etched my skin, sketching me from my shoulder, to my nape, to my jaw.

Moaning, I reached back and hauled my fingers into his hair, bolting him to me. That mouth indulged, opening and seizing on the delicate crook of my neck. A yelp blasted from me as the jester sucked my skin into the hot well of his mouth, his tongue sweeping over me.

The closures of my corset loosened. While his mouth worked me into a frenzy and his fingers gripped my neck, his free hand had dipped to the bodice, the flaps coming undone and flaring open under those skilled digits. My breasts spilled from the gap, the garment hanging at my sides.

Poet hummed like a night prowler—a deviant, unseemly, prohibited figment of lore. Proper princesses did not fantasize about such beings. Proper princesses did not sweep their heads farther back, granting their seducers greater access to their pulse points. But I hadn't been proper for a long time.

And so I keened enthusiastically as he released my throat and thumbed my nipples with both hands. Circling the pads of his digits, the jester caused the tiny studs to pucker. His groan rippled along my shoulder, which he drew on harder, sucking and licking and tasting as if dominated by an indispensable craving.

His fingers pinched my nipples, darkening and stiffening them to his satisfaction. My moans broke through the vault, the sound rising in octaves. Any second, and I might dissolve into particles. It would not be the first time, nor the last. Every sensuous encounter with this man took me apart, then put me back together, so that I discovered a new piece of myself along the way.

A distant shaft of light illuminated the recess. In a restricted archive such as this, outfitted with props and a variety of surfaces, I could not expect this jester to remain idle.

With his mouth attached to my neck and his palms spanning my breasts, Poet walked us forward. We swayed to the chaise, where the tapestries encircled the seat like observers, as if the almighty Seasons were watching us. Though even if that were true, I would not care. The pressure of Poet's mouth and the wet heat of his tongue transported me, melting my inhibitions like wax.

I would make love with him anywhere. I would let him fuck me until the world faded into a vine of smoke.

Ushering me before the chaise, Poet unlatched his mouth from my throat. A sigh floated from me as the jester planted a soft kiss to the swollen area. His palms traveled from my nipples to the haphazard corset, his digits shedding the vestment from my shoulders.

At a concentrated pace, Poet stripped the bodice. The prolonged act seemed ceremonious, despite the urgency of our respirations. We panted through it, paying attention as he progressed to my drawers. I glimpsed his black fingernails while he bunched the sides of my soaked undergarments, then pushed them down my quivering thighs. The scanty material sagged to the floor, and I nudged them aside with my toe.

As Poet exposed me to his gaze, he dragged his hands over my flesh like a sculptor, charting the sensitive areas. The touches urged whimpers from me, the contact painfully erotic. At his disposal, molded by his fingers, he made me feel sexy and extraordinary.

Priceless. Precious.

Like something irreplaceable.

His turn. The need to see my jester, to see his carved body, like one of the statues encased in this vault, drew arousal from my slit. Between my thighs, the flanks of my pussy clenched.

My restless feet shuffled. The jester radiated heat behind me.

Don't move until I tell you to.

Before I could defy that request, Poet stalked around my body. Putting himself on display, the jester faced me from across the chaise, his mask and jawline piebald in the half-light. I relished the look darkening his irises, from impish clover green to the shade of a dark forest. A sinful wilderness, the depths of which could engulf a person. He stared as if I was an appetizing target and a danger to his self-control, his pupils reflecting my naked breasts, my straight hips, and my glistening cunt.

Forgot how you affect me, is that it? Allow me to remind you.

Then he did. With devastating slowness, Poet undid the clasps of his vest. Every cobbled muscle flexed as he divested himself of the article, the motions sinuous and teasing. The sight reminded me of how he danced.

I felt a blush warm my cheeks. The jester was stripping for me.

His toned pectorals contorted, the contours of his whipcord frame smooth and strong. My digits prickled. I wanted to touch him everywhere. But if I started, I might never stop, and I would keep him down here forever.

Poet held my gaze, his expression intent. One by one, he plucked at the cords of his pants. The low waistline slumped around his narrow hips, then buckled under his grip. The vent spread open, and his cock sprang from the gap, lifting flush against his abdomen.

It rose between the V, the column thick and the roof wide. From here, I glimpsed the slit of his crown, a thin delineation much darker than the rest of his length. His veins inflated, and the sac tucked under his cock weighty.

This was how I affected him. This was the result.

Seasons forgive me. I'd had that glorious appendage in my mouth, clutched between the folds of my core, and buried so deep in my pussy. Yet it was never enough.

The jester lowered his pants to the ground. Despite the close fit, the garment fell with little effort. I savored each rigid inch of his erection, the bulbous crown expanding under my gaze.

Scars from punching that mannequin today pockmarked his knuckles. He stood there, naked but for the scarlet ribbon and the black mask.

Quietly, he pointed a solitary finger toward the floor. I approached, waiting with bated breath as the jester prowled to his original position at my rear. My pulse skipped when he drew along my spinal column with the back of one fingernail.

"Lie down for me, princess," he murmured.

The instant I stepped forward, Poet guided me onto the chaise, where I sprawled sideways on the cushions. Lowering himself behind me and realigning his chest with my spine, he caught my hip and folded my buttocks into his turgid cock.

"Wonderful," he praised. "Now relax your thigh, my thorn."

Nervous excitement sizzled through my veins. I suspected this would not be a familiar position. And based on his husky timbre, it required a practiced partner with flexibility and stamina.

Despite my interest, I wavered in self-consciousness before letting his voice soak into me. Poet was an attentive lover who knew the extent of my abilities. He would not engage unless he believed I could ride his movements, unless he knew it would bring me pleasure. So I unfurled into his body, giving myself over.

Poet growled quietly. Hooking his arm around my thigh, he bent and raised my limb aloft, suspending it parallel to the rest of my body. Like this, he anchored me in place, with my knee steepled.

The arrangement splayed me wide, exhibiting every intimate inch of flesh. Over my shoulder, Poet glimpsed the swells of my pussy, the damp indentation between them, and the nib of my clitoris, which extended from a crisp patch of hair. Candidly, he saw me dripping for him.

"Such a lovely little cunt," he crooned. "I wager you feel as perfect as you look."

Heat flushed my cheeks, though not out of the shyness I would have felt eons ago. Instead, avid curiosity suffused my complexion. That, and pride. I liked him seeing me this way, simultaneously at his behest and empowered by his appetite. Although the jester sought to claim me, I could never feel more dominant than this. I had lost count of how often he made me feel this way.

It took a moment to relax into the position. When I did, a stag-

310

gering amount of fluid melted from my core.

Effortlessly, Poet tilted his body, enabling his cock to reach my entrance. The tip probed my cleft, his bare length poised to fill me, the gentle abrasion making my head swim. On a whine, I squirmed and arched my backside into his pelvis.

The stem broadened, rising high in the seat between us. And when I gyrated harder over the crown, air sliced between the jester's molars. At the sound, I envisioned his snaggletooth poking out like a knife.

"Now," he hissed. "Let's see if you can remember, shall we?"

I twisted a fraction, slicing my mouth along his strained jawline. "I remember every time you take me." My tongue licked his skin. "I remember every way you've fucked me." Then my lips dropped a sweet kiss beneath his hard chin. "I remember all the ways we've made love, all the things we've done to each other, every time you've corrupted me, and every way I've ruined you."

A growl rumbled from the solid expanse of his chest. "Then re-member this."

His buttocks swept forward, and the pome of his cock slid between my walls, stretching pussy so that it flared around him. My mouth gaped, a cry of surprise lodging in my throat. Only a few inches in, and the slant of his cock was already tipped in a way I'd never felt before.

Poet groaned, his body shuddering along with mine. He sloped his backside forward and broached another few inches, then deeper, and deeper, and—"Oh," I whimpered—deeper. The weight and width of his phallus drew my folds apart, coaxing me to spread far around him.

My pussy acclimated, dilating over Poet's cock, suctioning him into me. The jester moved his erection steadily, neither rough nor tender. He rowed into me with heady precision, attentive to my body's response, timing each pitch of his length with my gasps. In this way, he marked and serviced me.

Every thrust seemed to say, *Mine*.

Every moan seemed to confess, *Yours*.

With another beat of his hips, Poet's cock slung to the hilt. The firm heat of his flesh beat against a narrow point that wrung a host of brittle cries from me. My head flew backward and landed against his clavicles. I sensed him watching me, drinking in every crinkle of my brows, each quaver of my lips.

Never had I experienced him nocked inside me this way. With my right limb moored in the air, the angle created a new sort of friction, throwing bolts of pleasure through my limbs. Heavens, I felt it in my hip bones and behind my knees.

It should not be possible to join our bodies from this direction. It hardly seemed feasible, much less enjoyable. Yet this was Poet, who could bend himself into postures most humans failed to achieve.

Which justified why he was able to glide his cock back and shove delicately into me again. Another shaky moan frayed from my lungs. I bowed into Poet, the points of my nipples aching.

The abrasion was nothing short of stunning. My pussy gripped his cock from the crown to the base, wetting him anew. Seasons have pity, but I needed more. So much more.

The jester knew as much from how thoroughly I drenched him, how tightly my walls seized his cock. A purr of encouragement resounded from his tongue. "There's my resilient princess." His mouth hastened across my cheek. "All mine."

"Yours," I keened as he flexed his cock deeper, hitting that angle thoroughly.

My hand shot backward, grappling for the bracket of his shoulder. Fastening my fingers there, I braced myself for *longer*, *higher*, and *faster*. And as ever, Poet reacted.

His buttocks reeled, pumping his cock through my slot. My own frame rocked against his, riding every vault of his hips. Because he did not withdraw fully, the grinding sensation felt more compact, despite our position. It seemed like a different type of intimacy, prompting my private flesh to squeeze his cock deeper still.

Balling his free fingers with mine at the end of the chaise, he bolstered himself halfway off the cushions and watched. Like that, the jester hoisted his thick length into me, his lower half siphoning between my thighs and splitting them wider. Moans shook from my lungs, in tandem to his own growls, the noises unabashed.

With each agile swipe of his cock, cries dashed from my mouth, the cacophony growing in volume. My pussy contorted, grabbing his erection and soaking him to the brim. For a moment, Poet's forehead landed on my scalp, husky pants rushing against my nape, as if he was unable to endure it.

Yet he kept going, kept prodding me. The tilt of our bodies made everything new, the stimulation both aggravating and captivating.

The jester lifted his head and grunted, "Look down, sweeting." With a kiss at my temple, he added, "Watch how your pussy works my cock."

My eyes had briefly closed in rapture. But when they fluttered open, I glanced at my intimate folds sprawling and Poet's cock punting in and out. His length had darkened, the veins stood out, and a quick glimpse of his swollen crest abrading my clit mesmerized me. So this was how we looked together.

The exhilarating thought fired through my blood. Arousal puddled from my walls and poured freely over Poet, smearing his cock. I saw that too, how my desire glazed him and enhanced the width of his erection.

So hard and high. So bad for me.

My cries mounted, and I swiveled my backside into him. Our groins slammed together, my pussy thudding with his cock. A low roar tumbled from Poet's lips, resulting in a quicker pace.

"Mine," he demanded.

"Yours," I chanted.

Perspiration beaded down his torso and glazed the gulf between my breasts. His palm tacked my thigh higher, opening me to him. As my frame grew accustomed to the position, I moved with greater effect, bucking into my jester.

Everything felt so taut, so provocative, so wonderful. I chased after the stimulation. My whines pleaded for Poet to end it, to make it last, to take me with him.

On another hiss, the jester pulled his soaked cock from my body.

I sobbed in protest until he released my thigh, sat upright, and shifted across the cushions. Perpendicular to my legs, he scissored them apart once more. Balancing on his knees, Poet looped my right limb over his hip and pistoned into me again.

My sobs turned into wails. The inarticulate noises launched from my being and consumed the relic vault, the sounds echoing beyond the tapestries and surging down the remote aisles.

Oh, Seasons.

Oh. My. Seasons.

This had to be dangerous. Yet none of those cautions posed a threat to Poet's adaptable body, nor his ability to guide me. He tilted me just so and held fast, his sinuous cock plying me repeatedly. Using his knees for leverage, the jester hefted his hips into the split of my thighs, his torso clenching with effort.

My lips fell apart, a stream of moans and cries falling off my tongue. Slanted this way, my gaze consumed the view. My body, sideways and open. His body, balanced and whipping into me. And where I'd once judged such primal behavior as tawdry, I now felt only passionate consummation. He made every caress vital, every moan profound.

One moment, touching him was like touching a shadow—evasive, secretive, and forbidden. The next, it was like touching the sunlight— invigorating and teeming with life.

Whereas being touched *by* him was a collision of both. An explosion of darkness and lightness.

At last, my eyes landed on his and stayed there. As if helpless, the jester's shapely mouth hung ajar beneath the mask. Yet his dark brows slammed together, and his irises gleamed with purpose.

As we stared, his waist snapped, fucking me into the chaise. Slight but pleasurable stings accompanied the motion, but those quickly subsided. What was unfamiliar became second nature, the subtle twinges melting into elation. Each sharp pass of his cock shoved broken moans from me, pushing my tolerance closer to a precipice.

The sensations mounted, building in strength. Unable to stand the blissful agony, I sprinted into it like a famished princess, belting my hips with his.

On a howl, the jester accelerated his momentum. His muscles contracted, vibrating as if about to unleash, the bridge of his cock laboring so deeply into my pussy. "Mine," he groaned.

My core clamped onto him, spurred on by shocks of pleasure. I must have lost track of my voice, which presently engulfed the room. At some point, I'd started howling, "Yours."

We undulated over the chaise, its knotted wooden legs scraping the ground. Yet it didn't matter. Nothing else mattered but his body joined with mine, the force of his bellows, and the ribbons entwining our wrists, the scarlet cords relics of our own making.

The jester leaned down to snatch my hand, lacing our fingers once more atop the cushion. This spread me farther. Fleetingly, I glimpsed the profile of his buttocks as they lunged between my thighs. Fucking me sideways, with his cock aiming in this direction, Poet reached uncharted parts of me, the contact breathtaking. I felt how wet I'd become, my body spilling onto him, smothering his flesh.

Then my eyes sought his once more, clinging to his stare through the visor. Those infinite pupils glowed in the darkness, the green varnish of his irises engrossed in my features, hellbent on them. Merely from the sight, my clitoris tingled, and the muscles of my pussy constricted.

I writhed beneath him, and his spine hunched with effort, the vigor of his thrusts flinging me into the cushions. My cries increased in volume. They drowned the vault and then hardened into shouts, as if I were lost in the throes of a blasphemous act.

Heat and tension compressed between my walls. I whined, unspoken pleas vacating my lungs because I needed more, and wanted more, and fought for more. Yet however much I held back, Poet's skill made this impossible. And I knew enough about my body to recognize the signs of a climax.

The escalation. The temperature.

The devastation. The transcendence.

Yet I did not wish for it to be over. I would have begged for more, if I could utter a coherent word. Whenever I tried, only hoarse sounds flew from my lips.

The drenched clutch of my pussy told Poet how close I was to oblivion, and the broadening width of his cock signaled how near he was to the same nirvana.

My folds clung to his driving cock. They surged together, his pelvis and mine, colliding and agitating. Inside my walls, everything condensed and shook, the strain accumulating with every jut of the jester's waist. My blood simmered like the contents of a kettle, and so I gave in.

Like a wild princess, I charged forth with my jester. I pounded my hips with his until we were yelling. Down here, we could do this, disarm ourselves and lose our voices.

No one would hear us. No one would find us. No one would see us. Mine. Yours.

At length, Poet's lithe movements put me under a spell. The whisk of his hips unlocked my joints, urging me to let go, to give him leave. I unraveled into the chaise, helpless to resist, and let him ride my cunt.

Hissing in satisfaction, the jester set his entire frame into motion. He cast his hips between my thighs, his cock stroking my pussy with short, shallow jabs. I seized the nape of his neck and held on, my breasts jostling, my body unspooling along with my whines.

The crown of his erection struck a slender place that triggered every sexual corner of my being. My skin ignited, pressure coiled in my pussy, and my clit throbbed. Everywhere, I quivered.

My moans were punctuated by the rhythm of Poet's cock, and his groans matched the same tempo, so that we became one violent and continuous shout. Blackness swarmed my vision. Heat gushed from the slit of my thighs.

And I went up in flames. Euphoria blew through me like a storm, ripping me apart. Warmth burst from the pleat in my limbs, my pussy gripping Poet's thick cock. My spine curled inward, hunching toward the jester, the better to see his exquisite face slacken.

Seething, he lashed his body once more, twice more, then stalled. Watching me climax, Poet came with a rumbling bellow that tore through the vault. His waist shuddered, spurts of fluid draining from him and filling me.

Molten heat poured from us, his cock encased in my folds, both rippling with pleasure. All the while, our moans tangled, long and loud. And as the lingering orgasms vibrated through us, our damp chests slammed together, his pulse thrumming with my own.

It took considerable time for our hips to stop rowing, for the aftershocks to ebb. Wheezing, we waited for the palpitations to slow, his distended cock still primed inside me.

Slumping into the cushions, Poet gently detached my leg from over his hip. He planted a breathless kiss to my knee, then nipped the flesh until I gasped, before trailing more kisses up the side of my body. When he reached my lips, we grazed them over one another, the movement tender yet firm.

That was us. Precious but durable and lasting, like the emblems in this vault, like history itself.

Poet ripped off the mask and stared at me, his gaze equally covetous and vulnerable. He opened his mouth to speak, but nothing came out.

From my jester, nothing came out.

Yet I sensed what he longed to say, and what he hoped to hear in return. Smiling, I cradled his face close to mine, and I whispered, "Mine."

And his fiendish lips tilted into a grin. "Yours."

33

Briar

"Y ou look like you've been fucked within an inch of your life,"
Cadence remarked with a sideways smirk while ransacking
my lingerie drawer.

Meanwhile, Vale plucked a pair of lace-up heels from my shoe
recess and perched on a bench. She tucked her feet into them, the
oyster white contrasting beautifully with her dark skin. "Moot point,"
she commented. "Briar always looks like that."

"But more so these days," Posy said while shimmying into a chenille gown imported from her own closet. "Sex in a confidential
setting will do that, especially if it's with a jester who knows how to
contort his body in as many ways as Poet."

They did not know the half of it. The number of angles in which
Poet had bent, arched, and twisted me in the relic vault lingered in
my mind like a recurring fantasy. I might have been smiling openly
to myself without realizing it, although I'd remained willfully quiet
on the matter.

But now I wheeled from the rack of event attire that my seamstress
had delivered. "How on earth did you know—," I queried, then re-

membered which Season I was dealing with.

"Never mind," I relented.

"Where was it this time?" Cadence interrogated, still sifting through undergarments ranging from ribbed corsets to lace drawers. "Above ground, middle ground, or below ground?"

"Meaning location," Vale quipped. "Not position."

"We'll get to the latter afterward," Posy assured me.

A masculine throat cleared from the doorway. "Please tell me you're talking about military strategy."

We swiveled toward Eliot, who leaned his bulky shoulder against the jamb. A fitted, dark gray doublet accented the muscles of his body, with a deep fluted V collar that framed the lute tattoo stretching up his neck. The jacket blended with his pewter gray pants and corresponding boots, and his instrument case rested against his back.

As debonair as the ensemble was, it proved no match against the comically agonized expression on his face and the flush consuming his features. By no means was Eliot a chaste being. But from the looks of it, my oblivious best friend had waltzed in sometime between *fucked within an inch of my life* and *below ground*.

The ladies bunched their lips together, clogging what I only imagined was a year's worth of guffaws. Mortified, I opened my mouth to apologize.

Instead, Eliot shook his head, pushed himself off the jamb, and dropped onto an ottoman. "As much as I prefer to know everything about Briar, you three have taught me there's a limit. Spring origins aside, leave the positions, locations, and durations for my absence."

"Then get out," Cadence retorted, only half joking.

Posy and Vale snorted. "Sorry," Posy muttered between laughter.

"She did not mean that," I stressed.

"Oh, I bet she did," Eliot said, tossing Cadence a mock glare. "Just because I lived incognito with you in the forest, and we subsisted on a diet of gruel and baked raccoon, and I've seen you traipsing around in moth-eaten lingerie, it doesn't mean you have dibs on my princess."

Posy and Vale wheeled toward Cadence. "You didn't," Posy insisted in sympathetic horror, glancing from their friend to Eliot and me. "Baked raccoon? Moth-eaten lingerie?"

"He is a minstrel," I bantered. "He's used to exaggerating."

"Whatever," Cadence said to Eliot, resuming her audit of my lingerie. "If you're going to stay, make yourself useful and play some music."

The minstrel rolled his eyes and set the instrument on the ground beside him. "I'll play once you've earned the privilege. Until then, you're not entitled to shit, milady." His mouth twisted. "If you don't mind me saying so."

Cadence feigned a glower, then nodded. "Good. At least you know how to keep up with me."

Their spirited bickering and wisecracks had not ceased since our return. Whereas Eliot and I considered ourselves long-lost siblings, the minstrel and lady verbally roughhoused like loyal but antagonistic cousins.

I fisted my hands on my waist and pruned my mouth at Cadence, who'd been reviewing every private article I owned from the moment she'd joined us. "Under no circumstances are you permitted to borrow any of those."

"Relax," she dismissed, flapping her hand my way as if to shush me. "I'm not looking for myself. My expectations were low, but thankfully your stash isn't half as disappointing as I'd expected."

"In other words, she's impressed," Posy translated.

Well, I was not flattered. What exactly had she anticipated? Autumn typically donned knee and ankle-length bloomers beneath their clothes, the styles modest as well as practical for this climate. However, that did not mean those were the only cuts we wore. Not least of all, I was intimately attached with the most provocative man on the continent, who'd contributed to the contents of my wardrobe.

On that note, if they only knew that Poet had done more than merely dress me in this wardrobe, shortly after he'd fondled the same undergarments currently at Cadence's disposal. If I told them that, they'd make me repeat the story every time they strolled in here.

Cadence whistled, fluffing out a skimpy pair of sheer briefs. "Now this is what I call a power choice." With approval, she pitched the item toward me.

In reflex, I caught the fabric and huffed out an exasperated breath. Nonetheless, my frown melted despite myself, and Cadence grinned conspiratorially.

I should have been offended by her indiscretion. Less than a year ago, I would have been. Yet after everything that had happened, from the Peace Talks to our isolation in The Lost Treehouses, we had changed. She'd witnessed me depleted on forest floor, just after I'd scraped my nails through the earth, searching for my lost ribbon bracelet.

With Eliot, we had braved the wilderness and spent months in solitude, learning to survive outside the confines of a castle. And although the woman had acclimated back to her routine amid the court, we often found ourselves trading silent glances such as this. Together and with my best friend, the three of us remembered that brief spell, when we ceased to be Royal, lady, and minstrel.

Even before then, each member of this clan had seen me treated with scorn during the Lark's Night carnival. They'd beheld me covered in blood during the courtyard carnage against the Masters and were present for my political collapse. I had very little to hide from them now.

So no. I did not mind Cadence inspecting my daintiest clothes. Particularly not after she'd made the subtext of her intentions clear.

Now this is what I call a power choice.

Accurate, to be sure. From the first layer to the last, I would need the best armor for tonight. This evening marked the first celebration preluding Reaper's Fest. Because Poet had a hand in arranging the festivities, he'd departed early to prepare, leaving the task of my outfit to me and the ladies.

"Dazzle me," he'd instructed before sauntering from my suite.

I nibbled on my lower lip. For a start, the sheer briefs would do.

And in that regard, Eliot's presence made no difference. Having grown up together, we'd seen one another stripped to the barest essentials several times before, during afternoons when we tried on various Spring costumes in private. Until Poet, my best friend had always been my one exception to every rule. Understandably, Eliot wasn't interested in the specifics of my relations with the jester, but concealing my undergarments was no more necessary than in the company of these ladies.

Case in point, Posy wasn't completely dressed yet because the conversation had distracted her. At length, the lady wiggled the chenille gown up her frame. The exquisite design hugged her curvy body, accentuating the lady's hips to an enviable degree, and the chandelier poured light onto the floral tattoo germinating across her collarbone.

Kicking off the heels, Vale sashayed to her lover and fastened the neckline to Posy's nape. In the floor-to-ceiling mirror's reflection, Vale winked, and Posy blushed.

In tandem, their eyes swung to my reflection. "I suppose with Eliot's restrictions, we're not getting an answer to my original question?" Posy nudged. "Not even a peep?"

"No, you will not," I confirmed.

"Not sorry," Eliot replied, holding up his palms innocently.

"And for that, you're going to hell," Cadence ribbed.

Often, these ladies attempted to pry the wanton details from me. Most times, they failed. Yet occasionally, I acquiesced, wanting their feedback and companionship on matters of intimacy. Despite their teasing nature, I trusted them.

For Eliot's part, he had long since recovered from his heartbreak over Poet. In The Lost Treehouses, my friend had reassured me of that. Therefore, I didn't fret that his reactions were related to unrequited love. He was elated for me and Poet, and he wanted us to be happy.

Still, I would not make an exhibition of the situation. Most importantly, remembering the other night in the relic vault, I felt protective of that episode. Poet and I had just negotiated with Winter and staged our first appearance as a unit. Never had I interacted with the court while escorted by another man, and I hadn't liked the feeling, nor what it did to Poet. However experienced the jester was in deception, I had seen beyond the veneer, as he'd seen beyond mine.

The relic vault had been our moment, and ours alone. I would not share the memory of that night with anyone. Just as I would not share the memories of Poet and me in the storm at the treehouse enclave, nor the way his tongue had consoled me in the shower after my allergy poisoning. Nor any of our pivotal sexual interludes since I reentered this castle, for that matter.

But I would hint. "We needed a respite."

My friends sobered, reading into my words. They may have already gauged how the welcome feast for Winter had affected me and the jester.

Silence infested the wardrobe, with half of us dressed and the other half not there yet. Posy and Eliot were ready for tonight, but Vale had only made it to an underskirt and bandeau, Cadence sported a chemise, and I hadn't yet removed my dressing robe.

"Fuck," Eliot muttered. "Can someone please make a joke? Or at least a comment about the weather? We need a distraction."

"I have a better idea," Cadence replied. "How about we get our shit together and dress this princess to kill."

"Sounds like a plan," my friend said quietly. "A few ballads should relax the crowd, especially if it includes relevant Autumn history about a brief but pertinent era when the Seasons defined humanity differently."

I nodded. "Good thinking."

"Vale and I will take the upper nobles tonight," Posy volunteered. "They need a little charm."

"We'll talk up you and Poet," Vale expanded. "Commend you for winning over the prince."

"I've got the council," Cadence said while shrugging into a skin-tight strapless gown dyed in ruby. "After the fourth chalice, they'll be eating out of my Spring hand and agreeing with me on how marvelously you've held up since your return."

"If your goal is to woo the council, I'd suggest you don a turtleneck instead," Eliot gibed.

Posy took the advice in earnest, her features stricken as she raised her hand. "For the record, I will never be doing that."

We laughed. After a moment, Cadence sighed. "Too bad Jeryn of Winter eats from the same pig trough as Summer. No asshole should look that hot, much less wear a crown." She twisted her gaze toward me. "We stand by the one who earns it."

Posy and Vale nodded. Eliot's features reflected loyalty as he gazed at me.

On impulse, I strode toward a cabinet displaying my everyday jewels. Remembering Cadence's words during our journey to The Lost Treehouses, I fished out the belt she'd admired when I was in Spring. The lady gave a start as I strapped the belt around her middle and buckled the clasps, the ruby leaves sparkling around her waist and complimenting her dress to perfection.

"Thank you," I whispered.

Cadence faltered, at a loss for how to respond. By way of gratitude, she finally said, "I wasn't serious."

My lips slanted. "Yes, you were."

It was the least I could do. I had sworn I would repay her and Eliot, and while I planned to do better than a mere bauble when this was over, I hoped the accessory would suffice for now.

Slowly and sheepishly, Cadence traced the priceless belt. Then she curtsied. And when she rose, the lady batted the hair from her face and scoffed. "Okay, so what the fuck are we waiting for? Let's make our princess look as beautiful as a weapon." She beamed wolfishly. "And let's make sure it's something the jester has never seen you in."

With that, my friends sprang into action. I chuckled as each occupant rushed to the alcoves and hunted through the options.

34

Poet

Libraries were the last places that Spring would think to throw a soiree. Yet sauntering into the Autumn's repository that evening, the Season proved me wrong. In a matter of hours, the library wing had transformed from a studious and orderly place to a dark cavern of mysteries and folklore.

Amid five boxy levels of wainscoting and mezzanines, built-in shelves glinted with natural orange light from leaves that had been strung together, the garlands woven among leather and cloth-bound volumes. Some of the glowing cords cascaded from the railings and bookcase trimmings. Between exposed beams, bronze chandeliers pulsated with garnet-dyed candles, and more tapers pumped additional light from candelabras.

Chrysanthemum arrangements decorated the communal desks and reading tables, most of which were occupied by nobles deep in conversation whilst they sipped from chalices and goblets. Other guests sat in wing chairs, with tartan blankets draped over their laps and pedestal tables nestled between them. Each surface bore a study lamp that illuminated their faces from below.

I'd helped plan tonight's revelry, the first event preceding Reaper's Fest. Yet my task hadn't involved aesthetics. Rather, mine had been a matter of plotting out the diversions with Eliot, which hadn't taken long. The minstrel knew on his own how to captivate a room.

After that, he'd gone to Briar's suite, and I'd left to bid Nicu good-night. Unlike the rest of Reaper's Fest, this event started too late for children to attend.

Knowing Briar would tuck in my son once she was dressed, I had read Nicu a few pages of verse, then departed to change at the last minute. I may have sulked at having only a half hour to achieve perfection, but Nicu was my greatest exception to the rules of fashion. Gladly, I had surrendered any bonus grooming hours in favor of more time with my little fae.

Compared to Spring's glitzy, marbled extravaganzas, the library gleamed with a hushed sort of luminescence. Everything about this celebration screamed of Briar.

Though some of the revelers mingled throughout the aisles, most courtiers gathered in the main quarter. Pointed arch windows lined the sprawling room, and the mouth of a nine-foot-tall fireplace roared from the east wall.

Although Spring reigned when it came to artistry, every Season possessed musicians. Situated before the blaze, a cellist strummed her instrument, the sound rich and heavy as it carried along the bookshelves.

A considerable number of heads veered my way as I entered, numerous eyes dipping up and down my form. A few balked at the studded leather pants and long brown paisley jacket with its rolled-up sleeves, whilst admirers overlooked those infractions and favored instead the smoky eyes, fingerless gloves, and exceedingly low neckline.

Aire stood guard at the far end, opposite the fireplace, and tolerated a flock of women and men who couldn't resist vying for his attention. Cadence had lured a few council members into conversation. Posy and Vale accomplished the same with a clique of nobles near the history stacks, and Eliot's renown as a musician seemed to be luring another crowd. Our friends did their utmost, promoting their jester and princess.

The rest fastened their gazes on me. I stalked past the courtiers who ducked their heads and uttered "Master Jester" without a shred of hesitancy. Picking my battles, I forgave the odious title of Master since it appeared our ruse with Winter was working. At least enough for my observers to regard me with more than repentant lust, intimidated resentment, or bitter speculation. Now they addressed me willingly.

Still, my gaze burned past them, knowing she was already here. The princess would never arrive late to a library, especially on this evening. Prowling past the desks, I disappeared into the candlelit aisles, aware of which route to take. My boots thudded against the floor, my mouth tilted when I reached the botany section, and I caught a whiff of her scent. Notes of tart apples and parchment wafted from the narrow lane, with books crammed along the shelves.

When I found her, my damn breath caught. Briar was waiting for me, poised between the tomes, with her manicured fingers clasped. A medallion-colored, off-shoulder dress accentuated her slender clavicles, long fitted sleeves ended in points at her wrists, and a wide skirt flared from her hips. Whilst the revelers had shackled their tresses in netted headdresses, escoffions, crespines, hennins, veils, and gabled hoods, Briar's red hair hung loose, embellished only with a jeweled headband and that single, dangling leaf-strewn braid.

A curse cut across my tongue before I had the presence of mind to muffle it. If we were alone, I would spoil this woman rotten with all manner of vulgarities and obscenities.

But fuck. She had no business looking that proper, in this very proper place, and still managing to drain me of intellect. I could pin her to these bookcases, flip up the gown's skirt, and cover her mouth. Together, we could make the shelves quake until the whole wing crumbled.

Briar flushed, interpreting her jester's wily thoughts. As she glimpsed my unadorned chest peeking beneath the jacket, I stalked up to her. Matching the princess's pose and draping my shoulder against the books, I tipped my head down. "Soooo," I purred. "Are you thinking about the last time we christened a bookshelf?"

Spring's archive library. My words and the fantasy I'd murmured in her ears. Briar's hands tucked under her skirt, her sharp little fingers plying her cunt to the sound of my voice.

Her complexion deepened like a ripe piece of fruit. "No," she confided. "I'm thinking about when the next time will be."

Bloody hellish fuck. My cock responded to that. "Alas. 'Tis unfair of you to admit that during a formal event. I might cause some trouble for you."

"You already have." To illustrate her point, Briar indicated my outfit, cognizant by now of how frequently we tried to outseduce the other. "I see you're aiming to compete with me tonight."

"Just tonight?"

Her mouth twitched like cursive, the halfway point to a glorious smile. "You will not win."

"Splendid. I like losing against you. It means I'll have to forfeit something."

That almost-smile widened, shy but scolding. "We should not flirt in present company."

"You're right. How sacrilegious of us. Blame yourself for wearing that color." I cornered the princess, my shadow touching hers, and whispered, "I could suck on you like a butterscotch."

A miserable expression scrunched her features, as if I was tormenting her. Briar groaned hopelessly. "I should not have let my ladies and Eliot choose this gown," she muttered. "I should have opted for the taupe one."

I scoffed. "A drab and penitent shade—the way brown would look if it had the flu."

"You've given it abundant thought, I see."

Instead of confirming that, I grinned. "But when I said I'd suck on you like a butterscotch, who said I was talking about the gown?"

Her chest hitched as she registered which part of her body I'd been fetishizing. It would be easy to kneel for my sovereign, slither under the gown, and wrap my lips around her pert clit, tasting it like a delicacy.

Because Briar failed to speak, I pushed that button. "Are you wet under that confection? Thinking about how steeply I bent you the other night?"

The princess's throat reddened. "I cannot stop thinking about it." Yet promptly, her straight brows smacked together. "But we must concentrate."

For if we didn't, we wouldn't be able to work our magic among the court, despite the presence of Winter.

After a painstaking moment in which my cock suffered, I backed off. Still, the magnetic pull tightened. We stared, silent and still and so very fucking tempted.

Commotion from near the fireplace broke the spell. Taking Briar's hand, we hastened from the aisle and spilled back into reality, in which Winter appeared with Avalea. Every figure genuflected to the Royals, with Briar's mother pasting a genial expression on her face and Jeryn doing nothing of the sort.

Unfazed, Winter merely watched Autumn pay heed, having expected no less. After making the required entrance, the queen separated herself from the prince, nodding to me and Briar whilst heading to her seat.

For his part, Jeryn located us quickly, his attention slashing our way and resulting in a grimace. Resigned, he strode toward us. Lead gray knit layers stretched across his torso, and he'd leashed that dark blue mane into a ponytail. The same vial hung from his throat—albeit now empty of fluid and its exterior cracked—the tips of his boots flashed like spikes, and the blue lines beneath his eyes appeared darker tonight.

By the time he reached us, all eyes had cemented on our trio. Based on that, plus how the courtiers had greeted me earlier, news was indeed making the rounds fast. By now, the details will have reached the outlying villages of Autumn.

I pursed my lips, appraising Jeryn's garb. "Three out of five."

He frowned, sufficiently baited. "Three out of five what?"

"Private joke," Briar atoned whilst covertly elbowing me in the ribs. "Shall we take our seats?"

By way of an actual answer, the prince refrained from rolling his eyes and strode toward the wing chairs reserved for Royals. Every social interaction required a clever balance. Thus, I'd curated the entertainment but wouldn't take part in it. Too much of a good thing, and Autumn would feel smothered.

Similarly as Briar's lover, we didn't hide our bond. Yet nor did we flaunt it, however tormenting the consequences.

On that note, I stole Briar's hand and brushed my lips across her knuckles. She gasped as my tongue poked out for a naughty lick. Winking, I turned and sidled to the opposite side of the room, where I sprawled myself lazily across the wingback chair nearest to the three ladies, each of whom had observed the scene with relish.

For the performance, we had agreed for Briar to sit with her mother and the prince. Recovering from the aftermath of my tongue, Briar followed Jeryn to their seats, where the queen waited with tense shoulders beneath a plum ribbed gown.

A raised level had been erected, opulently carpeted and garnished in maple leaves for the Royals. Winter joined Her Majesty on the first landing. The princess situated herself behind them on the upper level, the arrangement similar to an elegant theater box.

As Briar sank into her chair, Avalea cast the princess a meaningful glance over one shoulder, eternally checking on her daughter's wellbeing. Silent communication drifted between them until the queen relaxed and touched Briar's knee. In kind, the princess reached down to squeeze their fingers briefly, in a gesture of reassurance.

Cadence, Posy, and Vale entangled themselves across their chairs. Aire repositioned himself near the Royals, then rested his back against one of the bookcases. Though his grip was nailed to the hilts of his broadswords, a wistful expression eased his surly features.

Per tradition, the first revel before Reaper's Fest involved public readings, with each recitation accompanied by music. I lounged in my chair, my eyes tacked with Briar's from across the library. As the candles were snuffed, the hall darkened like an amphitheater. Even so, we never turned away from one another, my gaze heavy on hers, a fitful current passing from Briar's end of the repository to mine.

Before the fireplace, a dozen nobles took turns narrating from historical accounts, ancient journals, folktales, fables, and myths. Eventually, Briar forced herself to concentrate. Her head swerved toward the readers, and her profile alighted, rapt by the performances.

Yet I watched her. Always, I watched her.

Whatever the fuck the prince was doing, I had no clue until stealing a glance. The man barely concealed his distaste beneath that veneer. Autumn invested itself in scholarship and factual texts as much as Winter did, but Jeryn's kingdom had no appetite for fiction or verse beyond research. That was the only reason the avians I'd dispatched had eventually located the final book in Briar's favorite series; the installment had been gathering dust in one of Winter's universities.

The prince lounged in his chair with one elbow propped on the armrest. The ankle of his boot rested on the opposite knee, and yet my gaze seized on a few notable details. Winter rubbed his fingers against his mouth, then scraped those digits into the hairline above his ear before emitting a heavy breath. Huh. Scarcely a display but it was there. For such a static disposition, some unknown preoccupation made him restless. I tapered my eyes, surveying his body language but failing to detect the source.

With Jeryn's mind drawn elsewhere and Avalea focused on the readings, agitation crawled up my limbs. I should have known my patience would wane. Like an addict, I paced myself until the right moment.

Courtiers applauded, then burst into a flurry of whispers as Eliot materialized, extracting himself from the cluster of narrators on the sidelines. Naturally, he'd generated his own fans across the continent. People had heard of him even before he came here, his voice and ballads renowned.

Now the court was able to put a face to the celebrity, further sweetening that dish. With his stubbled features, athletic physique, golden hair snared into a bun at his nape, and the lute tattoo blazing beneath the neckline of his knit pullover, the man could charm a cement wall. Indeed, Eliot's charisma walked the line between boyish and virile, cherubic and strapping, his good looks less intimidating or cautionary than Yours Truly. And like a good trickster, he'd learned in the past few months how to wield those attributes.

The roaring fire darkened Eliot's silhouette, yet I caught him wink conspiratorially at Briar. Hooking the lute to his chest, the minstrel's fingers swept over the strings. A current of music lifted from the instrument, the melody sailing through the library. Eliot's digits dove, swayed, and plucked, sending a ripple effect through the audience.

All of this before he'd even opened his mouth. But when he did, I swore every figure leaned forward, lapping up the honey of his tenor. That, and the words. Eliot and I had picked a verse for him to recite, then discerned the notes he needed to hit. And being of Spring, he sang the passages instead of simply reading them.

For once, I was fine not being the center of attention. As the minstrel's lute and voice drew everyone's gaze, I got sneaky. Easing from my chair, I skulked toward the fringes and passed the bookcases, taking the long way around to Briar's side of the room.

She beamed at Eliot, her lovely features engrossed in his tenor and the story. Because the princess sat alone, out of eyeshot from her mother and the prince, I cleared the distance without detection. Snatching a stool from a random corner, I ascended the platform, then set the stool beside her wing chair, making sure to install myself a few inches behind it.

Briar inhaled sharply. The flesh across her shoulders pebbled.

My lips twisted. I didn't need to speak. She knew me well enough.

Quickly, her frame relaxed into the chair. She kept her head averted, yet her voice came out faint and reverent. "You chose my book."

I had. However controversial to these people, the final book in her series included contents that proved necessary to share with the court. Eliot and I had compiled the main passages, then the minstrel did the rest.

Briar's fragrance drugged my senses, and although mischief and desire had glamoured me here, now I just wanted to be near her. Look at her. Soak in her essence. For a moment, I wanted to pretend we had nothing else to contemplate but the music, the tale, and its meaning.

When I didn't speak, *couldn't* speak, Briar whispered, "And you know the language."

Aye. That was another facet we'd added to the performance. For Eliot sang in the ancient tongue of our continent—as lilting as the wind, as fluid as water, as deep as the earth, and as encompassing as fire. Though a dying art, Autumn and Winter were the only Seasons that still embraced the language, the former for its traditional value, the latter for academic purposes.

Few in Spring spoke the archaic tongue. And whilst Briar wasn't surprised about Eliot's linguistic fluency, she hadn't known about my aptitude.

I lingered behind her, distant enough to avoid detection but close enough to rasp against the shell of her ear. As Eliot sang, I translated the words. *"Hear, my love, the tale of how we began."*

A gentle smile graced her lips. *"Long ago,"* she translated back, *"thousands of sunsets and sunrises before."*

The book started with our continent's history. Centuries ago, four seeds sprouted into being, from vast distances apart and containing the souls of four deities. One blossomed into a land of wild flora, another into islands and oceans, another into forests bursting with color, and another into a frosted landscape of alpine mountains. So these almighty souls named themselves Spring, Summer, Autumn, and Winter.

The Seasons.

From these stems, shorelines, roots, and flurries sprang new life, from humans to faeries, giants, satyrs, nymphs, merfolk, and countless other beings. The Seasons united them until a hostile age approached, when every culture—apart from humans—waged a battle for dominance. It showed the darkness and lightness of our very nature. Lightness was our creation, but darkness was our lesson. And so we became The Dark Seasons.

As the one group who remained neutral, humans survived the carnage after the rest had faded or killed themselves off. Our population grew, establishing courts and kingdoms. Traditions, cultures, and societies expanded. Spring became a nation of artistry and sexuality, Summer of ambition and shrewdness, Autumn of introspection and craftsmanship, and Winter of ingenuity and intelligence. These became our cornerstones, placing value on the mind above all else. A lack of control and sound judgment had destroyed our former neighbors, and we vowed not to make the same mistake.

Back then, no one was excluded or condemned. According to history, that changed when an unknown figure began to promote vitriol toward those who didn't hold up to this arbitrary standard. Alas, this person coined the phrase "born fool." And here was the fucking ignorant lapse. The so-called born—the alleged "mad" and "simpleton"—were deemed abominations, errors of nature whose souls didn't comply with the Seasons' cultural canon.

Burdens. Misfits. Dangers.

The uncontrollable and incomprehensible. Those who disrupted the presumed order of things.

The Almighty Seasons brought us nature, with all its beauty and horror, its growth and destruction. Yet our world believed natural disasters such as floods and avalanches were a necessary balance created by the Seasons. Humans couldn't control that.

But a supposed "abomination" in the form of an innocent person? Our ancestors had presumed it was essential to either correct this—without musing whether it even needed correcting—or find a way to benefit. The ancients felt it was their duty and right, just as they preserved the earth, all on nature's behalf.

Ridicule. Enslavement. Suffering.

That was how it began. Through speeches, writings, and oral tales infested with propaganda, this belief grew like a virus. It traveled across the continent and made its way into every household and scribed text.

That was how the first book in Briar's series started. Using this historical account as a backdrop, an unknown author had turned the timeline of events into fiction, a story about a rebellious queen. Only one copy of the collection existed. Few had heard of it until tonight.

Once, there was a Royal who reigned during that ancient time, a woman who embodied the description of a born soul. She suffered from constant panic and fear, yet she hid it well. But ultimately, the kingdom discovered the queen's condition, realizing she wasn't who they expected her to be. Rejected by her people, she lived in isolation among the trees, forging it into her own wild castle.

"From the sacred wild, she will reign."

"In the hidden trees, is her domain."

As Eliot sang those words, courtiers stirred in their seats. Yet they didn't rage or squint in displeasure. His tenor and the verse wouldn't allow it, both of which captivated them.

Briar leaned in closer to me. *"Lo, she fell to ruin. Then she fell in love."*

In a gruff tone, I translated, *"With a commoner."*

"Who saw in her strength, courage, and valor."

"Who saw naught but such loveliness," I murmured. *"Beyond words."*

"Beyond class."

"Beyond courts."

"Beyond cultures."

Briar's head twisted slightly in my direction, her hair burnished in lambent strands of red and gold, like Autumn leaves. *"She wonders if her lover is real or a figment, too divine to resist."*

I scooted forward, my mouth rushing across her ear. *"He fears this queen will bring him heartbreak, too high above his station."*

She shivered. *"Her fantasy."*

I swallowed. *"His dream."*

Briar squeezed the arm of her chair. *"Yet this forbidden love gave her the fortitude to persevere,"* she confided. *"And win back her throne."*

Because everyone had the capacity to love, no matter who they were. Everyone was made of lightness and darkness. Everyone was a sunset and a storm. The state of the queen's mind didn't diminish her humanity. Her pulse beat at the same rhythm, her heart pumped the same blood, and her soul desired the same inevitable things.

Our quiet voices drifted toward each other, stroking and caressing like a touch. Whilst the words transcended into lyrical dialogue between the queen and her lover, Briar's candlelit features twisted my way, her sterling gaze claiming mine.

Her, entranced by my features. Me, caught in the grip of her stare.

"Walk with me, my temptation," she uttered.

"Dance with me, my damnation," I husked.

"Sing with me, my beloved one."

"Live with me, my equal one."

"Let the world see, my only one."

"As we become eternity."

Her ardent expression swept over mine, the impact like a stake through the heart. I raked my own gaze across her visage, counting the freckles, worshiping the sharpness of her chin, transfixed by the slight bump in the bridge of her nose, soaking in the lush pink of her lips. And every pivotal emotion I'd ever felt combusted.

Fear. Pain. Sorrow.

Bliss. Hope. Joy.

Fury. Passion.

Love.

My chest jolted from the impact, as though she hurled those same emotions back at me.

There was my lightness and darkness. There was my sunset and my storm.

Heat swirled up my throat, and speech abandoned me, my tongue useless. For no words could do this moment justice.

Right then, she owned my pulse, my blood, and my breath. We stared and stared and fucking stared. I couldn't have looked away if the castle had crumbled to the ground.

Firelight blasted through the library, shattering the spell. We blinked, our gazes tearing apart as the room fell silent, all eyes on us.

Eliot stood motionless with his lute, gazing our way in wonder and pride. The ladies simpered, silently gushing as if they were about to collapse in a romantic fit. Over her shoulder, Avalea's wistful expression lingered on me and Briar. And Jeryn frowned, dubious and unnerved by whatever he saw between us.

How long ago had Eliot quit playing? When had the courtiers stopped applauding?

At some point, they must have heard Briar and me whispering, translating the story. They had witnessed our trance. And whilst we'd agreed not to flaunt our bond, it became abundantly clear. The harder this rule became, the more people saw through us. In the dim lighting, amidst a riveting performance, we hadn't held back a fucking thing.

Briar straightened, red flags of color surging across her cheeks. It took me longer to recover from the daze, too long for me to muster a clever remark and distract the room.

So the ladies did it for us. They sprang to their feet, clapped their hands, and whistled at Eliot. And whilst the display was more Spring than Autumn, it worked. The audience broke from their stupor and applauded the minstrel, who bowed and did his best to keep the attention off us.

During the cacophony, Aire appeared beside the dais. Bending forward, he muttered to me and Briar, "A hawk landed at the gate with urgent tidings. Summer is arriving early for Reaper's Fest."

Overhearing that, Avalea and Jeryn swerved toward the knight. Meanwhile, Briar stiffened. We had banked on Rhys coming, as well as Basil and Fatima from Spring. But how this visit would turn out, what happened during the fest, and who survived remained to be seen.

I spoke through my teeth, giving voice to everyone's unspoken question. "How early?"

Aire flattened his lips. "Tomorrow."

35

Briar

Sunset poured muted light onto the maple pasture. Fauna grazed amid the hulking trees, copper and red foxes traipsing across the grass, their titian irises glinting. Cows, mares, and stallions did the same, bowing their heads and nibbling from the earth.

Often, we took Nicu here at this time of day. He loved this picturesque hour, when the clouds yielded his favorite color. Shades of happy orange glazed every leaf and wheat stalk, and typically the fauna would flock to him. Poet's son had a remarkable way with the creatures of this world, his presence luring them.

In Autumn, the greater fox population dwelled with their keepers in The Fox Dell, deep in the outer wilderness. But some dens lived on the castle grounds. So when the resident foxes saw me, their ears perked in expectation. I shook my head as if they would understand. Nicu had not accompanied us this afternoon.

Instead, Eliot and my ladies were entertaining him while Poet and I strode to one of the makeshift buildings that had been erected for this evening's revels. Throughout the pasture, dining sheds and

338

shopping booths were scattered across the grass, with winding mulch paths and glowing pumpkins leading to each building. Traditionally, Autumn hosted a night market two days before Reaper's Fest, replete with all the wonders of this kingdom. Poet's son would adore the mystical ambience, but whether he would have the chance to attend depended on the next hour.

The notion spiked my blood with vitriol. Yet I remained quiet, my boots crunching the mulch while Poet made enough noise for the two of us.

"Nuisance of a motherfucker," he hissed, charging down the lane while clutching my hand. "'Tis adding insult to injury. His existence is tiresome enough, but by making a consistent habit of showing up unannounced, he might as well beg me to pick up where I left off the last time that I saw him. Only for this victory lap, I'll garnish the man's ashes on my dessert plate, with a side helping of his balls, fresh from the grill spit."

At last, I spoke. "You must calm down."

"I *am* calm!"

"That is not calm. That is self-destructive."

The jester halted, whipped toward me, and snarled, "He traded for Nicu in Spring. He blackmailed us in Autumn. He turned the Masters against you. He deemed you mad in front of the court. He had you dethroned and banished. He was sniffing out the castle's passages. He recruited a new cult of pissants and ordered them to poison you. He had them massacre a born soul in protest to your reign.

"And now he's here, forty-eight hours in advance, polluting the court with his bigoted stench, his shitty taste in clothes, and his vendetta. Alas for him, I don't take kindly to someone who targets my princess whilst also forgetting to arrive fashionably late. So tell me again to calm the fuck down."

Softening my features, I stepped closer to Poet, intending to reassure him. I opened my mouth to speak when a figure dashed across my periphery. My eyes jumped across the dining shed and shopping booths outfitting the pasture. Yet only the fauna and Aire's troops presently occupied the area, the soldiers' armored outlines visible as they scouted the vicinity. Every brewer, crafter, farmer, miller, and servant had finished setting up for eventide; they would return within the hour, whereas the nobles and lower town residents were busy readying themselves.

And yet ...

Poet tensed. "What is it?" he asked, following my gaze and bracing to fling me behind him at the first sign of danger.

I blinked, flummoxed. The figure had appeared cloaked and diminutive, prompting a certain memory. "I thought I saw ... Somebody."

"Who?" Poet misunderstood, his timbre honed like a knife.

"Somebody," I emphasized until awareness claimed his features.

The girl who had been forced to work for the Masters. The child who'd slain Merit at the guild's behest, on orders from Rhys. The one who avoided showing her face and had only answered to the name, Somebody.

At scarcely ten years of age, the girl had infiltrated a camp full of knights and beheaded one of their brethren with her axe. Albeit, she hadn't done so willingly. The Masters had placed Somebody in their debt, having something to do with her mother.

In any case, a terrible possibility took root in my mind. One that I refused to believe.

In the silence, Poet guessed the awful direction of my thoughts and shook his head. "It wasn't her, sweeting."

Exhaling, I nodded. "I know."

Somebody wasn't here. Ever since the courtyard battle, she had vanished without a trace. She'd befriended us and wouldn't have tried to poison me, nor harm a born soul. Although the child had been coerced to behead Merit, she wasn't a murderer by nature. Most unfairly, I never would have thought of it, had my vision not tricked me seconds ago. In actuality, I must have caught sight of a young animal roaming the pasture.

"I pray she is safe," I said.

"That feisty little tyke?" Poet intoned. "I suspect she is."

Firelight bloomed from inside one of the dining sheds. We kept walking that way, with our fingers netted. I could not blame Poet for his rage. Not when the same emotions broiled in my gut as I thought of Nicu and the likelihood that it might be too risky for him to attend the market. No matter what this conference yielded, we could not take a chance in Rhys's presence.

Striding down the pumpkin-lit path, Poet and I assessed the secret entrances camouflaged into the maple trunks. After the born soul's death, and considering Rhys's new agents must have breached the channels—first, to assassinate me; second, to extract one of the dungeon captives—we had debated the wisdom of hosting the market in this location. However, an alternate setting would have confounded the revelers, who desperately required stability, and alerted the traitors that we knew they had access to the passages. To that end, everything needed to proceed as normally as possible.

And this way, we could sleuth. Our clan would inspect everyone's behavior and note any suspicious behavior. Though at present, none of the hidden entrances appeared disturbed or tampered with.

A rustic shed loomed ahead, the facade painted a shade of carmine. The atmosphere would have been quaint, were it not being used as an outpost for a military conference between Mother, Aire, Jeryn, Poet, and myself. On the pretense of preparing for the night market, we would gather for a final recap on how to manage Rhys.

Instead of honoring our customs and making an appearance the morning of Reaper's Fest, Summer would roll into the courtyard soon. Moreover, Rhys withholding the precise time of his arrival hadn't been an oversight. Granted, we had foreseen this tactic and only hoped it wouldn't come to fruition.

In the interim, Poet and I had yet to settle a quandary, which had arisen after last night's reading. That we were lovers was certainly no secret, yet attendants had been chattering nonstop about that moment between Poet and me, as if they'd witnessed a phenomenon. Regardless, our trance had been severed by a disagreement shortly after learning of Rhys's travel plans.

With Spring expected to attend the revels as well, we hadn't decided how or when to tell Basil and Fatima about Rhys distributing spies in their court. In person would be the optimal choice. But with Summer in residence, and with threats surrounding us, the moment required discreet timing. That was one of the dilemmas our clan planned to debate now.

Poet and I had vowed to make decisions together. Therefore, I broached the subject once more in advance, before involving the rest of our group. "I still say we should tell Spring when we have concrete proof."

Poet grunted. "You know what I think about that."

"Yes, you were somewhat vocal after the reading when we cleared the library."

"The longer we wait, the graver the consequences. Do it forthwith, and do it in front of Rhys, and we have an advantage. He won't be expecting the charge and will splutter all over the place. His temper will spike, and he'll admit everything by accident."

"Or he'll rant, twist our words, and accuse us either of corruption or a grudge."

"No one twists words like me. I'm a juggler; he's just a piece of shit."

"You are underestimating his shrewdness, and you know it," I snapped. "Unless we have proof for Spring's benefit, alleging anything could backfire. At worst, it would grant Summer the leverage to declare war with Autumn."

"And whilst it would be glorious to see you lead an army, I would walk through hell to keep Nicu from living through a war. But you know Rhys doesn't want an armed battle. At least not a continental one," the jester reiterated. "He wants dominance by way of convenience, which is likely why he spends more time sucking his own cock than his wife does."

Snatching Poet's arm, I spun him toward me. We stalled again, not fifteen feet from the shed's entrance. "Fine, but I insist we need proof," I rehashed under my breath. "Something more than a verbal testimonial about the Masters."

"We didn't wait for witnesses or documentation to approach Winter."

"That was because we had to act quickly. We needed Jeryn to ally with us for the revels. We had to take that chance. A leap of faith, remember?" I summarized from our talk on the training lawn. "With Basil and Fatima, we can pace ourselves. By tonight, we may very well capture Rhys's cult at work."

"And if we don't?" Poet contested. "Suppose my ex-sovereigns find out on their own that we've been keeping intel from them, before we have a chance to inform them ourselves. Winter might even tell Spring, if we delay for too long. One Season as our enemy is enough, but having two is pushing for catastrophe on a long-term scale, if we hope to make headway in our campaign.

"Either that, or we rely on your intelligence and my tongue, and we call it a day. Some would consider those talents enough to convince Spring. By the way, have I mentioned I used to serve them and know a few tricks about how their minds work?"

Blood rushed to my head. "Stop being a smartass."

Poet's brow quirked. "Because that's bad? In case you've forgotten, a jester's lethal wit and a princess's perception are two things we excel at, which accounts for my confidence in us."

"I wholeheartedly agree with you, but—"

"But nothing," he interjected, sunset slicing across his face. "Rhys can deny, grovel, and scapegoat us as much as he wants. At this rate, the shithead is making up our so-called crimes as he goes along. We can handle that, but waiting to inform Basil and Fatima until after we have proof is a greater hazard. Our verbal savvy will have to supplement for evidence, and it wouldn't be the first time."

I flung my arm to the side. "We ran into this exact obstacle when deciding whether to prosecute the Masters, whom we've yet to find evidence against."

"We're not dealing with them anymore. We're dealing with the

Royals of The Dark Seasons, and whilst that sounds rather grandiose, we have intimate experience there. We persuaded Winter—"

"We bribed him."

"Minor details, sweeting. You act like I'm the only one in this relationship who's done a fair share of manipulating. What makes you think we can't persuade Basil and Fatima of what is, inextricably, the truth?"

"Because recent history hasn't warmed them to us," I disputed. "Spring has a bias. We duped and betrayed them. How has this escaped your memory? You're supposed to be the sly one."

"You dare challenge my trickster prowess?"

"This is not funny," I reprimanded, though Poet's face looked nothing close to mirthful.

My breasts mashed against his chest, the heat of his annoyance matching my own. At some point, we'd stomped nearer to one another without realizing it.

Poet's sensuous mouth curled, his livid voice carving through the inch of space separating us. "Careful, Sweet Thorn. Questioning a jester's methods, not to mention his sense of humor, is a gamble in and of itself. Walk that fine line, and you might trip."

I swallowed furiously. "Take heed, Sir. A princess does not bend in the face of such threats."

"Oh, believe this." He pushed into me, his torso beating against my own. "By now, I think I know what gets you to bend."

The temperature spiked between my thighs, and my core flexed with tension even while a scream lunged up my throat. I clamped my mouth shut to keep from lashing out, all the while my fingers shook against his, because despite our words reaching their boiling point, neither of us had released the other's hand.

I thought back to the last time we quarreled like this, the day after Rhys had turned up unannounced in Autumn to blackmail us. He'd created that rift, the jester's and my own strategies clashing.

The strain and frustration. The antagonist lengths to which we'd gone. The molten effects it had.

That night in the throne room. On my chair, with Poet tied down while I rode his cock.

Exasperated and overheated, I schooled myself to focus. "Are we going to do this again?"

"You're surprised?" Poet ground out, his voice thick and heady. "We do plenty of things again and again and *again*."

I scowled, and he glared. Yet my nipples pitted against his coat, and I felt the muscles of his body tighten in response.

A masculine cough interrupted from the sideline. Neither Poet nor I glanced toward the source, because we recognized its owner.

Aire must have quit the building to retrieve us. The First Knight's bulky outline materialized in my peripheral vision, and his tone was rueful but urgent. "Your Highness. Sir Jester. I've come to—"

"Tell everyone to fuck off for another three minutes," Poet instructed while we glowered at one another.

"Sir?" came the soldier's baffled reply.

"We'll be there shortly," I clarified.

"It's not that." The knight fell temporarily silent, as if bracing himself for an explosion. "There's been a change. Summer is already here. He arrived privately and without ceremony not ten minutes ago, then inquired after your whereabouts, to which the council notified him of our assembly." I heard rather than saw Aire compress his lips, anger brimming under the surface. "His Majesty is seated inside, insisting on participating in the meeting."

A shard of mulch cracked under my boot, and a feral hiss scraped from Poet's lungs. Slowly, our heads swerved toward Aire.

"He *what*?" we seethed in unison.

Three seconds later, Poet and I slammed through the shed doors.

36

Poet

ucking condemnation. I usually enjoyed making an impressive entrance, yet it appeared we'd been upstaged. Hence,
this was no exaggeration. The princess and I blasted into the
roundtable like cyclones.

The shed doors blew open and smacked the opposite wall with
a deafening thwack. Loose blades of straw flitted across the grassy
floor. Overhead lanterns punched the walls with a livid orange glow,
and trestle table chairs creaked as every occupant swiveled our way.

If the Summer King had made an entrance, we made an extrav-
aganza. With our fingers ensnared, Briar and I sliced a path to the
table's head like a force to be reckoned with.

My eyes sliced from one player to the next. Avalea stood behind
a chair at the table's head. Her fingers grasped the finial posts, and
her face reflected barely restrained animosity toward the figures
adjacent to her.

Giselle of Summer occupied one seat. Trussed up in a marigold
shawl, the Summer Queen's olive features mirrored consternation.
Though not at us.

Nay. At her husband.

Rhys's obnoxious form contaminated the chair beside his wife. A smug expression turned his features into a caricature, his upturned mouth lifting the shaggy mustache hanging like a cadaver from his face. As usual, I could only guess that a sneer hid beneath all the facial hair, with the outline of his lips struggling to peek out.

"Well if it isn't The Mad Princess herself," the wanker announced, his gaze lancing from Briar to me. "And her perpetual, pyromaniac whore."

Not three seconds into this, and he'd already let our waltz by the fire slip. Too bad the high-necked mantle and knuckle-length bell sleeves concealed the evidence, beneath which I imagined patches of his flesh resembled crusts of toasted bread.

A viper's hiss skated up my throat. I stalked closer to Briar's side, ready to plant myself in front of her. My tongue flexed, about to slash Rhys open with the response he deserved, when Briar's hand clenched mine in warning. Following her gaze, I understood why.

Across from Rhys and Giselle, two additional figures popped from their chairs. One of them clapped his hands and then spread his arms in greeting. "Poet!" Basil of Spring boomed, his voice as loud as a trumpet. "Poet, lad!"

Next to him, Fatima bumped her shoulder into the man. "Too much, too soon," the queen advised her husband.

Chagrined, Basil's jovial expression faltered, then smoothed out into a portrait of begrudging formality. "Er, Jester," he muttered. "You're looking well."

Hellfire. Apparently, this showdown had expanded from one Season to three. Like Summer, Basil and Fatima of Spring hadn't been expected until the day after tomorrow.

The First Knight trailed in behind us, offering me and Briar an apologetic look. Not that we'd given him a choice. Had the princess and I paced ourselves before storming inside, Aire would have prepared us.

The soldier closed the doors and stationed himself there. No need to guess whether he would foresee anyone else coming, for the warrior could detect signs of approach within a mile radius, and his troops were not only loyal but discreet. For this collision, voices could hurl like cannonballs across the room without the added concern of witnesses.

Spring's presence alongside Summer couldn't be random. Rhys must have finagled their cooperation, beguiling them to join him early. I knew these jolly, rosy-cheeked, and impulsive Royals well enough to bet they were unaware of any ulterior motive.

And fair enough. Why would they ever suspect Rhys of duplicity?

Briar and I swapped a quick glance, drawing the same conclusion. Not for the first time, we'd have to improvise until catching onto Rhys's agenda. For a start, Summer coming here early intended to throw us off guard.

Very well. A game and a dance. Challenge accepted.

Minutes ago outside, I'd been tempted to haul Briar against the nearest maple trunk and fuck the irritation out of us both. But now the memory of our feverish argument faded. Time to be the resourceful princess and sly jester. We released one another, our fingers unclasping as the princess strolled to one end of the table, whilst I remained across from her. Like this, we flanked our guests, the better to see everyone. And to be seen.

I bent my features into a mask and bowed to Spring. "At your service, Your Majesties," I charmed, the very picture of devotion and respect. "Enchanted, as always."

"Yes," Briar echoed, plucking her skirt and curtsying. "Your return to Autumn is most welcome."

"And so prompt," I added, my eyes clicking over to Rhys, who leered like an asshole.

"Indeed and ingenious," Basil exclaimed, parking his silk-encased rump onto the chair. "When we learned of Summer's plans to arrive early, Spring refused to be outdone. Even if this market is a tad—" he wiggled his fingers toward the door and the ambience beyond, "—a tad sober."

"Why is he doing that?" Rhys grumbled, gesturing to where I pranced across the shed, the firelight throwing my shadow onto the walls.

Only then did I register the additional knights and guards lining the perimeter like gargoyles, their attention stapled to the building's clapboard facade. Three soldiers hailed from Summer, their forms draped in animal-skin capes and armed with curved swords.

The other three were of Spring, their mantles dark green and their polished blades heavily ornamented. Odd that I didn't recognize any of them. Moreover, something struck me about their suits of armor, though I couldn't place it. Giving them a once-over, I ambled past the men and women-at-arms whilst filing those details in my mind.

No matter about the warriors. Aire's broad frame exceeded theirs, he kept his eyes on them, and I'd seen this man take down half a dozen soldiers without breaking a sweat.

Ignoring Rhys's first complaint of the evening, I prowled the vicinity like a carnivore waiting to strike. The motions did what I expected, distracting the king and making him agitated.

Instead of justifying my behavior, Avalea rounded her chair and lowered herself stiffly. I commended the queen for curbing her wrath. Considering Rhys had ordered a group of unknown peons to poison her daughter and then burn a prisoner alive, it was fortunate for the king that brass cutlery hadn't been set in front of the woman. Otherwise, he'd already have a steak knife lodged in his mouth.

Flattening her palms on the table, Avalea hinted, "Forgive us, but the revels have yet to begin."

"This is a private conference," Briar stated more plainly, moving to stand beside her mother's chair. "For invited participants."

Ah. Such barely restrained diplomacy hadn't satisfied my princess. Based on how those freckles stood out, her temperature had risen. How this woman thrived when she was furious.

Rhys put on a show of dramatic and imperious offense. Like a hardcore amateur, he groused, "Of all the cheek, audacity, and rudeness."

"Really?" I queried. "You couldn't stick to merely one noun?"

Naturally, the man failed to maintain the front. In one second flat, that short fuse went from contrived to actual, with trenches burrowing into his countenance. "If I were you—"

"Nonsense. No one could ever be me."

"—I would think before addressing my superiors with insolence."

"Our apologies," Giselle amended. "We regret the interruption."

"Speak for yourself, woman," Rhys griped.

The queen's eyebrows punched together, clearly done with her husband's shit. "And just what makes you think I would speak for anyone else?"

Halting beside an empty chair, I hitched my forearm onto the back and quirked my own brow at the Summer Queen. "You have our deepest condolences, as well."

Because according to her inflection, not to mention general common sense, this woman was married to quite the handful. One couldn't help but pity her.

Though cleanly delivered, the mockery proved difficult even for the king to miss. Anger ground into Summer's face as he glowered my way. "Once a cunt, always a cunt."

Cunt. Whore.

How trite. Also noteworthy, he spoke as though cunts weren't religious experiences and being a whore was a bad thing.

No strangers to profanities—etymologically speaking, Spring had invented most of them—Basil and Fatima shouldn't have been aghast. Yet their heads whisked toward Rhys in astonishment. The pair rarely experienced trouble exercising their tongues in Royal judgment, but breaking Nicu from the dungeon had been the only time they'd so much as thrown an insult my way. Not least of all, they'd never seen anyone be so foolish as to test the Court Jester.

From his vantage point, Aire glowered in moral repugnance. His fist landed on one of his broadswords.

Briar flung a vicious look at Rhys. Predicting her intention to verbally flay the king, I got there first. "Good boy," I condescended, sitting and crossing my ankles atop the table. "You had me worried this was going to be a difficult conversation. When really, you only have me stumped in one regard: The mere fact that you know what a cunt looks like."

The king's visage scrunched like a wad of wet paper. "You insufferable fuck—"

Briar strode forward and stamped her palms onto the tabletop. "What are you doing here?"

"Can't stay away from us," I taunted. "Can you, sweeting?"

"Can't stay where you belong," the king patronized, glaring at the princess. "Can you, Daughter of Autumn?"

Daughter of Autumn. The rank this court had adopted in place of Your Highness, apart from Aire's troops.

My sweet thorn refused to swallow the bait. As resilient and sharp as her namesake, she declared, "The court embraced my return. No thanks to you, Sire."

Triumph resurrected his mood, and he feigned innocence. "For a nation that values honesty, you seem to be implying something atrocious, as if I had anything to do with your conviction. For your sake, I hope the council and your queen mother have educated you on the laws of defamation and treason."

"No need. I'm familiar with the legislation of my Season. I've studied it extensively as part of my upbringing." The magnificent princess leveled him with a flat look. "Would you care to borrow my textbooks?"

"For shame. Do you hear this, Spring? It's not my fault if my timing was inconvenient for you that night. I was merely a witness to the courtyard's calamity." Like a tenderfoot, he shifted his attention to me and mock-rhymed, "Why, I can't decide if you look stupefied or mortified."

"And we can't decide if you're a dumbass or a dumbfuck," I replied smoothly. "That you dare to botch a single line of verse? Now that's offensive."

"You converted this nation against me," Briar contested to Rhys.

"Yet here you are, lecturing me about denigration."

The king gloated, leaned into the table, and steepled his fingers. "Except this isn't your kingdom any longer."

"Sire!" Avalea hissed.

"Rhys!" Giselle censured.

A threat snaked across my tongue. "Watch yourself, sweeting."

Basil glanced from his wife to the rest of us. "Should we perhaps—"

"Stay," Rhys requested without turning his waspish gaze from Briar.

Aye. It was obvious. The prick wanted Spring here as witnesses whilst he attempted to chew on Briar's reputation like a termite. He aimed to brand my thorn as an irredeemable, unfit heiress, thus riling her up and calling her sanity further into question.

What's more, he meant to twist our defenses and make it seem as though we were plotting a devious course. That way, it would irrevocably tarnish Autumn in Spring's eyes, ensuring we'd never receive support from our fellow Seasons.

So be it. If this pest wanted a verbal battle, he would get one.

Beneath that flapping mustache, his jowls moved, and his mouth continued to make noise, which increased in both speed and volume. "The Mad Princess," he harassed. "I believe you set that precedent the moment you opened your legs for this heathen—" he flung his arm toward me, "—then adopted his bastard fool of a son. And I haven't even gotten to the part where you took leave of your senses in the courtyard, ranting and raving, calling me a murderer, and threatening to 'fucking kill' me."

Inevitably, the man got carried away and rose to his sandaled feet. In a flash, I was out of my chair, the daggers in my coat beckoning my fingers. One more inch in the princess's direction, and this monarch would lose more than his leverage.

Recognizing the look on my face, Rhys huffed but shuffled backward. "Clearly hysteria and guilt caused you to misinterpret," he ridiculed Briar. "Yet what does it matter, when you're here now. I applaud your ambition." Pressing his palms together as though praying, he unpacked his trap. "I'm sure you did a thorough job of appealing to Autumn's generous nature upon your return. Moreover, the unfortunate sickly spell that followed worked wonders to stoke Autumn's sympathy, much like a prostitute fondling a cock. Oh yes, my wife and I heard about the poisoning."

And here, Giselle galled at her husband. The reaction indicated she'd known nothing of the sort, yet the man kept talking. "Such a relief to see you've recovered."

"Do us all a favor and spell bullshit," I told him. "Take your time. We'll wait."

"I say, Summer," Basil exclaimed, his attention wheeling between Briar and Rhys.

Fatima filed in her husband's blanks. "Surely, you're not insinuating the former princess orchestrated an assassination attempt on her own life."

"As a means to win back Autumn's approval? Evidently, you're both forgetting the mayhem these two criminals caused in Spring. According to reports, it's uncommon for victims to survive a poisoning of that magnitude." Rhys's eyes thinned on the princess like a snare. "Where did you get the proper remedy?"

Like a stab of frigid air, another male voice infiltrated the room. "From me."

37

Poet

Silence frosted the shed. A masculine silhouette ate up the doorway, his head nearly hitting the upper casing. The fibers of his fur coat bristled like needles against the setting sun, and his dark blue hair avalanched over his shoulders.

One time. Only this one time would I allow him to outrival my entrance.

Aire must have moved aside, because Jeryn stalked into the room with an expression hewn from stone. Unlike Rhys, whose emotions tore a burning hole in his face, the Winter Prince showed no such vulnerability. He could have walked in on us discussing the weather, plotting his death, or having an orgy, and I doubted his visage would have changed. That was his wild card, and fuck it all, but I couldn't say I hated it at the moment.

Rhys's tanned complexion drained like paint from his features, replaced by a wraith-like white. Whilst everyone else had the presence of mind to greet Winter, Summer merely decomposed into his chair. He shriveled quickly onto the seat and then remembered himself, rising again like a fledgling about to soil his loincloth. "Your Highness," he stammered. "I wasn't … I didn't realize … you were here."

"Am I interrupting?" Jeryn inquired, deadpan.

Basil consulted Avalea. "Is he?"

"Not at all," the queen said, gesturing for Jeryn to come forth. "He was expected."

That got Rhys's unbridled attention. Winter had been anticipated for this conference, yet the hypocrite was never late. Nonetheless, I wasn't about to complain, especially when Rhys's visceral reaction hit its breaking point.

Since when did Winter voluntarily partake in private meetings with Autumn?

I seized advantage of Summer's shock. "What little birdies told you about the poisoning?"

Rhys went from ashen to fuchsia. From an outsider's perspective, he couldn't have learned about the poisoning that fast. Not unless someone privy to that episode had sent a messenger avian to inform him, since Autumn raptors flew at breakneck speeds.

This implied unauthorized emissaries. The assassins themselves, for instance.

To say the least, Rhys hadn't expected us to call him out. We had unmasked the Masters as spies, and he'd insinuated to Briar and me about having additional minions scattered across the continent. Unfortunately for him, the man hadn't wagered on us exposing that and thus risking contention with Spring and Winter.

Speaking of Winter, the king's informants must have told him about Jeryn's presence. Whether residing inside the castle or not, the caravan of black carriages driving sleet through the lower town had been difficult to miss. That tidbit could have easily made its way into the message.

Drawing the obvious conclusion for Winter's attendance, Rhys evidently packed his trunks within hours and traveled by ocean, using Summer's accelerated ships to get here in record time. He must have assumed Winter healed Briar and then left. But what the fuckwit hadn't foreseen—because no one ever would—was that Jeryn had stayed longer than necessary. That attributed to the king's slackened jaw.

Hence. As an alternative to assassination, Rhys had planned to monopolize Briar's recovery in front of Spring. What he hadn't counted on was our other extended houseguest.

Debating whether to call my bluff, Summer recuperated enough to dodge the question and rationalize through his teeth, "Winter and its medicine." He regarded Jeryn with renewed presumption, the king's hubris slowly returning. "She's fully healed, so I can't fathom what keeps you in Autumn."

The prince sauntered to the table. The chains ornamenting his pants rattled like loose bones. "Fellowship."

Summer balked. "Excuse me?"

My tongue couldn't resist spelling out, "F-E-L-L-O—"

Rhys's fist hammered into the table, shaking the furnishing. "Fuck off, you diabolical shit!"

Giselle folded her lips inward, stifling her amusement. Fatima gaped, and Basil batted his eyelashes in puzzlement.

Like me, the prince hadn't blinked. "On the contrary, Summer. Since my arrival, I've grown rather taken with the princess and jester."

Taken with us. Not necessarily a lie. If one left semantics out of it.

Quickly, Briar summarized Jeryn's visit, how he'd treated her illness and then willingly accepted Autumn's invitation to remain for Reaper's Fest. It went without saying that she omitted our bargain with him.

Now Rhys's expression contorted. "You expect me to believe your courts are engaging socially with each other? Preposterous," he vented, gesturing at Briar and me like we were a contagion. "They stand for everything Winter scorns. Were this continent left in Autumn's hands, we would be overrun by an epidemic, with every unleashed maddened creature and simpleton in existence free to roam among normal society."

Because silence was Winter's weapon, the longer Jeryn remained deliberately quiet, the more Summer became the opposite. "Ordained by the almighty Seasons, it's our duty to preserve order before Autumn's ideals run rampant and *destroy us*."

To that predictable disclaimer, I mouthed the words along with him. Though only Briar noticed and fought to withhold a grin.

When Jeryn still said nothing, Rhys exploded. He rammed both fists into the table now, his spittle ejaculating like lava across the waxed surface. "Sire, you cannot be serious!" he clamored, from one asshole to another.

Like an impertinent bastard, I reminded him, "You do know what Season he's from, right?"

Jeryn flattened his hands on the tabletop, the shadows cleaving his features in half. "Caution, Your Majesty. It sounds like you're patronizing my court and postulating Winter's judgment, both of which are unwise."

"I would never!" Summer retracted. "What I meant—"

"At the risk of wasting my breath, I'm aware of what you fucking meant," Winter hissed, calmly enunciating every word. "As for your clumsy presumption, I'm in attendance because it appears Autumn and Winter have more in common than I estimated."

"What the fuck could you have in common?" Rhys blustered, his saliva flying as if he was suffering from heatstroke. "Autumn is a sentimental wasteland, on the brink of downfall because of this lawless bitch, her demonic jester, and their half-witted spawn—"

With a growl, I lunged his way. Briar reacted swiftly, grabbing my shoulders and wrestling me back.

Although his security detail wedged themselves closer, Rhys ignored the fact that he'd almost lost a kidney. Instead, his shrewd gaze dashed from me and the princess to Jeryn. "What have these sympathizing sluts offered His Highness?"

"How dare you!" Avalea said, launching from her chair.

"Husband," Giselle ordered, grabbing Rhys's ugly linen mantle. "That is enough!"

Winter simply cocked his head. "Offered me?"

The arctic edge in Jeryn's voice could have amputated a limb. Hearing it, Rhys backpedaled. "They ... they must have ..."

But he choked on his words as the prince scrutinized the king. "If I didn't know better, I'd say you're now questioning my integrity." Unintimidated by their disparities in rank, Jeryn flipped aside one panel of his coat and set his fingers on the scalpel-shaped knife at his hip. "Careful what you assume."

In other words, don't fuck with this prince. On that score, Jeryn's calculating pupils flashed on us. My own gaze narrowed; he was waiting for us to expose Rhys's spies. Either we acted now, or he would. One might expect Analytical Winter to side with Briar's logic, believing we needed proof. But then, I sensed Jeryn knew what the outcome would be.

Glimpsing Briar's expression, I caught the private shift in her bearing. The trust in our abilities. That leap of faith. All of this, plus the knowledge that Rhys was already on the verge of conniption. It wouldn't take much to tip him over.

I inclined my head. *Do the honors, Highness.*

Her chin rose. *Don't mind if I do, Jester.*

Briar turned to our rapt audience and dropped the next sentence like a guillotine. "Summer has been parceling spies across the Seasons."

That was all it took for Rhys to detonate. He barked and bleated whilst Briar spoke over his protests, explaining to a stunned Basil and Fatima all that had happened, starting with Merit's beheading and proceeding with Rhys's informants, the Masters' recruitment, the courtyard battle, and everything his minions had attempted since Briar's return to the castle.

In the end, Giselle slapped her palm over her husband's mouth, staunching his tirade.

After a thunderstruck moment, Fatima glowered at Rhys. "Is this true?"

Summer purpled, the color proof enough. Indeed, he hadn't thought we would make a move without a guarantee, certainly not in our position.

Aire stepped from the doors. "Autumn is a nation of virtue," he testified. "We mean what we say."

Jeryn rolled his eyes, clearly finding that affirmation to be insufficient. "Winter received an admission from one of its knights, which confirmed Summer's presence in my court."

"Ludicrous!" Rhys accused. "You intimidated him!"

"That would have been child's play," Jeryn dismissed, his baritone unrepentant. "I dismembered him."

Aire's horrified eyes widened. Avalea winced, not entirely surprised based on Jeryn's reputation. Basil turned green, and I had no fucking clue how Fatima reacted because I didn't bother checking.

"You barged in on Autumn with a demand once," Briar clipped to Summer. "Now we have one for you. Whatever you came here to achieve or accuse us of, quit while you're not ahead."

Rhys brayed, "An heiress doesn't command a king!"

"Then allow her queen to do it," Avalea said. "Stand down, Your Majesty."

"I've done nothing but protect this continent!" Rhys threw a malicious glower my way. "You were the one who—" But the coward cut himself off, his pride refusing to admit the pampered Court Jester had almost incinerated him to a crisp the last time he was here.

Behold, the power of an inflated ego. I should know.

"Filthy lies!" he spat at me and Briar. "And I will not be interrogated by a fucking inferior. Guards!"

Summer's knights hustled forward, steel ringing as they ripped out their swords. In the confusion, Spring's soldiers followed suit.

Yet my head whipped toward them, and they halted at the deadly cut of my stare. "Cute," I pretended to compliment before my features collapsed, darkening with the promise of violence. "But don't be absurd."

Briar's hands twitched, arrested in the act of reaching for her thorn quills. Aire and Jeryn had shoved closer. Basil and Fatima raised their palms in silent command, thus stalling their knights.

Avalea had leaped nearer to her daughter.

And Giselle did nothing. Neither did she defend her husband, nor did she object. At once, I recalled the perceptive frown she'd given Rhys, back when Briar was banished. Even then, she must have suspected the king of fuckery.

None of which the woman had contributed in. That much was clear.

My gaze swerved back to the knights, waiting until they disarmed. As they did, a feature about Spring's armor snagged my attention. Something hadn't sat right with me when I'd passed them earlier.

Now I saw it. And more.

The agitated looks on their faces. How the knights braced their weapons like cooking spoons. And most distinctly, the fucking ivy-strewn flora symbols on their surcoats.

My nostrils flared. Wordlessly, I summoned Briar's attention and jutted my chin toward the vestments. The princess's brows crinkled until she registered the details, then her frown unraveled with the same epiphany.

We might have had no evidence beyond what Jeryn got from his soldier, in addition to the proclamations we extracted from the Masters. But this would fix that.

Back on my first night in this castle, I'd invented hand signals with Briar, gestures to use whenever too many eyes and ears were aimed at us. We had employed this method on the Masters. Even before that, we'd exercised those gestures against Rhys when he blackmailed us.

Casually, Briar flicked an invisible speck of dust from her bodice. *Humor them.*

At the cue, my mouth tipped sideways. "Hmm," I murmured, easing my stance and pretending to admire the knights' wardrobes. "Such posh armor. I confess, I'm feeling rather nostalgic for my former nation. I'd forgotten how swanky you all look whilst defending your sovereigns. I especially appreciate the embellishments on your surcoats." Twirling my finger at the adornments, I asked, "Wherever did you acquire such intricately stitched patches?"

One of the knights wavered. When Basil reluctantly nodded to the man, commanding him to answer, the soldier muttered, "Tailor in the lower town. Near the west brothel."

"Close to the Dragonfly Pavilion," I praised. "Lovely. I know both establishments well."

Rhys barked out a malicious laugh, ignorant of the perceptive frowns Basil and Fatima traded. "Behold the pointlessness of a jester. A profession as burdensome and expendable as the creation of born fools. Trivia and frivolity will not win you clout in this argument."

"If you insist." Leaning over the table, I set my palms delicately on the surface. "'Tis a fact. Spring is an opulent citizenry, often fixating on wardrobes. Except for one problem." My head cocked, and my grin dropped. "A Spring knight wouldn't patronize a tailor."

The soldier blanched, as did his comrades.

Rhys's eyes bulged, and he threw an order at the knights despite not having the jurisdiction. "Out."

"For textiles, that knight would commission a needleworker." Casually, I gestured to the surcoats. "Who wouldn't be caught dead fabricating Spring symbols into cheap patches."

"Out now."

"Because the ivy and flora would be embroidered, as they are for every surcoat."

Rhys's octave blasted to the ceiling beams. "Leave. This. Building!"

Hay straws tumbled across the grass as the knights fled toward the doors. Aire moved with the velocity of a windstorm. He blocked the imposters' retreat, tipping his broadswords at their throats as if to say, *Try it.*

My eyes skewered Rhys. "You didn't even have the decency to cast Spring's most proficient performers. Instead, you went after a bunch of novices. 'Twas rather foolish of you, to assume amateurs could impersonate the real thing, even if the nation excels in artistry. Even more foolish to flaunt your sloppy mistakes in front of the Court Jester, who can tell the stage garb of a rookie thespian from the suit of an expert warrior. After all, this infamous *whore*—" I rested my palms on my chest, "—has bucked, sucked, and fucked plenty of the latter. Because let's not forget, Spring is first and foremost a court of sin and sex, two subjects you know shit about."

But when the king opened his beak, I murmured, "Whatever you're planning to say, I highly recommend against it. Our toys are sharper than yours."

"Arrest these frauds," Avalea commanded Aire, whilst Basil and Fatima gave their concession, and Giselle motioned for her own knights to do the same.

As Aire and the Summer troops corralled the faux Spring warriors from the building, I let my words cleave through the room and snatch Rhys by his testes. "Hear this, and listen well. Your advantages have become your disadvantages. Autumn has possession of them now. If you cross us, I'll spread those vulnerabilities out on the table like props to play with. Am I making myself clear?"

"Sympathetic scum!" Rhys blared. "If you think I'll quail before you, you're not only misguided but delusional. This isn't over!"

"Reveal your assassins," Briar ordered, striding ahead of me. "Tell us who's been violating Autumn."

The king's pupils reflected hatred and firelight from the lanterns. "You should have demanded that before exposing me!"

He cranked his arm, his palm swinging across the table to her face. My vision went up in flames. A primal sound erupted from my lungs, and my serpentine reflexes kicked in.

One arm catapulted Briar behind me. My other arm lashed out, my dagger spearing through the man's open palm before it breached the first inch. Rhys howled, the noise infantile as I twisted him into an inhuman angle and slammed his hand onto the table, pinning him there.

Blood splattered the surface. Basil and Fatima shrieked and bounded from their chairs.

My limbs tensed, ready to hurl over the furnishing so I could properly shear the flesh from Summer's bones. But when the king made a floppy attempt to dislodge my dagger, a glass object with a needle tip appeared from nowhere and stabbed the corner of Rhys's throat. The king buckled, his eyes flaring wide in shock. Beside him, Jeryn calmly held a syringe against Summer's neck.

"Contain yourself," the prince bit out, his features inscrutable as the king collapsed, unconscious, into his chair.

As Rhys flopped forward like a rag doll, silence suffocated the room. Basil and Fatima gawked at the crimson spritzing from where my dagger impaled Rhys's hand. Next to me, Avalea clutched Briar.

Summer's wife merely stared in a daze. Though for a moment, her gaze swiveled my way. A surreptitious light flickered in the woman's visage, telling me I was forgiven.

At length, Spring gawked at me and Briar. Then and there, my former sovereigns nodded, extending their gratitude for weeding out Spring's traitors.

Finished with Rhys, I yanked out the dagger, blood gushing from the king's wound. There was no point in cleaning up his mess. Let it smear the table and ruin my clothes as I drove the weapon into its sheath. For this was one stain I'd wear with relish.

Anyway, I'd only just begun. For this was the least I would do to him.

Until then, I bowed to Spring and Briar's mother. Then I snarled to the king's prone form, "As you were."

Taking Briar's hand, I led my princess to the doors. On our way out, Jeryn glared at us over his shoulder, that venomous look erasing whatever thanks we'd meant to show him. The prince hated what we stood for, despised aligning himself with us, and there was still no telling what the fuck he secretly planned to gain from it. He hadn't done any of this for our sake.

Whilst exiting the shed, I met his shit-list stare with a warning one of my own.

Walking the same path back to the castle, Briar remained eerily silent. At first, I thought it was due to shock. But then she whispered, "Fashion victim."

Glancing down, I caught the tilt of her lips before she rewarded me with a full view of that Royal smirk. Grinning wickedly, I raised her hand. With our fingers blotted by the king's blood, I kissed her knuckles and gave her a devious wink.

38

Briar

ur triumphs accumulated. We had exposed Rhys's criminal and treasonous actions to the Royals, which decimated his reputation amidst the Seasons and would not bode well for Summer's relations. What compensation all of us sought from Rhys remained to be seen, to be decided upon later. In the meantime, the king had been placed under house arrest, on the public pretense of illness.

My relief lasted into the night, after the sun dove behind the beechwood forests bordering Autumn's harvest fields. Hours after that overdue episode in the shed, I wandered through the crowds. Among the maples, booths pulsated with lantern light, and pumpkins glowed along the mulch paths. The classes mixed in celebration, decorous courtiers and jubilant tradesfolk strolling through the night market ambience.

At the glittering stalls, craftworkers sold their wood-carved wares. Bakers and millers offered warm sourdough loaves, their counters wafting with the scents of yeast and crust. Farmers exhibited fresh squash, turnips, and persimmons, which patrons would later use to prepare whatever dish they planned to contribute for the bonfire ball of Reaper's Fest. A brewer's stall peddled ale, mead, and hot spiced cider. While fiddlers and flutists played, guests strolled with baskets looped over their arms or lounged on the grass for eventide picnics. The world smelled of ripe apples and crisp leaves.

Revelers ignored me as I passed them, which meant the disguise was working. With my braided hair tucked beneath a felt cavalier hat, and the tiny jester diamonds tracking under my lower lashes, none of the attendants recognized my features. They strolled by, unaware of being watched.

Despite the altercation with Rhys, the identities and whereabouts of his residual cult remained obscure, their anonymity intact due to the king's silence. My gaze scanned the passersby yet found nothing alarming about their conduct. No signs of danger. No indication any of them knew about the secret passages. Everyone ate, drank, chatted, and enjoyed the lively music as Eliot joined the performers.

From across the distance, my best friend glimpsed my outfit. *Comely*, he mouthed while strumming.

Hunky, I quipped, to which his smirk broadened.

Near a carpenter's booth selling jewelry boxes, Vale, Posy, and Cadence tossed back tankards. Upon sighting me, they whistled and blew kisses, impersonating a clique of ladies beckoning a nobleman.

"Roarrr," Vale flirted.

"Hellooo sir," Posy cooed.

"Fancy a drink?" Cadence purred.

Lately, Cadence had been instructing the pair on how to hold and wield a knife. For this event, the trio hid their weapons beneath flouncy gowns and capes. Though apart from vigilance, their eyes gleamed, proud of the motley diamond pattern they'd applied to my eyes.

Biting back a chuckle, I played along. Puffing up my chest, I gave them a smoldering look.

In unison, they pretended to swoon. Mirthful, I left them to it. Our clan would revel with the guests while keeping alert eyes from our respective corners. Ignorant of their princess's proximity, the members of Rhys's cult would let their guard down and possibly expose themselves. With skill and luck, we would hear or see something out of the ordinary.

Aire patrolled the grounds with his troops. Every so often, I glimpsed his ashy hair, the flash of his vambraces, and the wingspan of his broadswords.

As for Winter, the prince hadn't yet made an appearance. Though he would, as part of our agreement.

I moseyed through the masses. Even if a few revelers registered my presence, the billowy men's breeches and loose shirt would be no surprise.

Like myself, many attendees sported costumes as part of the tradition. Most of the garments honored figures of Autumn, with revelers draped in makeshift cuirasses and helmets resembling ancient armor, the tasseled gowns of wheat goddesses, and fauna whiskers.

Throughout the congregation, I searched for that small figure whom I thought I'd seen prior to the market roundtable. Among the buoyant children racing around the trees, I sought out a youthful frame wrapped in a cloak, but none fit the vague memory. Truly, I must have been imagining them.

Nonetheless, seeing the people at ease lifted my mood. To be among them simultaneously filled my veins with warmth yet pinched me with sadness. I hated the thought of Nicu missing this, but after what had happened with Rhys, there was no way Poet or I could allow him to join the festivities. It stood to reason the king's cult had somehow learned of the meeting's outcome. Who knew what vengeful state of mind they would be in tonight, provided they were here. As much as it broke the jester and me to deny him this night, we would not leave Nicu's safety to chance.

Presently, he was with Mother and Tumble in the nursery. The queen had shoved me and Poet from the room, commanding us to attend the night market while she got to soak up the evening hours with Nicu and his furry familiar. Since the event took place out of view from Nicu's chambers, we did not have to worry about him experiencing the sorrow of being left out.

My gut twisted. Now I understood what Poet must have felt all those years in Spring when he'd been separated from his son, unable to show Nicu all this world had to offer, the brighter spots of this dark continent.

But someday, he would get to see and partake of these wonders. Together, Poet and I would ensure a future for him.

As the night progressed, other emotions unfolded. Namely frustration that our enemies seemed to be evading our clan. And anticipation because there was one person I hadn't yet found.

We'd parted ways to get ready after visiting Nicu's chambers, agreeing to meet at the market. Though we'd never designated a location.

Traveling down gourd paths nestled within the maple thickets, I scanned the mesh of bodies. I sidestepped noble couples, roaming servants, and laughing tradesfolk. Beneath the hat's brim, my eyes scrolled from one face to the next, yearning and annoyance clutching my chest.

Where are you?

Tingles rushed up my spine, the sensation electric as if he were answering.

Find me.

Any other person familiar with this man would conclude he intended to make an entrance. And they would otherwise be right. Yet intimate experience had taught me the jester would never allow hours to lapse on such a crucial night.

Neither would he leave me to fend for myself. Not for an instant.

No. My jester had been here for a while, a protective shadow observing the details.

Watching the crowd. Watching for enemies.

Watching me.

At the pasture's center, revelers formed two rows and struck a dance. Unlike the glamorous performances that were customary in Spring, the music here was rustic, especially when it originated from the outlying villages and lower town. Fiddlers plucked, pan flutists harmonized, and Eliot kept pace with the melody, perfecting a brisk tune that allowed the couples to sweep across the grass and wheel their partners.

The number of revelers in this area increased, either to clap with the beat or to participate in the jamboree. The pounding of feet shook the earth. And before I knew it, a pair of manicured hands grabbed mine.

"What—," I sputtered as Cadence yanked me into the fray.

"Shut up and get your ass in here," she demanded.

Posy and Vale were already at it, grinding their hips in an exuberant Spring fashion. Yet only on this occasion did revelers fail to notice or balk. As the line dance continued, I yielded with a laugh and paired with Cadence. The ladies proved knowledgeable about Autumn's footwork, acclimating quickly.

Having been raised on these steps, it was one of the rare dances I could manage without faltering. Even then, a certain male figure had inspired me to stop fretting over my lack of rhythm, so that I no longer cared and simply let the tempo guide me. The ladies and I hopped, looped arms and spun each other in circles, and clapped while shimmying our hips.

Pins kept my hair from tumbling, although a few errant tendrils broke free. Perspiration dashed down my nape. My skin heated with exertion and exhilaration, and my pulse skipped because I knew.

Oh, how I knew. He was staring. I felt it, the thick and intoxicating force of his gaze, like a gust of humid air.

In the midst of turning, I halted. My eyes crashed into a pair of fiendish green orbs. From across the press of bodies, a tall figure reclined beneath one of the maples, those hooded eyes penetrating the distance.

The music faded, replaced by the thrum of my pulse. The crowd vanished, erasing the yards between us as we locked gazes.

I sensed how I must look, flushed and elated and desperate to reach him. I let that desire swell across my features, hiding nothing.

In a trance, I stepped from the crowd and approached. The jester materialized into view, from the messy layers of dark hair to those clover irises lined in kohl. Instead of leather pants and whatever expensive coat he'd usually have commissioned for an event, a floor-length graphite skirt fanned around his boots, and the matching jacket hugged his frame like a glove, emphasizing his toned muscles.

The jester's pupils dipped up and down my shirt, breeches, and men's hat. Recognizing the ensemble from his closet, as well as the painted jester diamonds skipping beneath my lower lashes, his sensuous lips slanted. Amusement dashed across his visage, along with a more sinful glint meant only for me.

Seasons, this devil.

Breaking from the tree, Poet sauntered my way. We met on the fringes, separate from the assembly. For a moment, we admired one another in silence, our mouths tipping in mutual appreciation.

Poet's wardrobe would have drowned me. But just as I'd commissioned a replica from one of his outfits, the jester's skirt and jacket were clones from my own wardrobe, since anything I owned would have been shredded if he'd tried them on.

A divot formed in Poet's cheek. "Hi, beautiful."

A blush crept up my neck. "Hello, handsome."

He sidled forward, the skirt swishing. "Beguiling."

I sidled nearer, the pants rustling against my thighs. "Provoking."

But while the sight of him in my clothes threw titillating sparks across my flesh, something more unconditional and remarkable blossomed inside me.

How often we thought alike. How often we thought differently.

Despite wearing disguises, it had been effortless to pinpoint one another. In the dark, from a distance, and surrounded by a crowd, we'd never been able to hide from each other. Intrinsically I'd felt him here. Indeed, I would recognize him anywhere, in any guise.

My heart dripped from my mouth. "Have I ever told you why I love you?"

Poet had not been expecting that. The question struck him, those long eyelashes flapping, his jaw slackening at whatever he heard in my voice.

It came out of me like a confession, a benediction, and a vow. "Because with you, I'm foolish. Because with you, I'm fearless. Because you reunited me with the child I used to be. Because you've drawn from me the woman I can become. Because you're the other half that was missing from me."

My throat swelled. "Because of you, I want to stand for this world in ways I'd never expected. Because before you, I never thought I could. And I know you'll claim to have done nothing, that I became this person on my own, and I love you for that as well. And I'll never stop loving you. Because it's always been like this. Because I cannot stay away, and I've never been able to stay away, and I never will be able to stay away.

"Because with you, I relish darkness as much as lightness. Because no one else does that to me. Because no one else … is you."

I licked my lips, shivering when his attention tracked the movement. "But more than any of that, you have my heart for an unbreakable reason. Because now I care more about giving my love than receiving it. Because you gave me Nicu."

Poet's features had collapsed. Raw, explicit, and spellbound.

Perhaps I had expressed too much, too publicly. Perhaps I should not have taken leave of myself.

Perhaps none of this. Because what stared back at me wasn't restraint. It was all the things I felt. From wonder, to terror, to rapture.

Riveted, the jester said nothing. He remained uncharacteristically quiet, as if I had stripped him of the ability to speak. He merely kept staring until I shuffled in place.

Unable to abide it any longer, I squared my shoulders and affected a regal posture. Moving past him, I said, "We should continue scouting the market."

His fingers shot out, snatching my wrist and jolting me in place. A current of heat sizzled up my arm. Twisting my head toward him, I found the jester staring at his grip on me. But as the music eased into a slow theme, he aimed those molten eyes on mine and extended his hand, palm upturned.

I felt his request rather than heard it. *Dance with me.*

As we had once before in Spring. And because we hadn't yet done so in Autumn.

My hand floated like a feather and landed in his. Without looking away, we stepped into the pasture and turned to face one another.

The gentle slide of a fiddle drifted into the air, followed by the tender pluck of a lute, the instruments straying into a classic melody. This sort of dancing, I could manage. By Seasons, I could handle anything with him.

Raising and bending our arms parallel to one another, we aligned our palms. Although we didn't touch, the tips of our scarlet bracelets brushed. The contact slammed into me, a soft sort of heat flowing through my veins.

Like this, we circled each other. Our eyes fastened, the pasture beyond evaporating. Once, twice, then we wheeled the other way.

I thought back to the night we met. My attempt to dance in an empty hallway. His eyes tracking my movements from the shadows. How we had circuited around one another like enemies.

Now Poet's body revolved seamlessly, the motions fluid as we switched arms and pivoted in reverse. Memories of another dance scorched my flesh. That night after the labyrinth, in his chambers when we'd swayed and pumped our hips together. In the middle of his suite, then against his wall, articles of clothing had been discarded with each turn.

Me, sprawling on his floor, with the fire crackling beside us. The jester, looming above.

The first sensation of his cock against my pussy. The first taste of ecstasy. The way he'd opened me to a new existence until I was crying out for it.

More than that, the exquisite honesty. The trust.

With his gaze latched to mine, Poet led me over the grass. We swept through the steps, veering in one direction, then the other. It was a slow, methodic dance, in which the partners never made contact. Our fingers laced behind our backs, then hung at our sides as we rotated, always following the other, always just out of reach. Like something eternally forbidden.

Yet it did not matter. The jester held me in the grip of his stare, riveting his eyes on me as though nothing else existed, and I claimed his attention with the same vigor, so that we fell into the motions, the landscape blurring. Merely from this, I felt Poet's fingers across my parted lips, running down my back, and rushing into my hair.

With every move, I heard him speak. And I heard myself answer.

Marry me.

Yes.

My bones melted. My lungs hitched.

Blood and breath. Mind and soul.

Fear. Sorrow. Joy.

Rage. Grief. Desire.

All the ways to love someone. All of them inseparable.

We spun in opposite trajectories, then glided into one another again. Our palms hovered between us, the air seeming to crackle there.

As the instruments faded into wisps of sound, Poet and I stopped. Engrossed in one another, our chests heaved. The pasture materialized once more, with the area cleared of dancers.

I blinked, discovering everyone in our proximity idling on the margins. At some point, the revelers had vacated the expanse, the better to observe us. The awestruck crowd studied me and Poet wistfully, as if they'd just witnessed a mating ritual. Or a wedding dance.

Our clan beamed as they had during the library reading. Beyond Eliot and the ladies, the Winter Prince's silhouette idled on the outskirts. Jeryn's expression seemed muddled, speculative, and as disconcerted as it had been during the reading, when Poet and I were ensconced in our trance.

It became clear. Everyone finally identified us beneath the costumes, having viewed our hypnotic dance from beginning to end.

After the crowd dispersed in a daze, genuflecting and migrating across the market or converging into another dance, Poet and I stood still. Firelight from the gourds and lanterns laced the grass and maple leaves, transporting us into another haze. The jester's expression reflected the same sweet desperation scattering across my flesh.

As the activity resumed around us, Poet stalked my way. His torso radiated against my shirt, and our exhales rushed together. For the second time, he offered his hand. "Come with me."

Poet

Every ounce of breath held fast in my chest. I waited on tenterhooks for her to take my hand, a strange concoction of nervous anticipation running rampant across my flesh, to the point where my fingers shook with need. 'Twas as if we'd never done this before, never touched or even tried, never dared to make contact.

A chaste shade of pink bloomed across Briar's cheeks, like she was experiencing the same mystifying sensation. We gazed at one another, marveling at each other's features. She and I might as well be caught in a glass globe, isolated in time and space.

After an eternity, the princess settled her fingers in mine. And the world blackened, and it burst with firelight, and my veins ignited. A great exhalation flew from my lungs. My relief proved inexplicable, as though I was some besotted adolescent, inexperienced and smitten, unsure but hopeful that the woman of his dreams would accept him.

Such a simple thing, her hand landing in my own. Yet it became everything, the contact turning our fingers into the center of this forsaken universe. The crowd thinned, and the music dimmed. Nothing else existed but this.

Naturally my kind had a habit of hyperbolizing, however I gave no fucks how it sounded. This elation threatened to knock me to my fucking knees.

Briar's fingers trembled, equally overcome. Eagerness and something external—true and sure—ripened her complexion like forbidden fruit. In this heiress, I beheld the reverence of a virgin, the confidence of a lover, and the yearning of an equal. This impossible match, which we made into a reality, seizing it with abandon, refusing to relinquish it no matter the cost and regardless of the sacrifice.

Nay. Instead, we surrendered in another way.

My digits closed around hers, encasing my princess there. Mine. All mine. Just as every inch of me belonged to her.

With my heart pumping, I turned and guided Briar from the clearing. Wending through the pasture, I stalked around maple trunks and veered off the gourd-lit path. It might have seemed as if I was moving aimlessly, but my destination was clear. I knew where the fuck to take her.

And take her, I would.

Moving deeper, deeper, deeper into the thicket, I led us to a condensed area where the trees huddled close. Amid the maroon glint of maple leaves, a compact dining shed stood vacant, the building's door sketched in luminescence from the pumpkins and lanterns burning through the pasture. The woodworkers had been overly ambitious, a characteristic of this nation. To that end, an overabundance of structures meant several were unoccupied by merchants or revelers.

Spotting the edifice, we walked faster. The costumed skirt buffeted my limbs, and my boots ate up the distance. Briar's respirations came fast, keeping pace with my own.

To be safe, we should remove ourselves completely from the market. To avoid detection, I should haul her into the building and slam the deadbolt in place.

Yet I couldn't bother to care. If we didn't stop now, the pain would be too much, and I'd lose my cursed mind. Besides, I'd spent plenty of time scouring the market, finding no sign of a threat, and a surplus of weapons rested in various compartments under this jacket. Were someone to interrupt us, I would flay them to pieces.

Briar seemed to agree because her footfalls rushed alongside mine. She had weapons of her own pinned beneath that hat and strapped to her boots. Of this, I had no doubt.

Hence. We weren't making it inside the fucking shed.

I hoisted the princess to the back of the structure, trapped her in a fire-lit alley between the building and an empty vendor's booth. With maple branches arching overhead, I hefted her against my frame.

Briar hastened into me, her fingers dropping to my tailbone and clinging there like film. Her palms scorched through the costume, throwing embers up my spine. We pressed into one another, panting and overwhelmed.

Despite our feverish outtakes, our motions were sluggish and heavy with longing. My forehead pressed into hers, and my hands cradled her profile with such anguished delicacy, fearful of breaking this moment. Farther away, the fiddler strummed a tender melody, akin to the one we'd danced to.

Our eyes shut, and our breaths dashed together in a heady spell. My mouth sizzled, grazing against hers, sweeping one way, then the other. Her lips parted, lush and firm and quavering. I rowed up and down, tracing her mouth whilst she did the same. The gentle exploration robbed me of oxygen and depleted me of words.

For no blasted words could measure up to this. We'd passed the point of needing them. I heard every plea and desire without either of us speaking.

We rubbed our lips together as though discovering them for the first time, learning one another anew, only with the same history tethering us. We etched each other like we'd gone through it all—every deadly conflict and battle of wills—without touching.

Yet wanting to. For so long.

Briar's whimpers lifted my cock high. The secretive urgency of it broke my heart and split me open.

A secret and a scandal. A shadowed liaison and a force of nature.

That's what we were.

The greatest courage a person can have is to love another.

The memory of my speech, from the night we spent in a Spring jail, was both a torment and a comfort. I could lose this, or I could keep this forever. Either way, I would sacrifice myself to have her.

The tartness of Briar's mouth wrought an agonized sound from me. My teeth caressing the princess's lower lip coaxed a whine from her.

I thrived on those noises. Our gaping mouths lapped over each other with teasing restraint, on the brink of combustion. Finally, the muscles of our lips yielded, pressing together, swift and tempting.

Give me your mouth.

One peck led to another. My head anchored in the opposite direction, my lips folding against Briar's and pulling a sigh from her lungs.

Give me your tongue.

And again, and again. We met in a sequence of frenzied little pecks, the tension thick and hot, the taunting contact launching the blood to my cock, which broadened against her pants.

Give me your moan.

Ragged, I inched back and raced my thumbs across her freckles, then dragged down her throat and cupped her jaw. My thorn's eyes fluttered apart, those irises lined in jester diamonds and flashing like the steel of a blade. Latching onto my face, she repeated my actions, skating her fingertips over my features. We did this with a fragile type of lust, as if we were younger and meeting a fledgling age.

Her grip sank to my ass, wracking my muscles with shudders, the agony divine. The soft outline of her pussy abraded my erection, the steady throb of her cunt pulsing through her pants and my skirt, rendering the fabrics obsolete. In no time, my dick lengthened, and an obscenity sat on the knife's edge of my tongue.

Kiss me until I fucking die.

Shaking my head, I muttered that curse and swooped down. My palms clamped the sides of her face, holding her in place.

And then I kissed my princess.

Not roughly, nor swiftly. But with all the dedication of a fiendish man who'd fallen hard.

I slanted my lips and clamped them fully onto hers. At the same time, Briar sighed and launched onto her toes. Lunging her arms around my neck, she dove her fingers into my hair, clutching my scalp as I spread that mouth wide and whisked my tongue against hers.

My hands mirrored Briar's, sliding to the back of her head and fastening her there, the better to seal us together. Like this, I deepened the kiss, pistoning my tongue in a fraught tempo. Briar keened, her mouth sprawling beneath mine. That delicious tongue writhed languidly with my own, licking and savoring. I groaned, putting the strength of my jaw into it, putting my soul into it, the angst and sweetness of this night my undoing.

I kissed her to claim her. I kissed her to cherish her. I kissed her to love her.

On a tortured moan, Briar peeled her lips away, the flesh swollen and scarlet red from the onslaught of the kiss. The sudden movement pried our hands from each other, yet we remained pinned, with her chest adhered to mine.

Beneath the cavalier hat, a draft of wind rustled the burnished strands of Briar's hair. Those glazed eyes flapped at me, and I felt my own pupils inflating. Gales of oxygen heaved from our lungs, hot air siphoning between us.

Briar licked her lips, the sight doing calamitous things to my rigid cock. This time, she was the one to shake her head in wonder. And one passionate request came out. "Again—"

My palm seized the nape of her neck and yanked her forward. I hoisted the princess into me, my mouth crashing against hers, cutting off the plea.

The hat toppled from her head and hit the grass. Briar gasped in approval and flung her arms over my shoulders, her body coiling and the humidity between her thighs stoking my pulse like kindling.

Her wish was my command. Again and again. And fucking again. I would brand her and worship her. By Seasons, I would give it all.

My fingers dug into the princess's skin, and my free hand plunged to her ass, gripping one cheek and locking her to me. My tongue licked along the wobbly crease of her lips, splitting them open and pitching inside the intimate well of her mouth.

Briar sobbed against my tongue, her body pliant and melting against my frame. Her mouth rocked under me, kissing me back, wanting me back.

With a low growl, I tore away and descended to the crook of her neck. My lips seized the sensitive flesh and sucked until she arched, a suffocated noise falling from her. I prolonged that effect, the flat of my tongue lining her collarbones, the neckline of her shirt fluttering open. I suctioned Briar's skin between my teeth, plied her with open-mouthed kisses in the basin of her clavicles, and licked up the column of her throat before snatching that breathless mouth once more, probing it with my tongue and shattering when she met the rhythmic thrusts of my lips.

Enough and more. My mouth shaking, I forced myself to release the princess. Tacking my forehead once more to hers, I walked Briar backward, with our eyes welded together. Drugged, we made the long trek across the grass, feeling the brunt of every step as if it would never end.

Briar gave me an imploring look, silently begging me never to stop, never to let her go. I felt the sweet desperation of our movements. What I was about to do to her wouldn't be rough and fast, nor erotic and leisurely. Nay, this would be passionate and devastating.

Mutinous lovemaking. An excruciating fuck.

We remained in danger of being caught, with any number of revelers able to stroll by. With hundreds of people in proximity, we treaded a fine line. And we did it well, following that fucking line straight to the shed's clapboard wall.

Let them see who we are. Let them watch us. Let them judge.

I stalked the princess toward the facade, then thudded her against it. Briar emitted another savory noise, this one beseeching. My body hummed as I fenced her in, the bridge of my cock primed against the sumptuous heat filtering through her pants. How wet she was, the slickness dampening her costume straight through.

The jacket strained across my chest, far too constrictive. Briar squirmed, the looser clothing burdening her as well. Without glancing away, we unbuckled the closures, my fingers plucking open her shirt, and her hands brushing apart my jacket flaps.

With a quiet jolt, I batted open the shirt. Then I tugged down the bodice, and her exquisite tits sprang from the fabric.

At the motion, oxygen pushed from Briar's lungs, even as she reciprocated by unclasping my jacket. She did this slowly, unfastening the garment at a luxurious pace. Inch by inch, my torso expanded into view, and her attention riveted on the slab of muscle, which rippled with each beat of my lungs.

I could suck those nipples between my teeth, and she could destroy me with her mouth on my pecs. Instead, we intended something more. She pulled me to her, and I fell into Briar's body, wanting only to feel the rampant percussion of our hearts.

Remote firelight toasted the darkness. The distant fiddle played for us.

Breathing the same air, our hands sought the other out. Briar snuck her fingers into the waistband of my skirt, a whimper escaping her as she discovered my bare cock beneath. I groaned against her mouth as she wrapped her fingers around the column and pumped me from base to crown, her thumb stealing across the slit, where a droplet of cum leaked. My sac tightened, blood surging to the roof of my erection.

In kind, I flicked open the front panel of her pants and combed through the sprigs of hair thatching her pussy. Briar's mouth fell ajar, a silent moan lodging in her throat. Obsessed, I extracted more of those sounds as my fingers circled the stub of her clit, the dainty flesh enlarging, then traced the drenched slot of her cunt.

We moaned into one another, fondling and caressing and groping as though we'd had no idea until now what the other felt like. Her palm worked my cock, stroking my length, bloating the pome. My digits drew over her folds, cupping and massaging them. Tracing that tight oval between her walls, I scissored the lips of her pussy apart and probed Briar with three fingers, watching oblivion pull her features taut.

Fuck. Her cleft squeezed my fingers, her arousal pouring down to my knuckles.

Briar sobbed, her hips jutting to meet my hand. My own hips snapped gently, rolling my cock into her fist, the sensations threatening to disintegrate my limbs.

Groans splintered from my mouth, and I slapped one palm against the facade beside her head. I rode her hand, and she rode mine, our gazes unwavering. Moans quivered between us, the ache palpable, the pain lovely.

Unable to stand it, I hitched Briar's left thigh beneath my skirt and over my waist. My thorn nodded and released my cock, bracing herself harder into the wall and strapping one arm around my neck, urging me nearer. Her free hand bunched up the skirt, then surged to my ass, fixing me in place.

With her tits flush against my pecs, I rolled my waist into the vent of her legs. The front panels of her pants widened, enough for my erection to penetrate the gap. Without waiting, I nocked the bulbous tip at her entrance, the rift of her cunt soaking me. And I rocked my hips upward.

My cock pulsed into her, hefting Briar up the wall. A soft grunt emptied from her throat, and her eyes dipped to mine, the irises forged of mercury. My muscles quaked, the damp clench of her pussy wringing a groan from my chest, the noise rumbling and haggard.

Throbbing between her folds, I snapped my ass tenderly, bucking her up and down on my cock. In tandem, Briar swatted her waist, grinding herself on me.

Slowly. Softly. Sweetly.

Keeping the other in our sights, we paced ourselves. My hips lashed gradually, pumping through the princess. Her pussy clutched my flesh, the tender walls hot and pooling fluid down to my sac.

Briar's mouth hung ajar, small cries unraveling, in tune with the motions of my ass. She palmed me there, helping to push, spurring me to reach as deeply as possible. I measured my thrusts, whisking into the seat and flexing out to the tip, the friction producing a stream of low sobs from my thorn.

My lips parted in a fit of silent groans, heavy pants wrenching from my chest. We stared and pounded gently into one another, our hips fitting together and thumping, chasing every streak of sensation. Her eyes tensed, each pass of my cock sending a blissful pang through her, each contortion of her pussy ruining me.

We kept the noises between us, not because we feared being overheard. At that moment, we could have inundated the land with shouts. Rather, we confined the sounds between us like something sacred, meant for no one else.

And if there was an element of forbidden restraint involved, so be it. We'd long become well-versed in the illicit impression we gave to this continent. If the danger of being caught added a certain thrill to the risk, we allowed it to spur us on. These obstacles only fanned the flames, for the jester and princess had never played by the rules.

When would it be over? Did I need it to be?

Never. Nay.

If we built any sort of legacy, it would come to this. That I would live anywhere with this woman, be it in a castle tower or an exiled wilderness. That I would walk through fire to be with her. That I would slay a thousand kingdoms to stand by her side. But even if our story fizzled out someday, reduced to a mere line in a history book, I wouldn't give a shit. Between us alone, we had already outlived and outloved beyond expectation. That history was ours. No one else needed to remember us, so long as she loved me back.

With aplomb, I fucked into her, lunging my cock. Briar reciprocated, her cunt sealing around my flesh and spilling onto it. She gripped me so firmly, another low moan tore from my soul.

I relished the view of her tits splayed from the shirt, a replica from my wardrobe, the swells jutting lightly. The mottled flush of her skin hypnotized me, and the strain of her neck made my mouth water. I swooped in, my lips tucking into her throat and sucking.

A barely contained yelp jumped from Briar's mouth. Her head flew backward, thumping against the shed wall. Both sets of fingers dug into my scalp and buttocks, nailing me to her, encouraging me. Her body quaked as I licked her pulse point and kissed her skin as if it was her mouth, the flat of my tongue lapping.

I sampled every swallow, every gulp, every shudder of breath. When her pulse struck my tongue, sense abandoned me completely, the taste of her palpitations intoxicating.

That heart beat for me. It pounded with me. And by some miracle, it loved me.

Remembering her speech before our dance, I growled into her throat. Grabbing the princess's thigh harder and snatching the other, I launched her from the ground. She complied, releasing my ass and scalp before linking both legs over my waist, knotting them at the ankles. Like this, Briar wound her arms around me, anchoring herself as I fucked her, made love to her, took her.

She fucked me back, made love back, took back. Her hips swiveled onto me, the taut muscles of her pussy dripping and catching my thrusts.

Helpless to this woman's effect, I veered from her throat to watch, fusing my eyes to her once more, drowning in those features. That tenacious mouth and those unhinged moans. The points of her nipples rubbing my own. The stubborn chin, loose and relaxed. That single oak braid cascading down her shoulder, the freckles springing across her cheeks, and the rings of her irises. All of it.

Briar's eyes searched my own, something reflecting there that seemed to captivate her. Mayhap she knew what was happening to me. By fucking Seasons, let it be the same emotions.

Eyes glistening, she grabbed the sides of my face. Burrowing down on me, the princess seized my lips. Our tongues thrashed, kissing in a gentle frenzy. All this time, we made love without haste, beating our hips in a sinuous rhythm, my cock striking her pussy with tender precision.

I lost myself in the sweep of her mouth, slanting my lips with hers and tugging. Each lick traveled to my sac, my balls tightening and bumping against her crease. Briar whined into my mouth, and I hummed in return, the sounds rushing together.

Her fingers spread over my jaw, that darling touch scalding my flesh. It entreated me to quicken the pace of my cock, but only marginally. Under no circumstances would I cease until the sun rose. Between now and then, I would squeeze every possible cry, sob, and moan from her. For my privileged ears only.

I thudded Briar into the wall, the patient swipe of my cock abutting a glorious spot inside her. She grunted into my mouth, enabling me to sample how I made her feel. Reaching behind, I snatched her wrists and stamped them overhead, then plied my cock upward, hitting her pussy at a new angle.

Sundering the kiss, Briar's lips catapulted from mine and split wider. The span of my waist opened her thighs, so that my princess straddled me fully, her knees bracketing against the facade. Shocked agony crinkled her brows, and frayed moans quaked from her lungs.

Fuck, she mouthed.

Wicked hell. The sight of my thorn on the brink, with her cunt gushing on my cock, was nothing short of transcendent.

Reinvigorated, I pitched into her deeper, higher. And she bobbed on me, her slit dousing my erection. I felt myself thicken to unfathomable proportions, the roof of my cock twitching, heat charging through my blood.

Sweat coated my torso, the backs of my knees burned, and the skirt material was crushed between us. Briar's shirt flapped around her breasts, and the pants slumped. We banded our hands together, the nexus of our bodies joined, so good it hurt.

Everything about this hurt. The way I craved her. The way she consumed me. The reasons why she loved me, and the terror that she might one day stop. That not even an army, banishment, or the laws of the Seasons could sever us. The way we defied our courts and the fact that we had no other choice. This love was raw, real, and rapturous.

From the moment I first saw her. From every second since, I'd fallen deeper, harder, faster.

Aye, it hurt like hell. And I'd never been more euphoric.

Briar keened, her folds cinching me. Lost in the fever dream of her stare, I reeled into my princess with unbridled affection. Her quiet moans tangled with my ragged groans. Our hands fell apart, allowing us to wrap ourselves together, snaring tightly.

Hooking my arms under Briar's thighs, I palmed her ass. This braced her thighs even higher, knees steepling.

The seat of my cock stroked Briar's clit, and her arousal smeared me, both contorting with the first ripples of release. Her whines tapered, and growls rumbled from my chest, the echo of our lovemaking and the clamor of our fucking barely suppressed. The crest of my dick struck that lovely, condensed point inside the princess, unbolting moan after moan, her walls suctioning onto me.

We thrashed sweetly, in proximity to Autumn's revelers, unintimidated by the threat, indeed fueled by this. Briar's features crumpled in rhapsody. Her pleasure roused my blood, heat swirling in the base of my cock, so that I devoted myself to her release, as though my own survival depended on it.

I fucked her like she would live forever.

She made love like she wouldn't last another hour.

That was all. That was everything.

In the dim firelight, my forehead landed on hers for the third time tonight. Her eyelashes fluttered, those pupils clinging to me. All the whilst, the fiddle music enveloped us, and the world burned outside this enclosure.

As I deepened the brunt of my thrusts, Briar pressed her face into mine, fighting to keep the shouts at bay. She gazed at me like a shadow, something she yearned to disappear into, the better to see in the dark. I felt the screams she longed to unleash, the temptation to holler to the trees, her octave reaching the whole of this kingdom. And I sensed her withholding this luxury, the opportunity to shriek with pleasure, in favor of something just as meaningful—the liberty of privacy with her jester, regardless of the short distance that separated us from a crowd.

Oh, how I agreed. This defiance became its own aphrodisiac. And when we made each other come, the noises would be ours. Thusly, I worked into her pussy, determined to hear the princess break secretly alongside me.

My waist circled, my cock siphoning as Briar's pussy clamped on tightly. The lines around her eyes squinted, the impending orgasm flaring across her face. That stunning mouth dropped open, and her legs separated so willingly for me, and my hips jabbed in and out.

Then I saw it and fucking felt it. A wild sound leaped from Briar's throat, the flanks of her cunt clasping my length. Convulsing, she came like a firecracker on my cock, slickness puddling to my thighs.

Tireless, I ground my hips, fucking between the princess's thighs and palming her mouth to muffle the wails. Pleasure shot from my balls to the slit. The climax rocked up my legs as I hoisted my waist, then stalled when my cock shuddered, hot liquid spilling from me to her. Slamming my mouth onto Briar's, I gave her the sound of my bellow, letting the princess swallow the taste of it whilst my muscles rattled.

We continued to ride out the orgasms, my aching cock flooding her, and Briar's pussy clinging to me. Gasping and inhaling one another in, we slumped with our faces mashed together and our hands wandering over one another. Whilst coming, her fluttery moan met my stifled growl, and our lips brushed.

Breathless and bewitched, I pressed my grinning lips to hers. For once in my life, I held my silver tongue and let this sweetest of kisses speak for itself.

You, my thorn. You are my tale for campfires.

40

Briar

Reaper's Fest dawned. Two days after Poet and I had made love against the dining shed, I stood at a window alcove. From a hallway in the Royal wing, I rested my hands on the sill and gazed past the cattail boxes, beyond the castle and its maple pasture to the glowing lower town. Under a celestial sky, timber and plaster homes blazed with light, a succession of bonfires pulsating throughout the avenues. From the brewery and tavern, to the book-binder's emporium, to the mapmaker's stall, to streets ladened with carpentry establishments, the town pulsed like a torch.

Autumn divided the fest into two sections. Most courts would host the grandest affair in the castle. Instead, our culture did the opposite. In town, the bonfire ball would commence with modest pyres scattered amid the streets and culminating in a massive one at the square.

Soon fiddles would skip, mandolins would strum, flutes would pipe, and drums would pound. Game, bread, and produce from the harvest would weigh down the tables. As part of the tradition to abandon Autumn propriety, attendants would don masquerade masks and engage in lusher folk dancing than at the market, in a darkly mystical and less choreographed manner.

Whereas the castle courtyards provided quieter zones for revelers to indulge in conversation and drink among glittering orange candles. In the quads, foxes skulked, and maples frothed with vibrant leaves. In both areas, all was peaceful.

Though that would change in the next half hour.

Below, a few revelers left the castle in a flurry of tartan, cashmere, and merino wool extravagance. Watching them venture to town with visors in their hands, I could not help but grin wistfully. Despite all that had occurred over the past months, the sight bolstered my sense of hope.

The market had successfully concluded without incident, and Rhys was still restricted to the castle. Although prepared, with knights and guards patrolling every square inch of the fest, perhaps we would come out of this unscathed. I dared to believe this could mark the beginning of change.

Footfalls approached, and a pair of regal figures materialized at my side. "Ahem," a male voice grumbled. "We wish to ... thank you."

I twisted, surprised to find Basil and Fatima hovering with their arms looped. The king and queen wore their splendor well, draped in the dark green satin finery befitting their Season and carrying petal masks attached to long handles. Although the garments' lack of insulation concerned me, as it was rather chilly this evening, I made no comment.

"Your Majesties?" I sank into a curtsy, then gave them an inquiring look as I rose.

"The unfortunate state of affairs with Summer," Basil muttered, flitting a set of bejeweled fingers. "Most taxing. Therefore, Fatima and I extend our gratitude."

Spring's traitors had been unveiled, the performers posing as soldiers having confessed quickly. That left the informers in Autumn and Winter. Regardless of the pressure from the Seasons, Rhys would not speak on the matter, seeking instead to convince his fellow Royals that he'd taken essential precautions, acting for the welfare of his court. And while Spring and Winter sided with his prejudice, they didn't condone him breaching their lands with spies, whether or not Summer claimed he was doing it for the protection of his own nation.

It would take a while for the king to capitulate. Until then, he would exhaust himself by denying the charges, pardoning his actions, and justifying those transgressions to anyone who would listen. Done with his tantrums and nonsense, Mother, Basil, and Fatima had requested Poet be the one to interrogate Rhys later. The jester's tongue would either wear the man out or rile him into confessing the identities of his cult. And if need be, the Winter Prince would do the rest.

In any event, a multitude of reactions clashed inside me. Ambition fired through my chest, because we needed this kingdom as an ally instead of an adversary. Vitriol stoked my blood for the way Spring regarded born souls—mostly especially Nicu, whom they'd once imprisoned without remorse. And resentment pinched my flesh that our court required their endorsement in the first place, and that I must play this game to ensure it happened.

Yet determination eclipsed all of that, because someday those walls of intolerance would be dismantled. And for that to occur, we had to maintain an equilibrium. To that end, I summoned years of breeding and fought to maintain a humble expression instead of a scowl.

"There is no need," I assured them. "Though if I may be so bold, perhaps we might reach an understanding."

Basil and Fatima wavered, consulting one another in silence. Reaching a full-scale truce was too soon. But a proposal was a start.

"Perhaps," Fatima conceded, flapping her finger my way. "Mind, it won't change our positions on certain regulations."

"Yet it may grant Autumn the opportunity to start a dialogue," I ventured. "For example, at the next Peace Talks?"

It was a bold move, considering I'd been banished from the Talks. Yet I hadn't said I would physically be there. Thus, the mere implication upheld their authority on the matter.

Besides. Poet had taught me that a certain brazenness tended to charm Spring. On that score, the king and queen nodded in reluctant amusement, neither promising nor rejecting my suggestion. Nonetheless, an acknowledgment would do for now.

Fatima's eyes strayed to my hair, which I'd gathered in a sprawling bun atop my head. She noticed the rose planted there, recognition stunning her features. "That looks familiar."

It should. Poet had confessed to me how he'd stolen the rose from Spring when his former sovereigns were last here, bearing gifts for the invitation to Reaper's Fest.

Instead of feigning cluelessness, I touched the rose. Taking a cue from my ladies, I simpered, "It was a gift."

"Rare, stunning, and impervious to the fires of our continent," Basil listed, admiring the Spring blossom before affording me a perceptive look, his eyes twinkling with animated shrewdness like his wife. "As usual, our jester has exceptional taste."

Like a proper princess, I inclined my head as they took their leave. However, I spun in their direction at the last minute. "Sires," I called out when they were halfway down the corridor, where the trusted remains of their convoys awaited. "If there's a chance of war with Summer—"

"Pff," Basil dismissed with a swat of his hand. "And spoil the entertainment of retribution?"

"We have no idea what Winter intends with Rhys, but Jeryn and his grandaunts are logical rulers," Fatima clarified. "They're astute enough to align with us on the finer points."

"War won't punish Summer," her husband said just before his expression flattened. "Exclusion will."

Normally Spring behaved optimistically blithe even in the wake of conflict. Yet the monarchs' features tightened, illustrating just how ruthless any nation could be.

They were right. Combat did not frighten Rhys as much as humiliation and ostracism. This was precisely why he'd attempted that tactic with me, to inflict pain by having me expelled from my own nation.

Well. The king might be facing a taste of his own medicine in the near future. At least Spring, Autumn, and Winter agreed on this one course of action.

This time, my genuflection was more gracious. "Enjoy the revels, Your Majesties."

"And you." Despite herself, Fatima's lips twitched amicably. "Your Highness."

My heels clacked against the floor as I rushed through the corridors. Reaper's Fest would begin soon. Before then, I was eager to tell Poet what had transpired.

Rounding a corner, I hastened through a door and skidded to a halt. A long gallery had been renovated into a practice hall, with floor-to-ceiling mirrors affixed to the walls. It replicated the design of a Spring dance studio, where resident performers would train and rehearse.

But this hall belonged to only one person.

My heart vaulted into my throat at the sight of him. Leaning against the jamb, I watched the jester spin and twist across the polished floor like a sculpture in motion. Bare-chested and garbed in nothing but a pair of loose pants, his arms and legs synchronized, those cobbled muscles inflating and flexing as he veered from one end of the space to the other. The man moved like liquid, like shadows, and like the air itself.

A mixture of concentration and intensity strung across his face, akin to how I felt whenever I opened a book, harvested, or led Autumn's people. We'd talked late into the night about our passions many times, yet his affinities still captivated me.

I would marry him someday soon. But he would always remain this way to me.

My jester.

He spun like a disk, spiraling in full rotations, before launching into a sequence of complex flips. The mirror's reflection enhanced his attributes, so that I could not resist lingering on those powerful forearms, the clench of his shoulder blades, or the tightness of his backside. No man should be this embellished or striking. Even when disheveled, he looked impeccable.

His panting ceased. My eyes jumped from Poet's buttocks to his mischievous eyes, which gleamed at me in the mirror's surface. Mid-twirl, he'd caught me snooping.

He couldn't have been training for long. Otherwise, perspiration would have laminated his torso, yet he hadn't yet broken a sweat. With his chest rising and caving, that smooth abdomen rippled down to the slender trail of hair abutting his waistband.

In the mirror's reflection, Poet's lips tilted. "Don't princesses knock?"

Caught in the act, I flushed. "I'm sor—"

"Nay." He wheeled toward me and sauntered my way. "Never apologize for admiring this specimen."

"You rarely cease to amaze me," I pretended to scold, despite the bashful heat racing up my throat.

Poet nodded, as if that had been his plan. Amber and vetiver stirred my senses as he halted inches from me. His pupils expand-ed, brushing up and down my form. In addition to the wide bun at my crown, encircled by the oak leaf braid and the rose in my hair—with the thorns carefully pinned away from my scalp—I'd chosen a black, sleeveless gown with a high collar of ruffled lace that flounced around my neck.

No jewelry. Only the scarlet ribbon.

Poet took in the ensemble, his attention lingering on the rose he'd given me, pleasure alighting his gaze. The breath in his chest hitched. And I thought of the last time he looked at me this way, during our spellbinding dance at the market, then when he fucked me lovingly against the shed, and afterward when he gave my lips the gentlest kiss I'd ever known.

"Behold, an enchantress." Slipping an arm around my middle, Poet tugged me against him. "You devastate me, Highness."

My grin broadened. I could not stop thinking about the night market. Rather, I wanted him like that again, a thousand times, in a million more ways. I wanted my body to break his until he came so loudly, the noise cracked through the sky. Seasons, this jester made me feel like an innocent one moment and a temptress the next.

And always, a leader. Always, his counterpart.

I opened my mouth to reciprocate when an elated voice chimed into the room. "Papa! Briar Patch!"

We turned as Nicu bounded into the dance gallery. Jubilation sparkled in his wide eyes, and Tumble galloped in the boy's wake. In preparation for tonight, a stag mask swung from a harness at Nicu's belt. Dressed in an outfit of bronze and sage, and with the ferret squeaking beside him, the jovial child looked every bit the little Royal fae.

I chuckled as Nicu slammed into my side and clasped me into a tight hug before sprinting to his father, those scanty arms outstretched. Poet squatted, snatched his son, and hoisted the child into his arms. Meanwhile, Tumble ran circles around them.

"That's quite the spiffy attire," Poet complimented. "Dare I say, you'll outshine us all."

"You picked it for me," Nicu said, poking his father in the chest.

"Mmm. That, I did. Isn't it nice having the consultation of a connoisseur?"

"You're a bragger, Papa," the boy giggled.

"And you're in a good mood," Poet teased. "What could possibly be the reason?"

"Giant fireflies," Nicu chirped as if his father was silly for forgetting. "Remember? Aire said they're flying through town and making flames."

"Ah, that's right," Poet pretended to recall. "Reaper's Fest and the bonfire ball."

"Are you excited?" I asked while combing through Nicu's shaggy hair, which had grown long and now swept his shoulders.

Because the library reading and night market had proceeded without a disruption, we had cautiously deemed it safe enough to bring

Nicu. He deserved to have fun, and despite lingering reservations about his well-being, I could not wait to show him the revels.

The one great sorrow to the evening was the absence of those who had a right to be there as well. Born souls were locked up and kept out of sight. By contrast, Lark's Night in Spring had done the opposite, to an equally heinous degree by exhibiting them at the carnival for ridicule and sport.

At least here, Nicu would not suffer such degradation.

Yet I thought of the prisoners trapped throughout Autumn, particularly Flare. Perhaps it was the drawing she'd created in that mound of dirt, but the young woman had a dreamy nature to her. I suspected she would marvel at the fest, were she permitted to join. And it pained me to imagine Flare isolated, confined in a solitary cell at the Winter Prince's behest, merely because her defiance had insulted him.

As for Jeryn's whereabouts, I predicted he would turn up without fanfare in the lower town. At which point, he would make the obligatory rounds with us and then slip away when he'd had enough.

How the future king planned on hosting events in Winter was beyond me. But neither did I concern myself. So long as he refrained from directing any contemptuous looks toward Nicu, we would get on fine.

With their masks in hand, Vale, Posy, Cadence, and Eliot spilled through the door, laughing and joking. Eliot carried his lute and dropped a kiss on my cheek, and the ladies inspected the expanse of Poet's naked chest, though they wisely refrained from remarking on it. Instead, they gathered around Nicu, played with Tumble, and cooed over the pair.

Aire followed behind Mother, the knight's features at ease for once. He smiled and ruffled Nicu's hair, then positioned himself at the door.

My mother beamed at Poet's son and scooped the child from his father's arms. "Ready to see the bonfires?" she whispered.

Excitement eddied through me at Nicu's grin. Telling Poet about my chat with Spring could wait. With all of us gathered and secretly armed, and with surveillance measures in place in case of a breach, it was time to head out.

Except for one hindrance, which Poet gave voice to. "I'll need to freshen up and fetch a shirt and coat first."

"Please don't," Posy begged without shame.

Cadence snorted and raised her hands to ward off my frown. "At least it wasn't me this time."

"You were thinking it," I said, crossing my arms.

"Hon, everyone was thinking it," Vale remarked, winding her arm around Posy.

Avalea rolled her eyes. "We shall wait in the courtyard." She set Nicu on the ground, enabling Tumble to scamper up the boy's frame and drape that furry body across the child's shoulders. Taking Mother's hand, Nicu skipped out the door.

Before turning to follow them, Aire grunted to the group, "*I* was not thinking it."

The women smothered their hysterics and trailed the knight from the room.

Poet idled with me in the gallery, the mirrors and sconces painting our shadows in candlelight. I shuffled, torn between savoring our moment alone and catching up with Nicu.

The jester's lips turned up, and the kohl lining his eyes creased. "Go on, sweeting. You know you want to."

I wavered. "He will be safe tonight. Won't he?"

Poet's grin dropped, his face hardened, and he cupped my jaw. Banding his arm around me once more, the jester pulled my body flush against his. "Nothing will happen to either of you. I swear it."

"And will he have fun?"

"'Tis ever the goal."

Yes, it was. I melted into Poet, strapped my arms around his neck, and mussed his hair. "Never stop telling me what I need to hear."

"Never say never," he flirted, searing his mouth against mine.

Those lips scattered hot prickles beneath my gown. His devilish fingers burned through the garment. If we did not vacate the premises, I would have my way with him against the mirrors.

A low, masculine purr radiated from the jester's throat, as if he'd heard my wanton thoughts. "Be careful, my thorn."

I skated my mouth over his. "Don't make rules I won't follow, my jester."

On a tormented growl, he pulled back to absorb the sight of me, his other hand still clasping my face, his thumb stroking my chin. "You are so fucking beautiful." And my respirations thinned as he asked, "May I kiss you again, Princess?"

"Always," I whispered, delirious.

Yet instead of snatching my lips, Poet released me. In a gallant motion, he swept my fingers in his grip. Bowing, the jester caressed my knuckles with his mouth, planting a teasing kiss there.

My hand trembled. I trailed after him as he stalked backward and gently tugged me along. "On second thought, you could delay for a few minutes. Care to watch me get dressed?"

By now, our clan had made it outside to the primary courtyard, where they would delay until we met up with them. "I'd love to—"

"But a certain little fae awaits," Poet predicted. "They're likely exiting the castle by now. In which case, I'll walk you outside."

I shook my head. "Across a dozen intersections? That will delay you."

"Ask me if I give a shit. Aire and the rest of Avalea's security detail accompanied them, so you're not going anywhere without—"

"I shall be fine," I assured him as we reached the threshold leading into the corridor. "My own guards are stationed at the end of the hall. They will guide me."

Poet wavered. His features tightened with objection when I pressed my fingers to his mouth. "I can look after myself for another thirty paces."

After a moment, the jester relented and dissolved into a smirk. "Stubborn, impenetrable woman. The ribbon, leaf braid, and rose suit you."

"*You* suit me." Giving him a wink of my own, I turned and ventured down the passage. Unable to help myself, I glanced over my shoulder once more to where Poet stood admiring my figure. "Don't be long," I called out.

The jester gave me a saucy bow and a sinful grin. "At your service."

I turned away, pressing a fist into my smiling mouth. Behind me, I felt his protective gaze follow my movement until I turned the corner. By the time I reached the mezzanine corridor where security awaited me, I guessed Poet would be heading to his suite, which wasn't far since the dance gallery was in the Royal wing.

But at the mezzanine railing, I stopped. My brows pinned together as I searched the area, my entourage nowhere in sight. Glancing about, I hesitated and then shook myself. It was rare for the knights to lose track of me unless I wanted to slip away, but perhaps they'd been misinformed about my location.

Quickening my steps, I crossed more passages and trotted down a flight of steps to a lower level. At the landing of another mezzanine, my pace slowed. True, the residents had departed to the lower town, but it seemed odd for the castle's thoroughfares to be this vacant, even on a night like this. The click of my heels echoed in the cavernous space, and the crinkling of sconce flames reverberated more loudly than usual.

But then my limbs stalled altogether. On a wainscoted wall, one of the sconces fizzled. Then another fixture snuffed out, as if a breeze had blown through the flame. But within seconds, a chandelier dissolved as well.

Not possible. Yet my vigilant gaze traveled, watching as each source of firelight evaporated. One by one, candles, chandeliers, and a roaring hearth died in the level below.

I gripped the nearest balcony railing, bracing myself. This was not a fluke, a blast of wind, or a trick of nature. Furthermore, this seemed to be happening throughout the stronghold, with every globe of light and every channel in the vicinity stamping out. My pulse skittered with foreboding as I thought of the spies we hadn't yet caught and the confidential passages into this fortress.

Distant halls fell into darkness. Chills crept up my spine. And the castle went black.

41

Poet

My thumb and forefinger hovered over a taper candle. I stalled in the act of cinching the wick. Crinkling my brows, I stared at the thread of smoke. Before I could pinch the flame and douse it, the tiny blaze had blown out, as if touched by the wind.

Except the windows to my suite were closed.

Perplexed, I snapped my brows together. My gaze swerved from the snuffed candle to the rest of my chambers. The bedroom's hearth had gone cold, the timbers half charred when they'd been flaring seconds ago. Likewise, the sconces had died.

With my frown deepening, I strode to the antechamber, passing bronze and brass fixtures. My open silk shirt hung off my frame. I'd been in a hurry to leave the suite, and since it wouldn't have been the first or last time that I arrived flawlessly disheveled, I had decided to clasp the garment and shrug on my choice of coat on the way out.

Instead, I ignored the outer vestment currently flopped over a wing chair and stalked from the threshold. In the foyer separating my door from the nursery and Briar's apartment, my eyes skewered the corridors. Darkness smothered every passage, blanketing the patterned rugs, wainscoting, and wall paintings.

The wicked fuck?

After stepping into the mezzanine off the foyer, ominous silence and absence greeted me. Autumn's coat-of-arms hung from the beamed rafters, the pennant immobile. Not a scant trace of a breeze, much less anything substantial enough to extinguish a fortress.

Nature and the almighty Seasons worked in mysterious ways. Nonetheless, I'd spent a fiendish portion of my life as a shadow lurking in and out of a castle.

Instinct sent me veering back into the suite and across the chambers. No need to linger. By now, Briar would be outside with Nicu, her mother, and our clan.

A selection of blades was sheathed in my boots and pants, but I could do better. On the way, I snatched my velvet coat off the chair and stabbed my hands into the sleeves, arming myself with an additional surplus of concealed daggers. Grabbing my staff from a wall hook, harnessing it across my back, and knocking open a hidden wall panel with my shoulder, I slipped into another void.

Navigating from one conduit to the next, I descended a handful of levels before emerging into one of a dozen quads. Voices and silhouettes idled through the area. Courtiers dressed in wool and cashmere finery craned their heads, glancing in befuddlement at the castle's brick monoliths. Unnerved, they spoke in hushed tones.

"What happened ..."

"The whole castle ..."

"Snuffed out ..."

I traveled past them, dismissing their looks and whispers when they noticed me. The coat slapped my calves, and my eyes clicked to the stifled bonfires surrounding the castle. By comparison, the lower town pulsated with light.

My footfalls quickened. Entering the main courtyard, I headed toward our clan, who huddled near the central maple.

Cadence, Posy, and Vale had gathered with Eliot, Aire, and Avalea.

My son leaned his runty body against the minstrel's legs and was petting Tumble, trying to calm the squirming, agitated creature. At the sight of Nicu, my muscles slumped in relief, then tensed once more.

One person was missing.

She must have stepped away to converse with the residents. That must be it.

Cadence propped her fists on her hips. From a distance, I heard the lady interrogate the First Knight, "Please tell me this is some type of creepy special effect for Reaper's Fest."

"It is not," the soldier replied, his features upturned and consulting a circle of hawks and falcons dicing through the clouds. "Neither is it a willful act of nature."

Dropping his gaze, the man ran his flat palm slowly through the air, as though sketching an invisible current, reading something there before curling his gloved fingers inward. Sensing my approach, Aire's attention shot to me. "It is a human disturbance. Something intentional."

"Papa!" Nicu piped, wrapping Tumble around his shoulders, hopping from Eliot's legs, and leaping into my arms.

Draped in a shimmering bronze gown, Avalea followed the child's trajectory, her eyes jumping from Nicu to the empty space around me. "Where's Briar?"

Cold dread splashed across my chest as I hefted Nicu off the ground. "She's not here?"

Silence. Everyone stared, apprehension dawning quickly. Fair enough, they had assumed the princess was with me. Yet the underlying panic in Avalea's voice was infectious, transferring to the rest of our clan as they drew the same conclusion.

My blood chilled. Whilst balancing my son, I swerved toward the castle. My eyes cut across the brick facade, scaling the towers in the Royal wing where I'd last seen her.

Something intentional.

Cold terror leached from my veins. In its place, fury set my retinas aflame, and a silent roar cannoned up my throat.

Briar!

All this time, we had suspected a potential plot occurring at Reaper's Fest. Aye, we'd hoped for the better after what happened to Summer. But we'd also kept ourselves ready and assigned more troops to the covert passages.

Yet the king's faction had fucking gotten in anyway. And as a bonus, they'd suffocated the castle fires. I had enough experience with targeting to guess why.

"Papa?" Nicu's voice trembled. "Are you hiding Briar Patch?"

Everyone stayed deathly quietly. Their expressions ranged from distraught to wrathful as the threat became clear. With bated breaths, they waited for me to explain this to my son.

A moment ago, Nicu had been regarding the castle without care. Likely, he hadn't comprehended the dark windows, hadn't interpreted them as a threat so much as a source of excitement. Nor had he translated Briar's absence as a problem, having not made the connection between the stronghold and its princess. He didn't register distances and locations that way.

But now, my son's face folded in confusion. The trauma of losing her once before claimed his features.

Fighting to stay calm, I cupped his face. "She's merely late. I'll get her for you."

The skin between Nicu's eyebrows pleated. Every moment, he was getting older, so that his gaze lanced through me and dissected the lie. My son was no fucking fool.

His chin wobbled, then he started to wheeze, which riled up his familiar. Tumble squeaked and wriggled on the boy's shoulders.

"Shush." I grappled my son's face. "Nicu, shush."

"Briar Patch. Papa, please—"

"I'll get her. I promise, I'll get her." Combing through his hair and planting a swift kiss on his head, I prompted, "You need to stay here and be a hero, remember? Keep Tumble calm."

Given this assignment, Nicu swallowed his impending tears. Hiccupping, he nodded and began stroking the ferret, easing the creature's movements.

Then suddenly, Nicu's face transformed. His visage tightened with resilience and protectiveness, the emotions smashing through his fragile exterior and displaying a strong will beneath. "Be the darkness, to beat the darkness," he whispered.

Be a shadow, to see through the shadows.

By Seasons. He would outshine us all someday.

In the quad, the residents grew antsy. Their octaves rose, merging with the unrest echoing from the lower town. Revelers from here to the fest square had noticed the unlit castle, the effect working like a brushfire, the makings of chaos percolating.

Eliot fished a garrote from his lute, rancor and protectiveness straining across his face. But before the minstrel could act, I set Nicu on the ground and urged him toward Eliot. "Get my son to safety," I bit out to our clan. "Do *not* let him out of your sight."

Without waiting for a reply, I spun and struck toward an adjoining quad. Footfalls thudded behind me, and Avalea's voice called out, "I'm coming with you."

"Out of the question," I snarled whilst charging across the bricks.

"She's my daughter," the queen hissed, the words stabbing my back like needles.

"She's our princess," Posy insisted.

"She's my fucking best friend," Eliot gritted.

"And Nicu is your priority," I snapped, charging back around to face them. "There's no one else I trust."

Eliot smashed his lips together but wrapped a bulky arm around Nicu's chest, securing him there. Cadence flared her nostrils, and Posy and Vale held back protests. The minstrel and Cadence had risked themselves to remain at Briar's side during her banishment. Posy and Vale had lost the chance to help numerous times. They wanted to brave whatever was inside the castle for Briar's sake, yet they also read my ferocious expression. My son came first, Briar would agree, and I would move faster without an entourage.

The queen was a different matter, storming forward and snapping, "I will not leave my child in there. You are a force of nature, but you're still one person. You need—"

"I will go with him," a baritone voice interrupted, the source of which stepped from the gloom in a froth of charcoal fur.

Jeryn of Winter didn't smash through the murk so much as slice through it, with his features honed enough to grate steel. The prince's dark blue mane was affixed to his nape, his skyscraping frame swallowed the backdrop, and his placid features blunted the scene like the strangest fucking palate cleanser.

He glanced at the castle as though inspecting it through a lens. "It's the ashes of Summer tinder," he said. "That's what caused the blackout."

"How the hell did you figure that out?" Cadence interrupted.

"A flame's glare changes when traces of Summer ash are present." The prince clicked his head to a nearby sconce. "Though it's barely perceivable unless you know what to look for."

Aire reached my side, his inflection dubious. "Are you certain?"

I couldn't say which did it more. The soldier forgetting to address the prince by title or the fact that he questioned the Royal's theory to begin with.

Jeryn's eyes slitted, his expression capable of beheading a lesser mortal. "Don't fucking insult me."

As much as I detested the man, Jeryn's conclusion held weight as I recalled something Rhys had said, back when I'd set him on fire.

We can't burn because we created fire!

He'd been bragging, tooting his tiny horn. Be that as it may, he wasn't merely being figurative. On his previous visit when Briar was banished, the king had brought Summer tinder with him, snippets of which I'd stolen and used to rotisserie his body during that lightning storm. However, spontaneous combustion wasn't the only organic magic of his court. Pepper any blaze with the ashes of Summer tinder, and those flames could be controlled from its source, triggered by an invisible link that even Aire's uncanny ability would fail to notice.

Anyone possessing the original kindling had the power to manipulate those corresponding fires, no matter how large or small. Nature and the almighty Seasons yielded an exuberance of elemental magic. Summer created fire, which meant whoever wielded that power could also extinguish it.

That left no other way to reignite the blazes and illuminate the fortress. Every hearth would require new timber, and every candle would need a replacement, and so forth. Until then, the complex would remain in darkness.

Rhys's cult. He'd armed them with an effective means to stamp out the stronghold, including the hidden passages, so they could travel undetected. Likely, they'd done so more than once over the past few days, often enough to distribute the tinder ashes onto every taper, sconce, and fireplace in the castle.

That stood to reason. Yet I found it harder to believe the absence of light would get them past an army of skilled warriors guarding the tunnels. Moreover, we'd received no reports of anything out of the ordinary, such as random blackouts in the channels.

Nay. There had to be more to this.

With a hiss, I ordered the clan to get Nicu out of here, then ripped a dagger from its sheath and extended it to Avalea. Because my tongue was desperate, my next words delivered a sucker punch, from one parent to another. "What would Briar want you to do?"

Avalea's visage collapsed. With a livid gasp, she swiped the blade's hilt and aimed the tip at my heart. "You bring her back," she commanded, her voice cracking like thunder. "One hour. I'm giving you one hour, or so help me, I'll tear down these walls myself."

Nodding, I tore around and stalked through the quad. My boots hit the ground, scorching a murderous trail to the outer west wing.

They wanted my thorn? They would have to play with her jester first.

Two pairs of heavy footfalls aligned with my own. One of them, I didn't need to question. The metal rings of Aire's hauberk rattled with his movements. Sentinels and troops already patrolled the exterior outlets leading to and from the castle. Enroute, the First Knight shouted additional instructions. "Remain at your posts!" he told them. "Disobey this order, and you'll answer to me!"

Once again, this warrior had accessed my thoughts. The invaders would expect a swarm of hornets, not a few lone panthers. Another reason I couldn't afford to do this with a squad; the element of surprise would throw off my targets.

But why the fuck Jeryn bothered tagging along remained to be seen. As usual, he didn't explain himself. Not that I had time to give a soulless shit.

Then again, this man kept his cards far too close for my taste. When I reached the nearest discreet entrance and halted by a nondescript door shrouded in foliage, I seethed a warning. "Hear this, Prince of Dark Medicine. If that scalpel knife gets within a centimeter of Briar's vital organs, I won't be merciful."

Jeryn's features hardened into a scowl. "My property is in there. I'd rather not have it tampered with."

Aire grimaced in disapproval but withheld his moral retort.

Ah. The maddened prisoners.

I would have flayed Winter for this statement, but every second apart from Briar was a second too long. I'd seen the brutality this sadistic prince was capable of, the swift edge of his knife alone could sever a trespasser's head in milliseconds, and I didn't have all night to cherry-pick an alternate reinforcement. At least, not one educated in anatomy and trained to deliver exacting cuts the way this man could.

Jeryn shrugged off his coat. Wisely concluding the extraneous material would cause a lag in movement, he tossed the fur garment aside.

Flattening my palm on the door, I pushed it open. We stepped into a hollow corridor, pitch black sucking us into its maw. I heard rather than saw the knight and prince pursue me, shutting the threshold behind us.

We might as well be walking through a tomb. Quiet descended, the dank air snuck through my open shirt and coat, and tar black swallowed us whole. Twisting sideways, I slithered along the wall whilst extracting the first dagger.

From behind, I listened as Aire unsheathed one sword whilst Jeryn unhitched his knife. Having memorized the fortress's layout, I counted my paces and traced my fingertips along the paneling. Like this, we ghosted between the halls and mezzanines, submerging ourselves deeper into the bowels of the castle.

This western sector was comprised of the Royal wing, the library wing, the relic vault, and the dance gallery where Briar had watched me train. All of which were obvious red flags. My thorn would have evacuated this area by now, having drawn the conclusion that enemies would search here first for her.

Despite that, I needed to be sure, needed to check this area before moving on. Verily, my fingers suffocated the dagger and staff as I recalled one other crucial fact. The king was the only other Royal occupying the complex, restricted to private house arrest by his wife and peers. Remembering this, I tamped down a growl.

Aire took the right wall, Jeryn the left, with me prowling down the center. Every so often, moonlight filtered through a window, and a raptor's wings battered one of the glass panes from outside.

Something shifted. A dozen feet ahead, an invisible weight crossed an intersection.

I paused. Aire and Jeryn clicked to a halt on either side of me. In a beam of twilight, I motioned to the knight and prince. Signaling forward and gesturing to the hallway flanks, I braced myself as they split and receded into the murk.

My fingers unhitched the staff whilst my other hand choked the dagger. Cautioning forward, I stalked my prey's movements. It wasn't her. Oh nay, I was fluent in the princess's motions, and these didn't match.

When another swatch of air hit my chest, I seized in place. With a fiendish curl of my lips, I counted. Then I windmilled the staff over my shoulder and blocked the incoming hammer that struck from behind. The impact caused the figure to grunt and stumble. Ducking another swipe, I twisted, juggled the staff mid-rotation, and intercepted additional blows.

More of the pack flooded the hall, steel and iron resounding. Mayhap nine of them, none making a sound other than panting and grumbling with exertion.

From the margin, Aire flew into the passage and brandished his swords. Wielding them like a set of tornadoes, the knight sliced through his opponents.

At the opposite end, Jeryn gutted into the attackers with a methodical, systematic technique that proved no less ruthless. Like an afterthought, he diced through several figures at once, blood gushing from their arteries and spraying the window. At one point, I caught a flash of his knife skewering someone's throat and popping out from the other side.

Two more shitheads joined my adversary. With a deadly hiss, I exploded into motion, whirling and slingshotting past them whilst crackling their limbs with my staff, then streaking my dagger across their stomachs. Spinning back the way I'd come, I swept the first attacker's hammer from their grip and rammed it into their skull.

Bone crunched. Bodies collapsed.

A team of voices howled with agony and something akin to righteous sacrifice. Rather than stealth, they fought with brawn and anger. Pity for them, though vaguely it didn't sit right with me.

By the time we were done with them, ten corpses littered the floor. Crimson drenched my chest as well as Jeryn's fur and Aire's hauberk. Some of our guests were missing a few body parts, compliments of Winter.

I knelt, trying to identify the men and women's lifeless features. Tragically, the meager light drizzling from the window denied me that luxury. My fingers stole out to feel the texture of a man's cloak when Aire's murmur snatched my attention.

"There's more of them," the knight heaved. "I sense a residue in their wake." He pointed down what appeared to be an abutting channel. "They passed through there recently. The east wing."

"That makes zero sense," Jeryn sneered, punctuating the last word by wiping his blood-soaked knife across his shirt and then aiming it in the corresponding direction. "Your trajectory leads to the throne room, the assembly halls, and the nobility apartments."

Despite himself, Aire bristled. "With all due respect, I know where the hell it leads, Sire."

"Then you would also know it's an idiotic choice. Anyone going there would hit a sequence of dead ends, plus a few trivial exits leading to a fucking vegetable garden."

"Fair enough, Your Highness. Except you're assuming the trespassers won't use the restricted passages in that vicinity."

"Which are among the most heavily guarded, irrespective of a blackout," the prince argued.

Aire lifted his virtuous chin. "East is the faithful way."

"Fuck the faithful way," Jeryn griped, disgusted by the mere concept. "North is the logical way."

"For fuck's sake," I sighed, jamming my blade into its case. "Infiltrate the east wing," I commanded to Aire before turning my lethal glower on the iceberg to my right. "And you can infest the north for all I give a shit. I'm for the south wing."

The knight and prince split, their outlines dissolving into the black. Aire knew these outlets, whereas I only guessed how the fuck Jeryn had figured it out. Though with Winter's reputation for being a walking encyclopedia, I wasn't about to question his trivia prowess. Routinely, this world gave the prince's malevolent brain credit for knowing more facts than any human on the continent.

Ergo, he was right. No trespassers would intentionally head to an area where the secret channels had the greatest number of guards apart from the Royal wing. Not if they wanted to quit the castle with a gagged—if not murdered—princess in tow.

Still, Aire's intuition wasn't unfounded. Not if there was a remote chance they already had Briar.

As for Winter's rational direction, it likely had to do with the servants' quarters in the north wing being the least patrolled area. Therefore, the easiest way out.

But one thing I had on them was this: Intimate knowledge of my princess.

I'd know if she was near. Her scent, her breath, and her heartbeat would alert me. Until then, I burrowed into her mind, attuning myself to how she thought. If I'd found her once before, deep in the wilds of this kingdom, I could find my thorn in this castle.

Stalking along the perimeter, I melted into the shadows. The bitter tang of blood coated my teeth, a glob of it having struck my mouth. Wiping my sleeve over my lips, I pursued the darkness, the silence and emptiness like a crypt.

Turning a corner, my boot slipped on an object—some type of cloth. Hunching over, I kept my eyes on the darkness ahead whilst snatching the item off the ground.

My fingers traced its slender shape, identifying the frayed texture of cotton. Bringing it to my nose, I inhaled the essence of tart apples. My pulse ceased, fear and fury converging. I hardly needed light to see what I held, for it would be thin and dyed the color of scarlet, a precious relic that belonged to her.

It was a ribbon.

Briar

Somebody was hunting me. Perhaps more than one.

I stumbled through a chasm, the air so thick with darkness I failed to see the tips of my fingers. The void reduced my senses, narrowing them to scent, sound, and touch. My nostrils inhaled the charred reek of a thousand snuffed flames, my rampant breaths chuffed louder than they should have, and the hard wainscoting dug into my back as I snaked along the passage.

Every so often, I flung my arms out, checking to make sure I wasn't about to bump into an object. A vase of cattails. A suit of armor on display. A body lunging toward me. No, I wasn't alone in here, and that circumstance was hardly by chance.

My eyes widened, straining to catch an image, a flicker, a shadow. Palpitations rapped against my breastbone, and the rustling of my gown filtered into the black, the noise sending prickles up my spine. As I inched along what I presumed to be a hallway, the runner muffled my footfalls until my heel clapped onto a polished surface.

Having reached the rug's edge, the clamor of my shoe charged down the corridor. Anyone within a thirty-yard-radius could hear it. Seizing against the wall, I pressed my scalp into the facade and mashed my lips together, waiting.

Nothing. The sound faded without consequence.

Kicking off my heels, I nudged the shoes into the corner and proceeded barefoot. The wood floor chilled my toes but made it easier to move silently. I padded into a bottomless pit, searching, speculating.

Rhys. Whoever had doused the castle, and by whatever unknown means, they must be working for Summer. They had to be the ones who'd poisoned me and massacred the born soul.

With every creak of the ceiling beams and stairs, panic fired through my chest. A gust of wind turned me in one direction. A shift of noise twisted me in another. Sweat coated my palms as they ran over the wall moldings behind me, seeking a makeshift weapon. Invisibility prevented me from aiming my thorn quills, limiting my options to whatever heavy or sharp object I could locate.

To my distress, my fingers encountered no such luxury. But with any luck, I would spot a blessed window.

Please. Please let me find one.

My toes bumped into something soft and slick. As my foot brushed the shape, recognition assaulted me, and vomit gushed up my throat. I shot a hand to my mouth and forced down the contents of my stomach.

A limp hand flopped across my ankle. As I padded around the dead body, my soles felt their clothing, the metal breastplates and leather vambraces familiar. I stepped over the prone form, then encountered another, and another.

My security detail. That was why they hadn't been present to escort me from the dance gallery.

Wetness seeped into my hem, likely from blood. I heard no breathing, nor perceived any sign of survivors among the entourage. Pressing my palm harder against my lips, I stifled a gasp and maneuvered past the deceased guards.

There was nothing I could do for them now. Yet it took ages to recover, to regain my equilibrium, to stop imagining their lifeless eyes gawking at the ceiling. Were it not for their duty to protect their princess, those men and women would still be alive.

The depths engulfed me like a catacomb, darkness swallowing everything in its jaws. My frantic mind invoked specters and ghouls. But no, my hunters were not phantoms.

I urged myself to concentrate. From the onset, we had expected Rhys to use the tunnels and infiltrate the castle. But we hadn't expected his cult to single me out this way, caging me inside these walls like prey.

I continued to move, schooling myself to calm down, to remember the complex's layout. I knew these halls and wings like my own pulse, had committed this stronghold to memory from childhood, starting with those nights exploring with Father. That knowledge had enabled me to sketch a map of the castle by heart, drafting with Poet a diagram of ribbon trails for Nicu, which we'd installed.

I longed to reach up and touch one of them. Tragically, they hovered too far overhead to make contact.

Instead, I monitored the path and consulted a blueprint in my head. Based on the turns I'd made thus far, my trajectory placed me in the south wing, the knowledge bolstering my confidence a fraction. I'd evacuated the west quickly, since the trespassers would try for the Royal quarters first. This, provided they knew their way around the castle.

I prayed to the Almighty Seasons they weren't familiar with the skeleton of this citadel like I was. If I could reach the lower level, it would guide me to the armory, the training lawn, and the soldiers' dormitories adjacent to the main courtyard. The place where I had given my speech. The place where the knights had welcomed me home. Few attackers would likely dare to venture where the soldiers of Autumn slept. Even if the warriors had quit the dorms, they must be stationed in droves around the exterior.

Or rather, I hoped as much. Regardless, that was the closest outlet from where I'd begun, the quickest accessible option.

The wall I'd been pressed against ended. I calculated my whereabouts, recognizing the hollow echo of four thoroughfares. If my estimation proved accurate, a stairwell door stood just across the intersection.

I clenched my eyes shut and pictured green irises. Two sets. One mischievous, the other precious.

Poet. Nicu.

Agony creased my features, but determination set my jaw. By Seasons, I would get to my family.

Taking a measured breath, I hunkered on my hands and knees, then crawled through the murk. With each trembling pace, my respirations quivered and grew shallow. My flat palms braced against the floor, grappling nothing until a hard facade manifested.

I patted the door, clutched the overhead knob, and eased open the threshold. A cavernous groan wended into a cavity so vast, it was hard to believe shapes and color had ever existed. I scurried into the stairwell and sat upright on the landing's rug liner. Clasping the rail bar would only get me so far before I stumbled and snapped my neck. The safest choice was to scoot down the steps on my backside.

Fumbling in the dark, I traced the thorn quills stacked in my hair and gown, then skimmed my wrist for a measure of reassurance. Yet when my fingers made purchase there, I felt nothing but bare skin. With hectic motions, I patted my arm, the action kindling an old fear.

No. *No.*

But yes. The ribbon was gone. As in the forest after my banishment, the scarlet bracelet must have unspooled and fallen during my trek.

For the second time, I'd lost it. But this time, I would not find it.

My face collapsed, a dry sob escaping my lungs—which I stifled as footfalls thudded into the corridor beyond the stairwell. Clamping a hand over my mouth, I peered through the crack, to no avail. I'd left the door ajar but couldn't see a thing, and attempting to shut it would only risk the antique hinges squeaking.

The footsteps grew louder, materializing from a few paces away. Terror gripped my throat. If I had remained out there, they would have found me.

Based on the rhythm, I counted five of them. Choppy intakes flared my nostrils. I grasped the landing, digging in my nails. With the other hand, I slowly withdrew a thorn quill, for all the good it would do without light to guide me.

Murmurs invaded the silence, then halted altogether. And then a coarse voice sang, "Come out, come out, princess."

"Enough," another one said. "She's not here, which means we're wasting time."

"You're telling me the scent of that expensive apple perfume isn't recent?"

"I'm saying she's not fucking here. Probably passed through, is all."

"The king said—"

"I know what he said, but the plan was to snatch both of them, and based on the carcasses in the Royal wing, it isn't smart to play a jester's game for longer than necessary."

The inflections didn't ring personally familiar. And how were they able to navigate freely, much less in the dark?

Poet. My heart leaped.

I'd searched the Royal wing for him but hadn't detected a trace in the shadows. My hope had been that he'd exited the castle safely and was protecting Nicu.

But of course. Of course the jester would find a way to shield his son and still come after me.

The voices and footfalls hushed for a moment, then stalked down one of the passages. With renewed energy, I crept backward. Slowly and carefully, I harnessed the thorn quill and snuck down the zig-zagging stairwell, needing both hands for balance and moving at a snail's pace down countless flights.

My fingers and limbs quaked. Wheezes threatened to trip from my lungs.

When I was a child, the first time Father took me exploring in the castle, I had cowered in the dark. Now his face floated through my mind.

Brave, loving, platinum eyes. The lopsided tilt of his beard whenever he smiled. The Y-shaped battle scar across his cheek.

I'm frightened, Father. I'm supposed to be fierce, but I'm so frightened.

Yet his gentle brogue filled my head, wrapping around me like a shawl. The words he'd spoken on that first night of exploring resurfaced like the sun.

Keep going, my girl. Even when you're frightened, you must keep going. That is how you reach the light.

Nodding, I did as he said. With every step, a name passed through my head.

Poet. Nicu. Mother.

Poet. Nicu. Mother.

Poet. Nicu. Mother.

At last, the final step leveled out. I crept from the stairwell and gained my feet.

Blessed moonlight dripped through a narrow window. Barely a sliver, yet it struck my vision, a thin strip of illumination plating the space in silver. My vision adjusted, then darted to an arrangement of lounge furnishings and the outline of a door across from me.

The armory.

I lurched forward—then yelped as a fist grabbed my hair and launched me backward. My spine rammed into a wall, and the toxic scent of brine defiled my senses. A male figure gripped me in a chokehold, and although I could not see him, that unmistakable voice crackled like burned paper.

"Little Royal bitch," Rhys snarled in my face, his fingers curling around my throat. "Filthy sympathizing whore." His grip vaulted my head forward and slammed me once more into the facade, my scalp exploding with pain. "I told you this wasn't over," the king spat through his teeth. "Did you think I was lying?"

Bandages encased one of his palms, where Poet had stabbed him during the roundtable, though the dressings did nothing to inhibit the king's movements. With his fingers locked on my windpipe, my thoughts swam. Lightheadedness overwhelmed me, and I gagged for air. Summoning the last vestiges of willpower, I thrashed my body against his, fighting to break free.

"Wanted to end me with flames, then with humiliation? Where's your lover now, eh? Not here to save his beloved slut?" Rhys taunted. "I warned that heathen jester when he failed the first time. Summer doesn't submit to fire. We have the power to create or snuff it out."

"Why?" I croaked. "Why are you ... doing this?"

Offense warped the king's features—right before his palm crashed against my cheek, the impact lashing my head sideways. The tang of blood clotted my tongue, and my temple throbbed.

With each restrained breath, my energy gave, and my arms flopped. And that was when my fingers caught onto a sharp object stashed under the skirt of my gown.

"Prudent Autumn. You should know the answer by now." Summer mashed me deeper into the wall. "I'm a superior of the Seasons."

My fingers flitted, bunching up my gown and slipping beneath the hem.

"I will not be overrun by abominations."

My digits snatched the hidden object from a garter around my thigh.

"I will not be undermined!"

My hand strapped around the hilt.

"This is my continent!"

And with a growl, I swung my arm, stabbing the thorn quill into his right ear. The king howled and staggered back, globs of crimson spurting from the side of his face. He released me so that I stumbled forward, air whooshing from my lips. I hacked, sucking oxygen down my throat while Rhys struck the same wall.

Against the king's hold, I hadn't been able to reach the cache of weapons in my hair. Thankfully, my gown had supplied me with additional places to store them. Whirling, I ripped out another quill just as the king bellowed and catapulted my way.

Swinging from his fist, I hurled a thorn at his chest, but the king ducked. I veered in the opposite direction while flinging another projectile, which only grazed his arm on account of the limited light. And before Summer could tackle me once more, I rolled and surged upright on my haunches, dispatching another quill, which rent the air above his head.

Curse him! The king's silhouette swiped my limbs from under me. I cried out and smacked the ground, my molars clattering. At the last second, the flash of a curved knife appeared from his mantle and aimed for my skull. With a yelp, I flung myself sideways and tumbled, snatching a mahogany chair by the legs and hauling it in front of me like a shield.

Rhys's knife punctured the seat. As he tore it free, I released the furnishing and scrambled backward like a crab, one hand fumbling for another quill.

The bleeding king charged at me, then skidded in place. He halted as a roaring figure catapulted over my body and landed in front of me. The male silhouette hit the ground on his knees, with one palm braced on the ground and the other clutching a staff in a protective stance.

43

Briar

The jester's form hunched forward like an alpha guarding his mate. "If you touch her," Poet growled, "I'll bleed you out until you're nothing but a husk." The last word ended on a feral hiss. "Fucking try me."

In the meager slash of window light, Rhys hesitated. But then another door flew open, and a team of bodies swarmed the room. I counted, identifying them as the ones who'd almost caught me before.

At their arrival, the king sneered and bolted toward the group. The coward melted into their outlines, guarded by them as they shot in our direction.

With a snarl, Poet sprang at the group. He pounced on them, whisking his staff and adding a surplus of daggers to the clamor. Bodies launched backward as he tore through the mass, and then another large form swooped into the battle while brandishing a pair of broadswords. The jester and knight cleaved through their opponents while I staggered to my feet. Doing my utmost to spot the assailants in this void, I released a thorn quill, the projectile shearing toward a figure who screeched and crashed to the floor.

In moments, the final attacker crashed in a heap. Silence descended, other than the gales of breath sawing through our lungs.

Poet's outline whirled my way. I felt, more than saw, his eyes crash into mine.

He dropped the staff. I dropped the next quill.

We raced across the distance and collided. His arms snared around me, crushing my frame to him, and I pasted myself to his solid form.

"Poet," I whimpered.

"Briar," he rasped.

The warmth of his skin threatened to buckle my limbs. An instant later, we pulled back, both of us checking one another for wounds. In the dark, I raced my hands over his body, not satisfied until I covered every inch of his torso. The slickness of blood saturated his clothes, but it didn't originate from him.

Quickly, the jester fished a scrap of fabric from his pocket. A dry sob fled my lips as he looped the ribbon around my wrist. "You found it," I rejoiced.

"As I'll always find you," he swore, knotting the scarlet bracelet.

Yet my relief was short-lived. Because when Poet brushed the place where Rhys had struck me, I winced. Whereupon, a murderous sound grated from his mouth. "I'll skin him alive."

I clasped the jester's face. "I'm all right."

Unfortunately, so was the king. One of the attackers might have led Rhys to safety, but more likely, Summer had fled and left his cult to fend for themselves.

Aire's silhouette lingered beside the casualties, where he mumbled an Autumn prayer. I swayed in the group's direction and knelt beside one of the figures. My heart clattered as I strained and failed to make out their features.

Poet squatted beside me and traced the texture of their blood-soaked attire. "Cashmere," he muttered before continuing to the next person. At which point, a hiss ripped from his throat. "Roughspun."

Cashmere and roughspun. Textiles worn by two distinct classes. Nobles comprised the first, and when I skimmed one of the fallen weapons, making out the teeth of a short saw blade, a cry fell from my lips. "Oh, Seasons." My head fell forward in remorse. "I'm sorry," I croaked. "I'm so sorry."

We had expected our enemies to be members of another organization, akin to the Masters. But from these garments and weapons, their identities left no room for question.

Courtiers. Harvesters.

Rhys had enlisted the nobility as well as the tenants of the lower town. He must have appealed to their combined sense of the greater good, as he had with the Masters. He'd inspired these people to lace my food with Willow Dime, to burn an innocent human in protest of my reign, and to hunt me through this castle. That explained how they'd moved confidently through these halls, despite the absence of light. Because half of them lived here, while the others had grown accustomed to sneaking in and out, presumably in the dead of night.

Poet and I had also theorized Rhys's cult might include figures dwelling both beyond and within these walls. Yet we hadn't been certain. These discoveries punctured my heart, and I mourned the victims regardless of what they'd done.

"We must hurry," Aire coaxed, though sympathy etched his voice.

Without a leaf to place on their foreheads, I mumbled the same words I'd bestowed on Merit in The Shadow Orchard, then rose with Poet. Yet as the jester harnessed his crimson-splattered staff and snatched my hand, I resisted.

"Wait," I said. "The prisoners."

Realization struck Poet's features. The born souls in the dungeon. They were still in here, unable to get out.

I had wanted to find and extract them. But I'd been alone, targeted, and unable to aim my weapon properly. Now I had backup.

In a faint slash of light, Aire's hair gleamed. After a moment's contemplation, he said, "They are not the intended quarry, Highness. I don't feel any disturbance in the air that signals additional infiltrators."

"Then helping them shouldn't be an obstacle."

"I also don't sense that the born souls are in peril."

"Not yet, you don't. And while I trust your power of perception, I must insist we go against it. I will never abandon my people."

"Then I will see to them," the knight vowed. "But you must go. Likely, Winter has already inspected the dungeon."

My brows furrowed, confusion tinting my words. "Winter?"

Quickly, Poet explained how the prince had joined them. Apparently, Jeryn had wanted to make sure his so-called property wasn't compromised.

"He hustled to the north wing," the jester said, but then his voice trailed off.

Suddenly, Poet's thoughts linked with my own. Dread lanced through my gut.

The north wing, where the servants' quarters were located. Additionally, the dungeons. And one isolated captive.

"Flare," Poet and I said in unison.

Grasping our weapons, we dashed from the area, relying on our combined memories to navigate the darkness. It took far longer to get there, but between the three of us, we managed while avoiding another raid. At the north wing's entrance, the First Knight broke away and headed for the dungeon and its born souls, to ensure their safety and seek out Winter.

As for Poet and me, we hastened in a different direction. For once, I was grateful we had separated Flare, even if we'd done so at the prince's cruel request. This action might have just spared her, provided we got to the female before Winter did.

We hadn't told Jeryn where to find her. Yet I wouldn't put it past him to figure it out. If he hadn't already, prior to the blackout, then he would during his present search. To that end, the methodical prince would cover every square foot of this wing.

Flare was dauntless and fierce but also sweet and compassionate. And something about her stoked the prince's ire, which would only damn Flare if left alone with that man.

The jester and I charted a path to the Royal cells. There, we blasted into a small hall of cubicles, also deprived of light but for the windows. Thank Seasons, moonbeams leaked into the confines. The place was deserted except for a lone figure who popped off the ground the moment we entered.

Shocked confusion inundated Flare's face as she gripped the bars. Her golden eyes speared through the darkness like a defiance.

In the shadows, Poet swiped a ring of keys from a wall bracket. We darted to the woman's cell, panting as the jester stabbed one key after another into the deadbolt while Flare watched in astonishment.

At last, the hinges squealed. The door swung open.

Flare skittered backward, her frown expressing skepticism. That, and a flicker of hope.

I extended my hand. "Come with us."

Behind the dark locks, the young woman's face pinched. And I knew why. She had trusted us, yet we'd ordered her to be transferred, to be cloistered without another soul to keep her company. The betrayal of it simmered in Flare's pupils.

"I'm sorry," I whispered. "He would have hurt you."

"He'll hurt you now, sweeting," Poet added. "Or he'll do it later. Winter isn't a merciful Season." A creaking noise from above caught the jester's attention, then he glanced at Flare again. "He's on his way."

"Please," I begged, my outstretched fingers trembling. "Please, let us be your friends. Please, trust us."

Flare wavered, glanced back to what I imagined was a pile of soil in which she'd drawn her sketch. After one final look, she twisted my way and slapped her hand in mine.

Warmth and calluses brushed my skin. I could have wept with relief. Together, we made slow but steady progress from the north wing, my hand latched with Flare's.

As we reached another generous shaft of light from a window, I glanced up. Finally, I spotted one of the ribbon trails we'd installed for Nicu.

Which brought my thoughts to him. Which conjured a memory.

While exploring the castle with Nicu and Poet one night, the child had discovered a random crack in the wall.

It's like a ribbon.

That's what he had said. At the time, I'd made note of the aperture, and so had Poet. Yet I reduced it to a rare architectural blemish that needed maintenance. But now ...

Like a ribbon. Like something to follow.

My tracks halted. Flare and Poet wheeled my way, their shadowed expressions impatient.

"It's like a ribbon," I murmured, thinking back on that rift. In hindsight, there had been something strange about the delineation, which had been seamless rather than crude. Not a natural occurrence or accidental flaw but an intentional marker.

"Rhys wasn't looking for a hidden passage on the Royal map." My head whipped toward Poet. "He was looking for one we didn't know about."

The jester's eyes flashed. "A deceptive outlet."

Yes. I gestured wildly to the ribbons, and Poet leaped upward, ripping the cord partially from the low ceiling. This way, we followed the garland's trail, each nail coming loose and freeing another length of ribbons.

While we crossed through the halls, I explained. "The ancient Masters must have created a channel for no one but them, then passed the knowledge to their successors."

"And their allies," Poet said.

Which included Rhys. That was the tunnel Summer had been hunting for, seeking to confirm its location.

In league with courtiers, that was also how the town residents had entered the castle undetected. With this advantage, they'd slipped past security and joined the nobles.

To poison me. To burn a born soul. To snuff out the fortress.

Recalling where we'd seen the crack, I directed our trio from one cord to the next, each one guiding us. Flare assisted, her eyes more adjusted to the darkness after having been imprisoned for who knew how long. Because I described the crack in detail, she was the first one to point it out when we reached the right corridor.

We paused by the rift; our fingers traced its shape. Now I understood why passersby would have dismissed this detail. It was discreet, blending in with the wainscoting like a grain of wood. But if this crevice worked like the other confidential passages …

My fingers hit a depression in the wall. The facade pitched inward like a revolving door, firelight casting through the fissure.

Poet stepped aside, ushering me and Flare past him, then sealed the partition behind us. The conduit dug into the earth for what seemed like an eternity, winding farther and farther. Mounted torches blazed along the root-laced walls, illuminating Flare's petite frame and Poet's tall physique.

"Fie and fuck," the jester groused. "Where the devil does this lead?"

By now, we must have passed the courtyards, the maple pasture, and The Wandering Fields. Knowing what came after those areas, trepidation prickled my flesh. Especially when pulsating hues outlined another door at the tunnel's end, where screams and crackles of flame reverberated beyond.

Flare released my hand and sprinted ahead. Poet grabbed my fingers as we barreled through the door and stumbled into another nightmare. Where there had been darkness before, now light and heat consumed our vision.

Months ago, the castle had fallen to ruin.

And now the lower town burned.

44

Briar

Flames. Everywhere.

The town had caught fire like kindling, scorching the night in wrathful hues of orange and blue. Bonfires meant for Reaper's Fest rose higher. Each blaze chewed on the facades, from brick avenues to alleys, from timber restaurants and taverns to forges and pitched houses, from hay wagons to leaf-strewn carriages and stables. Pyres bloated to impossible sizes and coughed embers into the sky.

No.

Thick pelts of smoke clogged the air. Immeasurable heat blasted against my skin. Charred odors singed my nostrils.

No.

Shouts and bellows sliced across the vicinity. Revelers dashed around us in a panic, some wailing people's names, others hollering threats. Castle and town residents flung stones, threw punches, and crossed weapons.

No.

Chaos ensued. Mass hysteria clashed with widespread confusion.

Perspiration leaked down my skin. Hacking, I swung this way and that, unable to process the anarchy.

My people. My home.

My nation was burning itself to the ground.

Among that, groups from the castle and town joined forces, shattering glass windows and thrusting torches against roofs while yelling, "For inheritance of the Seasons!" and "The Crown is a traitor!"

Half of the people sought to flee. The other half sought to entrap.

Poet yanked me against him and braced his staff. Beside us, Flare beheld the scene with a mixture of terror and awe, so much light and heat consuming her after years of deprivation.

My frantic gaze swept across the desolation. I had no time to shout, no time to stop the pandemonium. Only one thought rose to the forefront.

I lunged forward. "Nicu!" I screamed, my lungs shredding. "Nicu!"

Poet's arm slung around my middle, hauling me backward as a tongue of flame swatted past me. I scrambled to get loose, shrieking and kicking the air. A whistling noise arched overhead, and in a flash, the jester swerved me into a slender alley and jammed my body against the wall. Just as he covered my frame with his, a flaming globe crashed into the town square, ejected from one of the roofs.

The explosion cracked the world in half, the blast of noise harrowing. The ground quaked, chunks of masonry and bricks ramming into the foundation.

The jester shielded me, covering my head and hunching into my body as debris rained on us. When the collision halted, he jolted back. Dust and sweat coated his features, but those eyes flared like green scythes.

The jester seized my face. "He's with your mother!"

"But where?" I panicked.

"We'll find him," he growled. "We'll find them both!"

Over Poet's shoulder, I caught sight of Aire and his troops flooding the town, the knight's legion scattering too quickly for us to signal him. Yet the soldier must have reached the dungeons and confirmed the born souls' safety. The castle was now a more secure place than here—at least, for the time being.

As for Winter's whereabouts, I had no clue if the First Knight had encountered the prince in the north wing. But if one thing remained certain, the prince would not be idle or without purpose. He would eventually find his way here.

I whirled toward Flare. The young woman rose from where she'd hunkered beside us, her bare toes and shoulder-length waves caked in grime, either from the dungeon or the tumult or both.

I snatched her shoulders. "Go," I hissed.

The female's eyebrows crimped in bafflement, then her golden orbs flashed in understanding. I'd just handed her what she deserved. Poet and I could not give this to everyone, but we could do this for her.

Flare hedged, glancing back at the destruction before steering her rapt attention to me. Her features bunched into a livid frown, and she shook her head. Mouthing something, she slapped a hand on her breast before transferring that touch to my own chest.

My throat swelled. She wanted to stay and help us. Despite everything, this woman refused to spare herself.

"He will find you," I implored. "If you stay, he will find you."

Hatred for the prince simmered in Flare's irises, the metallic reams flashing. Jeryn would shackle this woman, take her captive, and punish her for this defiance. Seasons only knew what he'd do to this beautiful soul, how the prince would exact retribution, how dark and cutting his actions would be.

My attention strayed to the sunburst collar tattooed around Flare's neck, then soared back to her. "You have suffered enough," I stressed, my words splintering with anguish and conviction. "You can go anywhere now."

Flare blinked, those eyes glistening. Her face crumpled, and she hoisted me into a hug, which I returned. Clutching her back, I inhaled the stunning fragrance of mystic ocean currents and fresh sand, as if they were imbued in this woman's blood.

My instructions came out fast. "Take the adjacent alley until you reach the beech forest, then head northwest. Eventually, you'll reach a creek. It will split into four directions and take you wherever on the continent you wish to go." Holding her tightly, I whispered, "Never look back."

Flare drew away and framed my cheeks, then glanced at Poet. Her lips moved again, and this time, I understood. *"Friends."*

Wordlessly, the jester unsheathed a dagger and handed it to Flare. With a grateful smile, she took it.

Swallowing tears, I watched her trot backward, her gaze latched to mine. Then my friend whirled and sprinted into the miasma.

"Come," Poet urged, snatching my fingers.

Clinging to him, I raced with the jester through the back streets. If we spilled into the quagmire, the public might spot us, and who knew what they would do. Neither of us would shrink away, but we needed to find Nicu and Mother first.

My gaze jumped from shadow to shadow, flame to flame. Beyond the lanes, I scanned the conflagration. Fear seized my heart, and fury lanced up my spine.

Summer could snuff out fire, as well as produce it. Rhys had said as much, and Poet had confirmed it, explaining about the ashes of Summer tinder on the way to Flare's cell. The king had supplied his cult not only with the means to extinguish the castle's flames but also to ignite the town.

The bonfires expanded in a way only Summer's resources could achieve, which reminded me of what the jester had also told me. When Poet tried to kill Rhys, he'd used stolen kindling from the king's suite, which was prone to spontaneous combustion when mixed with the right elements. During his last visit, the king hadn't merely brought the tinder as a personal preference. He'd done so to outfit his followers in advance.

The bonfires weren't of Autumn. This wasn't a natural disaster.

And this wasn't the doing of a small group like the Masters. Summer's cult had expanded beyond what we'd expected, having now taken on a life of its own, so that Rhys hadn't needed to lift another finger to incite mayhem.

Our attackers weren't an isolated faction. Our attackers were the people.

Rhys had gotten to Autumn's elite guild. When that hadn't worked, he'd mobilized both the courtiers and town residents who opposed the Crown's actions and beliefs. He rallied them like he'd done with the Masters, taking advantage of their sense of duty to this nation, their so-called definition of "normal" and the greater good.

Eventually, the propaganda had developed its own heartbeat. It provoked the citizens, dividing them in half—those who supported the monarchy, and those who didn't—and pitting them against each other until that became its own weapon.

I may have won over the knights. Poet and I may have staged a kinship with Winter. The Royals may have stood with us against Rhys during the roundtable.

But already this uprising had been building, like a fuse ready to blow. When Rhys had said this wasn't over, he hadn't meant that he would be the one retaliating. Rather, the king had implied something worse, more hurtful, exceeding the pain of betrayal from the guild.

Like the courtyard battle, Rhys had instigated this outcome. He'd been the spark, knowing it was only a matter of time before the public acted without his interference. All he'd needed to do was get them upset, get them nervous, get them motivated.

In the dark castle, Poet, Aire, and I had taken down the perpetrators who poisoned me and murdered the born soul. But they had been a mere fragment of a greater opposition.

That wasn't a castle invasion. This was a public riot.

Cries of anger scraped my eardrums. Nobles, servants, harvesters, and crafters collided in a fit of violence.

Pitchforks jabbed. Blades flashed. Arrows nocked into bows. Hammers slammed.

Blood spewed into the air. Houses and buildings sizzled. Cows, mares, and stallions galloped from the stables and headed toward the maple pasture beyond the fields, taking shelter among the resident foxes.

Several figures materialized among the havoc. I glimpsed a frenzied King Basil and a distraught Queen Fatima shielded by their guards. Members of our council rushed about, dodging looters and weapons.

Then a group of other figures skated past my vision. I skidded in place, a shout catapulting from my throat and getting eaten by the crackling flames.

Eliot. Cadence. Posy. Vale.

Poet had instructed our friends to help Mother protect Nicu. If they were here ...

The jester saw them too and uttered a harsh noise. In unison, we barreled toward our clan, only to be sucked into a vacuum. Few in this world matched Poet's reflexes. However, a mass of rioters proved to be another matter.

A wall of bodies crashed into us like a rapid river. Poet growled, his hand clamping onto mine. But the weight of everyone plowed between the jester and me, severing our grip.

"Poet!" I howled. "Poet!"

Wails and hollers smothered the jester's bellow as his fingers vanished from mine. Muscle and bone ground into me, the girth crushing my ribs. I scrambled for purchase, desperately seeking Poet's hand.

The mass dragged me along like detritus. Panic cinched my chest. I grunted, wedging my way through until I popped from the swarm and stumbled into the square. Wheeling in a full circle, then spinning the other way, I scrambled for the jester's outline or any familiar silhouettes. Gripping my hair, I searched and searched and searched.

And found. And my feet shuffled backward.

The ominous figure stood in the shadows near a water well, his view unobstructed. Those vengeful eyes gleamed, blood crusted his ear from where I'd stabbed him, and more crimson speckled his bandaged hand, the latter courtesy of Poet's dagger.

Rhys's leer fastened onto me. I froze, momentarily arrested by his gaze before rage curdled my blood. Baring my teeth, I yanked out a thorn quill.

But Summer only narrowed his eyes in pleasure. Then he spoke, his accusatory tone ringing across the square. "The Mad Princess!"

A host of revelers swerved my way, their grimaces stalling my movements. In their features, I saw resentment, treachery, and blame. Although half of the public sided our clan, the king's followers caught sight of me first. The scales tipped fully, the devastation of their homes, businesses, and kingdom too much for them to bear. They held me accountable.

I could not hurt my people. But if I didn't, they would hurt me.

Rhys muttered again, this time lower. "Punish her."

That did it. The mob stormed into motion, charging too quickly and from too many directions. Before I knew it, the quill tumbled from my grip. A hundred hands grabbed and pulled on my gown, my hair, my limbs.

The rioters drowned out my scream as they hauled me across the square. Chants chorused into the air, rising alongside plumes of smoke.

"Burn her!"

"Burn the princess!"

I thrashed against their grip. I bucked and sank my teeth into flesh.

The world rushed by, as if I were being carried by a rushing tide. Flames popped and fizzed. All at once, I found myself being lifted and lugged over a heap of logs. Ropes snagged around my wrists, binding me to a post, and my frazzled mind registered where they'd taken me.

It was a pyre.

My heart clattered in my chest. My gaze darted across the courtyard, past the surrounding faces, straining for a glimpse of green eyes.

On the fringes, Eliot materialized. Savagery contorted his features as he discovered what they'd done. Bellowing in fury, he lashed his garrote, twisted the wire, and snapped the neck of a noble who tried to block him from barreling my way. With my name tearing from his lungs, he bolted in my direction while slicing the wire across the gullets of anyone who intercepted him.

My ladies poured into the square and screeched. Cadence diced a path through the crowd with her knife, and Posy and Vale kicked and punched their way behind her.

Because the mob had snared me, the remaining crowd began to pack the area, my supporters howling and throwing fists in my defense. Aire raced into the onslaught with his troops. Drawing his swords, he battled a path toward me, combatting a horde of others including Summer's knights.

But no Poet. And no Nicu.

Not like this. I could not leave them like this.

My heart cracked open. Wheezing, I struggled and jerked my arms. The cords held fast, binding me to the post.

Then my respirations seized up. Out of nowhere, a slender pair of fingers skated over mine from behind, and the left bonds slackened. The knots unraveled and dropped, freeing one hand. I snapped my head to the side, my gaze landing on a pair of golden eyes.

"Flare," I gasped.

But the young woman just pressed a finger to her lips. Because of the smoke and haze, and due to her petite frame hidden behind the logs, no one had discerned her presence.

The knots had been deftly tightened and should have been impossible to untangle. Yet Flare worked quickly, plucking the cords apart with a confidence that struck me.

How? How did she manage this?

The right bond fell from my wrist. Yet I kept my arm pinned as if I were still manacled, cautious of alerting the crowd.

My chest pumped oxygen. "Thank you," I heaved. "Thank you, my friend."

Flare gave a fierce grin, then scowled toward the mob. My gaze followed in her wake, to where a flash of dark blue hair emerged among a pack of Winter knights.

I veered her way. "Now! Quickly!"

The young woman nodded and leaped off the pyre, disappearing for a second time. She'd done what she could. Now the rest was up to me, before the timbers ignited.

I braced myself when a voice shredded through the square. "Briar!"

My head wrenched up. "Poet," I whispered.

On a murderous roar, the jester blew past the throng like a cyclone. Nobles and tradesfolk launched backward, fountains of blood spraying the air as Poet sliced his way to me. "Briar!"

The front of the crowd brayed. Someone tossed a torch into the air.

I bolted forward, only to yelp and stagger as fire combusted around me. Threads of flame scrolled across the timbers and formed a cage. Heat scorched the logs as the wall grew higher, threatening to engulf my form.

The blaze writhed and snapped, its temperature incinerating the atmosphere. Captured within a corona of fire, I inhaled the scent of roasted fabric, then glimpsed my dress hem, which had split from the tumult, the edges blackening like soot.

Suddenly, childish laughter skipped into my head. Its owner's smile surfaced like a dream, with Nicu's face rising before me.

The setting beyond rippled, blurred by the searing blaze. Yet I saw my jester slaughtering his way to me. "Briar!"

My flesh stung, but the vision of him reminded me of other blazes we'd shared. A wick flickering. A taper held aloft by a male hand. Like a fantasy, Poet's face appeared, that wicked smirk curling across his features as he denied me a candle on the night we met.

A red hot scarlet ribbon. A rose whose thorns could not burn.

Whose thorns could not burn.

My chest hitched. The rose in my hair. Poet had said its thorns were impervious to fire, and if one drew in their essence, it protected that person. The effect did not work forever but long enough to create a temporary barrier.

That dark magic extends to you and everything you keep close.

His words reemerged from the day I'd recovered after my allergy poisoning. At the same time, the environment watered, the inferno growing stronger, the molten heatwaves compromising visibility. Yet as realization struck, I closed my eyes and pictured the faces that mattered. Then I opened my gaze and glared at the flames.

Summer created fire. But Autumn survived it.

Plucking the rose from my hair, I traced its petals and barbed stem. I winced as I pricked my thumb, a pearl of blood rising to the surface. Armed as best as possible, I sucked in a breath. Then I stepped forward.

I could have jumped, but that was my jester's style. Rather, I walked like a ruler.

Tenacious. Resilient.

The flames hit my skin. They lapped at my dress, stoking it like a hundred pokers. And yet.

They didn't penetrate the garment. They didn't burn me.

Poet slashed a path through the mob. When he finally breached the front, I broke into desperate motion. The jester glimpsed the rose in my hand, which wiped the terror from his face. Understanding dawned an instant before he charged, hurled himself into the flames with the agility of a jaguar, and landed millimeters from me.

On a furious cry, I threw myself at him. The jester mashed me against his frame, and my body became armor, screening him from being scorched.

... and everything you keep close.

Standing within the bonfire's heart, we held fast, held tight, held on. Never letting this go. Never letting *us* go. We clutched one another, engulfed in the blaze, which danced around us in a tableau of orange and blue. Sparks whisked overhead, yet the wall of heat and the laurel of slashing flames failed to reach us. They merely formed a wreath, an unbroken circle that felt more like a shield than a trap.

Like a ribbon. Like a crown.

As we inched apart, Poet's rage dissolved as he held my face. Relief, wonder, and love glittered in his eyes. I gripped his jaw, splaying my fingers over his skin and marveling at the molten light sketching his features.

For my Season, for my kingdom, for this man.

For them, I would walk through fire.

As would my jester.

To be safe, I nicked Poet's thumb with the thorn, a bead of crimson pressing through his flesh. Slowly, he slid the droplet across my lower lip. Then with a fractured groan, he snatched my mouth with his.

Enveloped in a circlet of flames, my jester kissed me. His mouth fused to mine, hard and harsh, licking his blood from my lips, sharing the taste of it with me. Seasons, I clasped his face and kissed him back, my mouth opening for the desperate lash of his tongue.

It lasted seconds, yet the fit of his lips penetrated the crux of my body, bestowing me with inexhaustible strength. Gasping out of the embrace, we heaved for oxygen. After another swift brush of the lips, Poet linked hands with me. Turning, we strode through the flames without so much as a blister.

The mob had stalled earlier, their expressions captivated as they'd witnessed me and the jester embracing in the nexus of a fire. My kin, my court, my people. Now they gazed as their princess and jester stepped through, our movements in tandem to one another, so that Poet and I sank to our knees in unison.

As one, we had survived their anger and fear. As one, we knelt for our Season.

Just like that, the riot ended. The mayhem disintegrated, and silence washed through the square, apart from the crackling flames.

They could have accused us of using some type of harrowing magic to defy the bonfire, whereas I could have explained about the rose. Yet they knew how almighty nature worked, and they must have comprehended. Somehow, the Season had blessed me and the jester, had protected us.

A speech flitted through my mind, only to disintegrate before it reached my lips. On the training lawn, my words had won the troops' fealty. But tonight, my actions alone would reach out to the people.

Mine and Poet's.

To kneel was to swear a vow. To kneel was to pledge oneself.

We did not seek to command. We sought to connect.

Regardless of the chaos, and no matter what they believed of me, this eventide did not need authoritative words. It needed kinship and understanding. Poet and I would serve them honorably if they let us. And if they trusted us.

Our bowed heads said many other things. This was Autumn, land of benevolence, and humbleness, and serenity. We did not solve our conflicts with bloodshed, destruction, and fire. We did not dismantle our homes in a fit of hatred and xenophobia. Rather, we crafters and harvesters built this kingdom from the earth, and we built it to last.

Perhaps there was one thing to be said. The only thing that needed to be said.

Finally, I let my voice carry. "I kneel for Autumn."

"Will you kneel with us?" Poet finished.

Their choice. Their kingdom.

And ours. Because we belonged to each other.

No murmurs or shouts. After a moment, shadows moved in concert, like its own brushfire. With our hands still clasped, Poet and I glanced up to witness nobles, courtiers, crafters, farmers, brewers, millers, servants, councilors, and soldiers lower themselves beside us.

Admiration. Penitence. Respect.

And yes, kinship. All of it reflected on us.

Basil and Fatima of Spring gawked. Jeryn of Winter stood among his soldiers, a dark frown cutting through his face.

Crimson stained Aire's armor, but the knight emanated with reverence. Eliot, Cadence, Posy, and Vale each bore contusions, welts, and grins. Our clan watched, their features alighting with triumph.

One glance at my best friend rinsed the final drop of terror. From across the distance, Eliot nodded to me and the jester. Slowly, he mouthed, *They're safe.*

Mother. Nicu.

My eyes stung. Unshed tears congested in my throat.

Two words chorused from the people, their tones hushed but

honest. "Your Highness," they murmured, their voices overlapping.

And for the first time in months, I took a deep Autumn breath. And then I released it.

Finally, our kingdom rose as one. For Autumn, we stood together.

Poet glanced at me, awe mingling with pride. That, and retribution. He might have commended us on that stroll through the fire, were we not preoccupied with a long overdue reckoning.

Slowly, we laced our fingers tighter. At the same time, the Summer King stumbled through the mass and then swayed on his feet. Astonishment whitened his features as our livid gazes aimed his way.

You're ours, bitch.

Poet

No surprise. Summer didn't waste time burning bridges. Rather than embark on a futile attempt to locate his lost soul, the man's face contorted. With a battle cry worthy of melodramatic operas, Rhys erupted.

The crowd gasped, parting in reflex as the king charged at us. Thundering into the motion, he barreled past the citizens whilst ripping out a knife and cranking his arm backward, the unmistakable direction of his weapon aimed at Briar.

Unfortunately for him, I was faster. Before the king had even sprung off his haunches, I'd already launched the princess behind me. Rhys barely got several feet across the bricks when my body plowed into his.

Touch the princess, and I turned into a full-fledged beast. And because my son wasn't here to see his father maim the enemy, I didn't need to hold back. My fingers grew talons, and my teeth grew fangs, and my vision grew black around the edges. Like a typhoon, my fists and daggers were on the motherfucker in less time than it took for him to squawk.

In a flurry of movement, I twisted, lashed, and pounded. The bittersweet tang of the king's blood spritzed my lips. The symphonic echo of his howls flooded my ears. At last, I finished what I'd started.

Summer squirmed on the ground, his body a pulp of arms and limbs. His left eye bloated to the size of a gourd and sealed shut. The burn scars on his chest oozed crimson, and scarlet red clotted the craters where I punctured him like a pincushion.

All the whilst, he shrieked in agony. He bellowed at his guards, not to protect him but to "Slay the princess!" and "Burn Autumn!"

I would dismember his tongue next. After that, I would saw off his prick. Then I'd snip his arteries, strand by strand.

But why delay the main event? With a growl, I snatched the king's knife, juggled it in one hand, and wielded my own dagger in the other. Crossing my arms, I braced both weapons inches above his throat. It would take one jolt, one reverse motion to slash his neck open with two blades.

Squatting over the king, I leaned on one upturned knee and snarled through my canines. "You've overstayed your welcome, sweeting."

My arms jerked—then froze.

Two different sets of hands had gripped my elbows, stalling the kill. I glanced toward the freckled wrist first, her touch gentle but firm, before traveling to her eyes. In that sterling gaze, I saw my homicidal reflection, how close I'd come to losing myself because of him.

Tenderly, Briar shook her head. "We are smarter than this."

Let us never be like him.

Recalling those words from the treehouse, I stayed my weapons. Aye, we could do better, cleverer, wiser than mutilating Summer.

He didn't deserve death. That would be too easy.

For Briar, I would tear the world to shreds. But that didn't mean I needed to carve the king apart to achieve the same result.

With every ounce of restraint I possessed, I channeled my princess's willpower. Whilst clenching my teeth so hard I could bite through iron, I maneuvered back.

Aire and his troops blocked Summer's knights, whereas Winter and Springs' forces remained neutral. That explained why no one had dragged me from Rhys's limp form.

As for the citizens, their gazes tripped between us and the king. Yet instead of abhorrence being directed at us, they visibly impaled Summer with righteous glowers and disgusted pity. He'd attempted to murder Autumn's heiress in front of them, whilst Briar was unarmed and seconds after she'd prostrated herself in the name of peace.

And however much the people historically valued pacifism over violence, they'd barely recovered from their own riotous actions, with the town flaming around them and broken glass carpeting the streets. They didn't have the time or right to judge my own rage. Especially not when I'd been defending their sovereign. Indeed, the denizens who had sided against my thorn, who'd chanted for her to burn, now directed their resentment at Rhys.

Some adults covered their children's eyes. Only then did I feel a jolt of shame. Thank Seasons, Nicu wasn't here.

Finally, Briar's attention strayed to the person hunched on my opposite side. I swerved toward the other hand braced on my forearm, taking in the deep olive skin, slender fingers, and signet ring. My head snapped up, my gaze colliding with a pair of steady but vehement eyes.

Giselle of Summer stared at me, her expression neither furious nor forgiving. Nay, she sounded too pissed off at her husband to bother with anything else. "If you don't mind," she said. "I'll take it from here."

Briar and I rose with Giselle, who nodded to Summer's troops, then swept her fingers toward what was left of Rhys. "Apprehend your king."

"Woman, you have no right to humiliate me!" the man gargled around a mouthful of blood.

Aire ordered his forces to disband. Summer's knights reluctantly followed their queen's orders by hauling the king off the ground.

All the whilst, Giselle branded her husband with a scathing look.

"You have committed continental treason. You attempted to murder a Royal in the name of *our* nation. You have broken our alliances, risked making an enemy of The Dark Seasons, and thus condemned our court to ruin. You have lied to my face, undermined my authority, and betrayed your marriage vow to act as my equal." The queen lifted a single, perfectly plucked eyebrow. "I have every fucking right."

At which point, she raised her voice and addressed the crowd. Every treacherous act against Autumn and The Dark Seasons poured from her lips, including every lie and fabrication Rhys had orchestrated, from his manipulation of the Masters to his recruitment of the harvesters, to his spies in Winter and Spring, to his hand in Briar's allergy poisoning and the born soul's murder. Without hesitation, Giselle left no crime unexposed.

Murmurs traveled across the expanse. The more people heard, the more they gaped at the king in repugnance. They may not support the liberation of born souls—not yet—but neither did they believe a Royal had immunity to do whatever the fuck they wanted.

Briar could attest to that. I tightened my arm around the princess, pulling her close. She gripped me in kind whilst our clan edged nearby. The ladies, Eliot, and Aire clustered beside us.

Rhys spluttered, a host of denials and accusations ejecting from his mouth like grenades, which struck like duds as everyone witnessed the cocksucker's downfall. He stabbed a finger in Briar's direction, his good eye slitting. "She's mad! This bitch, her jester whore, and their bastard child will be the end of our continent! I did my duty and exercised my right as a king!"

Switching tactics, Rhys petitioned Basil, Fatima, and Jeryn. "Spring. Winter. Tell everyone, curse you!"

But the prince only tapered his crystalline irises and lifted his imperial chin. Basil and Fatima squinted at Rhys in distaste. They weren't on our side regarding equality and tolerance. Yet when it came to authority, they weren't about to defend Summer either.

The king balked through his one good eye. The bloodshot white of his orb flickered in panic as it swung from the Royals to the public. Never mind which body parts I'd tear from him. One false move against this sea of bodies and weapons, and it wouldn't be pretty.

Giselle cast her gaze on Briar and me. "I imagine you have requests."

His heart in my fist would be appealing. Instead, I interpreted my thorn's deliberate silence. Stalking forward, I tightened my fingers around the hilt of my dagger and rasped, "Kneel to her."

Summer transferred his thunderstruck expression from me to the princess. Briar merely waited with a poker face. No gloating. No sympathy. Only her steely gaze expecting him to comply, to acknowledge her as a Royal before this nation.

His throat bobbed. Malice tinted his skin.

And yet. With every witness crowding in, the king clenched his teeth and sank to his knees. Knowing what should come next, he bit out, "Your Highness."

"And to him," Briar commanded, edging nearer to my side.

A low, rabid noise grated from his lungs. "Court Jester."

Good boy.

Neither of us told him to rise. After a prolonged moment, Giselle commanded her husband to seek mercy for his crimes. When the ignoramus did nothing of the sort, the queen sighed. "Stake him to the pyre."

After one cautionary look from the woman, the hesitant guards hopped to it. They swarmed Rhys, who spewed and thrashed as they lugged him to the mound of logs where Briar had been shackled.

Alas. My top three fantasies aside, this monarch wasn't about to go up in flames. As Briar had said, death would be the simple solution. Never mind that in the long-term, Rhys's execution could provoke his diehard followers in Summer. This man hadn't earned a quick end. Instead, karma became his fate.

The king flopped like a netted fish. At one point, he shoved two of the knights and momentarily freed himself.

Just before he could take a flying leap, a tumbling shape pierced the air. The weapon somersaulted, hooked onto the king's mantle sleeve, and flung him backward. Rhys slammed into the upright post, pinned there like a slab of meat.

People yelped, whirling about to spot the source. Briar seized my arm, recognizing the small axe tacking the king in place. Our gazes dashed across the square and landed on a hooded figure idling at the threshold of an alley. The little female adjusted the mantle, faintly exposing the grainy texture of her skin and a pair of hazel irises.

"Somebody," Briar whispered.

My lips tilted. "Wicked hell."

The child who'd worked for the Masters. We had believed she'd disappeared.

I thought back to the night market, just before Briar and I had attended the roundtable. The princess had thought she'd seen Somebody ghosting through the maple pasture, near where we'd been talking. Apparently, it hadn't been her imagination.

Across the distance, Somebody noticed us staring. When I tossed her a silent *Thank you*, her mouth slanted into a feisty smile.

Aire's head whipped toward the girl. His blue eyes narrowed in recognition, his gaze locking with hers. As if his attention had thrust a squall of wind in her direction, the child shuffled back. Though not before darting a glower the knight's way and sticking out her tongue, which made his affronted frown deepen.

Twisting back around, we beheld Summer's reckoning. Ousted by his wife, shackled by his own troops, denied allegiance by his Royal peers, and scarred by a certain jester and princess, the man flailed against the bonds.

Eventually, Giselle approached us. "I was with your Mother," she said to Briar. "And your son," she added to me. "And a small creature."

Tumble. She meant Tumble.

"We crossed paths in the maple pasture, where the queen was protecting the child," Giselle continued, taking over her husband's squawks. "That's why I arrived nearly too late to stop Rhys. And so, I'll say to you what I said to Avalea: I beg your forgiveness." She ducked her head. "I should have acted long ago."

After a moment, the queen glanced toward her writhing spouse. "Rhys will live. But his spirit will die."

A broken king. Indeed, humiliation and exclusion were harsher fates than a blade through the heart.

Sympathy for Her Majesty drew Briar's eyebrows together. Giselle had a right to remove her husband's skull from his neck, but that would risk the same civil unrest in their own nation. At least from Rhys's fanatic supporters. Best to live with a shunned spouse than a headless one.

Wordlessly, Briar curtsied, and I inclined my head. We watched the queen step toward Spring and Winter, doubtless to extend more apologies.

After that, we hastened to find Nicu and Avalea. Because they'd been hiding in the pasture with Tumble, guarded by a den of foxes and a contingent of Autumn troops, Nicu sprinted across the grass the moment we appeared. I lost count of how long we plastered him and Briar's mother to us, with Tumble wedged between our huddle.

Once we tucked Nicu and his familiar in a public stable, where they slept soundly amongst a bevy of other children, the queen joined me and the princess in the square.

Along with the people, our clan snuffed out the flames, worked around the battered and brittle king, corralled the dead for a mass burial, and cleared up the rubble. No one responded to Rhys's growls, which eventually became whines. No one glanced his way, having dealt enough with his shit. Throughout the night, we disregarded him in a manner he'd have to get used to. As if he didn't fucking exist.

46

Poet

Did we eventually untie him? Aye.

By then, the miserable shit had gone silent, with his eyes glazed and his fury diluted to the equivalent of a wet rag. This effect would last much longer than a quick beheading, the king's future as a social and political pariah set in stone not only throughout the continent but in his own court. Already Summer's knights responded only to Giselle, who ordered her husband's bulk deposited into a carriage separate from hers, upon Summer and Spring's departure the next morning.

Did Summer, Spring, and Winter still adhere to the same beliefs? Aye.

Likely that wouldn't change in the span of decades, much less in a few days. They would enact the dreaded Fools Decree and trade born souls, an exception in which the Seasons would still interact with Summer.

Although Giselle had begged our pardon regarding the spies, and although she despised the lengths to which her bigoted husband had gone, that didn't mean her mindset diverted from his. She believed as Basil and Fatima believed, as Doria and Silvia believed, and as the Winter heir believed.

Did this dissuade the jester and princess? Fuck nay.

Autumn's position with Spring had mended. Basil and Fatima invited Briar and me to the next Peace Talks, where the princess and I would renew our mission to sway the Seasons. That Giselle would attend without Rhys equipped us with a perk, one obstacle against our campaign eliminated.

It marked a new beginning, a clearer path. All change began with a spark.

Over the next few days, cleaning up the lower town and reestablishing a connection with the people consumed our clan. Helping to clear the debris and mountains of soot, in addition to donating all the supplies and food we had from the castle's stores, drained the last vestiges of tension and uncertainty from the denizens. Some still regarded Briar and me like anomalies, yet contrition, intrigue, cautious optimism, and awed respect supplanted the fury. They viewed us differently, the way Briar had once vowed they would.

Repentant glances. Hesitant smiles. Guarded hope.

There was that, plus the promise of more to come. Alongside the people, we set about rebuilding Autumn from the ground up, in a myriad of ways.

Mayhap it had been witnessing us walk through an inferno. Mayhap it had been the moment we'd knelt for this kingdom.

Either way, the change was palpable. This time, for the better.

Outside of the reconstruction, we spent our remaining hours with Nicu, who recovered from the blackout scare quite resiliently. Doubtless, he'd inherited that trait from the princess.

Amid savoring time with him and resurrecting the town, we squeezed in several forums. With the council, our closest armed forces, and the members of our clan, we made plans on where to go from here.

That consisted of instituting a new Masters guild, which allowed every crafter—regardless of their pedigree—to present themselves as a candidate. The structure gave all citizens the opportunity to apply themselves, which won over the public. That was the easy part.

The more difficult debate focused on the treatment of born souls. Briar and I laid out a proposal to remove the people from captivity. We would nurture their trade skills through apprenticeships and pay them in ways that the other courts didn't: good lodging, plenty of food, and physicians' care.

As for the mad, anyone deemed hostile—after a series of medical examinations—would be given residence in an outlying village established solely for them, guarded but with humane conditions and doctors. It would be complicated, and sometimes we might misjudge a person's capacity. Overestimate. Underestimate. Improving on that would take a lifetime of work.

Briar also talked about restoring The Lost Treehouses into a haven. That would require the forest's blessing, which would require a heap of trust in the wild to keep its occupants safe. Moreover, it would involve a whirlwind of renovations to the enclave, which might take decades to accomplish. But eventually, we'd get there.

At first, most of the advisors opposed our propositions. At which point, Briar, Avalea, and their jester talked the members in circles until they were too dizzy to object, much less recall when they'd last consulted their morals.

The princess scheduled with me a series of speaking tours, which would take us from here to the borders of Autumn. This way, we would reach out to the Season's greater population, crusading for a shift in tolerance, presenting stories and truths, urging our audience to reconsider the divinity of the Seasons—the continent's faith in the mystery of nature. We would speak to every villager, every tradesperson, and every noble. We'd hear them out, debate with them, learn, and educate. Slowly we'd inspire not just this court but every acre of this kingdom.

With any luck, the Seasons would join us someday. With Spring, we might have a chance now. Winter, who the fuck knew. Summer, well. Miracles did happen. If they somehow managed to set aside their shit in the future, each court had something to contribute, and we'd have a greater impact together than apart.

In time, we would dismantle the Fools Decree.

Change wouldn't happen overnight. But with Briar's tenacity and my tongue, we'd see a new day in our lifetime. More importantly, in Nicu's lifetime.

One year after another. One word after another.

And did our busy schedules leave less opportunities for more carnal endeavors? Had we ever given that impression? Perish the fucking thought.

47

Poet

Briar's tranquil sigh floated through the room, the sound tripping into a stunned gasp as my head dipped between her thighs. She'd already been on the cusp of waking up, for I knew her patterns, the slender exhale that always preceded her eyes opening. But now the princess jolted awake, her startled inhale trembling into a moan.

"Poet," she keened, her voice thick with the remnants of a dream.

"Morning, Princess," I purred. "Feel like behaving yourself?"

Her answer would be no. And my reply would be slow and torturous.

Except when she attempted to respond, an illicit sound burst from her lips. It might have had something to do with my fingers tracing the lips of her pussy, which had begun to slicken with arousal. A small cry broke from her throat as I etched and swabbed her walls with lazy strokes, my digit curling back and forth.

We'd ruined each other over the course of several hours last night, yet that had only stoked my cravings. Under the quilt, my naked body spanned hers, my face hovered inches from where damp heat radiated in the delicious slit of Briar's legs. The layers of my hair brushed her knees, which parted and granted me further access. On a hum, I hooked my palms around her calves and spread the princess, the motion inebriating my senses with the wet fragrance of her desire.

Sucking in another breath, Briar arched off the bed. Fluid soaked that dark, delicate opening, so ripe for my palate. Her spine curled higher as I ducked my lips into the tight rift of her body and gave her crease a single lick.

How I planned to suck this heiress dry and fuck her into the headboard.

Briar's fingers combed through my hair, then gripped the blanket and whipped it aside to expose us. Like this, she gazed down with bright eyes, telling me she wanted to watch. Oh, but then I would give her a show.

My cock thickened, the head broadening against my pelvis. A bead of liquid gathered at the roof like a temptation. Making a show of it, I swiped the cum droplet from the tip of my cock and pumped that same finger between her sodden walls, dabbing the fluid inside her.

Briar whimpered, staring as I added a finger to split her open. Baring her wide, I feasted my gaze on the cinched flesh, glossy and seeping with desire. The inflated clit poked from her cunt like a tiny bud.

Growling, I swept the flat of my tongue over the slot, from her entrance to the stud of sensitive flesh. Briar whipped her head backward. She clamped a palm over her mouth, then wrestled against my fingers as I reached up to pull her hand away, to free the erratic noises she made.

My tongue leaped between her folds, tasting her pleasure, swallowing it. Briar's hips reeled, her pussy riding my mouth as it siphoned in and out of her, the rhythm insolent and leisurely.

Still, the princess refused to release those cries. No matter, for I plied her so thoroughly she would soon have no choice but to scream past her hand, letting the whole castle know who took such excellent care of her.

Briar groaned into her palm. The muscles of her pussy clenched my lurching tongue as it fucked into her.

Flexing my tongue from her folds, I lapped up the drenched line of her body and then sealed my lips around her clit. Sucking and patting the swollen peg of skin, I bobbed my head to enhance the sensations. At the same moment Briar shrieked into her cupped hand, a fucking knock reverberated from the antechamber.

"Highness?" one of the guards stammered. "Princess?"

Briar's eyes flew open. She opened her mouth to reply, but another whine of pleasure slipped from her throat.

So I responded for her. Between flicks against her clit, I heightened my octave to imitate hers and called out, "I'm coming!"

Briar's scandalized expression dissolved quickly into a half-chortle, half-moan. This time when she squeezed a second hand over her mouth, it was to stifle the laughter. Slapping my shoulder, the princess scolded, "Wretched, wicked man."

"Wild, wanton heiress," I teased, momentarily releasing her pussy to snake up her body like a troublemaker.

Wrapping her arms around my shoulders and linking her ankles over my ass, Briar coiled herself into me. Her breasts pumped against my torso, her skin warmed, and those irises sparkled. "I shall have you punished for this."

"In other words, my plan is working." I relished my thorn's happy face. "For I plan to spoil you."

Briar's joy melted into another decadent moan when I angled my cock against her cunt and snapped my hips gently. She chanted my name, her pussy clutching my erection as I pistoned once, twice—then I grunted in surprise as she twisted her frame. Flipping me over, Briar straddled my cock to the hilt, her hair falling like a red curtain around us.

"Then start now," she demanded fiendishly.

I hissed as Briar swatted her hips, grinding her soaked folds on me before switching to wrap her mouth around my cock, devouring me to the base until I was the one hollering.

By the time we stumbled from the princess's suite and reached the private dining room abutting the assembly hall, Aire was guarding the entrance. Accustomed to our unbridled habits, the puritanical knight usually grunted whenever it made us late. Loyal and chivalrous Aire didn't judge a person's appetites, but he tended to grimace like a surly prude.

However this morning, his knowing expression only reflected joy. With a sideways grin, he bowed as we approached. "Your Highness," he greeted warmly. "Sir Jester."

"Poet," I corrected, grinning as the man flushed with pride.

"Aire." Briar took both of his hands in hers, then let go and regarded the exquisitely inked raptor tattoos peeking from the rolled sleeves of Aire's shirt, the soaring flock beginning at his forearm. "I've never said it before, but those are lovely."

Wistfulness stole across the soldier's features. "They were my brother's favorite fauna."

Empathy constricted my ribs. When I first met Aire, he confided to me and Briar about his brother, who had a similar condition as Nicu but died at a young age. What happened to that boy, the knight hadn't expanded on. But with time, mayhap he would.

Briar's expression softened. "You must miss him a great deal."

"I'd have given anything for him to see this day come." Aire inclined his head, his mouth slanting upward. "I'm heartened to know Nicu has experienced a different fate. Not without its tragedies, but still he lives. And while I breathe, he'll continue to do so."

This, I comprehended. The man hadn't been able to save his brother, so he spent his life as a warrior trying to save everyone else. Yet something told me he overextended himself, guarding his secrets the way he guarded this kingdom. It took a lot for the knight to confide in anyone, because we all wore disguises in some fashion.

I tipped my head to the side. "And what about you?"

Aire lifted his chin. "I have all I need."

Hardly. As I'd told him before, someday a person might prove him wrong. But that was for Aire to find out and not for me to assume.

Relieved of duty for the morning, Aire joined us for a meal. In this dining room, a maple trunk grew from the floor, cut through a rectangular table, and umbrellaed overhead.

With one hand on my fork and the other beneath the table, I coasted my fingers up Briar's thigh and rested my palm there. Seconds later, her own fingers threaded with mine, and a little smile graced her profile. Like this, we each ate with one hand. And what a fucking triumph to have a day when this was the only challenge.

Moments later, Eliot and the ladies strolled into the great hall in a flurry of linen, leather, and chiffon. Having been raised in a court of sin, it took the Spring ladies zero seconds to register how we'd spent our waking hours. One perceptive glance at Briar's face, which suddenly bloomed a calamitous shade of scarlet, then another glance at my depraved smirk, and glee spread across their features.

As the women did a raunchy dance behind the guards, their hips and pelvises thumping to imaginary music, Briar's expression scrunched into an exasperated and censorious frown. With a humorous grin, Eliot sauntered to his chair. Aire glowered at the exhibition, his capillaries bursting.

The doors opened again. Swiftly, the ladies ceased their dance and pranced to the table whilst concealing their mirth.

In their wake, Avalea stepped into the dining hall. Nicu trotted beside her, his hands laced with the queen's.

Briar's reprimanding expression faded, and her mouth broke into a smile. My gaze latched to Nicu, the sight of him moving freely through the castle—thanks to the ribbon installation—swarmed my chest.

My son's lack of height was uncommon for his age, so his arm extended more than usual to grasp Avalea's. But when he saw the rest of the company, life altered course. His eyes bloated with elation, and he proceeded to attack everyone with hugs.

The members of our group doted on him, each one beckoning Nicu and indirectly fighting over his attention. I savored the view of my son being welcomed, of everyone's features alighting on him as though the sun itself had just entered the room. Nicu had a gift for charm. Among this clan, he was an equal participant and a source of delight.

At one point, Cadence balanced her chin in her palm and mused, "So where do we go from here?"

The ladies and minstrel wavered. Basil and Fatima had pardoned their shift in allegiance to Autumn and invited them back to Spring. The Crown wanted its famed minstrel to return, the women had originally been part of Fatima's retinue, and it would be an insult not to accept. Unless they already had a standing contract in this kingdom.

Briar hesitated, looking to me and her queen for reassurance. When we nodded, the princess aimed a wistful grin at the ladies and her best friend. "It's your choice, of course. But um…" Timidity crossed her features. "We do have positions open as our Spring ambassadors. And this court could use an official minstrel."

The ladies had looked crestfallen a second ago. Now their features brimmed with excitement, though they withheld the squeals fighting to smash through.

Ambassadorships would enable them to live here but frequent Spring, allowing them to travel between the Seasons, to come and go as they wished. And if Eliot wanted to join the ladies during their jaunts to Spring, he could travel with them as a famous bard, delivering our message of humanity through his music. Moreover, it offered the group a greater role in this crusade.

"Sounds like we went from having one job to two," Vale beamed.

"Two?" Briar wondered.

"You don't think we plan to stop being your ladies, do you?" Posy insisted.

"And leave her to the mercy of an Autumn coterie? Not likely." Cadence scoffed before giving Briar an earnest smile. "You're stuck with us, Highness."

Pleasure kindled across the princess's face. "I'd love that."

After a moment, Eliot's low voice answered, "You know my answer."

His grin said everything. Thrilled, I watched Briar and her best friend reach across the table and clasp hands.

Eliot mouthed, *Monarch*.

Briar swallowed and replied, *Minstrel*.

She had told me of her plan to repay Cadence and Eliot for staying by her side in The Lost Treehouses. But whilst they didn't hold Briar in debt, she had aimed to give her friends something in return. Their new ranks granted them the opportunity to call both Seasons home.

At Nicu's request, Eliot retrieved his lute from the corner and strummed a melody. My son's voice sprang across the hall, his lilting tenor causing more than one jaw to drop, with everyone mesmerized by his singing.

Afterward, the occupants applauded. To which Nicu did something uncharacteristic. A bashful pink drenched his cheeks, so that he rushed over to me and buried his face in my shoulder.

Chuckling, I rubbed his back and shrugged at the amused group. "Never say this jester ever pampered his son with vanity."

As we tucked into our meal, Posy slanted her head. "The lines he was singing. I recognized the words, but I can't say from where."

Absently, Cadence waved her fork around while chewing. "It was yesterday's conversation with him. When Nicu asked why the leaves change color in Autumn."

"That's right," Vale exclaimed, then said to Nicu. "You have quite a memory, laddie."

"The Royal son remembers everything," Aire said. Swinging his head to Nicu, who'd migrated from my side to Briar's lap, the knight lifted a chalice to his lips. "Is that not right, Young Sir?"

Like his father, it took very little prodding. Eagerly, Nicu nodded. And then a quote bounced off his tongue before Briar could thrust a palm over his mouth.

"Bend farther, Sweet Thorn," he recited verbatim. *"Show me how deep you can take it."*

Every head in the room whipped up. Aire hacked on the remnants of his drink. Cadence lurched forward and spit out her coffee. At the same time, Briar's fork clattered to her plate.

From over Nicu's shoulder, the princess gawked across the table at me. Her mortified eyes ballooned, and her complexion looked as though a pomegranate had exploded in her face.

Shit. I'd groaned those words a few nights ago whilst I'd been lunging my cock into Briar. We had thought Nicu was asleep, but because my chambers adjoined his through the bathroom, my son must have awakened and heard us slamming up against the wall. Thank fuck, he hadn't followed the ribbon garland and walked in. If I had to guess, Nicu had merely disregarded the words, not realizing what was happening, and fell back into dreams.

I'd told Briar before that she was a loud minx. I hadn't been exaggerating.

Avalea clenched her eyes shut and massaged her temples. The ladies and Eliot compressed their mouths, clogging the hysterics. Aire was Aire, still coughing on his wine, wheezing as though someone had poured acid down his gullet.

Once he recovered, silence descended. Then everyone burst into laughter. I threw my head back, guffaws booming from my mouth. And despite herself, Briar's mouth collapsed into something resembling sheepish humor.

The only one who didn't participate was Aire, who crossed his arms as though we'd lost all fucking sense.

Kissing the top of Nicu's head, Briar's gaze clung to mine and stayed there for the rest of the meal.

After everyone left and Avalea took Nicu for a stroll in the orchard—with half a dozen soldiers flanking them—Briar and I remained, our attention fixed to one another. Separated by the dining table, neither of us moved, the tension straining from her seat to mine.

Briar leveled me with a look of feigned disapproval. "I blame you for that quote."

"By that logic, it also means you get to punish me," I replied smoothly.

"You know." She drew her finger back and forth across the polished surface. "At the rate we're going, it's fortunate we haven't been caught in a compromising position yet. We came close behind the shed, and eventually our luck shall run out. I propose we contain ourselves for at least the next twenty-four hours. Consider it a challenge." Her lashes fluttered. "I know you like those."

"Hmm." I slid my dagger from the harness at my hip. Tapping the hilt against the furnishing, I pretended to give her idea some thought. "Already worn out, are you? We haven't been that rowdy. Not by a jester's standards." My voice lowered to a sultry pitch. "I have far to go with you yet, sweeting."

"I beg your pardon, sir. But would you like me to tally the number of chambers we've christened thus far?"

"Please," I boasted. "I can count and don't need you to—"

"Or the number of surfaces perhaps?"

"That isn't necess—"

"Maybe I should tally the positions you've had me in as well."

"Briar—"

"Unless you'd rather I add up the number of climaxes," she goaded innocently. "I mean, that is a most impressive calculation."

Shameless princess. Her playful insinuations prompted my mischievous side. "Eighteen. Twenty-two. Thirteen. And ninety-nine." At the princess's stunned reaction, I flattened the blade on the table like a fallen chess piece. "Give or take."

Briar's eyebrows crinkled. After a staggered moment, she accused, "You made those numbers up."

Now *that* was a challenge. My trickster lips slanted, and my timbre deepened. "Did I?"

Never tempt a jester. Not an hour later, and on that same table, the number of fucks, positions, and orgasms went up by more than one.

48

Briar

Excited knocks resounded through my suite. Having just pulled a certain book from the shelf, I dashed from the athenaeum, with my dressing robe flouncing around my limbs. A smile split my face as I whipped open the antechamber door, sank to my knees, and flapped my free hand. "Come here," I gushed.

Nicu made a jubilant noise and hopped into my arms. Tumble had been slung over the boy's shoulders, but the ferret scurried to the ground and shot across the chambers to explore. As I held Nicu close, the scents of milk and sunshine wafted from his hair, along with something new and unique to him, a male essence I couldn't place other than to think of cedarwood.

As we pulled from the hug, Mother sidled into the room and beamed fondly at us. "He's been keeping me abreast of your reading progress."

Like everyone in our clan, Mother had learned how to interpret Nicu's expressive wordplay and lyrical vocabulary.

These days, she required less assistance from me or Poet to clarify meanings, and she'd become proficient in Nicu's needs, from leaving objects in the same spot to explaining distances and directions to him. In fact, the pair had become quite the duo. Sometimes Mother even accompanied us on our midnight excursions through the castle or to the harvest fields, where I liked to show Nicu the methods of reaping from our land.

I transferred my grin between them, then indicated the book I'd been clasping. "Are you ready to finish the story?"

The little fae bucked his head up and down. "Will Papa listen too?"

"He'll be here shortly," I assured him.

Poet would join us soon, once he finished meeting with Eliot and the court's resident musicians. We did not have an ensemble the likes of Spring, but the jester and my best friend sought to change that.

"I think the story'll teach me how to be a protector," Nicu mused, his wide-set eyes as brilliant as emeralds. "The one who saves us all, like you said."

"You can teach yourself that." I smoothed out the flaps of his toffee-dyed waistcoat. "Though yes, the book might contribute. It depends on which parts inspire you."

Nicu nodded. "Which parts make me feel honest," he interpreted.

After a moment, my throat contorted. "Precisely."

Mother and I stared at him in wonder. The painful parts. The blissful parts. The truest parts. Those would guide Nicu more than anything that merely thrilled him.

Raising Nicu could be strenuous at times. I would succumb to moments when I had to leave the room to contain myself, to keep from snapping when he refused to listen, or to scold myself when I'd fail to explain things the right way. Or I would be too tired to speak, to do more than hug him.

Poet had his moments of weakness too. When one of us needed a pause, the other took over. But always, the happy moments surpassed the obstacles. Nicu was spirited and creative and affectionate, his creativity and various ways of seeing the world often exceeding ours. Routinely, this child taught us more than we could hope to teach him.

And Seasons. He was growing up every day, in small but definitive ways. I could not wait to see more of it happen, to watch him forge his path, with the same liberties as anyone in this world deserved. The campaign to achieve that wouldn't be easy, but now we had a bridge, a foundation to make it a reality.

I handed the book to Nicu. Clutching it in one hand, he hastened to his ferret familiar, reaching Tumble just as the animal rolled like a hollow log across the rug. While the pair play-wrestled, Mother took my fingers in hers. "Your father would be so proud," she uttered. "*I'm* so proud."

I ducked my head and spoke to our linked hands. "I'm relieved you weren't there to see me tied to that pyre." Then I lifted my gaze to hers. "But I also wish you'd been there when the people knelt with us. I missed having you beside me."

Something haunted, wrathful, and protective lanced across her features. "I would have torn through that fire to reach you. I don't think I'd have been able to see this court the same way again." She sighed. "To be frank, I doubt I can now."

"Good. We shouldn't see Autumn the same way," I urged. "That is how things will get better."

Her features mellowed. She detached our fingers, framed my face, and whispered, "When they knelt, that was your moment." Glimpsing Nicu, Mother smiled with adoration. "And he was mine."

I swallowed, unable to have asked for a more heartening answer. Mother hadn't been there, but only because she'd been doing something more vital, protecting the person who mattered most.

"Thank you," I choked out.

Mother waved that off. "Oh, I did what any grandmother would do."

The word filled a gap in my chest. "Yes, but that isn't the only thing I meant." I waited until she swung her gaze back to mine, and then my voice cracked. "Thank you."

For everything. For every year, every day, every minute.

Mother read my expression, and her throat contorted. She nodded, then sucked in a practical breath. "It will always be an uphill battle, and there won't be perfect outcomes, but you'll endure."

"We'll all endure," I amended.

Father used to say everything began with a seed. Soon, I would take my seat with Mother and Poet at the Peace Talks, where Autumn would contest the Fools Decree. And someday, the document would be reduced to cinders, a moment in history that no longer existed.

Until then, we would move slowly, find a balance, and set an example. A juggling act, as my jester liked to say.

Mother's lips tilted in enthusiasm. "Not that Poet hasn't been a vocal asset since he first arrived, but I never thought Autumn would have a jester on its council. I'm quite looking forward to his contributions."

I perked up even more. "He's clever. He's shrewd. He's—"

"Briar," she said in amusement. "That wasn't an invitation to start a roundtable. I was convinced long ago, and I'm aware of his prowess and credentials. I have breakfast with him every morning. That is, when you two manage to leave the bedroom on time."

Heat sliced up my cheeks. She did not know. The bedroom was hardly the only place in this castle the jester had been inside me.

Mother flapped her hands and chuckled with agonized mirth. "Whatever supplementary information is going through your head, please. For the sake of your mother's heart rate. Do keep it to yourself."

After we exchanged a laugh, Mother said, "We're family. I adore them both, and I'm elated for you," she intoned, remembering about the engagement. Dipping her head, Mother raised her eyebrows and prompted, "Have you decided on a time and place?"

"Not yet," I replied, giddiness fluttering through my stomach.

Poet and I had promised it would happen when the time was right, when we were free to marry without threats or conflicts looming. Yet I could not resist imagining and anticipating that moment, wanting it more each day. Perhaps there would never be a safe time, and perhaps that was fine because we knew how to love and live amid the darkness and lightness.

Mother transferred her gaze to my bedchamber, her pupils gleaming as though a new thought had struck her. With a dramatic sigh, she floated past me, drifted across the suite, and draped herself across the mattress.

"Ahh, this bed," she fawned, running her flat palm over the quilt. "So cozy looking. And such plush feather cushions."

Strolling into the room, I leaned my shoulder against the wall and crossed my arms. The familiar scene played out, harkening to a Spring day not long ago when she'd done this exact thing. Only back then, I had responded differently to the display.

"Mother," I stated.

Mother feigned an innocent look and pouted her lips. "Yes, dearest daughter?"

I stepped forward. "Perhaps we could have a sleepover?" At her stunned expression, I pressed forth awkwardly. "Maybe stay up talking? We can brew tea, dress in our nightclothes, and gossip over our latest obsessions. And if we fall asleep, so be it." I fidgeted my fingers. "Would you care to have a females-only night?"

Mother mustered a generous smile, evidently misunderstanding. "If you and your ladies wouldn't mind the company of an elder queen, I'd be delighted."

I shook my head, approached the mattress, and perched on the edge. "We'll invite Cadence, Posy, and Vale another evening. Tonight, I was thinking ... just us?" My gaze clung to hers. "You and me."

Then it happened. My mother's face trembled in realization, and her eyes shimmered. She sucked in a breath, as though needing more air to get out the words. In a tremulous voice, she said, "Okay."

I felt those same tears heat the backs of my eyes. "All right."

Out of nowhere, Nicu sprang like a cat and crashed onto the bed between us, with the book tucked in his arm and Tumble scampering after him. Laughing, we gathered them close.

While flipping through the book, I said, "Perhaps until Papa gets here, we can recap. Where did we leave off?"

"She gets her crown back," Nicu piped, tapping the pleated bun atop my head. "Like yours."

I halted in realization. I'd pinned the rose into the weave, thread-ing it with the oak leaf braid and several of my thorn quills. Each frag-ment made up a whole that encircled my head like a band.

After swapping an inspired gaze with Mother, I cupped Nicu's face. "Like me."

I'd once vowed to forge my own crown. Yet it appeared, I didn't need to anymore.

49

Briar

Winter's silhouette loomed in a dark corner of the infirmary, his height throwing a knife-shaped shadow across the tile floor. In the bleak room, Jeryn's profile studied a tray of curved, serrated, and pronged surgical tools. His index finger meticulously traced the blades like components to a shrine.

I knew his stomach-curdling proclivities well. Though upon closer inspection, the prince's expression stood divided between reverence and … something else. I would say my eyes were deceiving me, because for an instant, he seemed haunted.

Physicians sought to save lives. But they didn't always succeed.

Numerous sections of this wing consisted of clinics and sanitariums. None of them rivaled Summer's whirlpools and healing waters, much less equaled the advanced medical halls of Winter's alpine castle. However, our facilities were sufficient to nurse the wounded.

Less than a week had passed since the riot. Knights, courtiers, and town residents currently populated several vast rooms, where our healers oversaw them. For this reason, Jeryn had delayed his journey home, in favor of doctoring the patients and thus relinquishing his sleep. And because of his help, a considerable number of patients would survive their injuries.

Including children. Jeryn had spent a large portion of his hours administering to them.

Yet our appreciation for this only went so far. His actions did not absolve the prince from other atrocities.

Unlike the rest of this wing, nothing but silence filled the vacant space where surgeries were performed. Though it hardly proved a surprise to locate the prince here. Apart from occupying his throne alongside Silvia and Doria, the man spent his days immersed in other obsessions.

Science. Experiments. Torture.

Winter's medicine resulted from practicing on born souls against their wills. Shuddering, I evicted the image of Jeryn cutting into patients while they screamed.

Currently, a fleet of black carriages and stags waited in the main courtyard. With most patients now stable, Jeryn was free to leave. Apart from his medical assistance, this man's departure could not come soon enough.

I only wished we could stop Winter from taking Summer's born souls. After spending days with Mother and Poet, trying to find a loophole in the agreement, reality crushed our hopes.

What would become of the prisoners? What would the prince do to them?

What would he have done to Flare?

At least we spared her from this prince. At least that.

Striding into the room with me, Poet must have sensed my repugnance. "Caution, sweeting," he advised under his breath. "This wolf can see through stone, and I'd hate to spill Royal blood before dinner."

"I want him gone," I snarled.

"Soon," Poet murmured while facing forward. "Very soon."

With the jester by my side, I folded my hands into a single fist and willed my countenance into one of decorum. One hour left, and we would be rid of Winter.

Jeryn heard us enter, yet he kept his gaze on the surgical blades. That meant he had something of importance to discuss, which Poet and I had prepared for.

"Leaving us already?" the jester pretended to sulk, right before his voice flattened. "Whatever shall we do without you? Though since this is my last chance, the suspense has been killing me. Finally, I must ask: How many wooly mammoths had to die for your tailors to make that coat?"

Jeryn twisted his head sideways. Those crystal eyes sheared through the darkness. "Who said anything about it being sourced from an animal?"

Poet seethed. Bile washed through my stomach.

Satisfied, the prince directed his gaze back to the tray. "Tell me," he said while sketching a fork-shaped apparatus. "Did you know this tool is used for extracting a person's tongue?"

"Did you know tongues were more lasting weapons?" the jester murmured with silken malice. "Perhaps that's why they're such a threat, as to require amputation."

The man's nostrils flared. His fingers pressed into the blade's pointed tips. "Where is she?" he inquired with deadly calm.

When we refused to answer, the prince straightened and turned our way, his towering form stalking in our direction. The closer he got, the more those blue crescents stood out under his eyes, like the kohl lining Poet's lashes. The chains ornamenting Jeryn's pants shivered, and the fang-shaped vial pendant—with a slight crack in the glass—hung down his shirt, the necklace jolting with his movements.

The prince halted on the opposite side of a table, the only barrier separating us. There, he flattened his palms on the surface. "Eighteen prisoners have been loaded into the carriages," he said between his teeth. "One of them is missing."

Indeed, she was.

Flare had vanished after the riot. Although I'd give her directions, the female's exact whereabouts were anyone's guess by now.

And even though we hadn't told the prince where we'd isolated her prior to that, he never demanded the information. This fiend loathed being proven wrong, clueless, or incompetent. Moreover, he despised needing anyone's assistance. Winter prided itself on highbrow intelligence and educated savvy, the Season's erudite ego preferring such challenges.

In fact, Jeryn had been searching for Flare's isolated cell during the night market, which accounted for his late arrival to that showdown with Rhys in the shed. This, according to the sentinels who had witnessed the prince searching.

How ironic that it took Jeryn a while to realize Flare had been in the Royal dungeon. So accustomed to complexities and overcomplicating things, this man hadn't made the simplest deduction. The jester and I had counted on that.

Nonetheless, Jeryn had made the connection during the blackout. We'd confirmed as much from Aire, who encountered the prince in the north wing's dungeon, just as His Highness came to the realization. And by then, we had rushed Flare from her cell, knowing he would try to retrieve her.

Poet's head cocked. Like him, one thing struck me harder than the rest.

From the onset, Jeryn had been referring to born souls as "plagues" instead of humans. With one exception.

Where is she?

She. Often, he referred to Flare as a person.

When we kept quiet, the prince's eyes tapered. "You might have successfully played with fire. But you don't want to trifle with ice."

"Over a captive?" Poet volleyed. "You must have a lot of time on your hands. And yet she wasn't your only objective."

On cue, I jumped in. "You had a second agenda. Something worth siding with Autumn, despite the social threat we pose to you."

Jeryn's attention narrowed further. "Threat," he enunciated. "I scorn Autumn for its choices. Your sympathizing faults and the people who follow you will not supplement your weaker defenses. However much damage your people have inflicted upon themselves, Autumn's troops are not vast." As if in fatal inquiry, the prince murmured, "Why the fuck would I ever consider you a threat?"

I set my palm on Poet's knuckles, stalling the jester's hand, which had bent toward one of his hidden daggers. If we interrupted now, the prince would stop talking.

Winter contemplated. "Rhys, on the other hand." He trailed off briefly. "While I detest your nation, I loathe Summer more. That moron is tempestuous, with larger defenses. As such, his temper might cause a tedious war involving my court. Winter would win, but at an inconvenient expense.

"With his army and natural resources for medicine, Summer is an essential annoyance, which needed to be put to heel." Jeryn leveled us with a look of contempt. "Whereas you, Dispensable Autumn, merely need to be disregarded."

Breaching enemy lines, the prince leaned across the table. "If I haven't made myself clear, you're beneath my notice after today. But make no mistake. We are not allies. If you try causing trouble for my court, I will act."

How I longed to embed a thousand thorn quills into this bastard. How I longed for Poet to do his worst.

By aligning with us against Summer, Jeryn had the same objective—to break the greater threat. Except Winter had been motivated by different principles. Scarcely a shock, but it wasn't the whole story.

We had suspected from the beginning that Jeryn had ulterior motives for bargaining with us. However merciless, and however the prince hated born souls, Flare's captivity and Rhys's submission couldn't have been the only impetuses for this Royal.

"Get to the punchline, sweeting," Poet mocked.

Something akin to intrigue, or perhaps hostile admiration, flickered in the prince's pupils. "I did have another incentive. Which you helped me to attain."

"Such as?" I demanded.

"The Fools Decree." Jeryn's mouth slanted. "This arrangement will make negotiating with Summer more productive. So thank you for that."

Abhorrence and shame overwhelmed me. During the Peace Talks, The Dark Seasons had sanctioned the trade amendment to that odious document. By breaking Rhys and reducing him to an outcast, it put Winter at an advantage when dealing with Summer. Jeryn had wanted the Crown desperate and groveling, which would now make it easier to drive a ruthless bargain.

Despite Winter's intimidating nature, everyone preferred a guarantee. Helping us to dismantle Summer's reputation among the continent meant Jeryn would have his pick of born souls. Neither court treated those people humanely, but Winter's captives suffered a much more violent fate. The room's surgical tools reminded us of that.

"My, my," Poet sneered. "And they call me a twisted fuck."

Jeryn brushed off the comment with a shrug. "In case you haven't noticed, your judgment of me is immaterial."

He might as well have extended an invitation. Leveling a shrewd gaze on Winter, Poet inquired, "Is that right? Then you shouldn't mind me asking this: What does Summer have on you?"

Of course! Summer's informants in Spring and Winter. Poet had finally gotten their identities out of Rhys before the king departed with Giselle. However, we hadn't been privy to the details, nor what information those spies has amassed.

Not that it was our business. The point was, it had been another motivation for Jeryn to go after Rhys.

The prince's mouth thinned. For such a careful man, it appeared he did have secrets after all. Poet had predicted this in the beginning. And from the way His Highness gutted that knight on the parapet, the particulars were substantial. Perhaps even fragile.

Instead of engaging, Jeryn hissed, "If you wish to remain in Winter's good graces, you will tell me where she went."

"You have no right to request anything more from us," I retorted. "We're done. You helped mollify a percentage of the people—"

"Yet they still rioted."

"The ones on Rhys's side rioted. Not the ones we influenced."

"I did shit to persuade them. It was all you." At our confounded silence, Jeryn grunted. "The reading and the dance at the night market. Did you honestly not see how the people watched you? Or is Autumn that naive? Because I certainly can't imagine Spring is oblivious to the reactions of its audience."

Poet's glower melted into understanding. "We seduced them," he said to me while keeping his vigilant eyes on Winter.

I recalled us translating Eliot's performance during the library reading, how lost we became in each other, then how the world disappeared while we danced. Thinking back, the people had stared in awe, mesmerized by some awareness that neither of us had recognized.

Winter may have influenced and pacified some citizens. But his false allegiance had not inspired the people.

Rather, the intensity between Poet and me had achieved that. Our raw and inhibited longing caused the shift. By not pretending, by letting our masks slip, they'd seen us as we truly were.

In general, what ultimately inspired people were the palpable fragments of life. Loss, pain, yearning, and passion. The open wounds, the scars, and the parts of us that healed. Nicu had said as much earlier today.

That was the reason half of the castle and town residents had defended me. That was also the reason others had not. The latter had grown angrier, increasingly frightened, and ultimately threatened by my bond with Poet.

And that explained Jeryn's puzzled reaction on both accounts. He had deduced the effect we'd had, even if he hadn't understood it. This desensitized prince wouldn't know how to define love, much less to discern the emotion.

I would have savored this discovery, had I been alone with the jester. Instead, I moved closer to him and latched our fingers together.

Poet squeezed my hand but regarded Winter with a quizzical expression. "So eager to deny your contribution. No bragging or imagining you had more of an effect."

Jeryn lifted a single brow. "I give credence to facts, not fairytales."

"Not even the ones with smut? That's when the story involves graphic fucking, which is when two people—"

"I know what fucking is," the prince stated in exasperation.

"Splendid," Poet replied. "Far be it from me to explain such mechanics to the heir of a know-it-all Season. Winter is a know-it-all Season, right?"

Jeryn refrained from stepping on that verbal trap. "Rather cunning for a baseborn, licensed fool," he commented instead.

Poet just gave him a lethal grin. "Try me."

Beyond the door, muffled groans of pain drifted from the wounded. Outside, carriage wheels creaked audibly over dry leaves, and stags clomped their cloven hooves. Winter's entourage awaited him.

Nonetheless, His Highness showed no sign of being in a hurry. "I want no credit for endorsing your crusade," he summarized with distaste. "My effect on Rhys is another matter."

The implication became clear. Jeryn helped bring down the Summer King, assisting us in cornering Rhys until he got sloppy and condemned himself, both at the roundtable and in the town square. Against the king, Winter had stood with and vouched for Autumn, which would have a lasting effect. This, the prince would accept recognition for.

And no matter how much I'd scorned doing so, we had isolated Flare at Jeryn's behest. Additionally, it appeared we'd unintentionally enabled Winter to bargain harder with Summer. A heinous prospect and the answer to the riddle of what else he gained from us.

"In any case, this makes us even," I retorted.

Jeryn aimed his chiseled gaze at me and Poet. "Does it?"

For now, it did. Autumn had established that it would not participate in the trade, other than to rescue born souls and bring them here as a haven. Still, Mother, Poet, and I would challenge the Fools Decree at the next Peace Talks, whether it made a nemesis of Winter or not.

From there, we would seek to abolish the document and every law contained within. Including the trade.

Until then, that left only one other evident problem. The fact that we'd reneged on our agreement. And the fact that he knew it.

Jeryn flipped back his fur coat, the scalpel knife at his hip flashing. "Now where the fuck is my prisoner?"

Poet extracted one of his daggers. "Take heed, sweeting. Mine is harder and longer. And I haven't begun to describe the size of Briar's."

Faintly, a muscle ticked in Winter's jaw. Finally, Poet had struck a few nerves.

Yet why had Jeryn wanted Flare caged? Why single her out for a minor offense?

Although we'd tried, neither of us had come up with an answer. This prince was far too skilled to let that reasoning slip in our proximity.

The possibility of anyone getting close enough to him, to expose his secrets fully, seemed implausible. What person could ever break this man to that extent?

In any event, I didn't know where Flare was. Neither did Poet. And so we let our silence do the work for us.

Jeryn's pupils flashed, the black wells reminiscent of a frozen lake—cold and impenetrable. Releasing the coat, he braced his hands once more on the table. That dark blue mane of hair slithered across the bridges of his shoulders, and his baritone voice deepened with intent. "Then I'll just have to hunt the little beast myself."

I stiffened. If Poet and I stayed out of it, Flare would have no allies. And I refused to abandon my friend, especially not after she risked discovery to untie me from the pyre.

But if we somehow located her and stepped in to help, it might expose the woman's whereabouts to Jeryn. Provided he didn't find her on his own.

Later, Poet and I watched from a balcony as the prince stalked to his carriage. The fur coat swatted his calves, and his steel boots glinted like spikes. Despite the spectacle, Winter moved through two rows of knights with haughty indifference, his gait nonetheless purposeful.

Dread chilled my blood. We might have toppled a temperamental king. But in doing so, we had unleashed a monstrous prince.

"Winter cannot get his hands on Flare," I stressed. "We can't let him."

"Nay," Poet gritted out, flipping one of the daggers absently between his fingers. "But neither will she. Don't forget, Sweet Thorn. That firecracker stood up to Winter. Not even Rhys had the balls to do that." In my periphery, the jester's mouth twitched. "That woman is a survivor like you. She might give her Royal enemy quite the difficult chase."

I thought of the expert way Flare had unraveled those knots to liberate me from the inferno. I thought of those fierce golden eyes. I thought of her kindness and courage.

In Summer, young born souls were forced to weave complex nets, to outfit ships. Perhaps that was how she'd picked up the skill to free me. Though that would also mean the woman had been imprisoned since childhood. The notion cinched my ribcage.

Yet Poet was right. Flare was a survivor. Captured or not, her fiery spirit wouldn't be so easily contained.

"But we'll help," I vowed. "Should Winter abduct her."

"Aye. When she needs us." The jester glanced at me and grinned like the devil. "I'm at your service."

50

Poet

It took half a dozen outfit changes to satisfy me. I'd ransacked my wardrobe, switching fabrics and accessories to the point where the closet no longer resembled itself, with piles of coats, jackets, doublets, shirts, vests, pants, and belts suffocating the floor. Alas, I lacked the nerves to clean up before the tower horn blasted.

"Fuck," I muttered, readjusting my neckcloth.

"Leave it, Papa," Nicu said from his perch on the rug, both hands flat on the ground behind his back and his legs crossed at the ankles. "No frills."

Quirking my eyebrow in the mirror, I speculated. "You think?"

My son's eyebrows crimped. "I know."

Now that expression, he hadn't gotten from me. Chuckling, I accused, "Bossy little fae."

"She'll like it better that way," Nicu lobbied. "It's a flame."

Meaning, it was more attractive. Scarcely six years old, and already he was noticing the difference between clothes that intimidated and garments that enticed. Thank Seasons he'd inherited my taste, albeit more refined and scaled back like someone else I knew.

For the second time, that bloody fucking brass instrument honked, announcing the hour. Taking my son's advice, I yanked the cloth from my throat, letting the ruffled neckline work its own magic. A black coat and shirt in contrasting fabrics, with corresponding leather pants and boots. No color but the ribbon bracelet. Nor any embellishments but the painted onyx diamond spearing through one eye.

Simple. Seductive.

Aye. She would do more than like it.

My lips tilted. "The world is waiting for us." Turning, I extended my hand to Nicu. "Shall we?"

Minutes later, we exited the castle. Fog licked the night sky, raptors cut across the firmament, and the maples glinted with maroon light. The crisp air smelled of merlot, lush spices, and woodsmoke.

With Tumble draped over his shoulders, Nicu hopped ahead and careened into Aire's leg. The knight grunted in amusement, then flashed me a rare but genuine grin before swinging my son and the familiar onto his shoulders.

Miniature globes of fire marked a trail through the pasture, then the harvest fields, and into the lower town. The newly reconstructed timber and plaster buildings rose higher than before, with leaf vines scaling the facades. Through alleys and thoroughfares, candles blazed in the windows, lantern garlands poured additional illumination onto the streets, and a team of bonfires writhed against the wind.

The largest pyre bloomed in the square, as it had the last time. Only now, revelers bounded and spun around the beacons, dancing freely instead of wielding weapons and tearing one another to shreds. They weren't the same people they'd been before, no longer congratulating themselves for representing the epitome of charity and benevolence.

Yet beneath the jeweled and glittering masquerade visors, their eyes seemed clearer and their gazes wider. As though a veil had been lifted, the people saw this nation's flaws as well as its strengths. Whilst the same traits still exemplified Autumn's culture, this kingdom of honesty had begun viewing itself with more rawness and criticism than before. The classes had become open to broader perspectives, including the nature of humanity and equality, which the princess and I spoke about publicly on a routine basis.

Slowly, we'd been integrating the people, freeing born souls from their confines and giving them wages, wellness care by the court physicians, housing on the castle grounds and lower town, and work in whichever skills they displayed.

Whilst that sometimes discomfited others, many of the denizens had grown used to it. We didn't live without the occasional outbreak of opposition from singular voices or small groups, but those infrequent conflicts hadn't led to carnage. Instead, the queen, princess, and I had established laws to prohibit hateful acts and invited the people to engage in a discourse rather than killing sprees.

One step. One day. One spark.

That was our beginning. And what a glorious one.

With the town rebuilt, the court recovered, and the Season restored, tonight we turned chaos into hope. One year later, 'twas time to host the Reaper's Fest bonfire ball the right way.

No Spring monarchs. No Summer pricks. No Winter princes.

According to the reports, Jeryn hadn't located Flare yet. But those reports also said he was still hunting for her. So the princess and I remained on guard, vigilant of news.

In the meantime, this fest belonged to Autumn. Blazes crackled, hurling embers into the air. To the beat of drums and fiddles, revelers pirouetted around the pits. Their masks varied from iridescent to woven of foliage, the shapes from slender to wide. Some visors sat upon long stems like scepters, and others fastened to the attendants' faces.

Not everybody wore one, though. I hadn't, opting instead for eye makeup.

The revelers not dancing tipped back flagons and hollered with laughter. Perhaps a few forbidden pairings here and there sidled into the shadows, mayhap influenced by the bold presence of former Spring citizens.

From atop Aire's shoulders, Nicu's face glowed with amazement. Behind his stag mask, a hundred flames swirled in his pupils.

I relished the sight, my chest constricting. Not only had Jinny's most recent letter arrived this morning—her tidings to Nicu had boosted his spirits—but several children waved to him. Since the riot, my son and those tykes had developed a kinship. Because they'd spent a night in the public stable, resting whilst our clan helped the town clear its wreckage, the episode had given Nicu an opportunity to charm the striplings.

Furthermore, the revelers no longer regarded him like a harbinger of some noxious plague. For my son, this had been a good day.

Beside the main bonfire, Eliot strummed his lute with the musicians. At one point, his fingers tripped, the notes faltering as one of the resident nobles caught his eye from across the expanse—a man with dark skin, slate gray hair, and a dragon scale mask. The minstrel's attention lingered on him, a heated flush stealing up his neck. It took a while for either of them to peel their gazes away. Even then, Eliot's head dipped, his mouth crooking.

Cadence, Posy, and Vale undulated and hooted as the minstrel played. Spotting the ladies despite their metallic floral visors and then getting a nod of permission from me, Nicu scrambled off the knight and launched in their direction with Tumble.

I knitted my eyes at the clique, my pulse ratcheting up. They'd kicked me out of Briar's suite earlier, shooing me off and hinting about a Royal wax treatment, a common practice in Spring. Not ten seconds after I'd vacated the suite, the sound of a rip and the princess's angry yelp had flooded the foyer.

I wouldn't lie. My tongue watered as I imagined the result, all that bare pink flesh at my disposal.

Soon. Very soon.

"You seem anxious," Aire remarked, lifting a chalice to his lips. "Any reason why?"

I caught the divot in his cheek just before he downed the wine. "Jesters don't get anxious."

"You've been fidgeting with that ribbon bracelet for the last ten minutes."

"Smug son of a bitch. I liked you better when you were surly."

Like a prompt, the knight grunted with humor. But because he hadn't opted for a mask, the crevices in his face deepened suddenly as a female shadow cut between us.

"Sassy," the girl commented, knocking her head toward the ladies who flocked around Nicu. "My kind of friends."

With that hood still flooding her features, the girl who called herself Somebody didn't need a visor. Yet I only made out the grains lacing her skin, a beauty mark studding her upper lip, and a pair of hazel eyes. "Ah," I mused. "The infamous hatchet vigilante. Fancy seeing you here. No axe tonight?"

"Not one that you can see."

"My favorite type of answer."

The girl snorted. Beneath the mirth however, a tinge of loneliness crept across her irises as she peeked once more at the ladies with my son and his familiar.

Occasionally, Somebody came and went. She made unexpected appearances in the lower town and then vanished to wherever she lived with her mother. Because this stripling never volunteered information about her life, seeing right through me every time I tried to wheedle details out of her, I had relented along with Briar. Although we only ever encountered her alone, with the random exception of a small bird sometimes followed her around, the tyke seemed taken care of. Her laundered clothes and the lack of hunger in her eyes confirmed as much.

But whatever reason she'd joined the Masters, and whatever it had to do with her mother, it was the girl's business to safeguard. And like most skilled players, she kept her secrets well. In the future, it would take a paragon to break down those walls, to see past the veneer and get this feisty, axe-wielding female to open.

Briefly, I mused who that person would be.

Aire squinted at the girl until she noticed him scrutinizing her. Twice, these two had interacted. Once, during the courtyard battle when Aire had blocked a knight from gutting her. Then again during the riot, when Somebody had hurled that axe and pinned Rhys to the pyre.

Since then, the First Knight was never around whenever Somebody showed up. Though from the way she tensed in his presence, I wondered if that was on purpose. Moreover, based on how they regarded one another with familiarity and speculation, these two remembered both incidents in vivid detail.

Pink crept across the places where the Somebody's flesh was visible. Nonetheless, the loneliness I'd spotted evaporated, replaced by a flash of defensiveness. "What?" she demanded.

Aire frowned, taken aback. "Were you hurt?" When she scrunched her face in confusion, the knight clarified, "During the riot, were you hurt?"

Fair enough, the girl balked as if she'd never been asked that question in her life, much less when it pertained to something that happened twelve months ago. The blush intensified, along with a healthy scoff. "I don't need to be rescued, asshole."

Appalled didn't begin to describe Aire's reaction, his blue eyes slitting in offense. "That is unsavory language for a—"

"A what?" The girl plopped her grainy hands on her hips and leaned forward in a taunting posture. "A noble?"

Huh. I couldn't blame the female. After a year, talk about a delayed question. Somebody had sprinted from the riot shortly after tacking the Summer King to the post, but who knew how long she'd been there amongst the mayhem.

Chivalry notwithstanding, had Aire been dwelling on her safety all this time? Even though I'd told him, on more than one occasion, that the girl was fine?

One wouldn't think so, considering how the pair scowled at one another. Such a shame that my princess wasn't yet here to see the bulky knight imbued in a face-off against a female who had to be more than a decade younger than him. To that end, I spent a prolonged amount of time observing the phenomenon until finally taking pity on them.

Because they'd never officially met after Nicu caught her passing through camp in The Shadow Orchard, I invited, "Care for an introduction?"

That worked. With effort, Somebody tore her gaze from the knight, glanced at my son, and shrugged. "I can't stay," she said by way of apology. "But maybe someday." Giving me a quick smile, she said, "Glad he's okay."

I inclined my head. "Until then, Somebody."

With another antagonistic look at Aire, the girl swung away. Then she halted and glanced over her shoulder, the folds of her hood ruffling in the breeze. "Aspen," she said. "You can call me Aspen."

Ah. That suited her better.

Since I'd once offered to share my real name with this stripling, I moved to answer, but she raised a palm to stop me. "Nope. I like when secrets stay that way."

This, I understood. Seconds after Aspen strutted into the crowd, Aire made a crusty noise. "Brazen creature."

Thank fuck for that. I chuckled like an asshole as the knight stalked in the opposite direction toward our clan, his shoulders level as if he had something to prove.

My lips twitched, and I turned to join them. Then my gait stalled, and my breath stalled, and everything stalled. Across the bonfires and the mass of dancing bodies, a figure stepped into view, firelight sketching the length of her cascading red hair.

She wore a copper gown with a square neckline, a corset bodice, and a wide, flaring skirt. The classic silhouette ended in quilted cap sleeves and swept the ground. Instead of a mask, a laurel of rust and bronze leaves looped across her head, with thorn quills strewn among the foliage and the rose I'd given her peeking from the cluster.

A crown she'd made for herself.

With the scarlet bracelet, gold and brown foliage painted in a crescent around one eye, and her tresses unbound except for that single dangling braid, this woman wasn't merely a daughter of Autumn, nor a princess of this court.

Nay. She was Autumn itself.

"Briar," I rasped.

A thousand other words died on my tongue. A thousand rampant heartbeats punched a crater through my chest.

Seasons all-fucking-mighty. My feet stapled to the bricks, unable to move as her gaze floated through the crowd and fused to mine.

A host of *oohs* and *ahhs* radiated from the attendants. They bowed and curtsied and murmured, "Your Highness," then jumped back into the revels.

All the whilst, our gazes never wavered. She erased the distance, intoxicating me with the scent of tart apples.

Her throat bobbed, freckles hopping across the flesh of her neck. "Jester."

"Princess," I husked, prowling nearer until our clothing brushed.

We stayed like that, hypnotized as the people spun and sang around us. At some point, shouts broke the spell. Cadence, Posy, and Vale hollered. Eliot and Nicu whistled, the clan beckoning us whilst Aire merely grinned and Avalea materialized with a nostalgic expression.

Pivoting and sauntering backward, I cupped my fingers at Briar in a beckoning gesture. "Can you handle me, sweeting?"

Leveling her chin, the princess cast me a daring look. "Let us find out."

We threw ourselves into it, letting loose around the bonfire. Spiraling from one pyre to the next, I watched the princess leap from partner to partner, stomping her heels in tune with the revelers, shaking her hips with the ladies and queen, linking arms with Eliot and Aire, and swinging Nicu in circles.

Then as we cycled back to each other, with her fingers clasping Nicu's, my son used his free hand to point overhead. "Mama, look."

And for the second time that night, I went still. Briar froze beside me, her eyes riveting on Nicu.

He said ...

He'd called her ...

Momentarily, the princess's eyes strayed to mine. Not long ago she'd insisted that Nicu should have the right to choose. However much she had craved hearing the word, she'd wanted to give him that power, to make the decision for himself, to change from being my son—to our son.

"Mama?" Nicu noticed Briar's glistening pupils, confusion etching his features. "Are you going to rain?"

Was she going to cry?

The princess returned her gaze to him and swallowed. "Not today," she whispered.

Nicu beamed and pointed. "Look."

Above, the lanterns glowed with different colored flames to show him the way. We'd installed this lighting effect for Reaper's Fest, with the orange trail leading home to the castle.

The ladies, queen, and knight swept our son into another dance. Eliot harnessed his lute and strolled across the square, where the nobleman met him halfway. Briar smiled, elated by the sights.

Feeling my ravenous gaze on her, the princess turned, the flames stroking her profile. Sweat bridged a heady trail to her bodice. Those lips parted, the vision robbing me of oxygen.

Fuck. My selfish fingers tingled, and my predatory instincts surfaced.

More than that, I felt the moment expand into something pivotal. Standing on the margins of the bonfire ball, the princess must have too, because she braced herself. "We once talked about how ancient cultures performed no ceremony."

They simply found a place that was meaningful to them.

And there they made a promise, traded a token, and fucked until dawn.

Air rushed from my lungs. "Aye. I do recall that."

"So then." Briar extended her hand. "Come and marry me."

51

Briar

Our horses pounded across the pasture, their hooves drumming into the earth. Tossing me a feral look, Poet leaned deep into his mount and kicked the creature into full speed beside me. My heart rammed into my chest, an all-encompassing need driving me forward. I matched the jester's pose, whispered to the mare, and flew through the maples.

Racing toward the glinting castle, our momentum matched. Together, we left the revels behind and galloped through the night fog at a ferocious pace. Poet threw himself into the ride, and I kept up with his velocity.

My loose hair flared behind me, the wind dashed through my dress, and my knees shook. I could have laughed out loud. I could have shouted with triumph. Instead, I kept quiet, hellbent on reaching the empty stronghold.

The castle stood uninhabited. Vacant. Secluded. No one there but us.

The jester's long black coat flapped behind him like wings, his corresponding leather pants outlined those powerful limbs, and his knuckles whitened as he gripped the reins. With that tousled dark hair and the painted diamond spearing through one eye, he resembled a phantom king, manifested from the pages of lore.

My sinful counterpart. My dark jester.

All. Fucking. Mine.

So easily, this man drew profanities to the edge of my tongue. So effortlessly, he inspired me to lustful cravings. So thoroughly, he owned my soul.

Perspiration bridged down my back. My joints tingled, heat swirled in the rift between my thighs, and every part of me throbbed to life.

Skidding to a halt in the main courtyard, I threw myself off the mare just as Poet's boots hit the ground. With a desperate gasp, I twisted his way at the same time the jester snatched my ass and hauled me against him. I grabbed his jaw and lunged his lips down to mine, our mouths crashing together.

Poet growled, his tongue flaying between my lips, prying me open. He swabbed into me, licking every moan that broke from my lungs. I hefted my own mouth against his, taking the kiss, taking all of it.

The jester pitched that hot tongue in and out, crushing his mouth to mine, feasting on my whimpers. Like this, we stumbled up the stairs and smashed through the castle doors. Our panting echoed into the cavernous halls, torches and towering fireplaces sketched us in molten light, and our heels scuffed the floor.

Kicking off our boots, we staggered from the entrance and into the west thoroughfare. With my mouth adhered to Poet's, I grabbed his collar and thrust him against the nearest wall.

His husky grunt melted into a chuckle. That sexy snaggletooth poked from his lips like a hidden gem.

My own laugh came out ravenous, breathless, and greedy. I grinned into that alluring mouth, then lapped my tongue over his slanted tooth. Sliding past his incisors, I ingested the flavor of red wine, a frenzy of decadent spices, and every indecent word he'd ever said to me. Seasons, I adored the taste of him.

I wanted all of it. The blasphemous and impure. The provocative and protective. The darkness and lightness. In kind, I wanted him to have all of me.

My fingers grasped the closures of his shirt and yanked. The fabric tore, the clamor of shredded velvet slicing down the passage. Poet hummed in enthusiasm, the masculine noise sent my temperature rising, and the folds of my pussy dampened, seeping through my drawers so that I felt my thighs go slick. His torso flared from the material, the stack of his abdomen clenching and those nipples toughening under my gaze.

Unable to stay still, we traveled down the dimly lit channel. On the way, we ripped off Poet's coat and shirt, firelight illuminating the expansive planes of his chest.

Passing through another hallway, I fastened him to a wood column. There, I spread my palms over his smooth skin, thumbing his nipples and skating down his ribs, the steel plate of his muscles hitching beneath my touch. That rampant pulse accelerated as I skidded my fingers along every sculpted inch, leaving no bit of flesh neglected.

Pushing me away, Poet stapled his forehead to mine, spanned my buttocks with one hand, and steered me backward through the corridor. Chuffing shallow air, we careened deeper into the wing. The jester's irises glittered, flooding my vision with fiendish green, the shade burning through this muted castle.

His free digits knifed into my hair and tightened on the roots. "Have I mentioned how cruel it is of you to wear this gown?"

I flicked my tongue against his lips. "Then take it off me."

Poet's gaze went up in flames. With a hiss, he wheeled me around, snaked his arm around my midriff, and severed the laces of my bodice in seconds. Black, glossy fingernails flashed in the half-light as he worked the top portion of my gown, the garment splaying apart to reveal a transparent camisole.

Rasping, the jester swooped in and burrowed his teeth into the crook of my neck. Sparks danced over my flesh where that warm, possessive mouth drew on me. I flung my head backward while he ushered us deeper, deeper, deeper into the isolated castle. He flayed my skin with his tongue, caressing me while dragging open the bodice, pushing the gown over my hips, and chucking the frock to the floor.

This left me in the sheer camisole, matching drawers, and a bronze lace garter harnessing a single thorn quill. Poet groaned as he slipped one strong palm into the neckline and seized a breast, my pointed nipple ruching against his skin. The other hand slithered into the front of my drawers and cupped my folds.

A savage noise rumbled from behind me when the jester discovered what I'd done. The hair that usually thatched my pussy was gone, leaving me bare and soft and wet. The ladies had assisted earlier, and while it had been unpleasant, I rather enjoyed Poet's feral reaction.

"Fuck," he uttered against the pulse point of my throat. "You will burn me."

"I think we'll burn each other," I uttered, feeling the high bridge of his cock against my backside. "Forever, I hope."

He made a noise of agreement, then curled his digit over my naked crease, flicking lightly atop my inflated clit. "Such a warm and willing pussy."

My stomach fluttered. Until him, I'd never felt more sexy, desired, worshiped.

When I stalled in place and uttered a plaintive sound, begging for him to trace me, Poet murmured, "Shhh" against my temple, then brushed a kiss there. "Keep going, love."

I struggled to walk, to let the jester guide me while he probed the slender cleft of my thighs, sketching the damp flesh and toying with the peg of skin, his ministrations igniting my body like kindling. Those dexterous fingers rubbed and skimmed each delicate fold yet never sank into my opening.

My knees shook, and my cries shivered down the complex. Poet's hoarse grunts followed closely behind, the sounds of us flooding the castle.

Finally, he showed mercy and released me. The instant he did, I whipped around and tugged Poet into me. Now I dragged him backward, with a trail of stripped clothes following in our wake. My corset disappeared, peeled from my body and landing on the rug, and my breasts popped into view.

Belting one arm around my waist, Poet focused on me while circling his thumb over one nipple, spreading my arousal over the budding skin. My mouth opened, a small cry escaping.

Baring down, the jester seized my lips and ate up the sound. At last, we blasted into the library wing, the doors whisking apart and striking the walls. With our mouths still clamped and our restless hands groping, we pitched past desks and study rooms. The giant mouth of the fireplace roared with heat and light, a great combustion of flames plating the space in metallic shades.

Among the whiffs of amber and vetiver, I inhaled woodsmoke and parchment. Suddenly, nervous anticipation gripped my chest.

Poet must have sensed this, because he pried his lips from mine. And that was when he finally registered the setting. We'd come here instinctively, without needing to verbalize our destination.

Yet hundreds of scarlet candles glimmered from every flat surface, highlighting the gold leaf spines, and the statuesque fireplace blazed like its own bonfire. In a facing indentation, niched between two built-in bookshelves, a pile of blankets and pillows awaited us.

I shifted, hopeful as Poet riveted on the atmosphere. That ardent gaze brimmed with recognition, then swung toward me. This man was so accustomed to furnishing the ambience, however he also knew his princess liked having control as much as she liked submitting. In his awestruck expression, I sensed him remembering the library reading, when we'd been ensconced in the stacks.

Are you thinking about the last time we christened a bookshelf?

No. I'm thinking about when the next time will be.

The captivated jester went still, the flames brushing that sensual jaw as he gazed at me, wonder deepening his timbre. "You planned this."

"Only the part where I fuck you until dawn," I confessed shyly, then pressed my bare breasts against his torso, my fervent words coasting across his lips. "The rest is our choice."

Our choice. Because whenever the ancients got married, they chose a special place to be alone. And while this wasn't the wildflower forest where we first shifted from enemies to allies, nor the meadow where we first kissed, nor the forest bower where the jester first made love to me, our life together had also been forged of written words.

The lines he'd recited in that mirrored hall where we first spoke, then the poetry he composed in a jail cell after we rescued Nicu. The decrees and documents we set out to challenge. Secret notes to meet one another. A book in my beloved series. The bathtub in my suite, where Poet had whispered verse as he made love to me, on the night before I was banished. An archive library in Spring, where his voice had wrought an orgasm from me as I fondled myself. And this Autumn repository, where we'd translated an ancient story to one another about enemies who became lovers.

Someplace meaningful for us. Someplace to make a vow and consummate until dawn.

Reading my thoughts, the jester stalked forward, his gaze penetrating me to the core. "Say it, sweeting."

He'd asked after we returned from the treehouse enclave. Now it was my turn.

My throat bobbed, my eyes stung, and my heart spilled off my tongue. "Marry me."

Slowly, Poet nodded. That devilish mouth slinked into a grin, and he husked between his teeth, "Aye."

Barely getting the reply out, the jester snared my hips and hoisted me against him. That wicked mouth snatched mine, his lips hauling on my own. That mischievous tongue pitched into me, stroking my palate and tasting my moan. I stood on my tiptoes, clung to his face, and yanked him down. Yielding beneath the strength of his mouth, I spread my lips and rocked them with his, urging the jester to deepen his entrance.

My breasts ground into the cliff of his chest, and my toughened nipples brushed his flesh. The jester's ragged groan vibrated from his tongue to mine. I savored the texture of his response, the gritty sound of his desire, then I pulled back to slant my own tongue across the seam of his lips.

Poet shuddered, his torso pebbling and his nipples erect. Empowered by this reaction, I burrowed my teeth into his plush lower lip and nibbled.

With a vicious snarl, Poet heaved his mouth into mine, sealed around my tongue and sucked. The hot wrap of his lips consumed my whimper. And then we were moving again.

Slipping his palms inside my drawers, the jester gripped my buttocks and steered me across the rug. As his feverish mouth clutched my tongue, we swayed into motion, Poet prowling me backward until we reached the built-in bookcases flanking the pile of blankets.

Uttering another harsh noise, he whipped me around and mashed my body against the shelves. Volumes trembled from the impact. Errant strands of hair flew around my face, which Poet swiped aside, the better to clamp onto my lips.

While his tongue swatted my own, the jester oozed his fingers to my pussy, flicked aside the gusset of my drawers, and sketched the swollen folds. I whined, my cleft leaking through the textile and seeping onto his digits. With a hum, Poet drew back to watch the effect.

His pupils dilated at the sight of my naked cunt peeking through the sheer fabric. The lack of hair exposed my distended clit and the tight line of my core, all of which dripped onto him.

"Wicked hell, Briar," he muttered while etching my intimate flesh.

My mouth opened on a slender cry. I gripped the overhead shelf and bucked my hips into his hand, both of us mesmerized by the sight, how the teasing abrasion of his touch wetted me thoroughly.

Unable to stand it, Poet grabbed the waistband of my drawers, intending to bunch the dainty material down my limbs. Instead, I jolted forward, brushed my mouth over his, and gusted out, "Rip them."

Unbridled could be gentle, frantic could be affectionate, and passionate could be poignant. There was no shame in urgency and no fragility in sweetness. We could be both, do both, and have both.

And now I understood this.

With this man, I could have everything.

Not needing to be told twice, Poet fisted the lace trim and yanked. The undergarments frayed, the shearing noise filling the stacks. Unveiling my private crease, I stood before him in nothing but the scarlet ribbon, the garter harnessing my thorn quill, and the laurel crown atop my head.

The jester relished the image, his dark gaze consuming me. One palm braced my cheek, his thumb lightly stroking the crescent of brown and gold foliage painted around my eye. "Mmm. I do believe this will become my favorite way to fuck you. Whilst you're wearing nothing but a crown and a weapon."

"Don't forget the bracelet," I reminded him. "Your target on me."

Composure lost, Poet snared my mouth, the sumptuous flicks of his tongue dissolving my knees. Deeply, he kissed me into the shelves and coasted his fingers once more to the drenched vent of my thighs. Instantly, he must have felt the drum of my pulse there, my pussy throbbing for him, because a growl wracked his muscles.

He lurched back, those green irises hooding, intent on observing what he did to me. An agonizing flurry of sensation coiled in the narrow slot of my body as he feathered his digits along my rift. I whined and squirmed, needing more friction.

Yet something better stole my attention. Poet's cock shoved into the front panel of his pants. Through the haze of pleasure, I imagined that long, hard stem of flesh and its bulbous head, all of it ruddy and straining for me. The fantasy sent a jolt through my cunt, which poured freely now.

Reaching out, my fingers broke open the flaps of the jester's pants and batted them aside. As usual, he wore nothing beneath the garment. Between the slope of his pelvis, the jester's flushed cock rose into view, high and hard, the crown bloated and the slit tight.

I had once thought he wouldn't fit, that I wouldn't be able to accommodate his girth. How elated I'd been to be proven wrong.

While he traced my cunt, I eased the pants from his hips. Poet stalked into me, granting my arms closer access until they shivered down the toned muscles of his navel. I glimpsed the taut profile of his buttocks and the faint scars he'd cultivated over the years. In response, he grazed his black fingertips from my pussy to my navel, then down again.

Bared to one another, we siphoned our hands. My fingers caught the stem of his erection and pumped him from the heavy sac to the pome, urging fluid to the surface. Poet's lips hung ajar, his features ravenous, yet those fiendish eyes glinted on me, and his own digits toyed with my clit, his thumb delicately skimming the crest.

We stared at one another and took our time, the movements hypnotic and reverent. Feeling, touching, giving. Never once holding back.

No restraint. No modesty.

The firelight blooming across his physique caused my mouth to water. At length, I released Poet's turgid cock and charged forth, the momentum detaching his hand from my core. Lunging to the opposite shelf, I stamped the jester into the facade, snatched his throat in my mouth, and sucked.

The jester emitted a harsh noise. Invigorated, I drew his flesh between my teeth and swabbed his pulse. Then I devoured the rest of his upper frame, dragging my lips and tongue down the center of his body, wandering across his pectorals and sinking to the grid of muscles that contracted above the sexy plank of his cock.

Parched, I yearned to sink my ivories into this man, to strap my lips around every inch of flesh and make him lose control. In his proximity, I wanted a thousand reactions, a thousand dark pleasures, a thousand endearments, and a thousand emotions.

Slow. Fast.

Soft. Rough.

Sweet. Wild.

My lips traveled, attentive and devout. I lavished his nipples as if they were his mouth. I strummed my tongue across his clavicles as though they were lifelines. I nipped his throat as if my own breath was stored there. Poet's chest beat in shallow pants, indicating that a string of obscenities and encouragements teetered on his lips.

Hissing, the jester manacled my wrists and hefted me into him. Books rattled on the shelves, one of them in danger of slipping. In the ambient light, his powerful fingers fastened my wrists on either side of his head.

Sweeping in, Poet pared his mouth across my trembling lips. "Kiss me, Briar."

Tears of rapture stung my eyes. "Fuck me, Poet."

Give yourself to me. Make love to me.

Trick me. Ruin me. Burn me.

We paused. Then we unraveled.

Poet captured my thighs and vaulted me off the ground. Instinctively, I bent my knees and hooked them over his waist. Snatching my laurel crown, I pulled it from my head and whisked it aside. My hair cascaded over my shoulders, the leaf braid falling down my back.

Anchored above him, I grabbed his face and burrowed down on his mouth, flinging myself into the kiss, taking the brunt of his tongue as it whipped into me.

The noises rumbling from Poet's chest bordered on savage. Bracing himself against the bookcase, the jester clasped my ass and splayed me wide, tacking me against him until I felt the broad, hot ridge of his cock.

Our gazes held fast. Pausing suddenly, he ghosted his fingers through my loose hair, combing out the strands with tender ferocity. His pupils smoldered—awestruck, covetous, and starved. As if in ceremony, I coasted my own digits across his jaw, then his cheekbones, the motions carefully precious.

At the same time, his touch scalded my flesh, and mine caused his orbs to flare. Pinning our foreheads together, we locked hips, with the crest of Poet's cock nocked at my wet opening. It never failed to stun my senses, the size and shape of him, and how it rose and thickened purely from need of me.

And then. Seasons, and *then*.

Poet gently lashed his backside upward. The broad head of his erection spread the pleats of my cunt, casting his full length into me.

Our mouths hung open, my devastated cry tangling with his ragged groan. The feel of his cock primed so completely, rooted so deeply into me, melted my body. My heart shattered, and my eyes prickled. I felt it everywhere, felt his firm heat encased to the brink, felt the tip anchored in a spot that threw sparks up my vertebrae.

Poet sucked in a fractured breath, then ran the sinful point of his tongue across my tremulous mouth. "Now fuck with me."

Nodding profusely, I braced my toes on the bookshelf behind him and used the leverage to vent my thighs wider. The instant I did, Poet's strong body hoisted upward, his buttocks snapping and his cock whisking into me. In tandem, the jester bobbed my frame up and down in a sinuous pace, my folds pumping over his length. Pleasure fired up my veins and doused my pussy in fluid, so that I wept aloud.

Swatting my hips with his, I moved in sync. Each pass withdrew him to the roof, then pivoted his erection high, enabling me to take every glorious inch. We bound our gazes to another one, my parted lips unleashing shrill noises, while Poet growled in cadence to his thrusts.

Like this, I fucked him into the bookcase. And he took me in mid-air, my frame hunching into him, my breasts jostling. We bowed steeply into one another, putting every part of our bodies into it, the point where my knees pitched against the tomes, and my fingernails dug into the shelf.

Perspiration lathered the jester's torso, the grid of his abdomen clenching with effort. He kept a measured pace, his stamina notorious for lasting until dawn. My lover tested and teased my limits, his cock hitting at one angle, then striking into me at another slope. I whined against his mouth and rowed my waist over his pelvis, determined to keep pace.

"How's that, Sweet Thorn?" Poet panted. "Do you like how my body makes you feel? Does my cock please you?"

"Yes," I keened. "Do you enjoy being claimed?"

In reply, a wolfish smile blasted through his moan. He circled his hips, lancing his cock into me at yet another angle, the stem of his flesh rubbing my clit.

"Oh!" I belted to the ceiling. "Poet!"

"That's right," he purred, pounding leisurely. "Praise your jester. Ride him into this shelf. And do it loudly."

My moans split through the library. Out of my mind with desire, I charged into Poet, galloping on his pelvis, hurling my cunt at him. A collection of books slipped from their perch and smacked the floor. The case shook against the wall.

My jester seethed, and his head thumped against the facade. He braced my bottom, encouraging every beat of my hips, my pussy clasping his cock, tightening him in a wet grip.

Those magnificent eyes scorched mine, the diamond painted over his eye creasing in blissful anguish. "Every time I couldn't touch you," he stressed, on the brink of another groan. "Every time it was forbidden. Every waking moment." His tongue swathed my mouth, then dropped a tender kiss there. "Every second. Every look."

I whimpered against his lips. "Every word you said."

"Every response you gave," he crooned.

"Every day," I implored.

"Every night," he rasped.

It was always him. It was always me. It was always us.

Uttering a primal sound, Poet unleashed. As if overcome by our words, he bundled me in his arms and catapulted off the shelf, standing upright in between the stacks. Anchoring me to his torso, he vaulted the straight ledge of his erection through my walls.

I yelped, my body jolting in tune with his waist. My spine arched, and I latched onto his damp nape, my waist gyrating atop him. Poet cupped the back of my scalp, banded one strong arm beneath my rear, and flung his hips.

Blood coursed through my limbs. The ecstasy filled me with vitality, set me aflame, and brought me to urgent life. I cried out in triumph and wonder, unmoored and uncensored.

Poet emitted the same noises, only rougher. The sounds ejecting from his lungs fragmented into the air, heady and harsh.

A tempest of sensation chipped me into fragments, my legs clinging to the jester's skillful joints, which revolved over and over. The force of his cock unraveled me until my arousal splashed down our thighs.

And when that didn't suffice, Poet sprang to the opposite case. Crushing me into the edifice, he stapled my wrists overhead and ducked his mouth to my left nipple. I shrieked, the hot tug of his lips mesmerizing. More hollers followed the rest when he switched to the other breast, sucking the tip raw and flexing his tongue over the peak.

All the while, his waist bucked, now with added momentum. The brunt of his cock widened me, my thighs bridging his hips and my ankles linking beneath his ass. He made love so thoroughly, so devotedly, so mercilessly that my scalp prickled, and my toes curled.

My navel abraded his stomach, softness and hardness rubbing together. My helpless moans inundated the library, and his silken growl followed, the sounds inebriating.

He intoxicated me like no one ever could. And he gazed at me as though I'd bewitched him.

Poet devoured my body whole. With a hum, he took my mouth and sucked me into another full-bodied kiss. His tongue flayed mine, the tempo erotic while he powered his cock in and out.

Releasing my wrists, he gripped my backside and fastened me in place, stalling my movements as his waist continued its onslaught. Fixing me to him, the jester jutted his cock, the gradual lash of his flesh creating new friction.

Astride his phallus, I chanted in astonishment and gave into the rhythm. The maneuver enabled me to feel the liquid pump of his erection, from the crown to the sac. Siphoning this way, Poet coaxed more wetness from me, the cleft of my pussy drenching him.

The jester hummed, his timbre skating over my flesh like satin. Alone in this castle, insulated in this dark library, we branded each other. My fingers dashed across his back, my nails scraping his shoulder blades, certain to draw blood. Yet the jester only murmured endearments and ground his cock deeper, harder, higher.

My hands landed on his ass. I clutched the divots, feeling the contours flexing, working into me. I squeezed my pussy around him and packed his buttocks in my hands, spurring him farther, faster.

There. There. *There.*

My touch begged for more. My cries pleaded for his cock to lodge itself entirely, to pull every drop of arousal from my body, to fill my lungs with shouts.

Poet cursed under his breath, his tone fervent and possessive. He sprang forth, accelerating his cock and spearing me with quick, shallow jabs.

I bowed into the shelves and yelled into the candlelit library. All the while, the jester worshiped me like an otherworldly shadow, like someone unattainable.

Yet he was mine. Just as I belonged to him.

The knowledge threw me into a tailspin. I joined his movements, my need to claim as great as my yearning to succumb. We barreled into one another, our hips crashing together, my cunt grasping his cock.

Slamming into the bookcase, I felt my voice go slack, then erupt into a scream. My body exploded at the same time Poet froze, then he came with a rupture, his muscles shuddering. A thunderous roar broke from his throat and joined my prolonged cry.

His mouth surged against mine, offering me the sound of his climax. In kind, I came long and loud into his mouth, my pussy rippling and soaking his cock. Our voices blasted into one another until it became a single, primitive sound.

Oxygen wheezed from my chest, my breathing shaky and threadbare. And yet, I didn't fall limply, nor did he collapse against me. Rather, Poet's head snapped to mine, and the green fire of his eyes intensified. Through his expression, I saw my own.

We weren't done yet. If we had our way, neither of us would ever be done with the other.

I scrambled, hooking myself around him as Poet wrenched me off the bookcase and carried me to the hill of blankets that I'd installed before Reaper's Fest began.

Kneeling, he dropped me onto the mound. An eager gasp chuffed from my mouth as I landed, then he snatched my calves to jerk me closer and scissored my thighs apart, exposing the oval of my cunt. Bare. Flushed. With my limbs flopped over his thighs, the jester loomed above, his cock solid against his navel and that remarkable body etched in flames from the fireplace dominating the adjacent wall. Hovering, he feasted his gaze on my pussy, my mouth, my eyes.

Swiping one finger along my crease, Poet collected a stream of my climax, then stroked the same digit along the slit of his length, mixing his fluid with mine. Hunching into me, he licked that finger and crooned, then glided it over my lower lip, spreading our combined slickness there.

"Taste us, sweeting," he coaxed.

My skin pebbled. Darting out my tongue, I licked the fluid, the flavor of sex and ardor seeping into my palate. Emboldened, I draped my lips around his finger and sucked on the rest.

Poet groaned and fell into me. In unison, I grabbed the side of his jaw and hastened his lips to mine, our mouths fusing and rowing. His hot tongue plied my own, rocking us into a deep kiss. With our lips tugging on one another, we sampled the taste of our bodies, the tang of our release, the way we affected each other.

I moaned into his mouth, dissolving against the blankets and pillows when Poet's weight descended. Our rampant breaths softened. Everything unspooled quietly now, the jester's sculpted form spanning my body, then linking my thigh over his ass and rolling onto his side, taking me with him.

We lay facing one another, my right leg crooked over his hip, the width of his pelvis spreading my thighs. Heat drifted from the grate and painted us in warm light. With his thick cock braced against my pussy, Poet verdant irises glowed.

The sight alone wetted me anew, my clit thrumming. Then we moved as one. The cap of his erection nudged apart my folds, and my mouth unhinged, and his eyes darkened.

"More," he murmured.

So I broadened my thighs, and he fitted his cock deeper.

"More," I sighed.

So he whisked those expert hips, and my pussy sucked him farther.

"More," he hissed.

So I pitched my leg higher, and his erection struck me to the hilt.

This way, I experienced the fullness of him. His shape and girth. Just as he felt the depth and tightness of me.

Our hips locked. Then his waist thudded into mine, leisurely stroking in and out, and I rode the motions, gradually beating my folds over him. Like this, we watched each other, watched our naked bodies pound slowly, watched our features contort, watched what we did to one another.

My moans grew heavy, punctuated by the deep sling of his cock. Poet groaned, the throaty sound stimulating my flesh, causing an outbreak down to my soles. My nipples rushed against his pectorals, and my clit tingled as the column of his length rubbed against my delicate skin, electrifying the tips of my being.

I sobbed enthusiastically. My hands rushed over his torso and dove into his hair, mussing the layers before gripping them for balance, lest I should fall apart.

He claimed me patiently, utterly. And I claimed him back, desperately, fervently.

Something happened then, consuming me to the core, pleasure and passion reaching bone deep. We'd made love in a thousand ways, in a thousand places. But always, we consummated during a time when risk, danger, and bloodshed lurked in proximity, when any moment was fraught with threats and gambles.

Tonight, no such impediments existed. Nothing deadly. Nothing forbidden. Just us, and here, and now. The controversial jester and princess, at liberty to love wherever, whenever, and however we wished.

A crown had bound me to this nation. A ribbon had set me free.

Who knew what would happen tomorrow. But one certainty remained. That we would face the morning as one, with no more boundaries between us.

This was the right time. This was the only time.

My equal. My eternity.

Mine. Yours.

"Husband," I breathed, the word slipping into a moan.

His pupils flashed. "Wife," he whispered.

Those sacred words seeped into me, even as Poet's hips lashed deeper. I cried out and grasped his hair, holding on for dear life as the jester accentuated his thrusts. The wide head of his cock pumped harder, drawing out my weeping, my cunt pouring down his sac.

He gripped my backside and hauled his ass slowly. Somehow, his cock expanded more, filling me to the seat, thumping between my thighs.

Time lost its meaning, the world outside this library reduced to a memory. Only this existed. The sight of my jester's face on the verge of collapse, his eyes intent on mine, his climax fueled by my own response.

At some point, my moans broke, the anguished noises spilling across the vast wing. The muscles of my pussy rippled around Poet's gliding cock. My jester growled and pistoned at a vicious angle, every swipe pushing me to the summit. Heavens, this man fucked into me so beautifully, so much.

His silken voice caressed my flesh. "Come, Sweet Thorn," he murmured, kissing my chin. "Come with your jester."

My drenched walls contorted, and his cock vibrated, and we burst into noise. My cry shattered into a wail, and his growl tore into a bellow, heat swarming my blood and the nexus of my body unspooling. I soaked him, the flanks of my pussy clenching around his cock, taking every drop of his cum.

Poet's muscles contracted with every spasm. As he came on a holler, the jester hauled me against him, my frame pinned to his, our bodies riding out the sensations.

Falling into the blankets, his heart rammed into mine, and my shaky breaths rushed against his lips. A husky, satisfied noise resounded from the jester's throat. Grinning, he swept his sexy mouth across my own and snatched another kiss.

Happiness like nothing I'd ever known pulled my lips into a smile. I curled into Poet as he twisted onto his back and tucked me against him, his hold firm as though he'd never let me go. And by Seasons, I was counting on that.

My cheek rested on his chest, with my red hair tousled and my leg slung over his thighs, the thorn quill flashing from the bronze garter. I strummed my fingers over his abs, content to stay here forever.

Poet took my hand, our scarlet ribbons brushing. Quietly, he unknotted his bracelet and tied it around my wrist. With my heart in my throat, I did the same, removing my own ribbon and affixing it to him.

The gesture said everything. In this place, where we'd married and claimed each other, our bracelets were the only tokens we needed to exchange.

We would tell everyone who mattered the most tomorrow, beginning with Nicu and Mother. Eventually, the announcement would extend to the people. We'd share our union once the timing was right and we could perform a ceremony.

Until then, this night belonged only to us.

"Sneaky princess," he teased, gathering me tighter against him. "Making me a Royal when I least expected it."

I chuckled into his torso and tossed him a sheepish look. "You could have turned me down."

"I'll never do that."

"Then I suppose you're mine from now on."

"Oh, but you're wrong." I yelped as the jester hoisted me atop his chest, my legs splayed on either side of his narrow hips. Speaking against my mouth, he whispered, "I was yours a long time ago, from the moment I set that ribbon on your pillow and fantasized about tying you up with it."

"Well, we might have time for that," I teased. "The sun isn't up yet."

"Never tempt a jester."

"Pity for me, because I plan on doing it often."

"Splendid," Poet said with a trickster smirk, then positioned me astride his cock. "Because we're nowhere near finished."

Before we threw ourselves at each other again, I peeked at the fire, then at him. "A tale for campfires."

That was also the reason I'd fashioned this makeshift camp in the library. Because we were made of countless stories, starting with the one Poet had recited to me long ago, narrating a passionate tale about how we met. From being enemies to becoming lovers, additional tales had arisen, with many more to come.

We had earned that now. A future together.

Uphill battles still lay ahead. Threats existed in the form of Winter. And our allies would need our help, as well as the people we fought to liberate.

Yet we'd prevailed thus far and found our home. Whatever came next, we would conquer it. And through it all, this man would always be more than my king. First and foremost, he was my jester.

My Fenien. My Poet.

Poet rubbed his nose over mine. "That is all."

"That is everything," I finished, crushing my mouth against his.

Poet

When I said we were nowhere near finished with each other, was I exaggerating? Fuck nay. And perish the thought.

After making a vow and exchanging those ribbons, I took her for hours in that library, and she claimed me back, each of us making the other arch and shatter to the bone. Indeed, the princess and her jester shouted so emphatically, the pleasured sounds had likely seeped into the walls.

We stayed there until the passing hours reduced to a mere wisp of thought. Indeed, that was fine. For we had all the time we wanted now.

Afterward, I retrieved Briar's laurel and savored the vision of this princess crowning herself. Then I snatched her off the ground. Linking both arms beneath my thorn's thighs, I hauled her into my frame and proceeded to scandalize her, carrying Briar from the library wing and through the vacant corridors.

The princess blushed and scolded me. And why? Because we were still naked.

Nonetheless, Briar's admonishments broke into shocked laughter, the exquisite sound filling the castle halls. She knew her sinful jester full well.

And yet she wanted him, married him, loved him.

Fuck, but this woman had tricked, ruined, and burned me for eternity.

Eventually, I set the princess on her feet, and we ran. Clasping hands, we became moving shadows through the passages, dashing in and out of candlelight.

Emerging at the highest tower where Autumn's great horn overlooked the fog-laced vista, I hoisted my willful wife into my arms. And there, I swayed her into a dance.

To dare, to dance, to do.

At these heights, the wind whipped through her locks, turning the loose cascade into red flames. The leaves painted under her lashes glinted, and those irises melted from sterling to mercury. To say nothing of the delectable freckles sprinkled across her cheeks and bare tits.

My expression must have turned feral because Briar's complexion went scarlet, excitement flashing through her pupils. Aye, she knew where my impure thoughts were headed, predicted what my smutty intentions would be in a matter of moments.

Come now. I hadn't brought my princess up here merely for the view. We weren't leaving this tower until she'd been kissed hard and fucked sweetly.

Until then, only this. Stripped and so very alive, we undulated to the music drifting from the lower town. Briar's fingers dove into my hair, and I snared one arm around her waist, with my free hand palming her ass and pressing her body flush against me.

Our campfire tale wouldn't end tonight. Nay, it would only begin anew. And it would last until this world faded, taking us with it. But before that, the days and nights would be long, and they would be ours.

Spinning her slowly under my arm, I twisted Briar toward the panorama. Her back nestled into my chest, and my jaw rested against her temple. Like this, we watched a mural of black skies, soaring maples, and gilded harvest fields.

Beyond that, countless blazes illuminated the town, where the revels would continue through dawn, and our family would be waiting. And whilst this kingdom ignited into bonfires, and the people flung aside their inhibitions, the princess and her jester stood at the top of the fucking world.

But although I loved holding Briar like this, I also loved tasting her. She chuckled as I lightly bit the freckles scattered along the side of her neck. "Wicked man. Behave yourself for at least another few minutes."

"Getting worn out already, Sweet Thorn?"

"Never," Briar swore, extending her throat for my mouth. "It will take a lot to exhaust this tenacious princess."

"What a coincidence. Jesters like a challenge."

"Then you've found the right partner."

"Indeed, I have."

With a naughty growl, I caressed my mouth over her throat, obsessed by the way it made her shiver. However, I did enjoy prolonging the desire. And I did fancy whispering enticements to my thorn, of which I planned to seize many more opportunities.

Fucking her beautifully could wait for a moment. But first, a simple pleasure.

"Now then." I wrapped my arms around Briar's middle, relished her smiling profile, and murmured into her ear, "Tell me how your day was."

Jeryn and Flare's scorching story is coming in book 4.

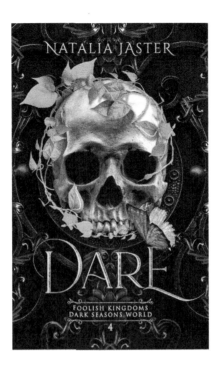

Want steamy NSFW character art of Poet and Briar's
reunion scene from Burn?

Sign up for my newsletter
to unlock an exclusive digital download,
for 18+ subscribers' eyes only:
https://nataliajaster.com/newsletter

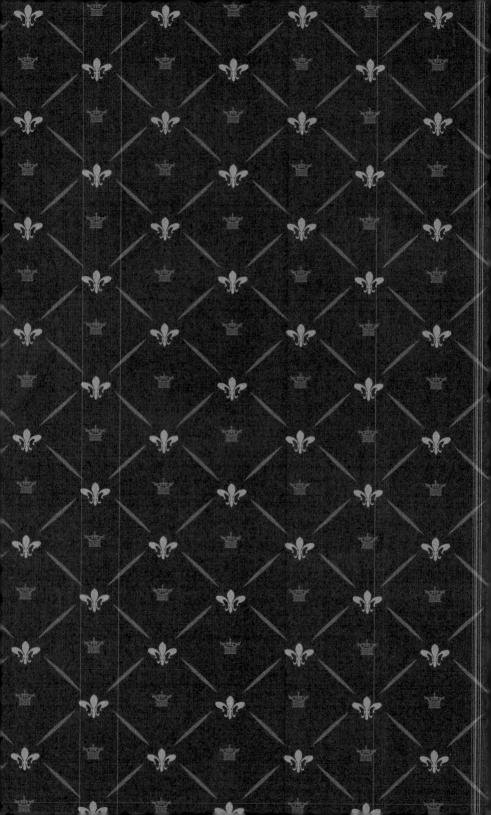

AUTHOR'S NOTE

icked hell, are you crying? Me too.

Happy tears. Wistful tears. All the tears.

When I first set out to work on Poet & Briar's story after *Trick*, I didn't know what to expect or where this passionate couple would take me. And whilst terrifying, my excitement knew no bounds. I trusted my jester and princess to take me on a breathtaking journey.

Oh, indeed they did.

And I'm elated you feel the same. Often, I receive such touching messages about Poet and Briar's strength, their spicy tension, and their unconditional devotion to each other. Readers have connected with them in a deep and profound way, and I couldn't be more delighted to know they've found a place in your hearts.

As I write this, my eyes are stinging. I feel blessed that these characters came into my life. For my wicked couple, I'd walk through fire.

More than anything, I hope their conclusion is everything you wanted.

Now you might be wondering: What comes next?

Is this the end of the series? Nay.

Burn marks the epic conclusion of Poet & Briar's campfire tale. However, there's more Dark Seasons: Foolish Kingdoms coming. There will be three additional books after this, each with a different couple, most of whom you've already met.

What's more, Poet and Briar will play key roles in each story (!!!) as the series builds to an ensemble. There's a larger world conflict that still needs resolving, after all.

With that in mind, you might have noticed some new characters in *Burn*, plus a few romantasy breadcrumbs. It's all part of my steamy plan, sweetings.

So: Jeryn and Flare are next!

Enemies to lovers. Forced proximity.

Villain gets the girl. He falls first.

Be ready for their scorching series continuation in *Dare* (Foolish Kingdoms #4). It's going to be one smoking hot tale.

And make sure to follow me on Amazon for release alerts.

In the meantime, I'm going to light a candle and celebrate my jester and princess. To the depth of my soul, I love these two.

That is all. That is everything.

XO,
Natalia

ACKNOWLEDGMENTS

All my gratitude to the court of beta and sensitivity readers, who generously offered feedback for this story.

Thank you to Ariella for being a champion of this series.

My wholehearted thanks to Michelle and Jacqueline for your beta prowess and friendship. It means so much.

To my family, eternally.

To Roman, my soul mate and silver-tongued troublemaker.

Always, to my ARC readers and the Myths & Tricksters FB group. And to everyone who has read, loved, and shared Poet and Briar with this bookish world.

You are kindred. You are Royals.

About Natalia

Natalia Jaster is a fantasy romance author who routinely swoons for the villain.

She lives in a dark forest, where she writes steamy New Adult tales about rakish jesters, immortal deities, and vicious fae. Wicked heroes are her weakness, and rebellious heroines are her best friends.

When she's not writing, you'll probably find her perched atop a castle tower, guzzling caramel apple tea, and counting the stars.

Come Say Hi!

Bookbub: www.bookbub.com/authors/natalia-jaster

Facebook: www.facebook.com/NataliaJasterAuthor

Instagram: www.instagram.com/nataliajaster

TikTok: www.tiktok.com/@nataliajasterauthor

Website: www.nataliajaster.com

See the boards for Natalia's novels on
Pinterest: www.pinterest.com/andshewaits

Printed in Great Britain
by Amazon

35433510R00290